Y0-CCJ-476

Leo
Africanus

Leo
Africanus

Amin Maalouf
Translated by Peter Sluglett

W · W · NORTON & COMPANY
New York   *London*

For Andrée

Copyright © by Amin Maalouf 1986
Translation copyright © by Peter Sluglett 1988

First American Edition, 1989

Originally published in French by Editions Jean-Claude Lattès
All rights reserved

Printed in the United States of America

Library of Congress Cataloging-in-Publication Data

Maalouf, Amin.
  LEO AFRICANUS.
  Translation of: Léon l'Africain.
  1. Leo Africanus, ca. 1492–ca. 1550–Fiction.
2. Renaissance—Fiction.   I. Title.
PQ3979.2.M28L413   1988   843   88–18027

ISBN 0-393-02630-2

W. W. Norton & Company, Inc., 500 Fifth Avenue, New York, N. Y. 10110
W. W. Norton & Company Ltd., 37 Great Russell Street, London WC1B 3NU

1 2 3 4 5 6 7 8 9 0

Table of Contents

I THE BOOK OF GRANADA

II THE BOOK OF FEZ

III THE BOOK OF CAIRO

IV THE BOOK OF ROME

'Yet do not doubt that I am also Leo Africanus the traveller'

W.B. YEATS

1865–1939

I, Hasan the son of Muhammad the weigh-master, I, Jean-Leon de Medici, circumcised at the hand of a barber and baptized at the hand of a pope, I am now called the African, but I am not from Africa, nor from Europe, nor from Arabia. I am also called the Granadan, the Fassi, the Zayyati, but I come from no country, from no city, no tribe. I am the son of the road, my country is the caravan, my life the most unexpected of voyages.

My wrists have experienced in turn the caresses of silk, the abuses of wool, the gold of princes and the chains of slaves. My fingers have parted a thousand veils, my lips have made a thousand virgins blush, and my eyes have seen cities die and empires perish.

From my mouth you will hear Arabic, Turkish, Castilian, Berber, Hebrew, Latin and vulgar Italian, because all tongues and all prayers belong to me. But I belong to none of them. I belong only to God and to the earth, and it is to them that I will one day soon return.

But you will remain after me, my son. And you will carry the memory of me with you. And you will read my books. And this scene will come back to you: your father, dressed in the Neapolitan style, aboard this galley which is conveying him towards the African coast, scribbling to himself, like a merchant working out his accounts at the end of a long journey.

But is this not in part what I am doing: what have I gained, what have I lost, what shall I say to the supreme Creator? He has granted me forty years of life, which I have spent where my travels have taken me: my wisdom has flourished in Rome, my passion in Cairo, my anguish in Fez, and my innocence still flourishes in Granada.

1

I
The Book of Granada

The Year of Salma al-Hurra
894 A.H.
5 December 1488 – 14 November 1489

In that year, the sacred month of Ramadan fell in high summer. My father rarely left the house before nightfall, as the people of Granada were short-tempered during the daytime. Quarrels were frequent, and a sombre bearing was regarded as a sign of piety; only a man who was not keeping the fast could smile under the fiery heat of the sun, and only a man who had no concern for the fate of the Muslims could remain cheerful and friendly in a town exhausted from within by civil war and threatened from without by the unbelievers.

I had just been born, by the unceasing grace of the Most High, in the last days of Sha'ban, just before the beginning of the sacred month. My mother Salma was excused from fasting while she recovered, and my father Muhammad was dispensed from groaning, even in the hours of heat and hunger, as the birth of a son who would bear his name, and one day bear his arms, is a matter of legitimate rejoicing for every man. Furthermore, I was the first born son, and when he heard himself called 'Abu'l-Hasan', my father's chest swelled imperceptibly; he stroked his moustache and slid his two thumbs slowly down his beard while glancing up at the alcove on the floor above, in which I lay. However, even his overwhelming joy was not as deep and intense as that of my mother Salma, who, in spite of her continuing pain and physical frailty, felt herself born again by my arrival in this world, as my birth transformed her into the first of the women of the household and assured her of my father's continuing regard in the long years ahead.

Long afterwards, she confided to me the fears which my

5

appearance had unwittingly assuaged, if not entirely banished. She and my father, cousins betrothed to each other since childhood, had been married for four years before she conceived, and had felt around them as early as the second year the buzzing of defamatory rumours. To the point that Muhammad came home with a beautiful Christian girl, with black braided hair, whom he had bought from a soldier who had captured her in the course of a raid into the country near Murcia. He called her Warda, set her up in a room overlooking the patio, and even talked of sending her to Ismail the Egyptian to teach her the lute, dancing and calligraphy, like any favourite of the sultans.

'I was free, and she was a slave,' said my mother, 'so we were not evenly matched. She had all the wiles of seduction at her disposal; she could go out unveiled, sing, dance, pour wine, wink her eyes, and take off her clothes, while I could never, as a wife, abandon my reserve, still less show the slightest interest in your father's pleasures. He used to call me "My cousin"; he would refer respectfully to me as *al-hurra*, the free, or *al-'arabiyya*, the Arab, and Warda herself showed me all the deference a servant girl owes to her mistress. But at night, she was the mistress.'

'One morning,' went on my mother, her voice still choking with emotion in spite of all the years that had passed, 'Gaudy Sarah came knocking at our door. Her lips were stained with walnut root, her eyes dripping with kohl, her fingernails steeped in henna, and she was enveloped from head to toe in a riot of ancient crumpled silks which breathed sweet-smelling perfumes. She used to come to see me – may God have mercy upon her, wherever she may be! – to sell amulets, bracelets, perfumes made from lemon, ambergris, jasmin and water lilies, and to tell fortunes. She immediately noticed my reddened eyes, and without me having to tell her the cause of my misery, began to read my palm like the crumpled page of an open book.

'Without lifting her eyes, she said these words, which I remember to this day: "For us, the women of Granada, freedom is a deceitful form of bondage, and slavery a subtle form of freedom." Then, saying no more, she took out a tiny greenish stoppered bottle from her wicker basket. "Tonight, you must pour three drops of this elixir into a glass of orgeat syrup, and offer it to your cousin with your own hand. He will come to you like a butterfly towards the light. Do it again after three nights, and again after seven."

6

'When Sarah came back a few weeks later I was already having my morning sicknesses. That day I gave her all the money I had on me, a great handful of square dirhams and maravedis, and I watched her dancing with joy, swaying her hips and tapping her feet loudly on the floor of my chamber, making the coins dance in her hands, the sound of their clinking together mingling with that of the juljul, the little bell which all Jewish women had to carry.'

It was indeed time that Salma became pregnant, since Providence had ordained that Warda had become pregnant already, though she had taken care to conceal her condition for her own protection. When this came to light, two months later, it became a contest as to which of them would bear a son, or, if both had sons, which would be the first to give birth. Salma was too full of apprehension to sleep, but Warda would have been quite content to give birth to a younger son, or even a daughter, since, according to our Law, the mere act of giving birth would entitle her to the status of a free woman, without having to give up the delicious frivolity which her slave origin permitted.

As for my father, he was so overjoyed at having been vouchsafed this double proof of his virility that he never had the slightest inkling of the bizarre competition taking place under his roof. Just before sunset one evening, when the condition of both his wives had become sufficiently advanced to be plainly visible, he commanded them both to accompany him to the threshold of the hostelry where he used to meet his friends, near the Flag Gate. They walked hand in hand several paces behind him, shrinking in shame, my mother in particular, from the inquisitive scrutiny of the men and the sniggering of the old gossips of our quarter, the most garrulous and most idle in the entire suburb of al-Baisin, who were watching them from the upper rooms of their houses, hidden behind curtains which parted as they walked past. Having shown them off sufficiently, and having no doubt himself felt the force of these glances, my father pretended to have forgotten something and took the same road back home, as darkness was beginning to obscure the countless dangers of the alleys of al-Baisin, some muddy and slippery in the spring rain, others paved but even more dangerous, as each gaping flagstone could turn into a fatal trap for the mothers-to-be.

Exhausted and disorientated, almost at breaking point, Salma and Warda, for once united, collapsed on to the same bed, the servant's bed, since *al-hurra* was unable to struggle up the stairs to her own. My father went back to the hostelry, quite unaware that he could have caused the loss of both his future children at the same time, hurrying, no doubt, according to my mother, to bask in his friends' admiration and in expectation of their good wishes for the birth of two fine sons, and to challenge our neighbour Hamza the barber to a game of chess.

When they heard the key turned in the lock, the two women burst out into in a fit of spontaneous laughter and it was a long time before they recovered their composure. Recalling the incident fifteen years later, my mother blushed at such childishness, drawing my attention somewhat shamefacedly to the fact that while Warda was barely sixteen, she herself was already twenty-one. After this a certain bond developed which softened the rivalry between them, so that when Gaudy Sarah paid Salma her monthly visit the next day, she asked the servant girl to come and have her stomach palpated by the pedlar-clairvoyant, who also doubled, when necessary, as midwife, masseuse, hairdresser and plucker of unwanted hair; she could also tell stories to her countless customers, shut up in their harems, of the thousand and one scandals of the city and the kingdom. Sarah swore to my mother that she had become exceedingly ugly, which made her very happy, since this was an unmistakable sign that she was carrying a boy, and complimented Warda pityingly on the exquisite freshness of her complexion.

Salma was so sure of the accuracy of this diagnosis that she was unable to refrain from telling Muhammad about it that very evening. She also felt she could bring up another rather more embarrassing notion of Sarah's, namely that a man should not come near either of his wives during pregnancy for fear of damaging the foetus or causing a premature birth. Even though obscured by circumlocutions and interspersed with long hesitations, the message was sufficiently direct to cause my father to flare up like a dry stick and launch into a stream of barely intelligible invective in which the words 'rubbish', 'old witches', 'she-devil' kept being repeated like the blows of a pestle in the hollow of a mortar, as well as a number of other generally uncomplimentary remarks about medicine, Jews and women's brains. Salma thought that he would have beaten her if she had not been pregnant, but also told herself that in that case the argument would of course not have taken place. To console herself, she concluded wisely to herself that the advantages of motherhood outweighed these passing inconveniences.

As a kind of punishment Muhammad strictly forbade her to receive 'that poisonous Sirah' in his house, hissing her name with the characteristic Granada accent which he was to retain all his life, which made him call my mother Silma, his concubine Wirda, the door '*bib*' instead of '*bab*', his town Ghirnata and the sultan's palace 'the Alhimra'. He remained in an extremely bad temper for several days, but with equal measures of prudence and vexation kept away from both his wives' bedrooms until after their confinements.

These took place within two days of each other. Warda was the first to feel the contractions, which then became less frequent in the evening and only became more intense at dawn; it was only then that she began to cry out loudly enough to be heard. My father ran to our neighbour Hamza, beat on his door and begged him to tell his mother, a worthy old lady of extreme piety and great skill, that the confinement was imminent. She appeared a few minutes later, wrapped in a white veil, carrying a broad-brimmed bowl, a towel and a piece of soap. She was said to have a lucky hand, and to have brought more boys into the world than girls.

My sister Mariam was born around noon; my father hardly looked at her. He had eyes only for Salma, who swore to him '*I* shall not disappoint you!' But she was not so sure, in spite of Sarah's infallible prescriptions and her repeated promises. She had to endure two further interminable days of anguish and suffering before her dearest wish was granted, to hear her cousin address her as Umm al-Hasan, the mother of Hasan.

On the seventh day after I was born my father called Hamza the barber to circumcise me, and invited all his friends to a banquet. Because of my mother's and Warda's condition, my two grandmothers and their servants took charge of the preparation of the meal. My mother did not take part in the ceremony, but she confessed to me that she slipped quietly out of her bedroom to see the guests and hear what they had to say. Her emotion was so great on that day that the most minute details became engraved upon her memory.

Gathered in the courtyard, around the carved white marble fountain, whose water refreshed the atmosphere with the noise of its splashing and with the thousands of droplets which it scattered, the guests ate with appetites made particularly healthy because it was the beginning of Ramadan, which meant that they were breaking their fast at the same time as celebrating my entry into the community of the believers. According to my mother, who had to be content with the left-overs the following day, the meal was a feast fit for a king. The main dish was *maruziya*, lamb prepared with honey, coriander, starch, almonds, and pears, and walnuts, as the season was just beginning. There was also green *tafaya*, goat's meat mixed with a bouquet of fresh coriander, and white *tafaya*, made with dried coriander. Not to mention the chickens, the young pigeons, and the larks, in garlic and cheese sauce, the baked hare, coated with saffron and vinegar, and dozens of other dishes which my mother so often enumerated, recalling the last great feast which took place in her house before the fury of Heaven rained down upon her and her own. Listening to her as a child, I always waited impatiently for her to reach the *mujabbanat*, hot pies made of soft white cheese, dusted with cinnamon and dripping with honey, cakes made of dates or almond paste, and pastries filled with pine kernels and nuts, and perfumed with rose water.

At this feast, my mother swore piously, the guests drank only orgeat syrup. She forbore to add that if no wine was poured, it was only out of respect for the holy month. In Andalus, the circumcision ceremony was always the excuse for celebrations whose original religious purpose was often entirely forgotten. The most sumptuous of all these occasions was still remembered in our day, the feast organized by the Amir Dhu'l-Nun of Toledo to celebrate the circumcision of his grandson, a feast which all the world sought to imitate but never managed to do. Wine and liqueur flowed like water, while hundreds of beautiful slave girls danced to the orchestra of Dany the Jew.

But at my circumcision too, my mother declared, there were also musicians and poets. She even remembered the verses which were recited in my father's honour:

By this circumcision your son's light glows more brilliant,
As the light of the candle increases when the wick is trimmed.

Recited and sung in every key by the barber himself, this couplet by an early poet of Saragossa marked the end of the meal and the beginning of the ceremony itself. My father went up on to the terrace to snatch me in his arms, while the guests gathered in silence around the barber and his assistant, a young beardless boy. Hamza made a sign to his assistant, who began to go round the courtyard, lantern in hand, stopping in front of each guest. A small present had to be offered to the barber, and according to custom everyone pressed the coins he gave on to the face of the boy, who announced the donor's name in a high voice and thanked him before passing on to his neighbour. When the money had all been collected, the barber asked for two powerful lamps, unsheathed his knife, recited some appropriate Qur'anic verses and leant towards me. My mother always said that the cry which I let out rang out over the whole quarter like a sign of precocious valour, and then, while I continued to scream with the whole of my tiny body, as if I had seen all the evils that were to come pass before my eyes, the celebrations began again with the sound of the lute, the flute, the rebeck and the tambourine until the *suhur*, the meal just before sunrise in Ramadan.

But not everyone was in the mood for the celebration. My maternal uncle, Abu Marwan, whom I always called Khali, then a member of the staff of the secretariat at the Alhambra, arrived late at the feast with a sad and downcast countenance. An enquiring circle formed around him, and my mother pricked up her ears. One sentence drifted across to her, which plunged her back for several long minutes into a nightmare which she believed she had forgotten for ever.

'We have not had a single year of happiness since the Great Parade!'

'That accursed Parade!' My mother was instantly overcome with nausea, just as in the first few weeks of her pregnancy. In her confused mind she saw herself once again a little girl of ten with bare feet, sitting in the mud in the middle of a deserted alley through which she had passed a hundred times but which she did not recognize any more, lifting the hem of her crumpled, wet and mud-flecked red dress, to cover her tearful face. 'I was the prettiest and most fussed over child in the whole quarter of al-Baisin, and your grandmother – may God forgive her – had sewn two identical charms on to my clothes, one on the outside, and the other hidden, to defeat the evil eye. But that day, nothing could be done.'

★ ★ ★

'The sultan of the day, Abu'l-Hasan 'Ali, had decided to hold pompous military parades, day after day and week after week, to show the world the extent of his power – but only God is powerful and He does not love the arrogant! The sultan had had stands built on the red hill of the Alhambra, near the Treason Gate, and every morning he and his retinue received visitors and dealt with affairs of state there, while innumerable detachments of troops from all corners of the kingdom, from Ronda to Basta and from Malaga to Almeria, marched past interminably, saluting the sultan and wishing him good health and long life. The inhabitants of Granada and the neighbouring villages both old and young, used to foregather on the slopes of Sabiqa at the foot of the Alhambra near the cemetery, from which they could see this continuous ceremonial taking place above them. Street sellers set themselves up nearby, selling slippers, or mergues, doughnuts or orange blossom syrup.'

On the tenth day of the Parade, as the Islamic year 882 was ending, the New Year celebrations, which were always unostentatious, passed almost unnoticed amid the hectic tide of these continuous festivities. These were going to continue through Muharram, the first month of the year, and my mother, who used to go along to Sabiqa every day with her brothers and cousins, noticed that the number of spectators was constantly increasing, and that there were always many new faces. Drunkards thronged the streets, thefts were commonplace, and fights broke out between gangs of youths beating each other with cudgels until the blood flowed. One man was killed and several wounded, which led the *muhtasib*, the provost of the merchants, to call the police.

It was at this point that the sultan finally decided to put an end to the festivities, evidently fearing further outbreaks of rioting and violence. Accordingly, he decreed that the last day of the Parade should be 22 Muharram 883, which fell on 25 April of the Christian year 1478, but he added that the final celebrations should be even more sumptuous than those of the preceding weeks. That day, on Sabiqa, the women of the popular quarters, both veiled and unveiled, were mingling with men of all classes. The children of the town, including my mother, had been out in their new clothes since the early morning, many of them clutching several copper coins with which they bought the famous dried figs of Malaga. Attracted by the swelling crowds, jugglers, conjurers, entertainers, tightrope walkers, acrobats, monkey-keepers, beggars, genuine and fake blind

12

men could be found throughout the entire Sabiqa quarter, and, as it was spring, the peasants were walking their stallions, taking fees for letting them mate with the mares that were brought to them.

'All morning,' my mother remembered, 'we had cheered and clapped our hands watching games of "tabla", during which one Zenata rider after another tried to hit the wooden target with staves which they threw standing up on the backs of their horses at a gallop. We could not see who was most successful, but the clamour which reached us from the hill, from the very place known as al-Tabla, gave an unerring indication of winners and losers.

'Suddenly a black cloud appeared above our heads. It came so quickly that we had the impression that the light of the sun had been extinguished like a lamp blown out by a jinn. It was night at midday, and without the sultan ordering it, the game ceased, because everyone felt the weight of the heavens on his shoulders.

'There was a flash, a sheet of lightning, another flash, a muffled rumbling, and then torrents of rain poured down upon us. I was a little less scared knowing that it was a storm rather than some grim curse, and like the other thousands congregating on Sabiqa, I looked for somewhere to shelter. My older brother took me by the hand, which reassured me but also forced me to run along a road which was already turning to mud. Suddenly, several paces in front of us, a number of children and old people fell down, and seeing that they were being trampled underfoot, the crowd panicked. It was still very dark, and shouts of fear were punctuated with cries of pain. I too lost my footing, and I let go my brother's hand and found myself trying to catch hold of the hem of one soaked dress after another without getting any purchase on any of them. The water was already up to my knees, and I was certainly yelling more loudly than the others.

'I fell down and picked myself up again about five or six times without being trampled on, until I found that the crowd had thinned out around me and was also moving more slowly, because the road was going uphill and the waves rushing down it were becoming larger. I did not recognize either people or places, and ceased to look for my brothers and my cousins. I threw myself down under a porch and fell asleep, from exhaustion as much as despair.

'I woke up an hour or two later; it was less dark, but it was still pouring with rain, and a deafening rumble assaulted my ears from all sides, causing the flagstone on which I was sitting to tremble. I had run down that alleyway countless times, but to see it deserted and divided by a torrent of water made me unable to work out where I was. I shivered from the cold, my clothes were soaked, I had lost my sandals in my flight, an icy stream of water ran down from my hair, pouring into my eyes which were burning with tears. I shivered again, and a fit of coughing seized my chest, when a woman's voice called out to me: "Up here, girl!" Searching all around with my eyes, I caught sight of a striped scarf and a hand waving from an arched window very high above me.

'My mother had warned me never to enter a strange house, and also that at my age I should begin to distrust not only men but also certain women as well. Thirty paces away, on the same side of the road, the woman who had called out to me came down and opened a heavy wooden door, making haste to say, in order to reassure me: "I know you; you are the daughter of Sulaiman the bookseller, a good man who walks in the fear of the Most High." I moved towards her as she was speaking. "I have seen you going past several times with him on your way to your maternal aunt Tamima, the wife of the lawyer who lives close by in the impasse Cognassier." Although there was no man in sight, she had wrapped a white veil over her face which she did not take off until she had locked the door behind me. Then, taking me by the hand, she made me go along a narrow corridor which turned at an angle, and then, without letting go of me, ran across a little courtyard in the rain before negotiating a narrow staircase with steep stairs which brought us to her room. She pulled me gently towards the window. "See, it is the anger of God!"

'I leaned out apprehensively. I was at the top of the hill of Mauror. On my right was the new *qasba* of the Alhambra, on my left, far in the distance, the old *qasba* with the white minarets of my own quarter of al-Baisin rising above the city walls. The rumbling which I had heard in the street was now deafening. Straining to see where the noise was coming from, I looked towards the ground and could not suppress a cry of horror. "May God take pity upon us, it is Noah's flood!" murmured my protectress behind me.'

My mother would never efface from her memory the terrified child's vision which lay before her, nor would any of those who had been in Granada on that accursed day of the Parade ever forget it. A raging torrent cascaded through the valley through which the bubbling but placid Darro normally flowed, sweeping away everything in its path, devastating gardens and orchards, uprooting thousands of trees, majestic elms, walnuts a century old, ash trees, almond trees and mountain ashes, before penetrating to the heart of the city, carrying all its trophies before it like a Tartar conqueror, swallowing up the central area, demolishing hundreds of houses, shops and warehouses, destroying the houses on the bridges, until, at the end of the day, because of the mass of debris which filled the river bed, an immense pool formed which covered the courtyard of the Great Mosque, the merchants' *qaisariyya*, and the suqs of the goldsmiths and the blacksmiths. No one ever knew how many were drowned, crushed under the debris or carried off by the waves. In the evening, when Heaven finally permitted the nightmare to fade, the flood carried the wreckage out of the city, while the water ebbed away more rapidly than it had flooded. At sunrise the agent of death was far away, although its victims were still strewn over the surface of the shining earth.

'It was a just punishment for the crimes of Granada,' said my mother, repeating a well-worn maxim. 'God desired to show that His power has no equal, and wanted to punish the arrogance of the rulers, their corruption, injustice and depravity. He wanted to warn us about the destiny which awaited us if we continued to walk in our impious ways, but our eyes and hearts remained closed.'

The day after the drama, all the inhabitants of the city were convinced that the man primarily responsible for their misfortune, the man who had brought down divine wrath upon them, was none other than the arrogant, corrupt, unjust, depraved Abu'l-Hasan 'Ali, the son of Sa'd the Nasrid, twenty-first and penultimate sultan of Granada, may the Most High erase his name from memory!

To obtain the throne, he had removed and imprisoned his own father. To consolidate himself in power, he had cut off the heads of the sons of the most noble families of the kingdom, including the valiant Abencerages. However, in my mother's eyes the sultan's most heinous crime was to have abandoned his freeborn wife, his cousin Fatima, daughter of Muhammad the Left-handed, for a Christian slave girl called Isabel de Solis whom he had named Soraya.

'It was said,' she told me, 'that one morning the sultan called the members of his court together in the Myrtle courtyard so that they could attend the Rumiyya's bath.' My mother was shocked to have to recount this ungodly act; 'May God forgive me!' she stammered, her eyes turned towards the heavens. 'May God forgive me!' she repeated (as she evidently intended to continue with her story).

'When the bath was over, the sultan invited all those present to drink a small bowl of the water which Soraya had left behind, and everyone rhapsodized, in prose or in verse, about the wonderful taste which the water had absorbed. Everyone, that is, except the vizir Abu'l-Qasim Venegas, who, far from leaning towards the bath remained proudly in his seat. This did not escape the notice of the sultan, who asked him why he did so. "Your Majesty," replied Abu'l-Qasim, "I fear that if I tasted the sauce I should immediately develop an appetite for the partridge." May God forgive me!' repeated my mother, unable to repress her laughter.

I have heard this story told about many of the notables of al-Andalus, and I do not know to whom it ought really to be attributed. However, at Granada on the morning after the accursed Parade everyone sought to find in the dissolute life of the master of the Alhambra the incident which could finally have exhausted the patience of the Most High. Everyone put forward their conclusive explanations, often only a verse, a riddle, or an ancient parable embellished with contemporary meaning.

The sultan's own reaction to the calamities which rained down upon his capital was more disturbing than this idle gossip. Far from regarding this devastating flood as a warning from the Most High, he chose to draw the conclusion that the pleasures of the world were ephemeral, that life was passing by and that he must drain the utmost from each moment. Such may have been the wisdom of a poet, but certainly not that of a ruler who had already reached the age of fifty and whose kingdom was threatened.

Accordingly he gave himself over to pleasure, in spite of the frequent warnings of his doctor Ishaq Hamun. He surrounded himself with beautiful slave girls and with poets of doubtful morals, poets who carved in verse after verse the forms of naked dancing girls and slender youths, who compared hashish to emeralds and its smoke to that of incense, and who nightly sang the praises of wine, red or white, mature yet always fresh. An immense gold loving cup passed from hand to hand, from lips to lips, and the one who drained it to the dregs was proud to summon the cup bearer to fill it to the brim once more. Countless little dishes were pressed upon the guests, almonds, pine kernels and nuts, dried and fresh fruits, artichokes and beans, pastries and preserves; it was not clear whether this was to satisfy hunger or to intensify thirst. I learned much later, in the course of my long sojourn in Rome, that this habit of nibbling while becoming intoxicated was already common among the ancient Romans, who called these dishes 'nucleus'; was it perhaps for that reason that in Granada such dishes were known as 'nukl'? God alone knows the origins of things!

Devoted entirely to pleasure, the sultan neglected the affairs of state, allowing those close to him to amass huge fortunes by illegal taxes and appropriations, while his soldiers, who did not receive their pay, were obliged to sell their clothes, their mounts and their arms to feed their families. In the city, where there was profound insecurity and fear for the future, where the rise or fall of each captain was rapidly known and commented upon, where news of the drinking sessions leaked out regularly through the indiscretions of servants or guests, the mere mention of the name of the sultan or Soraya brought forth oaths and curses and sometimes pushed the people to the very edge of revolt. Without needing to lay the blame directly on Abu'l-Hasan (which they only rarely dared to do) certain Friday preachers had only to rail against corruption, depravity and impiety for all the faithful to know, without a shadow of doubt, who was being criticized by implication, and they did their utmost to utter loud and recalcitrant cries of *'Allahu akbar!'*, to which the imam leading the prayer would sometimes reply, in falsely enigmatic tones, 'The hand of God is above their hands,' all the while darting looks of hatred in the direction of the Alhambra.

Although he was universally detested, the sultan still kept his eyes and ears in the crowd, who reported to him what was said, which made him the more mistrustful, brutal and unjust. 'How many notables, how many honourable burghers,' my mother recalled, 'were arrested because they had been denounced by some rival or even a jealous neighbour, accused of having insulted the prince or having besmirched his honour, and then made to parade through the streets sitting the wrong way round on a donkey before being thrown into a dungeon or even having their heads cut off!' Under the influence of Soraya, Abu'l-Hasan made his own wife Fatima and his two sons, Muhammad, called Abu Abdullah or Boabdil, and Yusuf, live under house arrest in the tower of Comares, an imposing square castle to the north east of the Alhambra, opposite the Generalife. In this way the mistress hoped to promote her own sons to power. The court was thus divided between the partisans of Fatima, numerous but necessarily discreet, and the partisans of Soraya, the only ones to have the prince's ear.

If the tales of these internecine struggles in the palace gave the common people a means of whiling away the boredom of the long cold evenings, the most dramatic consequence of the growing unpopularity of the sultan was his attitude towards Castile. Since he was accused of favouring a Rumiyya over his cousin, of neglecting the army, and of leading an inglorious life, Abu'l-Hasan, who was not lacking in physical courage, resolved to cross swords with the Christians.

Ignoring the warnings of certain wise counsellors who pointed out to him that Aragon had thrown in its lot with Castile as a result of the marriage of Ferdinand and Isabella, and that he should avoid giving them the slightest pretext to attack the Muslim kingdom, the sultan decided to put an end to the truce which existed between Granada and her powerful neighbours, by sending a detachment of three hundred horsemen to make a surprise attack on the castle of Zahara, which the Christians had occupied three quarters of a century earlier.

The first reaction at Granada was a great outburst of joy, and Abu'l-Hasan managed to regain some favour among his subjects. But, very soon, many began to ask themselves if, by involving the kingdom in a war where the outcome was by no means certain, the sultan was not guilty of criminal irresponsibility. The course of events was to prove them right; the Castilians replied by taking possession of Alhama, the most powerful fortress in the western part of the kingdom, in spite of its apparently impregnable position on a rocky peak. The desperate efforts of the sultan to recapture it were in vain.

A major war unfolded, which the Muslims could not win, but which, if they could not have avoided, they could at least have delayed. It was to last ten years and end in the most ignominious manner possible. In addition, it was accompanied by a bloody and demoralizing civil war, so often the fate of kingdoms on their way to extinction.

In fact, two hundred days precisely after his success at Zahara, Abu'l-Hasan was removed from power. The revolution took place on the 27th of the month of Jumada al-Ula 887, 14 July 1482. On that very day Ferdinand was at the head of the royal host on the banks of the river Genil, under the walls of the town of Loja, which he had besieged for five days, when he was attacked unexpectedly by a Muslim detachment commanded by 'Ali al-'Attar, one of the most experienced officers of Granada. This was a memorable day, of which Abu'l-Hasan could have been proud, especially as the hero of the hour, acting under his orders, had succeeded in sowing confusion and panic in the camp of the Christian king, who fled towards Cordoba, leaving cannons and ammunition behind him, as well as a great quantity of flour and hundreds of dead and captives. But it was too late. When the great news reached Granada, the revolt was already under way; Boabdil, the son of Fatima, had succeeded in escaping from the tower of Comares, it was said, by sliding down a rope. He was immediately acclaimed in the quarter of al-Baisin, and the next day his sympathizers enabled him to enter the Alhambra.

'God had ordained that Abu'l-Hasan should be overthrown on the very day of his victory, just as He sent down the flood on the day of the Parade, to make him bend his knee before his Creator,' observed Salma.

But the old sultan refused to acknowledge defeat. He took refuge in Malaga, rallied his supporters around him, and prepared to avenge himself upon his son. The kingdom was thenceforth divided into two principalities which proceeded to destroy each other under the amused gaze of the Castilians.

'Seven years of civil war,' mused my mother. 'Seven years of a war in which sons killed fathers and brothers strangled brothers, in which neighbours suspected and betrayed each other, seven years in which men from our quarter of al-Baisin could not venture alongside the Great Mosque without being jeered, maltreated, assaulted, or sometimes even having their throats cut.'

Her thoughts wandered far away from the circumcision ceremony taking place a few steps away from her, far from the voices and the clinking of cups which seemed strangely muffled, as in a dream. She found herself repeating 'That accursed Parade!' She sighed to herself, half asleep.

★   ★   ★

'Silma, my sister, still daydreaming?'

The harsh voice of Khali transformed my mother into a little girl again. She fell on her elder brother's neck and covered his forehead, his shoulders, and then his arms and hands with hot and furtive kisses. Touched but somewhat embarrassed by these demonstrations of affection which threatened to upset his grave demeanour, he remained standing, stiff in his long silk *jubba* with its flowing sleeves, his scarf, the *taylassan*, draped elegantly around his shoulders, his face only revealing the ghost of a protective smile as the sign of his happiness. But this apparent coolness did not discourage Salma in the slightest. She had always known that a man of quality could not reveal his feelings without giving an impression of levity which was not appropriate to his status.

'What were you thinking about?'

If the question had been asked by my father, Salma would have given an evasive answer, but Khali was the only man to whom she would reveal her heart as well as uncovering her head.

'I was thinking of the evils of our time, of the day of the Parade, of this endless war, of our divided city, of the people who die every day.'

With the flat of his thumb he wiped a solitary tear from his sister's cheek.

'These should not be the thoughts of a mother who has just given birth to her first son,' he declared without conviction, adding in a solemn but more sincere voice, ' "You will have the rulers you deserve," says the Prophet.'

She repeated the words after him: '*Kama takunu yuwalla alaikum.*'

Then, artlessly: 'What are you trying to tell me? Weren't you one of the foremost supporters of the present sultan? Didn't you raise al-Baisin in support of him? Aren't you highly respected in the Alhambra?'

Stung to the quick, Khali prepared to defend himself with a violent diatribe, but suddenly realized that his interlocutor was only his little sister, tired and ill, whom, in addition, he loved more than anyone else in the world.

'You haven't changed, Silma, I think I'm talking to a simple girl, but in fact it's the daughter of Sulaiman the bookseller that I'm dealing with, may God add to your age what He subtracted from his. And may He shorten your tongue as He lengthened his.'

Blessing the memory of their father, they burst out in peals of frank laughter. They were now accomplices, as they had always been. Khali hitched up the front of his *jubba* and sat cross-legged on a woven straw mat at the entrance to his sister's bedroom.

'Your questions pierce me with their softness like the snow of Mount Cholair, which burns even more surely than the desert sun.'

Suddenly confident and a little mischievous, Salma asked him bluntly:

'And what do you say?'

With a gesture which was not at all spontaneous she lowered her head, seized the edge of her brother's *taylassan* and hid her red eyes within it. Then, her face still hidden, she pronounced, like the sentence of a qadi:

'Tell me everything!'

Khali's words were few:

'This city is protected by those who seek to despoil it, and governed by those who are its enemies. Soon, my sister, we shall have to take refuge beyond the sea.'

His voice cracked, and so as not to betray his emotion he tore himself away from Salma and disappeared.

Devastated, she did not attempt to detain him. She did not even notice that he had gone. No further noise, no sound of voices, no laughter, no clinking of glasses came to her from the patio; no shaft of light.

The feast had ended.

The Year of the Amulets
895 A.H.
25 November 1489 – 13 November 1490

That year, for the sake of a smile, my maternal uncle took the path of exile. It was thus that he explained his decision to me many years later, while our caravan was traversing the vast Sahara, south of Sijilmassa, during a fresh and peaceful night which was lulled rather than disturbed by the far-off howling of jackals. A slight breeze obliged Khali to tell his tale in a loud voice, and his tone was so reassuring that it made me breathe once more the odours of the Granada of my birth, and his prose was so bewitching that my camel seemed to move forwards in time with the rise and fall of its rhythms.

I would have wished to report each one of his words, but my memory is short and my eloquence feeble, so that many of the illuminations of his story will never, alas, appear in any book.

'The first day of that year, I went up early to the Alhambra, not, as I usually did, to start work in the small office of the *diwan* where I drafted the sultan's letters, but, in company with various notables of my family, to offer New Year greetings. The *majlis*, the sultan's court, which was being held on this occasion in the Hall of the Ambassadors, was thronged with turbaned qadis, dignitaries wearing high felt skull caps, coloured red or green, and rich merchants with hair tinted with henna and separated, like my own, with a carefully drawn parting.

'After bowing before Boabdil, most of the guests withdrew to the Myrtle Court, where they wandered around the pool for some time dispensing their *salam alaikums*. The more senior notables sat on couches covered with carpets, backed against the walls of the immense room, edging their way forwards to get as close as possible to the sultan or his ministers to present them with some request, or simply to show their presence at court.

'As letter writer and calligrapher at the state secretariat, as the traces of red ink on my fingers bore witness, I had some small privileges, including that of sauntering as I wished between the *majlis* and the pool, and to stroll about with those who seemed most interesting, then going back to sit down before finding a new prey. This was an excellent way of collecting news and opinions about matters of immediate concern, the more so as people could speak freely under Boabdil, while in the time of his father they would look around seven times before voicing the least criticism, which would be expressed in ambiguous terms, in verses and proverbs, which could easily be retracted if they were denounced later. The sense of feeling freer and less spied upon only made the people of Granada more severe towards the sultan, even when they found themselves under his roof, even when they were there to wish him long life, health and victories. Our people are merciless towards sovereigns who do not behave towards them as sovereigns.

'On this autumn day, the yellowing leaves were more securely attached to the trees than the notables of Granada to their monarch. The city was divided, as it had been for years, between the peace party and the war party, neither of which called upon the sultan.

'Those who wanted peace with Castile said: We are weak and the Rumis are strong; we have been abandoned by our brothers in Egypt and the Maghrib, while our enemies have the support of Rome and all the Christians; we have lost Gibraltar, Alhama, Ronda, Marbella, Malaga, and so many other places, and as long as peace is not restored, the list will continue to increase; the orchards have been laid waste by the troops, and the peasants complain; the roads are no longer safe, the merchants cannot lay in their stocks, the *qaisariyya* and the suqs are empty, and the price of foodstuffs is rising, except that of meat, which is being sold at one dirham the pound, because thousands of animals have been slaughtered to prevent them being carried off by the enemy; Boabdil should do everything to silence the warmongers and reach a lasting peace with Castile, before Granada itself falls under siege.

'Those who wanted war said: The enemy has decided once and for all to annihilate us, and it is not by submitting that we will force them to withdraw. See how the people of Malaga have been forced into slavery after their surrender\ See how the Inquisition has raised pyres for the Jews of Seville, of Saragossa, of Valencia, of Teruel, of Toledo! Tomorrow the pyres will be raised in Granada, not just for the people of the Sabbath but for the Muslims as well! How can we stop this, except by resistance, mobilization, and *jihad*? Each time we have fought with a will, we have managed to check the advance of the Castilians, but after our victories traitors appear among us, who seek only to conciliate the enemy of God, pay him tribute, and open the gates of our cities to him. Has Boabdil himself not promised one day to hand over Granada to Ferdinand? It is more than three years since he signed a document to that effect at Loja. This sultan is a traitor, he must be replaced by a true Muslim who is determined to wage the holy war and to restore confidence to our army.

'It would have been difficult to find a soldier, an officer, the commander of a platoon of ten, or of a hundred or of a thousand, still less a man of religion, a qadi, a lawyer, an 'alim or the imam of a mosque who would not share the latter point of view, while the merchants and cultivators for the most part opted for peace. The court of Boabdil was itself divided. Left to himself, Boabdil would have made any truce at whatever price, because he was born a vassal and did not hope to do more than die as one; but he could not ignore the inclinations of his army, which regarded the heroic forays made by the other princes of the Nasrid house with ill-concealed impatience.

'A particularly telling example was always mentioned by the war party: that of Basta, a Muslim city to the east of Granada, encircled and bombarded by the Rumis for more than five months. The Christian kings – may the Most High demolish what they have built, and rebuild what they have demolished – had raised wooden towers which faced the outer walls and dug a ditch to prevent the inhabitants of the besieged city from communicating with the outside world. However, in spite of their overwhelming superiority in numbers and armaments, and in spite of the presence of Ferdinand himself, the Castilians were unable to prevail against the town, and the garrison was able to make bloody raids each night. Thus the relentless resistance of the defenders of Basta, commanded by the Nasrid amir Yahya al-Najjar, excited the passions of the people of Granada and inflamed their imagination.

'Boabdil was not particularly pleased at this, because Yahya, the hero of Basta, was one of his most bitter enemies. He even laid claim to the throne of Granada, which his grandfather had once occupied, and considered the present sultan a usurper.'

'The very evening before New Year's Day, a new exploit of the defenders of Basta reached the ears of the people of Granada. The Castilians, it was said, had got wind of the fact that foodstuffs were beginning to be in short supply in Basta. To persuade them that the opposite was the case, Yahya had devised a form of deception: to collect together all the remaining provisions, to display them prominently in the stalls of the suq, and then invite a delegation of Christians to come and negotiate with him. Entering the city, Ferdinand's envoys were amazed to see such a wealth of all kinds of goods, and hastened to report the fact to their king, recommending that he should not continue to try to starve out the inhabitants of Basta, but instead to propose an honourable settlement to the city's defenders.

'Within a few hours, at least ten people joyfully told me the same story, at the hammam, at the mosque, and in the corridors of the Alhambra; each time, I pretended not to have heard the story before so as not to offend the speaker, to give him the pleasure of adding his own embellishment. I smiled too, but a little less each time, because anxiety gnawed at my breast. I kept asking myself why Yahya had allowed Ferdinand's envoys to enter the besieged city, and above all how he could have hoped to conceal from them the penury which gripped the city, if everyone in Granada, and probably elsewhere, knew the truth and was laughing at the deception.

'My worst fears,' my uncle continued, 'were realized on New Year's Day, in the course of my conversations with visitors to the Alhambra. I then learned that Yahya, Fighter for the Faith, Sword of Islam, had not only decided to hand Basta over to the infidels, but even to join the Castilian troops to open the way to the other towns of the kingdom, especially Guadix and Almeria, and finally Granada. The particular skill of this prince had been to distract the Muslims by means of his pretended stratagem, to conceal the real purpose of his negotiations with Ferdinand. He had taken his decision, some said, in exchange for a substantial sum of money, and the promise that his soldiers and the citizens of the town would be spared. But he had obtained even more than this; converting to Christianity himself, this amir of the royal family, this grandson of the sultan, was to become a high-ranking notable of Castile. I shall speak of him

26

to you again.

'At the beginning of the year 895, it was clear that no one suspected that such a metamorphosis would be possible. But, from the first days of the month of Muharram, the most alarming news reached us. Basta fell, followed by Purcena, and then Guadix. All the eastern part of the kingdom, where the war party was strongest, fell into the hands of the Castilians without a blow being exchanged.

'The war party had lost its hero, and Boabdil had got rid of an inconvenient rival; however, the Castilians' victories had reduced his kingdom to very little, to Granada and its immediate surroundings, and this area was also subject to regular attacks. Was this a matter for rejoicing for the sultan, or lamentation?

'It is on such occasions,' said my uncle, 'that great-heartedness or small-mindedness reveals itself. And it was the latter that I perceived so clearly on the face of Boabdil on the first day of the year, in the Hall of the Ambassadors. I had just heard the cruel truth about Basta from a young Berber officer of the guard who had relatives in the besieged city. He often came to see me in the state secretariat, and he came to me because he did not dare to address the sultan directly, especially as the bearer of evil tidings. I led him straight to Boabdil, who commanded him to make his report to him in a low voice. Bending over towards the monarch's ear he stammered out the news he had received.

'But, while the officer was speaking, the sultan's face swelled into a broad, indecent and hideous smile. I can still see those fleshy lips opening in front of me, those hairy cheeks which seemed to stretch to his ears, those teeth, spaced wide apart to crunch up the victory, those eyes which closed slowly as if he was expecting the warm kiss of a lover, and that head which nodded with delight, backwards and forwards and forwards and backwards, as if he was listening to the most languorous of songs. As long as I live, I shall have the image of that smile before me, that terrible smile of pettiness and small-mindedness.'

Khali stopped. The night hid his face from me, but I heard him breathe deeply, sigh, and then murmur a number of prayers which I repeated after him. The yappings of the jackals seemed closer.

'Boabdil's attitude did not surprise me,' continued Khali, his equanimity restored. 'I was not unaware of the fickleness of the master of the Alhambra, nor of the feebleness of his character, nor even of his ambiguous relations with the Castilians. I knew that our

27

princes were corrupt, that they were not concerned to defend the kingdom, and that exile would soon be the fate of our people. But I had to see with my own eyes the bared soul of the last sultan of Andalus in order to feel myself forced to react. God shows to whom He will the right path, and to others the way to perdition.'

My uncle stayed only another three months in Granada, time to turn various goods and property discreetly into gold, which would be easy to carry. Then, one moonless night, he left with his mother, his wife, his four daughters and a servant, accompanied by a horse and several mules, for Almeria, where he obtained permission from the Castilians to sail to Tlemcen with other refugees. But he intended to set himself up at Fez, and it was there that my parents and I met him again, after the fall of Granada.

If my mother mourned Khali's departure unceasingly all that year, my father Muhammad, may God keep his memory fragrant, did not think of following the example of his brother-in-law. There was no sense of despair in the city. Throughout the year there were particularly encouraging tales in circulation, frequently spread about, my mother told me, by the ineffable Sarah. 'Each time Gaudy Sarah visited me, I knew that I would be able to tell your father tales which would make him happy and self-assured for a whole week. In the end it was he who asked me impatiently whether the juljul had tinkled in our house in his absence.'

One day, Sarah arrived, her eyes full of news. Even before she could sit down, she began to tell her stories with a thousand gestures. She had just heard, from a cousin in Seville, that King Ferdinand had received two messengers from the sultan of Egypt, monks from Jerusalem, in circumstances of the greatest secrecy, who, it was said, had been charged with conveying a solemn warning to him from the master of Cairo: if the attacks against Granada did not cease, the anger of the Mamluke sultan would be terrible indeed!

In a few hours the news went the rounds of the city, being enlarged out of all proportion and being constantly embellished with fresh details, so much so that the next day, from the Alhambra to Mauror and from al-Baisin to the suburb of the Potters, anyone who dared to cast doubt on the imminent arrival of a massive body of Egyptian troops was regarded with great distrust and profound suspicion. Some were even declaring that a huge Muslim fleet had appeared off al-Rabita, south of Granada, and that the Turks and

Maghribis had joined forces with the Egyptians. If this news was not true, people said to the remaining sceptics, how else could they explain that the Castilians had suddenly ceased their attacks against the kingdom some weeks ago, while Boabdil, so fearful only a short time ago, now launched raid after raid on the territory controlled by the Christians without incurring any reprisals? A curious intoxication seemed to have taken possession of the dying city.

I was at that stage a child at the breast, privy neither to the wisdom, nor to the folly of men, which meant that I did not participate in the general credulity. Very much later, when I was a man and proud to carry the name 'of Granada' to remind everyone of the noble and prestigious city from which I had been exiled, I found it difficult to stop myself reflecting on this blindness on the part of the people of my country, including my own parents, who had been able to persuade themselves of the imminent arrival of an army of salvation when only death, defeat and shame awaited them.

★　★　★

That year was also one of the most dangerous of all those that I would pass through. Not only because of the dangers hanging over my city and those nearest to me, but also because for all the sons of Adam the first year is the one in which illnesses are most deadly, in which so many disappear without leaving a trace of what they might have been or might have done. How many great kings, or inspired poets, or intrepid travellers have never been able to attain the destiny which seemed promised to them, because they were not able to come through his first difficult journey, so simple and yet so deadly! How many mothers do not dare to become attached to their children because they fear that one day they might find themselves embracing a shadow.

'Death,' says the poet, 'holds our life by two extremities:
Old age is no closer to death than infancy.'

It was always said at Granada that the most dangerous time in the life of a nursing baby is the period immediately after its weaning, towards the end of the first year. Deprived of their mother's milk, so many children did not manage to survive for long, and it was customary to sew into their clothes amulets made of jet, and charms, wrapped up in leather sachets, sometimes containing mysterious writings which were thought to protect the bearer against the evil eye and various illnesses; one particular charm, called 'wolfstone', was even supposed to tame wild animals if placed upon their heads. At a time when it was not uncommon to encounter wild lions in the region of Fez, I often regretted not having been able to lay my hands on such a stone, although I do not believe that I would have dared to get sufficiently close to these creatures to place the charm on their manes.

The pious considered these beliefs and practices contrary to religion, although their own children often carried amulets, because such men rarely managed to persuade their wives or mothers to listen to reason.

I cannot deny this in my own case. I have never been parted from the piece of jet which Sarah sold to Salma on the eve of my first birthday, which has cabbalistic signs traced upon it which I have never been able to decipher. I do not believe that this amulet really has magical powers, but man is so vulnerable in the face of Destiny that he cannot help himself being attracted to objects which are shrouded in mystery.

Will God, Who has created me so weak, one day reprove me for my weakness?

The Year of Astaghfirullah
896 A.H.
14 November 1490 – 3 November 1491

Shaikh Astaghfirullah had a wide turban, narrow shoulders and the grating voice of the preachers of the Great Mosque, and, that year, his dense reddish beard turned grey, giving his bony face the appearance of perpetual anger, which was the entire extent of the baggage which he carried with him into exile. He would never again colour his hair with henna; he had decided on this in a moment of lassitude, and woe to anyone who asked him why: 'When your Creator asks you what you were doing during the siege of Granada, will you dare to tell Him that you were prettifying yourself?'

Every morning, at the time of the call to prayer, he climbed to the roof of his house, one of the highest in the city, not to call the believers to prayer, as he had done for several years, but to inspect, from afar, the object of his righteous anger.

'Don't you see,' he cried out to his sleeping neighbours, 'that it's your own tomb that is being built down there, on the road to Loja, and you go on sleeping here waiting for someone to come along and bury you! Come and see, if it is God's will that your eyes be opened. Come and see the walls which have been raised up in a single day by the might of Iblis the Evil One!'

With his hand stretched westwards, he pointed with his tapered fingers to the citadel of Santa Fé which the Catholic kings had begun to build in the spring and which had already taken on the appearance of a city.

In this country, where men had long adopted the odious practice of going into the street with their heads bare, or just covering themselves with a simple scarf thrown carelessly over their hair, which slid slowly on to their shoulders in the course of the day, everyone could distinguish the mushroom-shaped silhouette of Shaikh Astaghfirullah from far away. But few of the men of Granada knew his real name. It was said that his own mother had been the first to bestow this soubriquet upon him, because of the horrified cries which he used to utter from earliest childhood whenever anyone mentioned in front of him an object or an action which he considered improper: '*Astaghfirullah! Astaghfirullah!* I implore the pardon of God!' he would cry at the mere mention of wine, murder, or women's clothing.

There was a time when people teased him, gently or savagely. My father confessed to me that long before I was born he would often gather together with a group of friends on Fridays, just before the solemn midday prayer, in a little bookshop not far from the Great Mosque, to take bets; how many times would the shaikh utter his favourite phrase in the course of his sermon? The figure ranged between fifteen and seventy-five, and throughout the ceremony one of the young conspirators would carefully keep count, exchanging amused winks with the others.

'But, at the time of the siege of Granada no one poked fun at Astaghfirullah,' continued my father, thoughtful and disturbed at the memory of his former pranks. 'In the eyes of the great mass of the people, the shaikh came to be regarded as a respected personality. Age had not caused him to abandon the words and the bearing for which he was famous; rather, on the contrary, the characteristics we used to laugh at had become accentuated. But the soul of our city had altered.

'You must understand, Hasan my son, that this man had spent his life warning people that if they continued to live as they did, the Most High would punish them both in this world and in the next; he had used misfortune to arouse them as a beater arouses game. I still remember one of his sermons which began along these lines:

' "On my way to the mosque this morning, through the Sand Gate and the suq of the clothes dealers, I passed four taverns, *Astaghfirullah!*, where Malaga wine is sold with only the merest pretence at concealment, *Astaghfirullah!* and other forbidden beverages whose names I do not wish to know." '

In a grating and heavily affected voice, my father began to imitate the preacher, embroidering his sentences with countless *Astaghfirul-*

lah!, mostly pronounced so quickly as to be almost incomprehensible, apart from a few which were probably the only authentic ones. This exaggeration apart the words seemed to me as if they were fairly close to the original.

' "Have not those who patronize these infamous haunts learned, from their earliest childhood, that God has cursed those who sell wine and those who buy it? That He has cursed the drinker and he who gives him to drink? They know, but they have forgotten, or otherwise they prefer drink which turns man into a rampaging animal to the Word which promises him Paradise. One of these taverns is owned by a Jewess, but the three others are owned, *Astaghfirullah!* by Muslims. And in addition, their clients are not Jews or Christians, as I know full well! Some of them are perhaps among us this Friday, humbly inclining their heads before their Creator, while only last night they were prostrate in their cups, slumped in the arms of a prostitute, or, even, when their brains were clouded and their tongues unbridled, cursing Him Who has forbidden wine, Him Who has said, 'Do not come to the prayer in a state of drunkenness!' *Astaghfirullah!*" '

My father Muhammad cleared his throat, which was irritated by the shrill tone he had put on, before continuing:

' "Yes, my brother believers, these things have come to pass in your city, before your eyes, and you do not react, as if God was not awaiting you on the Day of Judgement to call you to account. As if God will continue to support you against your enemies when you scoff at His Word and that of His Messenger, may God grant him his prayers and his salvation! When, in the swarming streets of your city, your women wander abroad unveiled, offering their faces and their hair to the lustful gaze of hundreds of men who are not all, I dare say, their husbands, fathers, sons or brothers. Why should God preserve Granada from the dangers which threaten it, when the inhabitants of the city have brought back the practices of the age of ignorance, the customs of pre-Islamic times, such as wailing at funerals, pride in one's race, the practice of divination, belief in omens and the efficacy of relics, and the use of epithets and soubriquets against which the Most High has most clearly given warning." '

My father gave me a knowing look, but without interrupting the sermon, without even pausing for breath:

' "When, in contravention of the most stringent prohibitions, you bring into your own houses marble statues and ivory figurines, reproducing the male and female and animal form in a sacrilegious fashion, as if the Creator had need of the assistance of His creatures to perfect His Creation: when pernicious and impious doubt creeps into your spirits and those of your sons, doubt which separates you from the Creator, from His Book, from His Messenger and the Community of the Believers, doubt which shatters the walls and the very foundations of Granada?" '

As my father continued, his tone became noticeably less mocking, his movements less exaggerated and wild, his *astaghfirullahs* less frequent:

" 'When you spend for your own pleasure without shame and moderation sums which would have assuaged the hunger of a thousand poor men, and brought a smile to the cheeks of a thousand orphans? When you behave as if the houses and the lands you enjoy were yours, while all ownership belongs to the Most High, to Him alone, comes from Him and returns to Him at the time that He ordains, just as we return to Him ourselves, bearing no other treasure than our shrouds and our good deeds? Riches, my brother believers, consist not in the things which one possesses but in the things one can do without. Fear God! Fear God! Fear Him when you are old, but also when you are young! Fear Him when you are weak, but also when you are strong! Indeed you should fear Him even more when you are strong, because God will be the more merciless, and you must know that His eye passes as well through the imposing façade of a palace as through the clay wall of a hovel. And what does His eye encounter within the walls of palaces?" '

At this point, my father's tone was no longer that of a mimic, but that of a teacher in a Qur'anic school: his words flowed without artifice, and his eyes were fixed towards a point somewhere in the distance, like those of a sleepwalker:

' "When the eye of the Most High passes through the thick walls of palaces, he sees that women singers are listened to more attentively than the doctors of the law, that the sound of the lute prevents men from hearing the call to prayer, that men cannot be distinguished from women, neither in their dress nor in their gait, and that the money extorted from the faithful is thrown at the feet of dancing girls. Brothers! Just as, with the fish that is caught, it is the head which begins to rot first, it is the same in human societies, where rottenness spreads from the top to the bottom." '

A long silence followed, and when I wanted to ask a question, my father interrupted me with a gesture. I waited until he had completely returned from his memories and had begun to speak to me again:

'These words which I have repeated to you, Hasan, were parts of the shaikh's sermon delivered a few months before the fall of Granada. Whether I agree with his words or not, I am still shaken by them, even when I recall them ten years later. You can imagine, then, the effect which his sermons produced on the hard-pressed city of Granada in the year 896.

'At the same time as they realized that the end was near, and that the evils which Astaghfirullah had always predicted were beginning to rain down upon them, the citizens of Granada became persuaded that the shaikh had been correct all along, and that it was heaven that had always spoken through his voice. Even in the poorest quarters, no woman's face was thenceforth seen in the streets. Some, even little girls who had hardly reached puberty, covered themselves through the fear of God, but others through the fear of men, because groups of youngsters were formed, armed with clubs to call the people to do good and to distance themselves from evil. Not a single tavern dared open its doors, even on the sly. The prostitutes left the city en masse and took themselves off to the camp of the besiegers, where the soldiers made them very welcome. The librarians hid from view those works which cast doubt on dogma and traditions, those collections of poems where wine and pleasure were celebrated, and treaties of astrology or geomancy. One day some books were even seized and burnt in the courtyard of the Great Mosque. I was walking past there by chance, when the pyre was beginning to go out, and the passers-by were dispersing with the smoke. A piece of paper flying in the wind revealed that the pile contained the works of a doctor poet of time gone by, known as al-Kalandar. On this paper, half consumed by the flames, I could just read these words:

That which is the best in my life, I draw from drunkenness.
Wine runs in my veins like blood.

★   ★   ★

The books burnt in public that day, my father explained to me, belonged to another doctor, one of the most relentless adversaries of Astaghfirullah. He was called Abu Amr, but the friends of the shaikh changed his name to Abu Khamr, 'Father of Wine'.

The preacher and the doctor had only one thing in common, the habit of speaking frankly, and it was exactly this trait which stirred up the disputes whose unfolding was followed so avidly by the citizens of Granada. Apart from this, it seemed that the Most High had amused himself by creating two beings as unlike one another as possible.

Astaghfirullah was the son of a Christian convert, and it was undoubtedly this which explained his zeal, while Abu Khamr was the son and grandson of qadis, which meant that he did not find it necessary to give continual proof of his attachment to dogma and tradition. The shaikh was fair, lean and choleric, while the doctor was as brown as a ripe date, fatter than a sheep on the eve of the 'Id, and an ironical and contented smile rarely left his lips.

He had studied medicine from the old books, from the works of Hippocrates, Galen, Averroes, Avicenna, Abu'l-Qassis, Abenzoar and Maimonides, as well as more recent texts on leprosy and the plague, may God distance both of them from us. Every day he would distribute freely to both rich and poor dozens of bottles of theriac which he had prepared himself. But this was simply to check the effect of viper's flesh or of the electuary, because he was far more interested in scientific experiments than in medical practice. Besides, how could he have been able, with hands which alcohol made constantly tremble, to operate upon an eye afflicted with a cataract, or even stitch up a wound? And would he have been able to prescribe diets – 'diet is the beginning of all treatment', the Prophet has said – or to advise patients not to gorge themselves upon food and drink, when he devoted himself without restraint to all the pleasures of the table. At the very most he could recommend old wine to assuage the sicknesses of the liver, as other doctors had done before him. If he was called 'tabib', it was because of all the scientific disciplines which interested him, which ranged from astronomy to botany by way of alchemy and algebra, medicine was the one in which he was least confined to the role of a mere dabbler. But he never took a single dirham from it, because that was not how he earned his living; he owned about a dozen villages in the rich Vega of Granada, not far from the lands of the sultan, surrounded by fields of wheat and barley, olive groves and above all by fine orchards. His harvest of wheat, pears, citrons, oranges, bananas, saffron and sugar cane brought him, it was said, three thousand gold dinars each season, more than a doctor would earn in thirty years. In addition, he owned an immense villa on the same hill as the Alhambra, a marvellous *carmen* surrounded by vines.

When Astaghfirullah held up the rich to public obloquy, he was often alluding to Abu Khamr, and it was the picture of the pot-bellied doctor dressed in silk that the poor people would call to mind. Because even those who benefited from his generosity without giving him a penny sensed a certain unease in his presence, either because some of his activities seemed to relate to magic, or because of the language of his discourse, so embroidered with learned words that it was often incomprehensible, except to a little group of learned idlers who spent their days and nights drinking with him and discussing mithridate, the astrolabe and metempsychosis. Princes of the royal family were often to be found among them, and Boabdil himself occasionally frequented their sessions, at least until the atmosphere created in the city by Astaghfirullah obliged the sultan to be more circumspect in his choice of companions.

'They were men of science and recklessness,' recalled my father. 'They often said sensible things when they were not in their cups, but in a way which exasperated ordinary people, because of its obscurity as much as its ungodliness. When a man is rich, whether in gold or in knowledge, he must treat the poverty of others with consideration.'

Then, in a confiding tone:

'Your maternal grandfather, Sulaiman the bookseller, may God have mercy upon him, occasionally went with these people. It was not of course for their wine, but for their conversation. And indeed the doctor was his best customer. He used to order rare books for him from Cairo, Baghdad or Isfahan, and sometimes even from Rome, Venice or Barcelona. Besides Abu Khamr used to complain that the Muslim lands produced fewer books than they used to, and that they were mostly repetitions or summaries of older books. On that your grandfather always agreed; in the first centuries of Islam, he would say bitterly, one could hardly count the treatises on philosophy, mathematics, medicine or astronomy. The poets themselves were far more numerous and innovative, both in style and in content.

'In Andalus too intellectual activity was flourishing, and its fruits were the books which were patiently copied and circulated among learned men from China to the far West. And then came the drying up of the spirit and of the pen. To defend themselves against the ideas and customs of the Franks, men turned Tradition into a citadel in which they shut themselves up. Granada could only produce imitators without talent or boldness.

'Abu Khamr lamented this, but Astaghfirullah accepted it. For him, searching for new ideas at all costs was simply a vice; what was important was to follow the teachings of the Most High as they had been understood and commented upon by the ancients. "Who dares to pretend that he is closer to the Truth than the Prophet and his companions? It is because they have stepped aside from the path of righteousness and because they have allowed morals and ideas to become corrupt that the Muslims have become weak in the face of their enemies." For the doctor, on the other hand, the lessons of History were quite otherwise. "The greatest epoch of Islam," he would say, "was when the caliphs would distribute their gold to wise men and translators, and would spend their evenings discussing philosophy and medicine in the company of half-drunk poets. And did not Andalusia flourish in the days when the vizier 'Abd al-Rahman used to say jokingly: 'O you who cry "Hasten to the prayer!" You would do better to cry: "Hasten to the bottle!" ' The Muslims only became weak when silence, fear and conformity darkened their spirits." '

It seemed to me that my father had closely followed all these discussions, but without ever having made a definite judgement upon them. Ten years later, his words were still uncertain.

'Few people followed the doctor's godless ways, but some of his ideas swayed them. As witness the business of the cannon. Did I ever tell you about it?

'This happened towards the end of the year 896. All the roads leading to the Vega were in the hands of the Castilians, and supplies were becoming scarce. In Granada the hours of daylight were marked only by the whistling of bullets and fragments of rock raining down on the houses, and by the lamentations of weeping women; in the public gardens, hundreds of destitute people in rags, impoverished at the beginning of a winter which promised to be long and hard, fought over the last branches of the last withered tree; the shaikh's followers, unleashed and distraught, roamed the streets looking for some mischief-maker to punish.

'Around the besieged city, the fighting was less intense, even less violent. The horsemen and footsoldiers of Granada, decimated by the Castilian artillery each time they sallied forth, no longer dared to venture in a body far from the ramparts. They were content with small operations at night, ambushing an enemy squadron, stealing some arms or rustling some cattle, bold but essentially pointless acts, because they were not sufficient to loosen the noose, nor provision the city, nor even to put new heart into it.

'Suddenly, there was a rumour. Not one of those which scattered like fine rain from a thick cloud, but one which poured down like a summer shower, covering the misery of daily noises with its deafening tumult. A rumour which brought to our city that element of absurdity from which no drama can escape.

' "Abu Khamr has just got hold of a cannon, seized from the enemy by a handful of reckless soldiers who agreed to drag it to his garden for ten gold pieces!" '

My father drew a cup of orgeat syrup to his lips and swallowed several mouthfuls slowly before continuing his story, unaware of my total incomprehension:

'The citizens of Granada had never possessed a cannon, and, as Astaghfirullah never ceased to repeat to them that this devilish invention made more noise than it did harm, they were resigned to the notion that only the enemy could have such a new and complicated piece of apparatus. Hence the doctor's initiative plunged them into considerable confusion. A continual procession of young and old filed past "the thing", keeping a respectful distance from it and remarking in subdued voices about its well-rounded contours and its menacing jaw. As for Abu Khamr, he was there, with his own roundness, savouring his revenge. "Tell the shaikh to come here rather than passing his days in prayer! Ask him if he knows how to light a fuse as well as he knows how to burn books!" The more pious distanced themselves immediately, murmuring some oath or other under their breath, while the others persistently questioned the doctor about how the cannon worked, and the effects it would have if it was used against Santa Fé. Of course he himself had no idea, and his explanations were all the more impressive.

'As you will have guessed, Hasan my son, this cannon was never used. Abu Khamr had neither bullets nor gunpowder nor artillery-men, and some of his visitors began to snigger. Happily for him, the *muhtasib*, who was responsible for public order, alerted by the crowds, organized a gang of men to take the object away and drag it to the Alhambra to show it to the sultan. No one ever saw it again. But we continued to hear about it long afterwards, from the doctor himself, naturally enough, who never ceased to say that it was only with the aid of cannons that the Muslims could defeat their enemies, and that as long as they did not agree either to acquire or to make a great number of these machines, their kingdoms would be in danger. For his part Astaghfirullah preached exactly the opposite: it was through the martyrdom of the soldiers of the faith that the besiegers would be overcome.

'The sultan Boabdil eventually brought them into accord, since he desired neither cannons nor martyrdom. While the shaikh and the doctor quibbled endlessly, and the whole of Granada around them pondered its fate, the master of the city could only think of how to avoid confrontation. He sent message after message to King Ferdinand, in which the only question was that of the date of the surrender of the city, the besieger talking in terms of weeks and the besieged in terms of months, hoping perhaps that the hand of the Most High would wipe out the feeble arrangements of men by some sudden decree, a storm, a cataclysm or a plague, which would decimate the grandees of Spain.'

But Heaven had other destinies for us.

The Year of the Fall
897 A.H.
④November 1491 – 22 October 1492

'It was cold that year in Granada, fearfully cold, and the snow was black with freshly dug earth and blood. O, the familiarity of death, the imminence of exile, how the joys of the past were painful to remember!'

A great change came over my mother whenever she used to speak of the fall of our city; for this drama she assumed a particular tone of voice, a look, words, tears, which I never knew in any other circumstances. I myself was less than three years old in those tumultuous days, and I do not know whether the cries that came to my ears at that moment were the memory of what I had actually heard at the time or simply the echo of the thousands of accounts of the story that I had heard since.

These tales did not always begin in the same way. Those of my mother spoke first of hunger and anguish.

'From the very beginning of the year,' she used to say, 'the snows had come to cut off the few roads which the besiegers had spared, making Granada completely isolated from the rest of the country, particularly the Vega and the Alpujarras mountains in the south, from which wheat, oats, millet, oil and raisins still used to reach us. People in our neighbourhood were afraid, even the least poor of them; every day they bought anything they could lay their hands on, and instead of being reassured at the sight of the earthenware jars of provisions stacked up along the walls of their rooms they became even more afraid of famine, rats and looters. Everyone said that if the roads opened up again they would leave immediately for some village or other where they had relatives. In the first months of the siege it had been the inhabitants of the surrounding villages who sought asylum in Granada, meeting up with the refugees from Guadix and Gibraltar. They accommodated themselves as best they could with their relatives, in the outbuildings of mosques or in deserted houses; during the previous summer they were even living in gardens and on waste ground, under makeshift tents. The streets were choked with beggars of all descriptions, sometimes grouped in whole families, father, mother, children and old people, all haggard and skeletal, but also often gathered in gangs of youngsters of menacing appearance; and men of honour who could not bear either to throw themselves upon charity or into a life of crime were dying slowly in their homes, away from prying eyes.'

This was not to be the fate of my family. Even in the worst moments of penury, our house never lacked for anything, thanks to my father's position. He had inherited an important municipal function from his own father, that of chief public weigh-master, in charge of the weighing of grains and the regulation of proper commercial practice. It was this function which entitled members of my family to the name of al-Wazzan, the weigh-master, which I still bear; in the Maghrib, no one knows that I now call myself Leo or John-Leo de Medici, no one has ever addressed me as the African; there I was Hasan, son of Muhammad al-Wazzan, and in official documents the name 'al-Zayyati' was added, the name of my tribe of origin, 'al-Gharnati', the Granadan, and if I was far off from Fez I would be called 'al-Fassi' referring to my first country of adoption, which was not to be the last.

As weigh-master, my father could have taken as much as he wished from the foodstuffs submitted to him for inspection, provided he did not do this to excess, or even receive payment in gold dinars as the price of his silence on the frauds perpetrated by the merchants; I do not believe that he thought to enrich himself, but his function meant that the spectre of famine was always distant for him and his family.

'You were such a chubby little boy,' my mother used to tell me, 'that I did not dare to take you for walks in the streets in case you attracted the evil eye'. It was also important not to reveal our relative affluence.

Concerned not to alienate those of his neighbours who were in more straitened circumstances, my father would often offer them some of his acquisitions, particularly meat or spring produce, but he always gave within limits and with modesty, because any largesse might have been provocative, any condescension humiliating. And when the people of the capital had no strength or illusions left, and showed their anger and helplessness in the streets, and when a delegation was to be sent to the sultan to charge him to put an end to the war at all costs, my father agreed to join the representatives of al-Baisin.

Thus, when he would retell the tale of the fall of Granada, his account would always begin in the tapestried rooms of the Alhambra.

'There were thirty of us, from all the corners of the city, from Najd to the Fountain of Tears, from the Potters' quarter to the Almond Field, and those who were shouting loudly did not tremble any less than the others. I will not pretend to you that I was not terrified, and I would have certainly gone back if I had not feared to lose face. But imagine the folly of what we did; for two whole days thousands of townspeople had sown disorder in the streets, yelling the worst curses against the sultan, abusing his counsellors and making ironic remarks about his wives, beseeching him either to fight or make peace rather than prolong a situation indefinitely in which there was no joy in living and no glory in dying. So, as if to bring directly to his ears the insults which his spies had certainly already reported to him, we, a group of strange, dishevelled and vociferous parliamentarians, were coming to defy him in his own palace, before his chamberlain, his ministers and the officers of his guard. And there I was, an official from the *muhtasib*'s office, charged with maintaining respect for the law and public order, in the company of the ring-leaders of the riots, while the enemy stood at the very gates of the city. Thinking of all this in my confusion, I told myself that I would find myself inside a dungeon, beaten with a bull's pizzle until the blood came, or even crucified on one of the crenellations in the city walls.

'My fears turned out to be groundless, and shame soon replaced fright. Fortunately, none of my companions was aware of either the one or the other. You will soon understand, Hasan my son, why I have told you about this moment of weakness, which I have never spoken of before to any member of my family. I want you to know what really took place in our city of Granada during that calamitous year; perhaps this may prevent you allowing yourself to be misused by those who have the destiny of multitudes in their hands. For my part, everything of value that I have learned about life has been revealed to me while unveiling the hearts of princes and women.

'Our delegation passed into the Hall of the Ambassadors, where Boabdil was enthroned in his usual place, surrounded by two armed soldiers and several advisers. He had astonishingly deep wrinkles for a man of thirty, his beard flecked with grey and his eyelids withered; an enormous carved copper brazier standing in front of him concealed his legs and chest from our sight. It was the end of Muharram, which corresponded that year with the beginning of the Christian month of December, and it was so cold at the time that one recalled the arrogant words of the poet Ibn Sara de Santarem when he visited Granada:

> People of this land, do not pray,
> Do not turn away from that which is forbidden.
> Thus you will win your place in Hell
> Where the fire is so comforting
> When the north wind blows.

'The sultan welcomed us with a smile hovering on his lips, which seemed to me to be benevolent. He motioned us to sit down, which I did very gingerly. But, before the discussion could even begin, I saw pass by, to my great surprise, a large number of dignitaries, officers, *ulama*, notables from almost everywhere, including shaikh Astagh-firullah, the vizier al-Mulih, doctor Abu Khamr, almost a hundred people, some of whom had always avoided one another.

'Boabdil spoke slowly, in a low voice which forced his visitors to be quiet and strain their ears in his direction, barely able to breathe. "In the name of God, the Compassionate, the Merciful, I have commanded that all those with an opinion on the disturbing situation in which fate has placed our city should meet here in the Alhambra Palace. Put forward your opinions and make up your minds on the course of action which should be adopted for the good of all, and I undertake to act according to your advice. Our vizier al-Mulih will give his opinion first; I shall not speak until the end." Upon which he leaned his back on the cushions arranged along the wall and did not say another word.

'Al-Mulih was the sultan's principal confidant, and it was expected that he would deliver some words of praise in rhyming prose of the stand taken by his master. He did nothing of the kind. Although he addressed his speech to the "glorious descendant of the glorious Nasrid dynasty" he continued in very different tones: "My Lord, will you guarantee me immunity from punishment, *aman*, if I say to you fully and frankly what I think at this moment?" Boabdil indicated his assent with a slight movement of his head. "My opinion," continued the vizier, "is that the policy we are pursuing serves neither God nor those who worship Him. We can hold forth here for ten days and ten nights, but this will not put a single grain of rice into the empty bowls of the children of Granada. Let us look the truth in the face, even if it is hideous, and let us scorn untruth, even if it is decked out in jewels. Our city is large, and even in time of peace it is not easy to provision it with the supplies that it needs. Every day which passes takes its toll of victims, and one day the Most High will call us to account for all those innocents whom we have allowed to perish. We could demand sacrifices of the inhabitants of the city if we could promise them a swift deliverance, if a powerful Muslim army was on its way to liberate Granada and punish its besiegers, but, as we now know, no one is coming to succour us. You, Lord of this kingdom, have written to the Sultan of Cairo, and to the Ottoman sultan; have they replied to you?" Boabdil raised his eyebrows to indicate that they had not. "And more recently, have you not written to the Muslim rulers of Fez and Tlemcen asking them to hasten here with their armies? What has been their reaction? Your noble blood, O Boabdil, forbids you to speak, but I will do so in your place. In fact, the rulers of Fez and Tlemcen have sent messengers laden with gifts, not to us but to Ferdinand, swearing that they will never take up arms against him! Today Granada is alone, because the other cities of the kingdom are already lost and because the Muslims of other lands are deaf to our appeals. What solution remains open to us?"

'A weary silence came over the assembly, which contented itself with occasional rumblings of approval. Al-Mulih opened his mouth as if about to continue his argument. But he said nothing, stepped backwards and sat down, his face fixed on the ground. Three speakers of no particular distinction then got up in turn to say that the surrender of the town should be negotiated immediately, and that those in charge had lost too much time, and had been insensitive to the sufferings of the ordinary people.

'It was now the turn of Astaghfirullah, who had been sitting impatiently in his seat since the meeting began. He got up, made a mechanical movement with both hands to adjust his turban, and directed his gaze towards the ceiling, which was decorated with arabesques. "The vizier al-Mulih is a man well known for his intelligence and his skill, and when he wishes to implant an idea in the minds of his audience, he can manage it with ease. He wants to give us a message, and he has prepared our minds to receive it and now he is silent, because he does not wish to give us with his own hands the bitter cup from which he wishes us to drink. What is there in this cup? If he does not want to tell us from his own mouth, I will do it myself: the vizier wants us to agree to hand over Granada to Ferdinand. He has told us that all further resistance is useless, that no help will reach us from Andalus or elsewhere; he has revealed to us that the envoys of the Muslim princes have compromised themselves with our enemies, may God punish them and the others as He alone knows how! But al-Mulih has not told us everything! He has not said that he has himself been negotiating with the Rumis for weeks. He has not confessed that he has already agreed to open the gates of Granada to them."

'Astaghfirullah raised his voice to speak above the mounting uproar. "Al-Mulih has not told us that he has even agreed to bring forward the date of the surrender, that this will take place within the next few days, and that he has only sought a delay to prepare the minds of the people of Granada for defeat. It is to force us to capitulate that the food warehouses have been closed for several days; it is to deepen our discouragement that the demonstrations in the streets have been organized by the vizier's agents; and if we have been invited to come to the Alhambra today, it is not to criticize the actions of our governors, as the vizier would have us believe, but to give our backing to their impious decision to surrender Granada." The shaikh was almost shouting; his beard shook with rage and bitter sarcasm. "Do not be indignant, my brother believers, because if al-Mulih has concealed the truth from us it is certainly not because he wished to deceive us; it is only because he lacked the time. But, by God, let us interrupt him no more, let him tell us in detail what he has been doing these past few days, and then we can agree on the course of action to be followed." He finished abruptly and sat down, gathering the hem of his stained gown with a trembling hand, while a deathly silence came over the room, and all eyes turned towards al-Mulih.

'The latter expected that one of the others present would intervene; in vain. Then he rose up with a burst of energy. "The shaikh is a man of piety and courage, as we all know; his love for this city is the more meritorious since he was not born here, and his zeal for Islam is the more praiseworthy since it was not the religion into which he was born. Furthermore he is a man of vast knowledge, well versed in the sciences of religion and of the world, and does not hesitate to seek knowledge at its source, however far away that may be. Listening to him relate what has passed between myself, the envoy of the mighty sultan of Andalus, and the emissary of King Ferdinand, I cannot conceal my admiration, astonishment and surprise, since it was not I who have told him these things. Moreoever, I must acknowledge that what he has said is not far from the truth. I would reproach him only in so far as he has presented the situation in the way that our enemies describe it. For them, what is important is the date of the peace treaty, since the siege costs them dear. For us, the point is not to delay the inevitable for a few days or even a few weeks, after which the Castilians would throw themselves upon us with even greater fury; given that victory is out of the question, by an irrevocable decree of He who orders all things, we must try to obtain the best possible terms. That is to say, a safe conduct for ourselves, our wives and our children; the preservation of our properties, our fields, our houses and our animals; the right of every one of us to continue to live in Granada, according to the religion of God and of His prophet, praying in our mosques and paying no other taxes than the *zakat* and the tithe, as prescribed by our Law; equally, the right for those who wish to do so to depart across the sea towards the Maghrib, taking all their property with them, with a period of three years to choose, and with the right to sell their possessions at a just price to Muslims or to Christians. Those are the terms on which I have been attempting to obtain Ferdinand's agreement, making him swear on the Gospel that he would respect it until his death and that his successors would respect it after him. Was I wrong to do so?"

'Without waiting to hear their replies, al-Mulih continued: "Dignitaries and notables of Granada, I do not bring you news of victory, but I wish to save you from the bitter cup of humiliating defeat, from massacre, the violation of women and young girls, from dishonour, slavery, pillage and destruction. For this I need your agreement and your support. If you ask me to do so, I can break off the negotiations, or make them last longer; that is what I would do if I sought only the praise of fools and hypocrites. I could give Ferdinand's envoys a thousand excuses for delaying the peace treaty. But would this really be in the interests of the Muslims? Now it is winter; the enemy's forces are more scattered, and the snow has forced him to reduce his attacks. He shelters behind the walls of Santa Fé and the fortifications he has constructed, satisfied with preventing us from using the roads. In three months, it will be spring, Ferdinand will have fresh troops, ready to launch the decisive attack against our city which hunger will have rendered almost lifeless. It is now that we must negotiate! It is now that Ferdinand will accept our conditions, while we can still offer him something in return."

'Abu Khamr, who had remained silent since the beginning of the discussion, leaped up suddenly from his place, jostling his neighbours with his massive shoulders: "We can offer him something, you say, but what? Why do the words stick in your throat? What you want to offer to Ferdinand is not a golden candlestick, nor a robe of honour, nor a fifteen-year-old slavegirl. That which you wish to present to Ferdinand is this city, about which the poet has written:

Granada, no city is your equal,
Not in Egypt, not in Syria, not in Iraq,
You are the bride
And these lands are only your dowry.

' "What you want to offer to Ferdinand, O Vizier, is this palace of the Alhambra, glory of glories and marvel of marvels. Look around you, my brothers! Let your eyes wander slowly around this room, every section of whose walls has been patiently carved by our fathers and grandfathers like a rare and delicate jewel! May it remain for ever in your memories, this holy place where none of you will ever set foot again, except perhaps as a slave."

'The doctor was weeping, and many men hid their faces. "For eight centuries," he continued in a broken and breathless voice, "we have illuminated this earth with our knowledge, but our sun is at its eclipse, and everything is becoming dark. And as for you, O Granada, I know that your flame will flicker a last time before being extinguished, but do not count on me to blow it out, as my descendants would spit upon my memory until the Day of

Judgement." He collapsed rather than sat down, and several seconds passed, slowly, heavily, before the silence was broken, once more by Astaghfirullah, who forgot, for once, his enmity towards Abu Khamr. "What the doctor says is true. That which the vizier is offering to the king of the infidels is our town, with its mosques which will become churches, its schools where the Qur'an will never penetrate again, its houses where no prohibition will be respected. What he is also offering to Ferdinand is the right of life and death over us and ours, because we know very well how much faith we can place in the treaties and oaths of Rum. Did they not promise respect and safe-conduct for the inhabitants of Malaga four years ago, before entering the city and leading the women and children into captivity? Can you assure me, al-Mulih, that it will not be the same at Granada?"

'The vizier replied in exasperation: "I can assure you of nothing, except that I shall remain in this city myself, that I shall share the fate of its sons and I shall use all the energy that the Most High will see fit to give me to make sure that the agreements are respected. It is not in the hands of Ferdinand that our destiny lies, but in the hands of God, and it is He alone who can one day give us the victory that He has not vouchsafed to us today. For the time being, you know what the situation is, and it is pointless to prolong this discussion. We must come to a decision. Those who approve the conclusion of an agreement with the Castilians should pronounce the motto of the Nasrid dynasty!"

'From all the corners of the Hall of the Ambassadors,' my father recalled, 'came the same words, "Only God can grant the victory," said with determination but with no joy, because that which had but a short while ago been a war cry had become, that year, a formula of resignation; perhaps even also, in the mouths of some, a reproach addressed to the Creator, may He preserve us from doubt and unbelief!

'When it was clear that he had the support of the majority of those present, Boabdil decided to take over from the vizier. He quietened his subjects with an imperious gesture of his hands, to say in a sententious tone: "The believers have agreed among themselves, and their decision has been made. We will follow the way of peace, sure in the knowledge that God will guide us towards that which is the best for us. It is He who listens, He who replies."

'Before the sultan had finished his sentence, Astaghfirullah strode towards the door, his anger making his limp more pronounced, his lips uttering the terrible words: "Was it of us that God has said in His Book: You are the best nation that has ever been given to mankind?'"

★ ★ ★

The very evening of the meeting in the Alhambra all Granada knew exactly what had been said there. Then began the harsh ordeal of waiting, with its daily batch of rumours, always centring on one despairingly unique theme: the day and the hour of the entry of the Castilians into the city.

'During the last week of the month of Safar,' my mother told me, 'the day after the feast of the birth of 'Issa the Messiah – peace upon him – Gaudy Sarah came to see me with a little book carefully wrapped up in a mauve silk scarf which she took gingerly from the bottom of her wicker basket. "Neither you nor I can read," I said to her, forcing a smile, but she seemed to have lost all her gaiety. "I brought this to show to your cousin," she said in the coldest voice. "It is a treatise written by one of the wise men of our community, Rabbi Ishaq Ben Yahuda. He says that a flood is about to pour down upon us, a flood of blood and fire, a chastisement which will afflict all those who have abandoned the life of nature for the corruption of the city." Her delivery was halting and her hands trembled.

'You were sitting on my knees, my son; I held you very close and kissed your warmly on the neck. "Foreteller of evil tidings!" I snapped at Sarah, more from irritation than malice. "Are our daily sufferings not overwhelming enough? Do you really need to prophesy an even worse fate for us?" But the Jewess would not be distracted from her theme. "Rabbi Ishaq is a regular visitor to King Ferdinand, he knows many secrets, and if he uses the language of the prophets it is to make us understand things which he would not otherwise be able to divulge." – "Perhaps he is trying to warn you that Granada will be taken, but that is no longer a secret." – "His words go farther than that. He maintains that, for the Jews, there will be no more air to breathe or water to drink in this land of Safarad."

'Normally so exuberant, she was now so distressed that she could only speak with great difficulty. "Is it your book that has so upset you?" – "There is something else. I heard this morning that one of my nephews was burnt alive at the stake at La Guardia, near Toledo, with ten other people. They were accused of having practised black magic, of having kidnapped a Christian child and crucified him like 'Issa. The inquisitors could not prove anything; they could not give the name of the child who was alleged to have been murdered, nor produce a body, nor even establish that a child in the area had disappeared; but under the water torture and the rack Yusuf and his friends must have confessed to anything." "Do you think that such a fate could befall your people here in Granada?" – She gave me a look which seemed full of hatred. I did not know how I had offended her, but in the state she was in, I decided to apologize. She did not give me the chance. "When this city is taken, do you think that your lands, your houses and your gold will be less coveted than ours? Do you believe that your Faith will be more tolerated than ours? Do you believe that the fire burning at the stake will be kinder to one of the sons of Shem than to the other? In Granada it is as if we were on an ark, we have floated together and we shall sink together. Tomorrow, on the road to exile . . ."

'Realizing that she had gone too far, she stopped abruptly, and in an attempt to mitigate the effect of her words, put her arms around me with their wide sleeves and the perfume of musk, and began to sob against my shoulder. However, I did not begrudge her this, because the same images that were terrifying her were haunting my mind both in dreams and in wakefulness, and in that respect we were both sisters, orphans of the same dying city.

'We were still bemoaning our fate when I heard your father's steps returning home. I called him from my bedroom, and while he climbed the stairs I wiped my cheeks with the hem of my dress, while Sarah quickly covered her head and face. Muhammad's eyes were bloodshot, but I pretended not to notice to save him embarrassment. "Sarah has brought you a book so that you can explain to us what is in it." Your father had long since ceased to entertain the slighest prejudice against Gaudy Sarah, who now came to our house almost every day; he enjoyed exchanging opinions and news with her, and also liked to tease her about her appearance, and she would laugh good-naturedly. That day, however, he had no more heart to laugh than she. He took the book from her hands without saying a word and sat cross-legged in the doorway leafing through it. He immersed himself in it for more than an hour, while we watched him in silence; then he closed it and remained pensive. He looked towards me as if not seeing me: "Your father Sulaiman the bookseller once told me long ago that on the eve of all great happenings books like this appear which predict the end of the world, seeking to explain the severe decrees of the Most High in terms of the movements of the stars and the disobedience of men. People pass them to each other in secret, and they are comforted by reading them, because the misfortune of each of them becomes lost and forgotten like a drop of water in a raging torrent. This book says that your people should leave, Sarah, without waiting for fate to knock at their door. As soon as you can do so, take your children and go away from this land." Sarah uncovered her face to show her suffering. "Where shall I go?" It was less a question than a cry of distress, but your father replied by leafing through the book: "This man suggests Italy, or the land of the Ottomans, but you can even go to the Maghrib across the sea, which is nearer. That is where we shall go ourselves." He put down the book and went out without looking at us.

'That was the first time that your father mentioned exile, and I would have liked to question him further about this decision and the arrangements he had made, but I did not dare to do so. He himself only spoke to me about it once more, the next day, to tell me in low tones not to raise the subject in front of Warda.'

Over the next few days, the cannons and the mangonels stayed silent; snow fell continuously upon Granada, covering it with a veil of peace and serenity which nothing seemed able to destroy. There was no fighting, and only the cries of children could be heard in the streets. How much would the city have wished that time would forget it! But it was on the move; the Christian year 1492 began on the last day of the month of Safar 897, and before dawn there came a loud knocking at our door. My mother woke with a start and called my father, who was sleeping with Warda that night. He went to open the door. Outside were some of the sultan's officers, who asked him to follow them on his horse. They had already collected several dozen people together, including some very young boys whose beardless faces were lit up by the snow. Muhammad went back into his house to put on some warm clothing, and then, accompanied by two soldiers, went to fetch his horse from the barn behind the house. Standing in the half-open door, with me half-asleep on her arm, and Warda's head peering over her shoulder, my mother questioned the officers to find out where her husband was being taken. They replied that the vizier al-Mulih had given them a list of people whom he wished to see urgently; they added that she had nothing to fear. My father also did his best to reassure her as he left.

When he reached the Plaza de la Tabla in front of the Alhambra, Muhammad could make out some five hundred prisoners as daylight was breaking, all on horseback, all wrapped in heavy woollen cloaks, surrounded by a thousand soldiers on foot or on horseback, who manifested no violence towards them, even verbally, simply surrounding them to prevent them escaping. Then the immense convoy moved off in silence, a veiled rider at its head, the soldiers walking in line alongside. It passed before the Gate of the Seven Stages, went along the ramparts, and left the city by the Najd Gate to arrive at the Genil, which was frozen over. A cherry orchard on the river bank was the first halting place of the silent and trembling caravan.

It was already daylight, but the fine crescent moon of the new month could still be seen in the sky. The veiled man uncovered his face and summoned to his side a dozen high dignitaries chosen from among the prisoners. To no one's surprise it was al-Mulih. He began by asking them not to be alarmed and apologized for not having explained the situation to them earlier.

'We had to leave the city to avoid any incident, any incautious reaction. Ferdinand has asked that five hundred notables from the great families of Granada should be left with him as hostages so that he can bring his troops into the city without fearing a trap. We too have every interest in the surrender taking place without the slightest violence. Reassure the others, tell them that they will be well treated and that it will all pass very quickly.'

The news was imparted to everyone without provoking more than a few inconsequential murmurs, since most felt proud to have been chosen as well as a certain sense of security in not being in the city when it would be invaded, which largely compensated for the irritation of temporary confinement. Others, like my father, would have preferred to be with their wives and their children at that crucial moment, but they knew that they could do nothing for them, and that the will of the Almighty must be fulfilled to the end.

They did not stop for more than half an hour, and then began to move on towards the west, always keeping within a stone's throw from the Genil. Soon a troop of Castilians appeared on the horizon, and when it drew level with the convoy, its leader took al-Mulih to one side and then, on an order from him, the soldiers of Granada turned their horses round and trotted back to the city, while Ferdinand's cavalry took their place around the hostages. The crescent had now disappeared from the sky. The convoy went on, even more silent, even more overcome with emotion, to the walls of Santa Fe.

'How strange, their new city built from our old stones,' thought Muhammad as he passed into this encampment which he had so often seen in the distance with a mixture of fear and curiosity. On all sides there was the bustle and commotion heralding a major attack, · Ferdinand's soldiers preparing ostensibly to engage in the final combat, or rather to slaughter the city which they were now holding at bay, as a bull is destroyed in the arenas of Granada after being torn to pieces by a pack of dogs.

The same evening, of the first of January 1492, the vizier, who had stayed with the hostages, went back to Granada, accompanied this time by several Christian officers whom he was to bring into the city in accordance with the agreements. They went in at night, by the road which my father and his companions in captivity had taken, which had the advantage of not arousing the suspicions of the people of the city too early. The following day they appeared at the tower of Comares, where Boabdil handed them the keys of the fortress. Using the same secret road, several hundred Castilian soldiers soon arrived, and secured the ramparts. A bishop hoisted up a cross on the watch tower, and the soldiers cheered him, crying 'Castile', 'Castile', 'Castile', three times, which was their custom when they occupied a place. Hearing these cries, the people of Granada understood that the unthinkable had already taken place, and, astounded that an event of such magnitude could have come to pass with so little disturbance, began to pray and chant, their eyes misted over and their knees weak.

As the news spread, the inhabitants came out into the streets, men and women together, Muslims and Jews, rich and poor, wandering around in a daze, jumping with a start at the slightest sound. My mother took me through one alleyway to another as far as Sabiqa, where she took up her position for several hours, observing everything that was happening around the Alhambra. I think I can remember having seen the Castilian soldiers that day, singing, shouting and strutting about on the walls. Towards noon, already drunk, they began to spread themselves out over the city, and Salma resigned herself to having to wait for her husband at home.

Three days later, one of our neighbours, a notary who was over seventy, who had been taken hostage with my father, was brought back to his house. He had feigned illness, and the Castilians had been afraid that he would die on them. From him my mother learned which way they had gone, and she decided to go at dawn the next morning and stand watch at the Najd Gate, right at the south of the city not far from the Genil. She judged it prudent to take Warda with her since she could talk to her co-religionists in case they challenged us.

So we left at the first hour of daylight, my mother carrying me and my sister Mariam in her mother's arms, both going slowly so as not to slip on the frozen snow. We passed through the old qasba, the Bridge of the Qadi, the Mauror quarter, Granada-of-the-Jews, the Potters' Gate, without passing a soul; only the metallic sounds of kitchen utensils being moved about reminded us from time to time that we were not in an abandoned encampment, haunted by ghosts, but in fact in a city where human beings of flesh and blood still felt the need to bang cooking pots together.

'It is true that it is barely daylight, but does that explain why no sentry is on duty at the Najd Gate?' asked my mother in a high voice.

She put me down on the ground and pushed one of the doors, which yielded easily, as it was already half open. We left the city, without really knowing which road to take.

We were still only a few steps from the walls when a strange sight presented itself to our astonished gaze. Two troops of horsemen seemed to be coming towards us, one from our right, coming up from the Genil at a brisk trot in spite of the slope, and the other from our left, coming from the direction of the Alhambra, moving awkwardly. Soon a rider detached himself from the latter group and went off at a faster pace. Returning quickly towards the city, we passed through the Najd Gate once more, without shutting the door behind us, in order to continue to watch without being seen. When the rider from the Alhambra was very close to us my mother stifled a cry:

'It is Boabdil!' she said, and fearing she had spoken too loudly put her hand to my mouth to keep me quiet, although I was completely silent and my sister too, both of us absorbed in the strange scene that was unfolding in front of us.

I could only see the sultan's turban which was wrapped round his head and covered his forehead down to his eyebrows. His horse looked somewhat colourless to me, in contrast to the two royal palfreys which now advanced from the other side at walking pace, covered with gold and silks. Boabdil made as if to dismount from his horse, but Ferdinand stopped him with a reassuring gesture. The sultan went towards his vanquisher and tried to seize his hand to kiss it, but the king withdrew it, and Boabdil, who was leaning towards him, could only embrace his shoulder, showing that he was still treated as a prince. Not as prince of Granada, however; the new masters of the city had granted him a small estate in the Alpujarra mountains where he was allowed to set himself up with his family.

The scene at the Najd Gate lasted only a few seconds, after which Ferdinand and Isabella made their way towards the Alhambra while Boabdil, taken aback for a moment, turned round once in the opposite direction before resuming his journey. He rode so slowly that he was soon caught up by his train, which consisted of more than a hundred horses and mules carrying men, women and children and a large number of coffers and objects wrapped up in cloths. The next day it was said that he had disinterred the corpses of his ancestors and had taken them with him to prevent them falling into the hands of the enemy.

It was also claimed that he had not been able to take all his goods with him, and that he had caused an immense fortune to be hidden in the caves of Mount Cholair. How many people vowed to find it! Will anyone believe me when I say that all my life I have met men whose sole dream was this vanished gold? I have even met people who are known everywhere as *kannazin*, who have no other occupation than seeking treasure, particularly that of Boabdil; at Fez they are so numerous that they hold regular meetings, and when I was living in that city they even elected a representative to concern himself with the legal cases constantly brought against them by the owners of the buildings whose foundations they weakened in the course of their excavations. These *kannazin* are convinced that the riches abandoned in the past by princes have been put under a spell to prevent them being discovered; this explains their constant recourse to sorcerers whom they employ to unravel the spell. It is impossible to have a conversation with a *kannaz* without him swearing that he has already seen heaps of gold and silver in an underground passage, but could not lay his hands on them because he did not know the correct incantations or because he did not have the proper perfumes on him. And he will show you, without letting you leaf through it, a book which describes the places where treasure is to be found!

For my part I do not know whether the treasure which the Nasrid rulers had amassed over the centuries is still buried in the land of Andalus, but I do not think so, since Boabdil went into exile with no hope of ever returning, and the Rumis had allowed him to take away all that he desired. He departed into oblivion, rich but miserable, and as he passed over the last ridge from which he could still see Granada, he stood motionless for a long time, with troubled mien and his spirit frozen in torpor; the Castilians called this place 'The Moor's last sigh', because, it was said, the fallen sultan had shed tears there, of shame and remorse. 'You weep like a woman for the kingdom which you did not defend like man,' his mother Fatima would have said.

'In the eyes of this woman,' my father would tell me later, 'what had just taken place was not only the victory of Castile; it was also, and perhaps primarily, her rival's revenge. Sultan's daughter, sultan's wife, sultan's mother, Fatima was steeped in politicking and intrigue, far more than Boabdil, who would have been perfectly content with a life of pleasure without ambition or risk. It was she who had propelled her son to power, in order that he should dethrone her own husband Abu'l-Hasan, who was guilty of having deserted her for the beautiful Christian captive Soraya. It was Fatima who made Boabdil escape from the tower of Comares and organized in minute detail his rebellion against the old monarch. It was she who had ousted the concubine and excluded her young children from power for ever.

'But destiny is more changeable than the skin of a chameleon, as one of the poets of Denia used to say. Thus while Fatima was escaping from the abandoned city, Soraya promptly resumed her former name, Isabella de Solis, and had her two children Sa'd and Nasr baptized, becoming Don Fernando and Don Juan, infantes of Granada. They were not the only members of the royal family to abandon the faith of their fathers to become grandees of Spain; Yahya al-Najjar, briefly the hero of the "war party", had done so before them, and was given the title of Duke of Granada-Venegas. After the fall of the city Yahya was made "alguazil mayor", chief of police, which amply demonstrated that he had gained the full confidence of the victors. Other people followed his example, among whom was a secretary of the sultan, named Ahmad, whom people had long suspected of being a spy in Ferdinand's service.

'The days which follow defeat often lay bare the corruption of souls. Here I am thinking less of Yahya than of the vizier al-Mulih. Because, while negotiating, as he had explained to us at such length, the welfare of the widows and orphans of Granada, this man had not forgotten himself; he had obtained from Ferdinand, as the price of the surrender which he had hastened so cleverly, twenty thousand gold castilians, or nearly ten thousand thousands of maravedis, as well as vast estates. Other dignitaries of the regime also accommodated themselves without difficulty to the domination of the Rumis.'

In fact life immediately began again in occupied Granada, as if Ferdinand had wanted to prevent the Muslims departing for exile en masse. The hostages returned to their families the very day after the entry of the king and queen into the city, and my father told us that he had been treated with more consideration than if he had been the guest of a prince. At Santa Fé he and his companions were not confined to prison; they could go to the market and walked around the streets in small groups, although accompanied by guards whose task was both to keep them under surveillance and to protect them against outbursts on the part of any drunken or overexcited soldiers. It was during one of these strolls that someone pointed out to my father at the door of a tavern a Genoese sailor whom all Santa Fé was talking about and making fun of. People called him 'Cristobal Colon'. He wanted, he said, to fit out caravels to sail westwards to the Indies, since the earth was round, and he made no secret of his hope to obtain part of the treasure of the Alhambra for this expedition. He had been in Santa Fé for weeks, insisting on meeting the king or the queen, who avoided him, although he had been recommended to them by eminent personages. While waiting to be received, he sent them a stream of messages and supplications, which, in these warlike times, did not fail to irritate them. Muhammad never saw this Genoese again, but I myself often had occasion to hear men speak of him.

A few days after my father's return, Duke Yahya summoned him to resume his functions as weigh-master, because, he told him, foodstuffs would soon be returning to the markets in abundance, and it was essential to take care that any fraud should be repressed. Initially disgusted by the mere sight of the renegade, my father ended up by working with him just as he had done with all other police chiefs, not without murmuring curses from time to time when he remembered the hope that this man had once symbolized for the Muslims. The presence of Yahya also had the effect of reassuring the city's notables; while some already knew him well, all began to court him more assiduously than they had done when he was the unfortunate rival of Boabdil.

'In his anxiety to calm the fears of the vanquished for their fate,' my father recalled, 'Ferdinand used to make regular visits to Granada to make sure that his men were faithfully carrying out the agreements. Although concerned for his own safety in the first few days, the king soon began to move freely round the city, visiting the market, under close escort of course, and inspecting the old walls. It is true that he avoided staying the night in our city for months, preferring to return to Santa Fé before sunset, but his unease, though perfectly understandable, was not accompanied by any iniquitous or discriminatory measure or any violation of the treaty of surrender. Ferdinand's solicitude, whether sincere or feigned, was such that the Christians who visited Granada used to say to the Muslims: "You are now more dear to the heart of our sovereign than we ourselves have ever been." Some were even as malevolent as to say that the Moors had bewitched the king to make him stop the Christians taking their property from them.

'Our sufferings,' sighed Muhammad, 'were soon going to absolve us and make us recall that even when free we would henceforth be chained fast to our humiliation. However, in the months immediately after the fall of Granada – may God deliver her! – we were spared the worst, because before it was let loose upon us, the law of the conquerors rained down upon the Jews. To her great misfortune, Sarah had been correct.'

★   ★   ★

In Jumada al-Thania of that year, three months after the fall of Granada, the royal heralds came to the centre of the city, proclaiming, to a roll of drums and in both Arabic and Castilian, an edict of Ferdinand and Isabella decreeing the 'formal termination of all relations between Christians and Jews, which can only be accomplished by the expulsion of all the Jews from our kingdom'.

Henceforth they would have to choose between baptism and exile. If they chose the latter, they had four months to sell their properties and belongings, but they could take with them neither gold nor silver.

When Sarah came to see us on the day after this proclamation, her face was swollen after a long night of weeping, but from her eyes, now dry, shone that serenity which often accompanies the coming to pass of a long-anticipated drama. She was even able to make fun of the royal edict, reciting the sentences she remembered in a hoarse man's voice:

'We have been told by the inquisitors and others that commerce between Jews and Christians leads to the most shocking evils. The Jews seek to win back the newly-converted Christians and their children by handing them books of Jewish prayers, by obtaining unleavened bread for them at Easter, by instructing them in the forbidden foods and by persuading them to conform to the Law of Moses. Our Holy Catholic Faith is becoming diminished and debased.'

Twice my mother asked her to keep her voice down, because we were seated in the courtyard that spring morning and she did not want this sarcasm to reach the ears of a spiteful neighbour. Very fortunately, Warda had gone to the market with my father and sister, because I do not know how she would have reacted to hearing the words 'Holy Catholic Faith' pronounced with such disdain.

As soon as Sarah had finished her imitation my mother asked her the only important question:

'What have you decided to do? Are you going to choose conversion or exile?'

A feigned smile greeted this question, then a feignedly casual 'I still have time!' My mother waited several weeks before broaching the subject again, but the reply was the same.

But at the beginning of the summer, when three-quarters of the time allowed to the Jews had expired, Gaudy Sarah herself came to say:

'I have heard that the Grand Rabbi of all Spain, Abraham Senior, has just had himself baptized with his sons and all his relatives. At first I was appalled, and then I said to myself, "Sarah, widow of Jacob Perdoniel, perfume seller of Granada, are you a better Jew than Rabbi Abraham?" So I have decided to have myself baptized, together with my five children, leaving it to the God of Moses to judge what is in my heart.'

Sarah's anguish was voluble that day, and my mother looked at her tenderly:

'I am glad that you are not leaving. I shall also stay in the city, because my cousin has not mentioned exile again.'

However, less than a week later, Sarah had changed her mind. One evening she arrived at our house with three of her children, the youngest hardly bigger than myself.

'I have come to bid you farewell. I have finally decided to go. There is a caravan leaving for Portugal tomorrow morning; I am going to join it. Yesterday I married my two oldest girls, aged fourteen and thirteen, so that their husbands can look after them, and I sold my house to one of the king's soldiers for the price of four mules.'

Then she added, in an attempt at an excuse:

'Salma, if I stay, I shall be afraid every day until I die, and every day I shall think of leaving and shall not be able to.'

'Even if you have been baptized?' my mother was astounded.

In reply, Gaudy Sarah told a story which had been going the rounds of the Jewish quarter of Granada over the last few days, which had finally decided her to choose exile.

'It is said that a wise man of our community put three pigeons on a window of his house. One was killed and plucked, and he had attached a little label to it which read: "This convert was the last to leave." The second pigeon, plucked but still alive, had a label saying "This convert left a little earlier," while the third was still alive and still had feathers, and its label read: "This one was the first to leave." '

Sarah and her family went away without looking back; it was written that we were soon to join them on the path of exile.

The Year of Mihrajan
898 A.H.
22 October 1492 – 11 October 1493

Never more, since that year, did I dare pronounce the word Mihrajan in the presence of my father, since its mention would plunge him into the saddest of memories. And my family would never celebrate that feast again.

It all happened on the ninth day of the holy month of Ramadan, or rather, I should say, on St John's Day, the twenty-fourth of June, since Mihrajan was celebrated not in accordance with the Muslim year but following the Christian calendar. The day marks the summer solstice, which punctuates the cycle of the sun, and thus has no place in our lunar year. At Granada, and, by the way, at Fez, we followed both calendars at once. If one works the land, if one needs to know when to graft the apple trees, cut the sugar cane or round up hands for the harvest, only the solar months make sense; at the approach of Mihrajan, for instance, it was known that it was time to pick the late-flowering roses, which some women wear at their breast. On the other hand, when leaving on a journey, it is not the solar cycle which is consulted, but the lunar one; is the moon full or new, waxing or waning, because it is thus that the stages of a caravan are calculated.

This said, I should not be faithful to the truth if I did not add that the Christian calendar was not used only for agricultural purposes, but that it also provided numerous occasions for feasting, of which my compatriots never deprived themselves. It was not sufficient to celebrate the birth of the Prophet, al-Mawlud, with great poetry competitions in public places and the distribution of food to the needy; the birth of the Messiah was also celebrated, with special dishes prepared from wheat, beans, chick-peas and vegetables. And if the first day of the Islamic year, Ras al-Sana, was marked particularly by the presentation of formal congratulations and good wishes at the Alhambra, the first day of the Christian year was the occasion for celebrations which children would wait for impatiently; they would sport masks, and would go and knock at rich people's houses, singing rounds, which would win them several handfuls of dried fruit, less as a reward than as a way of stopping the racket; again, Nawruz, the Persian New Year, was welcomed with pomp; the day before, countless marriages were performed, since, it was said, the season was propitious for fertility, and on the day itself, toys made out of baked clay or glazed pottery were sold on every corner, shaped like horses or giraffes, in spite of the Islamic interdiction. There were of course also the major Muslim festivals: 'al-Adha, the most important of the '*ids*, for which many of the people of Granada would ruin themselves to sacrifice a sheep or to buy new clothes; the Breaking of the Fast at the end of Ramadan, when even the poorest could not feast with fewer than ten different dishes; al-Ashura, when the dead were remembered, but also the occasion on which expensive presents were exchanged. To all these festivals should be added Easter, al-Asir, the beginning of autumn, and above all the famous Mihrajan.

On the latter occasion it was customary to light great fires of straw; people used to say with a smile that as this was the shortest night of the year, there was no point in sleeping. In addition it was useless to seek any rest at all, as bands of youths roamed through the city until morning, singing at the tops of their voices. They also had the dreadful habit of drenching all the streets with water, which made them slippery for the next three days.

That year, these hooligans were joined by hundreds of Castilian soldiers, who had since early in the morning been frequenting the numerous taverns which had been opened since the fall of the city, before wandering out into the various suburbs. So my father had not the slightest desire to take part in the rejoicing. But my tears, and those of my sister, and the pleadings of Warda and my mother persuaded him to take us for a stroll, 'without leaving al-Baisin', he insisted. So he waited for sunset, since it was the month of the Fast, quickly swallowed down a well-deserved bowl of lentil soup – how unbearable Ramadan is when the days are so long – and then took us to the Flag Gate, where temporary stalls had been set up by vendors of sponge doughnuts, dried figs and apricot sorbets, made with snow brought on the backs of mules from the heights of Mount Cholair.

Fate had given us an appointment in the street of the Old Castle Wall. My father was walking in front, holding Mariam in one hand and me in the other, exchanging a word or two with each neighbour that he passed; my mother was a couple of steps behind, closely followed by Warda, when suddenly Warda cried 'Juan!' and stood stock still. On our right, a young moustachioed soldier stopped in turn, with a little drunken hiccup, trying with some difficulty to identify the veiled woman who had addressed him thus. My father immediately sensed the danger, and leaped towards his concubine, seized her urgently by the elbow, and said in a low voice:

'Let's go home, Warda! In the name of Jesus the Messiah, let's go home!'

His tone was imploring, because the said Juan was accompanied by four other soldiers, all visibly drunk and armed, like him, with imposing halberds; all the other passers-by had drawn aside, in order to watch the drama without being involved in it. Warda explained with a cry:

'It's my brother!'

Then she advanced towards the young man, who was still dumbfounded:

'Juan, I am Esmeralda, your sister!'

With these words she pulled her right hand from Muhammad's clenched fist and deftly raised her veil. The soldier stepped forward, held her for several moments by the shoulders, and held her closely to him. My father turned pale and began to tremble. He realized that he was about to lose Warda, and even more serious, that he would be humiliated in front of the whole quarter, his virility impugned.

As for me, I did not understand anything of the drama unfolding before my childish eyes. I can only remember clearly the moment when the soldier grabbed hold of me. He had just said to Warda that she should accompany him and return to their village, which he called Alcantarilla. She suddenly began to hesitate. Although she had expressed her spontaneous delight at finding her brother again after five years in captivity, she was not sure that she wanted to leave my father's house to go back to her own family, burdened with a daughter which a Moor had fathered upon her. She would certainly no longer find a husband. She had not been unhappy in the house of

Muhammad the weigh-master, who had fed her, clothed her, and not left her on her own more than two nights on end. And then, after having lived in a city like Granada, even in times of desolation, the prospect of returning to bury herself in a little village near Murcia was not enticing. It could be imagined that such thoughts were running through her head when her brother shook her impatiently:

'Are these children yours?'

She leant unsteadily against a wall, and stammered out a 'No', immediately followed by a 'Yes'. Hearing the 'yes', Juan leapt towards me and snatched me in his arms.

How shall I ever forget the cry which my mother let out? She threw herself on the soldier, scratching him, raining down blows upon him, while I wrestled as best I could. But the young man was not put off. He quickly got rid of me and glanced at his sister reproachfully:

'So only the girl is yours?'

She said nothing, which was answer enough for Juan.

'Will you take her with you or leave her to them?'

His tone was so severe that the unfortunate girl took fright.

'Calm yourself, Juan,' she begged him, 'I don't want a scandal. Tomorrow I will take my belongings and I will leave for Alcantarilla.'

But the soldier would not listen to this.

'You're my sister, and you're going to collect your baggage immediately and follow me.'

Encouraged by Warda's about-turn, my father came closer, saying:

'She is my wife!'

He said it in Arabic and then in bad Castilian. Juan slapped him with all his might, sending him flying across the muddy street. My mother began to wail like a hired mourner, while Warda cried out:

'Don't hurt him! He has always treated me well. He is my husband!'

The soldier, who had grabbed hold of his sister roughly, hesitated a moment before saying in softer tones:

'As far as I'm concerned, you were his captive, and you no longer belong to him since we have taken possession of this city. If you tell me that he is your husband, he can keep you, but he must be baptized immediately and a priest must bless your marriage.'

Warda now directed her entreaties towards my father:

'Accept, Muhammad, otherwise we shall be separated!'

There was a silence. Someone in the crowd cried out:

'God is great!'

My father, who was still on the ground, got up slowly, walked with dignity towards Warda and said, in a shaking voice: 'I will give you your clothes and your daughter' before walking towards the house past a line of approving murmurs.

'He wanted to save face before the neighbours,' said my mother in a detached tone, 'but all the same he felt diminished and impotent.'

Then she added, doing her best not to be sarcastic:

'For your father, it was at that moment that Granada really fell into the hands of the enemy.'

★ ★ ★

For days, Muhammad stayed at home prostrate and inconsolable, refusing even to join his friends for the meals at the breaking of the Fast, the traditional *iftars*; no one begrudged him this however, because his misfortune was known to all the very evening of Mihrajan, and more than once the neighbours came to bring him, as if to a sick man, the dishes which he had not been able to taste at their houses. Salma made herself inconspicuous, only speaking to him to answer his questions, forbidding me to bother him, not imposing her presence upon him but never being so far from him that he had to ask for anything twice.

If my mother was upset, she kept her spirits up, because she was convinced that time would bring her cousin's sadness to an end. What upset her was to see Muhammad so devoted to his concubine, and especially that this attachment had been so flaunted in front of all the gossips of al-Baisin. When, as a youth, I asked her whether, in spite of everything, she had not been pleased when her rival departed, she denied it vigorously:

'A sensible wife seeks to be the first of her husband's women, because it is a delusion to wish to be the only one.'

Adding, with feigned cheerfulness:

'Whatever anyone says about it, being the only wife is no more pleasant than being an only child. You work more, you become bored, and you have to put up with the temper and the demands of the husband by yourself. It is true that there is jealousy and intrigue, and argument, but at least this takes place at home, because when the husband begins to take his pleasures outside, he is lost to all his wives.'

It was no doubt for this reason that Salma began to panic on the last day of Ramadan, when Muhammad leaped up from his usual place and went out of the house with a determined step. She only learned two days later that he had been to see Hamid, called *al-fakkak*, the old 'deliverer' of Granada, who had for more than twenty years been involved in the difficult but lucrative task of ransoming Muslim captives in Christian territory.

There had always been, in the land of Andalus, people responsible for looking for prisoners and obtaining their release. They existed not only among our people but also among the Christians, who had long had the custom of nominating an 'alfaqueque mayor', often a high state official, assisted by numerous other 'deliverers'. The families of the captives would report their disappearance – a soldier fallen into the hands of the enemy, an inhabitant of a city which had been invested, a peasant girl captured after a raid. The *fakkak*, or one of his representatives, would then begin his investigations, going himself into enemy territory, sometimes to distant lands, disguised as a merchant, or sometimes taking advantage of his rank, to find those who had been lost and discuss the sum required as ransom. Since many families could not pay the sums required, collections were organized, and no alms were more valued by the believers than those which were given to assist in the release of the faithful from captivity. Many pious individuals used to ruin themselves by ransoming captives whom they had often never seen, hoping for no other reward than the benevolence of the Most High. On the other hand, some deliverers were no more than vultures who fed on the misery of families by extorting from them the little money that they had.

Hamid was not of that kind; his modest demeanour bore witness.

'He welcomed me with the formal courtesy of those accustomed to receive streams of requests,' my father told me, with hesitations which the years had not swept away. 'He invited me to sit down on a comfortable cushion, and after having duly asked about my health, he begged me to tell him what had led me to him. When I told him, he could not stop himself letting out a loud laugh, which ended with a prolonged burst of coughing. Much offended, I rose to take my leave, but Hamid took me by the sleeve. "I am your father's age," he said, "you should not hold it against me. Do not take my laughter as an insult but as a tribute to your incredible effrontery. So, the person you want to recover is not a Muslim girl but a Castilian Christian girl whom you dared to keep captive in your house eighteen months after the fall of Granada, when the first decision taken by the conquerors was to set free, with great ceremony, the seven hundred last Christian captives remaining in our city." I could only answer "Yes". He looked at me, regarded my clothes for some time, and judging me to be a respectable person, began to speak slowly and kindly. "My son, I can well understand that you are attached to this woman, and if you tell me that you have always treated her with consideration, and that you cherish the daughter you have had by her, I truly believe you. But as you well know, not all slaves were treated thus, neither here nor in Castile. Most of them passed their days carrying water or making sandals, and at night they were stalled like animals, chains around their feet or necks, in squalid underground caves. Thousands of our brothers still endure this fate, and no one bothers about their deliverance. Think of them, my son, and help me buy some of them back, rather than pursuing a chimera, because, of this you must be certain, never more in the land of Andalus can a Muslim give orders to a Christian man, nor even to a Christian woman. If you are minded to get this woman back, you will have to go through a church." He uttered an oath, passed the palms of this hands across his face before continuing: "Take refuge in God, and ask Him to grant you patience and resignation."

'As I was getting up to go, disappointed and angry,' continued my father, 'Hamid offered me a final piece of advice in a confidential tone: "In this city there are many war widows, many impoverished orphan girls, many disabled women. There are almost certainly some in your own family. Has not the Book stipulated that those men who can do so should shield them with their protection? It is at the time of the greatest tragedies, such as those which are raining down upon us, that a generous Muslim should take to himself two, three or four wives, because, while increasing his own pleasures, he carries out a praiseworthy act which serves the whole community. Tomorrow is the 'id; think of all those women who will celebrate in tears." I left the old fakkak not knowing whether it was Heaven or Hell that had guided me to his door.'

Even today, I am quite incapable of saying. Because in the end Hamid went about his task with such skill, such devotion, such zeal, that the life of all my family was to be turned upside down by it for many long years to come.

The Year of the Crossing
899 A.H.
12 October 1493 – 1 October 1494

'A lost homeland is like the corpse of a near relative; bury it with respect and believe in eternal life.'

The words of Astaghfirullah sounded in time to the rhythm of the amber rosary which his thin pious fingers told incessantly. Around the preacher were four serious bearded faces, including that of my father Muhammad, four long faces each showing the same distress which the shaikh was stirring up without mercy.

'Go, emigrate, let God guide your steps, for if you accept to live under submission and humiliation, if you accept to live in a country where the precepts of the Faith are held up to ridicule, where the Book and the Prophet – on whom be prayers and peace! – are insulted daily you will give a shameful image of Islam for which the Most High will call you to account on the Day of Judgement. It is said in the Book that on that Day the angel of death will ask you: "Is not the land of God vast enough? Could you not have left your homeland to seek asylum elsewhere?" Henceforth the fires of hell will be your dwelling place.'

It was in that year of ordeals and heartbreaks that the period of three years allowed to the citizens of Granada to choose between submission and exile came to an end. According to the surrender agreement, we had until the beginning of the Christian year 1495 to decide, but as the crossing to the Maghrib beyond the sea might prove hazardous after the month of October, it was considered better to leave in spring, or, at the latest, in summer. Those who wished to remain behind were known by the epithet already in use to indicate

Muslims living in Christian territory, 'tamed', 'mudajjan', corrupted in Castilian to 'mudejar'. In spite of this derogatory adjective, many of the citizens of Granada still hesitated.

The confabulation taking place in the courtyard of our house in al-Baisin – may God restore it to us – was like a thousand others held that year to discuss the fate of the community, sometimes even of a single one of its members. Astaghfirullah took part whenever he could, his tone lofty but his voice low to indicate that he was now in enemy territory. If he himself had still not taken the road to exile, he hastened to explain, it was solely to turn aside the waverers from the way to perdition.

Waverers were plenty among those present, beginning with my father Muhammad, who had not despaired of retrieving Warda and his daughter, who had sworn that he would not leave without taking them with him, under the very noses of all the soldiers of Aragon and Castile. By dint of insisting, on visit after visit, he had managed to extract a promise from Hamid the deliverer to get a message through to his concubine. In return for a large sum of money he had also succeeded in charging a Genoese merchant called Bartolomeo with a similar mission; he had been living in Granada for a long time, and had made his fortune by ransoming captives. Hence he did not want to leave before he had reaped the fruit of his costly undertakings. His misfortune had turned him into a different person. Oblivious both to the general disapproval and to Salma's tears, he took refuge in his own misery from the miseries encompassing him.

Our neighbour Hamza the barber had other reasons for wavering. He had estates, which he had bought plot by plot, the fruit of twenty years of delicate and lucrative circumcisions, and had vowed not to depart until he had resold everything at a good price, down to the last vine; for that he had to wait, because so many of those who wished to leave, anxious to be on their way, were selling their lands for a song, and would-be buyers were like kings.

'I want to make those accursed Rumis pay through the nose,' he said in justification.

Astaghfirullah, whom Hamza had always admired, did not want him to remain in a state of impurity, since his blade had purified half the boys of al-Baisin.

Another of our neighbours, Sa'd, an old gardener who had recently been struck blind, did not feel able to leave.

'You can't plant an old tree in alien soil,' he would say.

Pious, humble, and fearing God in all things, he had come to hear from the mouth of the shaikh himself that which the *ulama* versed in the Word and in the righteous Tradition recommended for cases like his own.

'Hamza and Sa'd arrived at our house just after the midday prayer,' my mother remembered. 'Muhammad let them in, while I withdrew with you upstairs to my part of the house. They had pallid cheeks and false smiles, just like your father, who sat them on some old cushions in a shady corner of the courtyard, only communicating with them in inaudible mumbles. The shaikh arrived an hour later, and it was only then that Muhammad called me to make some fresh syrup.'

Astaghfirullah was accompanied by Hamid, of whose links with the master of the house he was well aware. The old deliverer had been touched by my father's folly, and if he had seen him often over the past year, it was less from a desire to reason with him than to experience his boldness, his youth and his turbulent passions. That day however, the visit of the *fakkak* had a solemn air about it. He had once more become the religious dignitary which he was known to be, his withered eyelids screwed up in an attempt at severity, his words the fruit of his long commerce with adversity.

'All my life I have had to do with captives who dream only to be free, and I cannot understand how a free man of sound mind can voluntarily choose captivity.'

Old Sa'd was the first to reply:

'If we all depart, Islam will be rooted out from this land for ever, and when, by the grace of God, the Turks arrive to cross swords with the Rumis, we shall not be there to assist them.'

The solemn voice of Astaghfirullah silenced the gardener:

'To live in a land conquered by the infidels is forbidden by our religion, just as it is forbidden to eat the flesh of dead animals, blood, and pork, just as murder is forbidden.'

He added, resting his hand heavily on Sa'd's shoulder:

'Every Muslim who stays in Granada increases the number of inhabitants in the land of the infidels and helps to strengthen the enemies of God and His Prophet.'

A tear trickled down the old man's cheek until it edged its way timidly into the hairs of his beard.

'I am too old, too ill and too poor to limp along the roads and across the seas. Has not the Prophet said: "Do what is easy for you and do not seek out what is difficult in vain?"'

Hamid took pity on the gardener, and at the risk of contradicting the shaikh, recited a comforting verse from the Sura of Women in a singsong voice:

'. . . except for those who are incapable, men, women and children, who have no means at their disposal and for whom no way is open, to them God can grant absolution, He is the Lord of absolution, the Lord of forgiveness.'

Sa'd hastened to add:

'He has spoken the truth, Almighty God.'

Astaghfirullah did not deny the obvious:

'God is good and his patience is limitless. He does not ask the same things from those who can and those who cannot. If you wish to obey Him by emigrating, but find that you cannot, He knows to read in your heart and to judge you for your intentions. He will not condemn you to hell, but your own hell could well be on this earth and in this land. Your hell will be the daily humiliation for you and the women of your family.'

Suddenly pressing the palms of his hands on the warm ground he turned his whole body round towards my father and then towards the barber, looking at them fixedly:

'And you, Muhammad? and you, Hamza? Are you also poor and ill? Are you not important people, prominent in the community? What excuse do you have for not obeying the commandments of Islam? Do not hope for pardon or forgiveness if you follow the path of Yahya the renegade, for the Most High is demanding towards those on whom He has showered his blessings.'

The two men, both exceedingly embarrassed, swore that they had no intention of remaining for ever in the land of the infidels, and that they desired only to regulate their affairs so as to depart in good order.

'Woe to him who trades paradise for earthly things!' cried Astaghfirullah, while the deliverer, not wanting to attack Muhammad, whom he knew to be in a tense state of mind and capable of foolishness, addressed the two recalcitrants in a fatherly way:

'Since it has fallen into the hands of the infidels, this city has become a place of infamy for us all. It is a prison, and its door is being slowly closed again. Why not take advantage of this last chance to escape?'

Neither the curses of the preacher nor the remonstrations of the deliverer persuaded my father to leave his city. The day after their meeting, he went to Hamid's house asking for news of his beloved. Salma suffered in silence and hoped for exile.

'We were already experiencing,' she said, 'the first of the summer heat, but in the gardens of Granada there were few strollers and the flowers had no radiance. The finest houses of the city had been emptied, the shops in the suqs did not display their wares; there was no more hubbub in the streets, even in the poorer quarters. In the public places the Castilian soldiers rubbed shoulders only with beggars, since all the Muslims who valued their honour and had not left were ashamed of exposing themselves to view.'

And she added in a voice full of grief:

'When one disobeys the Most High, it is better to do so in secret, because to strut about with one's sin is to sin twofold.'

She repeated this constantly to my father without managing to shake him.

'The only eyes which see me in the streets of Granada belong to those who have not departed. How can they dare to reproach me?'

Furthermore, he contended, his dearest wish was to distance himself from this city where his honour as a man had been held to ridicule; but he would not flee like a jackal. He would leave with head high and a disdainful air.

Soon came Dhu'l-Qa'da, the penultimate month of the year, and it was Hamza's turn to take to the road; urged on by his old mother the midwife, who bombarded him with her lamentations, accusing him of wanting to drag his whole family down to Gehenna, he left without selling his lands, promising to come back by himself in a few months to find a buyer. For Astaghfirullah too the hour of exile had come; he took with him neither gold nor clothing, only a Qur'an and provisions for the journey.

'Then came Dhu'l-Hijja; the sky became more clouded over and the nights cooler. Your father still persisted obstinately, passing his days between the deliverer and the Genoese, returning in the evenings either exhausted or over-excited, worried or serene, but with never a word about our departure. Then all at once, less than two weeks before the new year, he was possessed by a disconcerting feverishness; he had to go immediately, he had to be in Almeria in three days. Why Almeria? Were there no ports closer at hand, such as Adra, from which Boabdil had embarked, or La Rabita, or Salobrena, or Almunecar? No, it had to be Almeria, and we had to

75

get there in three days. The evening before our departure, Hamid came to wish us a good journey, and I understood that he was privy to Muhammad's high spirits. I asked him if he too would emigrate. "No", he replied, "I shall not go until the release of the last Muslim from captivity."'

Salma replied:

'You risk having to stay in the land of the infidel for a long time yet!'

The deliverer smiled enigmatically, but not without an air of melancholy:

'Sometimes it is necessary to disobey the Most High to obey Him more effectively,' he murmured, as if only speaking to himself – or perhaps directly to his Creator.

We left the next day before the dawn prayer, my father on horseback, my mother and myself on a mule, our baggage distributed on the backs of five other animals. Near the Najd Gate on the southern side of the city we joined several dozen other travellers, with whom we journeyed the better to ensure our safety. There were many bandits in the neighbourhood of the city and in the mountain passes, because everyone knew that great wealth was constantly being brought down to the coast.

★   ★   ★

The great confusion which prevailed in the port of Almeria left an indelible impression on my childish eyes. Like ourselves, many people seemed to have decided to leave at the last moment, and they crowded together to take the smallest boat by storm. Here and there a few Castilian soldiers attempted to calm down troublesome mischief-makers by shouting threats at them; others checked the contents of a trunk with greedy eyes. It had been agreed that the emigrants could take all their property with them without restriction, but it was often not unhelpful to leave a piece of gold between the fingers of an over-zealous officer. On the beach, business was in full swing, the owners of the boats being subjected to endless sermons on the fate which God reserves for those who profit from the misfortunes of the Muslims, apparently to no effect, since the fares for the crossing continued to increase by the hour. The lure of gain lulls consciences to sleep, and moments of panic are not the most opportune for arousing generosity. Resignedly, the men emptied their purses and signalled to their families to make haste. Once on board, they did their best to keep their wives and daughters from being exposed to promiscuous encounters, a difficult task when three hundred people were stuffed into a small galley which had never carried more than a hundred.

When we arrived my father refused to mix with the crowd. From the back of his horse he surveyed the scene around the port, before making for a little wooden cabin, at the doorway of which a well-dressed man welcomed him eagerly. We followed him at a distance; he signalled to us to come closer. A few minutes later we were seated comfortably on top of our luggage in an empty galley on which we had embarked by means of a gangway which was drawn up behind us. The man, who was none other than Hamid's brother, was the director of customs of Almeria, a post which the Castilians had not yet taken away from him. The little boat belonged to him, and it would not be taking on passengers until the next day. My mother gave my father and myself a piece of ginger to chew to prevent sea-sickness, and she herself took a large chunk. Soon night fell and we all went to sleep, after having eaten several meatballs which our host had had brought to us.

Shouts and commotion awoke us at dawn. Dozens of shouting men, women veiled in black and white, and dazed or squealing children seemed to be taking our galley by storm. We had to cling to our luggage not to be pushed aside or perhaps even thrown overboard. My mother held me to her as the boat began to get further from the shore. Around us, women and old men prayed and wept, their voices barely drowned by the sounds of the sea.

Only my father remained serene on this journey into exile, and Salma could even see a strange smile playing on his lips the whole length of the journey. For, in the very heart of defeat, he had managed to achieve his own tiny field of victory.

II
The Book of Fez

I was your age, my son, and I have never seen Granada again. God did not ordain that my destiny should be written completely in a single book, but that it should unfold, wave after wave, to the rhythm of the seas. At each crossing, destiny jettisoned the ballast of one future to endow me with another; on each new shore, it attached to my name the name of a homeland left behind.

Between Almeria and Melilla, in the space of a day and a night, my existence was overturned. But the sea was calm, and the wind mild; it was in the hearts of my family that the storm was swelling.

Hamid the deliverer had performed his duty well, may God pardon him. When the coast of Andalus was no more than a thin streak of remorse behind us, a woman ran towards our corner of the galley, stepping eagerly over both luggage and travellers. Her joyful step was in strange contrast with her appearance; her veils were so sombre and thick that we should have been hard put to recognize her if Mariam had not been in her arms.

The only cries of joy were uttered by my sister and myself. Muhammad and Warda were struck dumb with emotion, as well as by the hundred curious glances which beset them. As for Salma, she held me a little more tightly against her breast. From her restrained breathing and the occasional sighs which escaped her I knew that she was suffering. Her tears were probably flowing beneath the shelter of her veil, and these were not misplaced, as my father's unbridled passion would soon bring us all to the edge of catastrophe.

Muhammad the weigh-master, at once so serene and so uncontrolled! It so happened that I lost him in my youth, only to find him again in my maturer years, when he was no longer there. And I had to await my first white hairs, my first regrets, before becoming convinced that every man, including my father, had the right to take the wrong road if he believed he was pursuing happiness. From that time I began to cherish his erring ways, just as I hope that you will cherish mine, my son. I wish that you too will sometimes get lost in your turn. And I hope that, like him, you will love to the point of tyranny, and that you will long remain receptive to the noble temptations of life.

The Year of the Hostelries
900 A.H.
2 October 1494 – 20 September 1495

Before Fez, I had never set foot in a city, never observed the
swarming activity of the alleyways, never felt that powerful breath
on my face, like the wind from the sea, heavy with cries and smells.
Of course, I was born in Granada, the stately capital of the kingdom
of Andalus, but it was already late in the century, and I knew it only
in its death agonies, emptied of its citizens and its souls, humiliated,
faded, and when I left our quarter of al-Baisin it was no longer
anything for my family but a vast encampment, hostile and ruined.

Fez was entirely different, and I had the whole of my youth to
discover it. I have only hazy memories of our first encounter with the
city that year. I came towards it on the back of a mule, a poor sort of
conqueror, half-asleep, held up by my father's firm hand, because all
the roads sloped, sometimes so steeply that the animal only moved
with a shaky and hesitant step. Every jolt made me sit bolt upright
before nodding off again. Suddenly my father's voice rang out:

'Hasan, wake up if you want to see your city!'

Coming out of my torpor, I became conscious that our little
convoy was already at the foot of a sand-coloured wall, high and
massive, bristling with a large number of menacing pointed
battlements. A coin pushed into the hand of a gatekeeper caused the
door to be opened. We were within the walls.

'Look around you,' insisted Muhammad.

All round Fez, as far as the eye could see, were ranges of hills
ornamented with countless houses in brick and stone, many of which
were decorated with glazed tiles like the houses of Granada.

'Down there, in that plain crossed by the wadi, is the heart of the city. On the left is the quarter of the Andalusians, founded centuries ago by emigrants from Cordoba; on the right is the quarter of the people of Qairawan, with the mosque and the school of the Qarawiyyin in the middle, that huge building with green tiles, where, if God accepts, you will receive instruction from the *ulama*.'

I only listened to these learned explanations with half an ear, because it was the sight of the roofs in particular which filled my gaze: on that autumn afternoon, the sun was made milder by thick clouds, and everywhere thousands of people were sitting on the roofs as if on terraces, talking to one another, shouting, drinking, laughing, their voices mingling in a tremendous hubbub. All around them, hanging up and stretched out, was the washing of the rich and the poor billowing in the breeze, like the sails of the same boat.

An exhilarating rumour, a vessel which sails through storm after storm, and which is sometimes wrecked, is that not what a city is? During my adolescence it often happened that I passed whole days gazing at this scene, daydreaming without restraint. The day of my entry to Fez was only a passing rapture. The journey from Melilla had exhausted me, and I was in a hurry to reach Khali's house. Of course I had no recollection of my uncle, since he had emigrated to Barbary when I was only a year old, nor of my grandmother, who had left with him, the oldest of her sons. But I was sure that their warm welcome would make us forget the horrors of the journey.

Warm it certainly was, for Salma and myself. While she disappeared completely into the all-enveloping veils of her mother, I found myself in the arms of Khali, who looked at me for a long time without saying a word before planting on my forehead the most affectionate of kisses.

'He loves you as a man loves the son of his sister,' my mother used to tell me. 'More than that, since he only has daughters, he considers you his own son.'

He was to prove the truth of this to me on several occasions. But, that day, his solicitude had awful consequences for me.

After having put me down on the ground, Khali turned towards Muhammad.

'I have been waiting for you for a long time,' he said in a tone full of reproach, since no one was unaware of the embarrassing idyll which had delayed the weigh-master's departure.

Nevertheless, the two men embraced each other. Then my uncle

84

turned for the first time towards Warda, who had until then kept herself in the background. His gaze did not alight upon her, but veered off into the distance. He had chosen not to see her. She was not welcome in his house. Even Mariam, adorable, smiling, chubby little girl, did not have the right to the least display of affection.

'I dreaded this welcome, and this was why I was so unhappy when Warda appeared on the boat,' my mother explained to me later. 'I had always put up with Muhammad's misdemeanours in silence. His behaviour had humiliated me in front of all the neighbourhood, and in the end all Granada made fun of his passions. In spite of that, I always told myself: "Salma, you are his wife and you owe him obedience; one day, when he is weary of fighting, he will return to you!" While waiting I resigned myself to bow my head patiently. My brother, so proud, so haughty, could not do so. He would certainly have forgotten the past if the three of us had arrived alone. But to welcome under his roof the Rumiyya whom all the world accused of having bewitched his brother-in-law would have made him the laughing stock of all the *émigrés* from Granada, of whom there were not less than six thousand in Fez, all of whom knew and respected him.'

Apart from myself, showered with attentions and already dreaming of delicious little treats, my family barely dared to breathe.

'It was as if we were taking part in a ceremony which a baleful jinn had changed from a marriage into a funeral,' said Muhammad. 'I always considered your uncle like a brother, and I wanted to shout aloud that Warda had fled from her village to find me, risking her life, that she had left the land of the Rumis to come to us, that we no longer had the right to consider her as a captive, that we did not even have the right to call her Rumiyya. But no sound issued from my lips. I could do no more than turn round and go out, in the silence of the grave.'

Salma followed him without a moment's hesitation, although she was almost fainting. Of them all, she was the most affected, even more than Warda. The concubine had been humiliated, certainly. But at least she had the consolation of knowing that henceforth Muhammad could never abandon her without losing face, and while she was trembling in her corner she had the soothing feeling of having been the victim of injustice. A feeling which wounds, but which puts balm on wounds, a feeling which sometimes kills, but one which much more often gives women powerful reasons to live and to struggle. Salma had none of this.

'I felt myself crushed by adversity. For me that day was the Day of Judgement; I was about to lose your father after having lost the city of my birth and the house in which I had given birth.'

★ ★ ★

So we got back on to our mules without knowing which direction to take. Muhammad muttered to himself as he hammered the beast's withers with his fist:

'By the earth that covers my father and my ancestors, if I had been told that I would be received in such a fashion in this kingdom of Fez, I would never have left Granada.'

His words rang out in our frightened ears.

'To leave, to abandon one's house and lands, to run across mountains and seas, only to encounter closed doors, bandits on the roads and the fear of contagion!'

It was true that since our arrival in the land of Africa misfortunes and miseries had not ceased to rain down upon us, indeed since the very moment our galley drew up alongside the quay at Melilla. We thought that we should find there a haven of Islam, where reassuring hands would be stretched out towards us to wipe away the fatigue of the old and the tears of the weak. But only anxious questions had greeted us on the quayside: 'Is it true that the Castilians are coming? Have you seen their galleys?' For those who questioned us thus there was no question of preparing the defences of the port, but rather of not wasting any time before taking flight. Seeing that it was for us, the refugees, to offer words of comfort, we were only the more anxious to put a mountain or a desert between ourselves and this coast which presented itself so openly to the invaders.

A man came up to us. He was a muleteer, he said, and he wanted to leave for Fez immediately. If we wished, he would hire his services to us for a modest sum, a few dozen silver dirhams. Wishing to leave Melilla before nightfall, and probably tempted by the low price, Muhammad accepted without bargaining. However, he asked the muleteer to take the coast road as far as Bedis before striking due south towards Fez; but the man had a better idea, a short cut which, he swore, would save us two whole days. He went that way every month, he knew every bump like the back of his mule. He was so persuasive that half an hour after having disembarked we were already on our way, my father and me on one animal, my mother on another with most of the luggage, and Warda and Mariam on another, the muleteer walking alongside us with his son, an unpleasant urchin of about twelve, barefoot, with filthy fingers and a shifty look.

We had hardly gone three miles when two horsemen veiled in blue suddenly came into view in front of us, holding curved daggers in their hands. As if they had only been waiting for a signal, the muleteer and his son made off as fast as their legs would carry them. The bandits came closer. Seeing that they only had to deal with one man protecting two women and two children, and thus feeling themselves in complete control, they began to run experienced hands over the load on the backs of the mules. Their first trophy was a mother-of-pearl casket in which Salma had unwisely packed all her jewellery. Then they began to unpack one superb silk dress after another, as well as an embroidered sheet which had been part of my mother's trousseau.

Then, going up to Warda, one of the bandits commanded her: 'Jump up and down!'

As she remained dumbstruck with fear, he went up to Muhammad and held the point of his dagger to his neck. In mortal fear, the concubine shook herself and gesticulated like a contorted puppet, but without leaving the ground. Not fully comprehending the seriousness of the situation, I let out a loud laugh which my father silenced with a frown. The thief shouted:

'Jump higher!'

Warda threw herself into the air as best she could, and a light tinkling of coins could be heard.

'Give all that to me!'

Putting her hand under her dress, she drew out a small purse which she sent rolling on the ground with a disdainful gesture. The bandit picked it up without taking offence, and turned towards my mother:

'Your turn now.'

At that moment, the call to prayer rang out from a distant village. My father glanced up at the sun standing high in the heavens, and deftly pulled his prayer rug from the side of his mount, spreading it out on the sand, and then, falling to his knees, his face turned towards Mecca, began to recite his midday prayer in a loud voice.

This was all done in the twinkling of an eye and in such a matter-of-fact manner that the bandits did not know how to react. While they were exchanging glances with one another, as if by a miracle a thick cloud of dust appeared in the road less than a mile in front of us. The bandits just had time to mount their horses before making off in the opposite direction. We were saved, and my mother did not have to do their bidding.

'If I had had to do that, it would not have been a jingling that would have been heard but a regular fusillade, because your father had made me carry hundreds of dinars, sewn up in ten fat purses, which I had attached all over me, convinced that no man would ever dare to search so far.'

When the providential arrivals on the scene caught up with us, we saw that they formed a detachment of soldiers. Muhammad hastened to describe to them in detail the stratagem to which we had fallen victims. Precisely for such reasons, their commander explained with a smile on his lips, he and his men had been ordered to patrol this road, which had become overrun with brigands since the Andalusians began to disembark by the boatload at Melilla. Generally, he said in the mildest of tones, the travellers would have their throats cut and the muleteer would get his animals back as well as the share of the booty which would have been left for him. According to the officer, many of the people of Granada travelling to Fez or Tlemcen had met with similar misfortunes, although those making for Tunis, Tetouan, Sale or the Mitidja of Algiers had not been bothered.

'Go back to the harbour,' he advised us, 'and wait. When a merchant caravan forms up, leave with it. It will certainly be guarded, and you will be safe.'

When my mother asked whether she had any chance of retrieving her precious casket, he replied, like any wise man, with a verse from the Qur'an:

'It may be that you detest something, but that it shows benefit to you; it may be that you rejoice over something and it brings harm to you; because God knows, and you, you do not know.'

Before continuing:

'The mules which the bandits were forced to leave with you will be much more use to you than the jewels; they will carry you and your baggage, and they will not attract thieves.'

We followed this man's advice to the letter, and it was thus that we arrived at our destination at the end of ten days, exhausted but safe.

To find that our relatives refused us hospitality.

* * *

It was thus essential to find a roof under which we could shelter,
which was not easy as the Andalusian emigrants, arriving in wave
after wave in Fez, had taken over all the houses available. When
Boabdil had landed, three years beforehand, he had been accompanied, it was said, by seven hundred people, who now had their own
quarter where life was still lived in the style of the Alhambra, pride
apart. Normally, the newcomers would put up for a while in the
houses of their closest relatives, which we would certainly have done
without Warda. As things were, there was no question of spending a
single night in Khali's house, where my father considered, with
justice, that he had been held up to ridicule.

There remained the hostelries, the *funduqs*. There were not less
than two hundred of them at Fez, most of them very clean, each with
fountains and latrines with swiftly running water flowing through
them, taking the sewage towards the river in a thousand canals.
Some had more than a hundred and twenty spacious rooms, all
giving on to corridors. The rooms were let out completely empty,
without even a bed, the landlord only providing his customers with a
covering and a mat to sleep on, leaving them to buy their own food,
which would be cooked for them. Many made the best of such
places, however, because the hostelries were not only for the
accommodation of travellers but also provided dwelling places for
certain widowers of Fez, who had neither family nor sufficient
money to pay for a house and servants, who sometimes lodged
together in the same room to share the rent and the daily tasks, and
also to keep each other company in their misery. We had to set up
house ourselves in this way for several days, the time it took to find
more suitable accommodation.

It was not, however, the proximity of these unfortunates that
upset my father, but the presence of a very different group of people.
Having visited Fez in his youth, he still remembered the reputation
of certain hostelries, which was so disgusting that no honest man
would cross their thresholds or address a word to their proprietors,
because they were inhabited by those men who were called *al-hiwa*.
As I have written in my *Description of Africa*, the manuscript of

which remains at Rome, these were men who habitually dressed as women, with make up and adornments, who shaved their beards, spoke only in high voices and spent their days spinning wool. The people of Fez only saw them at funerals, because it was customary to hire them alongside the female mourners to heighten the sadness. It must be said that each of them had his own male concubine with whom he carried on like a wife with her husband. May the Most High guide us from the paths of error!

Far more dangerous were the outlaws who frequented these same hostelries. Murderers, brigands, smugglers, procurers, those engaged in every vice felt themselves secure there, as if they were in a territory outside the kingdom, freely organizing the sale of wine, kif-smoking sessions and prostitution, combining together to perpetuate their misdeeds. I wondered for a long time why the police at Fez, always so ready to punish the greed of a shopkeeper or the hunger of a man stealing bread, never went into these places to grab hold of the criminals and put an end to activities which were as displeasing to God as to men. It did not take many years for me to discover the reason: every time the sultan's army left on campaign, the innkeepers were made to supply all the staff necessary to cook for the soldiers, without being paid. In exchange for this contribution to the war effort, the sovereign left them to their own devices. It seems that in all wars order is the natural accomplice of disorder.

To be sure not to find ourselves in one of these infamous places, we had to find a hostelry near the Qarawiyyin mosque, where rich travelling merchants used to stay. Although the price of rooms there was more expensive than elsewhere, these establishments were never empty; whole caravans of customers would take them over at a time. The evening of our arrival we had the very good fortune to find a lodging in a hostelry run by an emigrant from Granada. He sent one of his slaves to the Smoke Market to buy us some small fried fish, meat fritters, olives and bunches of grapes. He also put a pitcher of fresh water on our doorstep for the night.

Instead of staying there a few days, we passed six weeks in this inn, until the landlord himself found us a narrow house at the bottom of a cul-de-sac not far from the flower market. It was half the size of our house in Granada, and the entrance door was low and somewhat sordid, the more so as one could not get inside without wading through a muddy puddle. When he suggested it to us he explained that it had been lived in by an Andalusian merchant who had decided to move to Constantinople in order to develop his business. But the reality was quite different, as our neighbours hastened to inform us: our predecessor, constantly confined to his bed, unable to carry on his business, and not having known a single day's happiness during the three years he had spent in Fez, had simply gone back to Granada. Two of his children had died of the plague and his eldest son had contracted a shameful disease known as 'the spots'. When we arrived, the whole of Fez was living in fear of this disease; it spread so quickly that no man seemed able to escape it. At first those who were afflicted by it were isolated in special houses, like lepers, but their number soon became so great that they had to be brought back to the bosom of their families. The whole town became an enormous infected area, and no medicine proved effective against it.

Hardly less deadly than the disease itself was the rumour that surrounded it. The people of the city whispered that it had never been seen among them until the arrival of the Andalusians. The latter in their turn defended themselves by claiming that 'the spots' had been spread, without any doubt, by the Jews and their women; they in their turn accused the Castilians, the Portuguese, sometimes even the Genoese or Venetian sailors. In Italy, this same scourge is called 'the French evil'.

★   ★   ★

That year, I think in the springtime, my father began to talk to me about Granada. He was to do so frequently in the future, keeping me at his side for hours, not always looking at me, not always knowing whether I was listening, or whether I understood, or whether I knew the people or the places. He used to sit cross-legged, his face lit up, his voice softened, his tiredness and his anger abated. For several minutes, or several hours, he became a story-teller. He was no longer at Fez, no longer within these walls that breathed plague and mould. He travelled back in his memory and only came back from it with regret.

Salma watched him with compassion, with worry, and sometimes with fear. She considered that his moods were not brought on by homesickness nor the difficulties of his life in exile. For her, my father had ceased to be himself since the day that Warda had left, and the return of the concubine had settled nothing. Those absent eyes, that self-conscious voice, that attraction towards the land of the Rumis, these obsessions which made him act against all common sense all led her to suppose that Muhammad had been put under a spell. She determined to rid him of it, even if she had to consult all the soothsayers of Fez one by one.

The Year of the Soothsayers
901 A.H.
21 September 1495 – 8 September 1496

When the honest women of Fez have to cross the flower market they quicken their step, wrap their veils more closely around themselves, and glance to left and right like hunted animals, because, although the company of myrtle or narcissus has nothing reprehensible about it, everyone knows that the citizens of Fez have the strange habit of surrounding themselves with flowers, both planted and picked, when they give themselves over to the forbidden pleasures of alcohol. For certain pious people, the very purchase of a perfumed bouquet became only a little less reprehensible than buying a carafe of wine, and the flower sellers seemed to them to be no better than the innkeepers, the more so as both were very often Andalusians, prosperous and dissolute.

Salma herself always quickened her pace as soon as she passed across the square in which the flower market was located, though less out of bigotry than out of a legitimate concern for her respectability. I had eventually noticed that she quickened her gait, and as if to amuse myself with a new game, pretended to challenge her to a race, trotting along by her side.

One day that year, as we were crossing the square, my mother quickened her pace. Laughing my head off, I began to run, but instead of holding me back as she usually did, she began to run in her turn, more and more quickly. As I could no longer keep up with her, she turned round for a moment, swept me up in her arms and ran on with even greater vigour, screaming a word into my ear which I could not catch. It was only when she stopped at the other side of the square that I understood the reason for her haste and the name she was calling: 'Sarah!'

Gaudy Sarah. I still often heard her speak of the Jewess, but her features no longer said anything to me.

'God Himself has sent you to this country,' gasped Salma as she caught up with her.

Sarah gave her an amused pout.

'That is what our rabbi says every day. As for me, I'm not so sure.'

Everything about her seemed bizarre to me: her pealing laughter, her many-coloured clothes, her gold-filled teeth, her voluminous earrings and above all the overpowering perfume which hit me full in the nostrils when she clasped me to her bosom. While I stared shamelessly at her she began to tell the tale, with a thousand gestures and a thousand exclamations, of what had befallen her since she had left the quarter of al-Baisin, a little before our own departure.

'Every day I thank the Creator for having pointed me towards exile, because those who chose baptism are now victims of the most dreadful persecutions. Seven of my cousins are in prison and one of my nieces was burnt alive with her husband, both accused of having remained Jews in secret.'

She put me down on the ground before continuing in a lowered tone:

'All the converts are suspected of continuing to be Jews; no Spaniard can escape the Inquisition unless he can prove that he is of "pure blood", that is, that he can count no Jew and no Moor among his ancestors, as far back as his family goes. Even so, their King Ferdinand himself has Jewish blood, as has Torquemada the Inquisitor. May the flames of Hell pursue them until the end of time!'

Thus Sarah did not regret having fled to Portugal with her family, although she soon realized that only rich Jews could take up residence there, and then only on the further condition that they showered gold upon the king and his advisers. As for the poorer members of the community, they were soon to have to choose, as in Castile, between conversion and flight.

'So I hastened to take ship for Tetuan, where I stayed several months. Then I came to Fez with my eldest daughter and my son-in-law, who had decided to set himself up here with an uncle who is a jeweller. My second daughter and her husband went, like most of our people, to the land of the Grand Turk, our protector.

May the Most High prolong his life and grant him victory over our enemies!'

'That is what we all devoutly hope,' said my mother approvingly. 'If God has the goodness to give us back our country one day, the Grand Turk will be His instrument.'

Revenge upon the Castilians was certainly one of Salma's most cherished desires. But at that moment her thoughts were less concerned with the fate of Granada than with that of her own family circle. If she was showing so much joy at having found Sarah again it was because she remembered how successfully she had assisted her to get Muhammad back when he had nearly eluded her shortly before my birth. This time a magic potion would not suffice; Salma wanted to consult soothsayers, and as her mother was seriously ill and could not accompany her, she was counting on the reassuring presence of Gaudy Sarah.

'How is your cousin?' asked Sarah.

'As God disposes him to conduct himself!'

The ambiguity of this formulation was evidently not lost on the Jewess. She put her hand on my mother's arm. Glancing at me at the same time out of the corners of their eyes, they took a step aside and spoke to each other in low tones, so that I could hear only occasional snatches of the conversation. The words 'Rumiyya' and 'sorcery', perhaps also 'drug' kept appearing on Salma's lips; the Jewess was attentive and reassuring.

The two women agreed to meet again in the same place two days later to go the rounds of the soothsayers. I knew about it that day because my mother had decided that I should accompany her. Perhaps she did not want to leave me with Warda; perhaps she judged it more fitting, in the eyes of my father and the neighbours, to take a child with her, as living proof of the honesty of her comings and goings. At all events, for a seven-year-old boy it was an experience as wonderful as it was unexpected, and, I must admit, sometimes agonizing as well.

Our first visit was to a clairvoyant named Umm Bassar. It was said that the sultan of Fez would consult her at each new moon, and that she had put a spell upon an amir who had threatened him, striking him blind. In spite of her renown, she lived in a house as modest as our own, situated in the perfume suq, at the end of a narrow arcaded gallery. We had only to push past a hanging to make our way inside. A black maidservant made us sit down in a small chamber before leading us down a dark corridor to a room which was only a little larger. Umm Bassar was seated on an enormous green cushion, her hair covered with a scarf of the same colour, fringed with golden threads. Behind her back was a tapestry with a picture of the twenty-eight tabernacles of the moon; in front of her was a low table on which there was a glazed earthenware vessel.

My mother sat opposite the clairvoyant and explained her business to her in a low voice. Sarah and I stayed behind, standing up. Umm Bassar poured some water into the vessel, added a drop of oil, and then blew on it three times. She recited several incomprehensible formulae, and then thrust her face towards the vessel, saying, in a cavernous voice:

'The jinns are there; some come by land, others by sea.'

Suddenly she turned towards me and beckoned me:

'Come closer!'

Suspicious, I did not move.

'Come, don't be frightened.'

My mother gave me a reassuring look. I came up to the table timidly.

'Lean over the table!'

The sight was, I swear, astonishing enough. The dancing reflections of the droplets of oil on the polished surface of the amphora gave the impression of ceaseless movement. Looking at it for several seconds, and allowing one's imagination free rein, one could make out all manner of beings and objects.

'Did you see the jinns moving about?'

Of course I said 'Yes'.

I would have said yes whatever the question had been, but my mother was all ears. For the objective she had in mind, and for the price she was paying, she did not want to be disappointed. At Umm Bassar's command I returned to my place. The clairvoyant remained for several minutes without moving.

'We must wait until the jinns become calmer; they are too troubled,' she explained in a confident voice.

There was a long period of silence, and then she began to talk to her jinns. She murmured questions to them and then leant over the vessel to observe the gestures they made with their hands and eyes.

'Your cousin will return to you after three periods of time,' she declared, without specifying whether it would be three days, three weeks, three months, or three years.

My mother took out a gold piece and left, pensive and bewildered. On the way back she asked me not to tell anyone about the visit, not even my father, for fear of seeing the jinns climbing on top of me in my sleep.

A week later we met Gaudy Sarah again on the square close to our house. This time our visit led us to an imposing residence situated not far from the sultan's palace. We were received in an immense lofty room, with a ceiling painted azure and gold. There were several women there, all fat and unveiled, who seemed not at all pleased to see me. They talked about me for several minutes, and then one of them got up heavily, took me by the hand and led me to a far corner of the room, promising to bring me some toys. I did not see a single one, but I had no time to be bored, because after a few minutes Salma and Sarah came back to fetch me.

I must say immediately that I had to wait several years before I learned the truth about what happened that day; I only remember my mother and Gaudy Sarah grumbling incessantly as they left, but also that between outbursts of anger they joked with each other and laughed out loud. I also remember having heard mention, in the salon, of al-Amira, the princess.

She was a strange person. The widow of one of the sultan's cousins, deeply versed in all the occult sciences, she had founded a peculiar circle, formed only of women, some chosen for their gifts of clairvoyance, others for their beauty. People with great experience of life call these women *sahasat*, because they are accustomed to use one another, and I know no more appropriate term to express it. When a woman comes to see them, they make her believe that they have friendly relations with certain demons, whom they divide into several species: red demons, white demons, black demons. They themselves alter their voices to make it seem as if the demons are speaking through their mouths, as I have set forth in my *Description of Africa*. These demons often order their fair visitors, if they are of comely appearance, to take off all their clothes and to exchange loving kisses with themselves, meaning, of course, with the princess and her acolytes. If the woman is prepared to go along with this game, whether out of stupidity or inclination, she is invited to become a member of the sisterhood, and a sumptuous banquet is organized in her honour, at which all the women dance together to a negro orchestra.

It was at the age of sixteen or seventeen that I learned the story of the princess and the demons. It was only then that I guessed what it was that had made my mother and Sarah take flight so quickly.

★ ★ ★

In spite of this misadventure, Salma had no wish to interrupt her quest. But for her next visit she showed greater circumspection in her choice of soothsayer. Hence, some weeks later, the three of us found ourselves at the house of a highly respected man of the city, an astrologer and bookseller who kept a shop near the Great Mosque of the Qarawiyyin. He received us on the first floor, in a room which was furnished only with books along the walls and a mat on the floor. He was at pains to point out as soon as we arrived that he was neither a magician nor an alchemist, and that he sought only to decipher the signs sent by God to His creatures. In support of his words he cited these verses from the Qur'an:

There are signs on earth for those whose faith is solid.
There are signs in yourselves, do you not see them?
There are also good things in Heaven which are destined for you.
And also those by which you are threatened.

Having thus reassured us of his faith and his honesty, he asked us to withdraw to the far corner of the room, rolled up the mat and traced several concentric circles on the floor with a piece of chalk. He drew a cross in the first one, and indicated the four cardinal points on the extremities of the cross, writing the names of the four elements on the inside. He then divided the second circle into four quadrants, and each quadrant into seven parts, making twenty-eight altogether, in which he wrote the twenty-eight letters of the Arabic alphabet. In the other circles he put the seven plants, the twelve months of the Latin year and various other signs. This procedure, known as *zairaja*, is long and complicated, and I would not have remembered the slightest detail if I had not seen it done three times in front of me. I only regret that I did not learn to do it myself, for of all the occult sciences it is the only one where the results are not open to discussion, even in the eyes of certain *ulama*.

After having finished his drawing, the astrologer asked my mother what she was seeking. He took the letters of her question one by one, translated them into numerical values, and after a very complicated calculation, found the natural element to which the letter corresponded. After an hour's scribbling, his reply came in the form of a verse:

Death will come, and then the waves of the sea,
Then the woman and her fruit will return.

My mother was so upset that her words choked, and the man tried to calm her:

'If one seeks to know the future, one must expect sometimes to encounter death. Is death not at the end of every destiny?'

Salma found the strength to reply, trembling, almost beseeching him:

'At the end, probably, but here it appears at the very beginning of the prediction.'

The man's only reply was to turn his eyes and his palms towards heaven. No more words passed his lips, and when my mother attempted to pay him he refused with a gesture which brooked no argument.

★ ★ ★

The fourth visit was to be Salma's undoing. This time it was to one of those people known as *mu'azzimin*, famous for their ability to cast out demons. My grandmother, may God take pity upon her! had praised this man exceedingly; according to her, he had solved a thousand problems far more complicated than our own. In fact, he was so sought after that we had to wait two hours in his antechamber while he dealt with six other clients.

As soon as Salma explained her situation to him a condescending smile came over his face, and he swore that within seven days her problem would be forgotten.

'Your cousin has a tiny demon in his head which must be cast out. If he were here I would cure him immediately. But I shall pass to you the power to exorcize him yourself. I will teach you a spell which you should recite over his head while he sleeps tonight, tomorrow and the next night; I will also give you this phial of perfume. You must pour out a drop when you pronounce the spell.'

The first evening, my father slept in Salma's room, and she had no difficulty in reciting the words and pouring out a drop of the elixir. On the second evening, however, there came to pass what any intelligent being might have foreseen. Muhammad was with Warda, and my mother slipped trembling into their bedroom. She was about to pour out the liquid when the concubine let out a piercing cry, at which my father awoke, and with an instinctive movement seized his frail aggressor by the ankle. Salma fell sobbing to the ground.

Seeing the phial in her hand, Muhammad accused his wife of sorcery, of madness, and of attempting to poison him. Without waiting for dawn he at once cried out to her three times in succession: '*Anti taliqa, anti taliqa, anti taliqa*', declaring thus that she was henceforth free of him and divorced.

The Year of the Mourners

902 A.H.

9 September 1496 – 29 August 1497

That year, Boabdil himself came to our house for the condolence ceremonies. I should say to Khali's house, because I went to live with him after my father had repudiated Salma. The deposed sultan entered the room, followed by a chamberlain, a secretary, and six guards dressed in the style of the Alhambra. He murmured various appropriate words to my uncle, who shook his hand for a long time before giving him his high divan, the only one in the house. His retainers remained standing.

My grandmother had died in the night, and the Granadans resident in Fez had begun to gather since the morning. Boabdil had arrived unannounced, well before the midday prayer. None of those present had a particularly high opinion of him, but his titles, however hollow, continued to make a certain impression upon his former subjects. Furthermore, the occasion was not a suitable one either for recriminations or for the settlement of accounts. Except, that is, for Astaghfirullah, who came into the room shortly after the sultan, but did not favour him even with a glance. He sat down on the first empty cushion, and began to recite aloud in his rasping voice the Qur'anic verses appropriate to the occasion.

Several lips followed the prayers, while others seemed set in a dreamy pout, amused at times, while still others chattered incessantly. In the men's reception room, only Khali was weeping. I can see him still, as if he was taking shape before my eyes. I can see myself too, sitting on the floor, not happy, certainly, but not particularly sad either, my dry and carefree eyes roaming avidly around the company. From Boabdil, who had become immensely fat, to the shaikh, whom exile and the years had rendered skeletal and angular. His turban appeared more immense than ever, out of all proportion. Every time he became silent the raucous screams of the women mourners rang out, their faces damp with sweat, their hair dishevelled, their faces scratched until the blood came, while in a corner of the courtyard the male mourners dressed in women's clothes, clean-shaven and made up, were feverishly shaking their square tambourines. To make them keep quiet, Astaghfirullah began to chant again, more loudly, more off key, with greater fervour. From time to time a street poet would get up and recite in a triumphal tone an elegy which had already been used for a hundred other departed souls. Outside, there was the clanging of cooking pots; the women of the neighbourhood were bringing in food, since nothing is cooked in a house where someone has died.

Death is a celebration. A spectacle.

My father did not arrive until midday, explaining rather confusedly that he had just learned of the sad news. Everyone eyed him curiously, thinking themselves obliged to greet him coldly or even to ignore him. I felt mortified; I would have wished that he had not been there, that he were not my father. Ashamed of my thoughts, I went towards him, leant my head against his shoulder and stood there without moving. But while he slowly caressed the nape of my neck I began to remember, I do not know why, the astrologer-bookseller and his prediction.

So the death had taken place. Without really admitting it to myself, I was somewhat relieved that the victim had been neither my mother nor my father. Salma told me later that she was afraid that it would be me. That which she could not voice, even in the very depths of her heart, only old Astaghfirullah dared to put into words, in the form of a parable.

Raising himself up to pronounce an elegy for the departed, he addressed himself first to my uncle:

'The story is told that one of the caliphs of long ago had lost his mother, whom he cherished as you used to cherish your mother, and he began to weep without restraint. A wise man came up to him. "Prince of the Believers," he said, "you should give thanks to the Most High, since he has favoured your mother by making you weep over her mortal remains instead of humiliating her by making her weep over yours." We must thank God when death follows the natural order of things, and trust in His Wisdom when, alas, it is otherwise.'

He began to intone a prayer, which the company murmured in time with him. Then without any transition he picked up the thread of his discourse:

'Too often, at funerals, I hear men and women believers cursing death. But death is a gift from the Most High, and one cannot curse that which comes from Him. Does the word "gift" seem incongruous to you? It is nevertheless the absolute truth. If death was not inevitable, man would have wasted his whole life attempting to avoid it. He would have risked nothing, attempted nothing, undertaken nothing, invented nothing, built nothing. Life would have been a perpetual convalescence. Yes my brothers, let us thank God for having made us this gift of death, so that life is to have meaning; of night, that day is to have meaning; silence, that speech is to have meaning; illness, that health is to have meaning; war, that peace is to have meaning. Let us give thanks to Him for having given us weariness and pain, so that rest and joy are to have meaning. Let us give thanks to Him, Whose wisdom is infinite.'

The assembly gave thanks in unison: '*Al-hamd ul-illah, al-hamd ul-illah!*' I noticed that at least one man had remained silent; his lips cracked, his hands clenched together; it was Khali.

'I was afraid,' he told me later. 'I thought to myself: "If only he can restrain himself!" Unfortunately I knew Astaghfirullah too well to nurture the least illusion in that direction.'

In fact, the sense of the allocution was beginning to change:

'If God had offered me death as a gift, if He had called me to Him instead of letting me live through the agony of my city, would He have been cruel towards me? If God had spared me to see with my own eyes Granada falling into captivity and the believers into dishonour, would He have been cruel towards me?'

The shaikh raised his voice sharply, startling the company:

'Am I the only one present to think that death is worth more than dishonour? Am I the only one to cry out: "O God, if I have failed in my duty towards the Community of the Believers, crush me with Your powerful hand, sweep me away from the surface of the earth like some baleful vermin. O God, judge me even today, for my conscience is too heavy to bear. You have entrusted me with the fairest of Your cities, You have put in my hands the life and honour of the Muslims; will You not summon me to render my accounts?"'

Khali was bathed in sweat, as were all those seated near Boabdil. The latter was deathly pale, like a turmeric stalk. It might have been said that his royal blood had abandoned him so as not to share in his shame. If, acting on the advice of some counsellor, he had come to re-establish his links with his former subjects, in order to be in a position to ask them to contribute to the expenses of his court, the enterprise was ending in utter disaster. Another one. His eyes roamed desperately towards the way out, while his heavy body appeared to have collapsed.

Was it out of pity, or exhaustion or simply by chance, that Astaghfirullah suddenly decided to interrupt his accusations and to resume his prayers? My uncle regarded this, he said, as an intervention from Heaven. The moment that the shaikh pronounced the words 'I bear witness that there is no other God but God, and that Muhammad is the Messenger of God', Khali seized the opportunity literally to jump out of his place and to give the signal for the departure of the cortège to the cemetery. The women accompanied the shroud to the threshold of the gate, waving white handkerchiefs as a symbol of desolation and farewell. Boabdil slipped away through a side door. Henceforth the Granadans of Fez could die in peace; the flabby silhouette of the fallen sultan would appear no more to plague their final journey.

*　*　*

The condolence ceremonies continued for another six days. What better remedy is there than exhaustion for the pain caused by the death of a loved one? The first visitors would come at dawn, the last would leave after nightfall. After the third evening, the relatives had no more tears, and sometimes forgot themselves sufficiently to smile or to laugh, which those present did not fail to criticize. The only ones to behave properly were the hired mourners, who sought to increase their pay by intensifying their wailing. Forty days after the decease, the condolences resumed once more in the same fashion, for three further days.

These weeks of mourning gave opportunities for my father and my uncle to exchange various conciliatory words. It was not yet a reunion, far from it, and my mother took care not to cross the path of the man who had repudiated her. But, from the vantage point of my eight years, I believed I could discern a glimmer of hope on the horizon.

Among other matters, my father and my uncle had discussed my future. They had agreed that it was time for me to start school. Other children went to school later, but it seemed that I was already showing signs of precocious intelligence, and it was pointless to leave me at home all day in the company of women. I might grow soft, and my virility might suffer. They each came to me in turn to explain this, and one morning they both solemnly accompanied me to the local mosque.

The teacher, a young turbaned shaikh with a beard which was almost blond, asked me to recite the *Fatiha*, the first *sura* of the Book. I did this without a mistake, without the slightest hesitation. He appeared satisfied with this:

'His elocution is good and his memory is precise. He will not need more than four or five years to memorize the Qur'an.'

I was not a little proud, since I knew that many pupils took six years, even seven. After having learned the Qur'an by heart, I would be able to enter the college, where the various sciences were taught.

'I will also instruct him in the principles of orthography, grammar and calligraphy,' the teacher explained.

When asked what payment he required, he took a step backwards:

'My only payment comes from the Most High.'

However, he added that each parent gave what he could to the school on the various feast days, with a more substantial gift at the end of the final year, after the Great Recitation.

Promising myself to memorize the hundred and fourteen *suras* as soon as possible I began to attend the shaikh's classes assiduously five days a week. There were no fewer than eighty boys in my class, aged between seven and fourteen. Each pupil came to school in whatever clothes he pleased, but no one would have thought of coming to school dressed in sumptuous garments, silk, or embroidery, except on special occasions. In any case, the sons of princes and of the grandees of the kingdom did not go to the mosque schools. They received the instruction of a shaikh in their own homes. But with that exception, the boys who attended the school came from a variety of backgrounds: sons of qadis, notaries, officers, royal and municipal functionaries, shopkeepers and artisans, even some sons of slaves sent by their masters.

The room was large, and arranged in tiers. The bigger boys sat at the back, the smaller ones in front, each with a little board on which he would write the day's verses, taken down at the master's dictation. The latter often had a rod in his hand, which he would not hesitate to use if one of us swore or made some serious mistake. But none of the pupils held it against him, and he himself never harboured a grudge from one day to the next.

On the day of my arrival at the school, I found a seat in the third row, I believe. Close enough to see and hear the teacher, but far enough away to protect myself from his questions and his inevitable outbursts of anger. Next to me sat the most mischievous of all the children of the quarter, Harun, known as the Ferret. He was my age, with a very brown complexion, with clothes that were worn and patched but always clean. After the first scuffle we became inseparable friends, bound together in life and death. No one who saw him would fail to ask him for news of me, and no one would see me without being astonished that he was not with me. At his side, I was to explore both Fez and my own adolescence. I felt an outsider; he knew the city was his, created for him, only for his eyes, for his limbs, for his heart. And he offered to share it with me.

It is true that he belonged, by birth, to the most generous of companies.

The Year of Harun the Ferret
903 A.H.
30 August 1497 – 18 August 1498

It was in that year that Melilla fell into the hands of the Castilians. A fleet had been sent to attack it, but found it deserted, abandoned by its inhabitants, who had fled into the neighbouring hills, taking their possessions with them. The Christians seized the city and began to fortify it. God knows if they will leave it one day!

At Fez, the refugees from Granada became afraid. They had the sensation that the enemy was at their heels, that he would pursue them to the very heart of the lands of Islam, even to the ends of the earth.

My family's worries increased, but I was still only slightly affected, absorbed in my studies and in my budding friendships.

★　★　★

When Harun came to my house for the first time, still very shy, and when I introduced him to my uncle, mentioning the guild to which his family belonged, Khali took my friend's hands, more slender than his, but already more roughened, in his own, and pronounced these words, which made me smile at the time:

'If the fair Scheherazade had known them, she would have devoted a long night to telling their story; she would have added jinns, flying carpets and magic lanterns, and before dawn, by some miraculous means, she would have changed their chief into a caliph, their hovels into palaces, and their penitential garb into ceremonial robes.'

These were the porters of Fez. Three hundred men, simple, poor, almost all of them illiterate, but who had nevertheless managed to become the most respected, most fraternal and best organized of all the guilds of the city.

Each year, until today, they appoint a leader, a consul, who regulates their activities down to the minutest detail. Each week he decides which of them will work and which will rest, according to the arrival of the caravans, the situation in the suqs, and the availability of his fellows. That which a porter earns for his day's work he does not take home, but deposits the whole of it in a communal chest. At the end of the week the money is divided out equally among those who have worked, except for a part which is kept aside for the good works of the guild, which are both manifold and munificent; when any of their number dies, they take over the responsibility for his family, help his widow to find a new husband and take care of his children until they are of an age to have a profession. The son of one is the son of all. The money from the fund is also used for those who marry; all the members contribute to assure them of a sum which will enable them to set up house.

The consul of the porters negotiates on their behalf with the sultan and his advisers. In this way he has managed to secure their immunity both from tribute and the salt tax, and to ensure that their bread is baked for them free of charge in the municipal ovens. Furthermore, if any of them should by some misfortune commit a murder punishable by death, he is not executed in public like other criminals, in order not to bring the guild into disrepute. In exchange, the consul must make a rigorous and unbiased examination of the probity of each new candidate, to exclude anyone who might be suspect. In this way the reputation of the porters has become so high that the merchants are obliged to have recourse to them to clear their stock. Thus the vendors of oil, who arrive in the suqs from the countryside with containers of all sizes, resort to special porters who will themselves confirm the capacity of the containers as well as the quality of the contents, and even give guarantees for the purchasers. In the same way, when a merchant imports a new kind of cloth, he asks the criers among the porters to proclaim the high quality of the merchandise. The porters charge a fixed sum for each of these functions, according to a scale fixed by the consul.

No man, be he even a prince, ever dares to lay hands on any of their number, because he knows that he would have to fight against the entire company. Their motto is a sentence of the Prophet's: 'Assist your brother, whether he is the oppressor or the oppressed,' but they interpret these words in the same way as the Messenger himself, when someone said to him, 'We shall assist the oppressed, that goes without saying. But in what way should we come to the aid of the oppressor?' And he replied: 'By getting the upper hand over him and by preventing him from doing harm.' Thus it was rare for a porter to start a fight in the suqs of Fez, and there was always a wise man among his brothers to reason with him.

Such were these men. Humble, yet proud, impoverished, yet generous. So far from palaces and citadels, yet so capable of running their affairs. Yes, this was the stock from which my best friend sprang.

Every day at first light Harun the Ferret would call for me to walk at my side the few hundred paces which separated Khali's house from the school. Sometimes we told each other tall stories, sometimes we repeated the verses we had studied the previous evening. Often we said nothing at all, walking in companionable silence.

Opening my eyes one morning I saw him in my bedroom, sitting at the foot of the box bed on which I slept. Fearing that I was late for school, I jumped up, already thinking of the teacher's cane about to whistle down across my calves. Harun reassured me with a smile.

'It's Friday, the school is closed, but the streets are open and the gardens too. Take a piece of bread and a banana and meet me on the corner.'

God alone knows the number of expeditions we made together after that. We often began our walks at the Square of Wonders. I do not know if that was its real name, but that was what Harun used to call it. There was nothing for us to buy there, or pick, or eat. We could only look around us, breathe in the air, and listen.

In particular, there were those pretending to be ill. Some pretended to be affected by epilepsy, holding their head in both hands and shaking it vigorously, letting their lips and jaws hang down, and then rolling around on the ground in such a practised fashion that they never even scratched themselves or upset the begging bowl by their side. Others pretended to be plagued with stones, and moaned incessantly, apparently in the most fearful pain, unless Harun and I were the only spectators. Still others displayed wounds and sores. From these I swiftly turned away, for I had been told that the mere sight of them was enough to become similarly afflicted oneself.

There were numerous tumblers on the square, who sang silly romances and sold little pieces of paper to the credulous, on which were written, so they claimed, magic spells to cure all manner of illnesses. There were itinerant quacks, who boasted of their miraculous medicines and took care not to appear twice in the same town. There were also monkey-keepers, who delighted in frightening pregnant women, and snake charmers who wound their creatures around their necks. Harun was not afraid to go up to them. But for my part I was as much frightened as disgusted.

On the feast days, there were story-tellers. I particularly remember a blind man whose stick danced to the rhythm of the adventures of Hallul, the hero of the wars of Andalus, and the renowned Antar ibn Shaddad, the most valorous of the Arabs. On one occasion, when he was telling the tale of the loves of black Antar and the fair Abla, he stopped to ask whether there were any women or children in the audience. Greatly disappointed, the women and children withdrew. I waited several moments to soothe my dignity. A hundred disapproving eyes were turned towards me. Unable to brazen it out, I was about to leave, when, with a glare, Harun signalled that there was no question of our doing so. He put one hand on my shoulder and the other on his hip and did not move an inch. The story-teller continued his tale, and we listened until the last embrace. Only after the crowd dispersed did we resume our walk.

The Square of Wonders was the crossroads of a number of busy streets. One of them, which was cluttered with the stalls of booksellers and public letter-writers, led to the entrance of the Great Mosque; another accommodated boot and shoe shops, a third the vendors of bridles, saddles and stirrups, but the fourth at last was the one we always had to take. Here were the milk sellers, whose shops were decked out with majolica vases far more valuable than the goods they sold. But we did not go to these shops but to those who would buy up unsold milk each evening at a low price at their doors, take it home, let it curdle overnight, and sell it the next day, chilled and diluted with water. A thirst-quenching and satisfying drink which strained neither the pockets nor the consciences of the Believers.

For Harun and I the discovery of Fez was just beginning. We would uncover its layers veil by veil, like a bride in her marriage chamber. I have kept a thousand memories of that year, which take me back to the carefree candour of my nine years each time I evoke them. But it is the most painful of them all that I feel obliged to relate here, since, if I did not mention it, I would be failing in my role of faithful witness.

That day, the walk had begun like any other; Harun wanted to nose around, and I was no less curious. We knew that there was a little suburb called al-Mars lying to the west of the city, the mention of which always brought a troubled look to our schoolmaster's face. Was it far off? Was it dangerous? Others would have asked no further; we were happy to set out.

When we arrived at this suburb around midday, we immediately understood its function. In the streets, women were lounging against the shopfronts, or by the open doors of establishments which could only be taverns. Harun mimicked the beckoning stance of a prostitute. I laughed and imitated the swaying gait of a stout matron.

And what if we went to see what went on in the taverns? We knew that it would be impossible for us to go inside, but we could always have a quick look.

So we go towards the first one. The door is half open, and we poke our two little heads inside. It's dark, and we can only see a crowd of customers. In the midst of them a shock of flaming red hair stands out. We see nothing else, because someone has already spotted us, and we quickly take to our heels, straight towards the tavern on the adjoining street. It's no lighter, but our eyes adjust more quickly. We count four heads of hair, about fifteen customers. In the third we have time to make out several faces, a number of gleaming cups, several wine jars. The game continues. Our reckless heads dive into the fourth. It seems lighter. Quite close to the door, we make out a face. That beard, that profile, that stance? I pull back my head and begin to run along the street, fleeing neither the tavern keepers nor their bully boys. The image which I want to leave far behind me is that of my father, seated in the tavern, at a table, with a shock of hair at his side. I have seen him. Harun has certainly recognized him. Has he seen us? I don't think so.

Since then it has happened to me more than once to go into taverns and streets more sordid than those of al-Mars. But that day the earth opened beneath my feet. It might have been the Day of

Judgement. I was ashamed, I was in pain. I did not stop running, the tears pouring down my cheeks, my eyes half closed, my throat hoarse, choking for breath.

Harun followed me, without speaking to me, without touching me, without coming too close. He waited until I was exhausted, until I sat down on the steps of an empty shop. He sat down by my side, still without a word. And then, at the end of an interminable hour, during which I gradually came to myself and calmed down, he stood up, and directed me imperceptibly towards the way home. It was only when we came in sight of Khali's house at dusk that Harun spoke for the first time:

'All men have always frequented taverns; all men have always loved wine. Otherwise, why should God have needed to forbid it?'

The very next day, I saw Harun the Ferret again without pain; it was meeting my father that I dreaded. By a happy chance he had to leave for the countryside where he was looking for a plot of land to rent. He came back several weeks later, but by then destiny had already drowned my sufferings and his own in even greater miseries.

The Year of the Inquisitors
904 A.H.
19 August 1498 – 7 August 1499

That year, Hasan the deliverer died under torture in one of the dungeons of the Alhambra; he was no less than eighty years old. There was none more skilled than he in obtaining the release of a captive, but when it came to his own liberation his words seem to have lost their weight. He was a devout and pious man, and if he sometimes made errors of judgement, his intentions were as pure as those of a child until his dying day. He died poor; may God now reveal to him the riches of Eden!

Thousands of others were tortured at the same time. For several months the most dreadful news had been reaching us from our former homeland, but few foresaw the calamity which was to engulf the last Muslims of Andalus.

It all began with the arrival at Granada of a party of inquisitors, religious fanatics who immediately issued a proclamation that all Christians who had converted to Islam should return to their original religion. Some of them reluctantly agreed, but the majority refused, pointing to the agreement concluded before the fall of the city, which expressly guaranteed the converts the right to remain Muslims. To no avail. As far as the inquisitors were concerned, this clause was null and void. Any man who had been baptized and who refused to return to Christianity was considered as a traitor and thus liable to be condemned to death. Several pyres were erected to intimidate the recalcitrant, as had been done for the Jews. Several citizens recanted. A lesser number told themselves that it was better to take flight, even at this late stage, before the trap closed on them again. They were able to take with them only the clothes on their backs.

The inquisitors then decreed that anyone having a Christian ancestor must be compulsorily baptized. One of the first to be affected by this was Hamid, whose grandfather was a Christian captive who had chosen to declare himself for the Witness of Islam. One evening some Castilian soldiers, accompanied by one of the inquisitors, came to his house in our quarter, al-Baisin. Warned in advance, the old man's neighbours went down into the street to try to prevent his arrest. In vain. The next day, a number of people, including two women, were arrested in other parts of the city. Each time, crowds gathered and the soldiers were obliged to draw their swords to force their way through. Most of the incidents took place in al-Baisin. A newly-built church not far from the house where we used to live was set on fire; in return, two mosques were pillaged. Everyone's faith was like a raw nerve.

One day, the news came that Hamid had succumbed in his dungeon as a result of the tortures inflicted upon him by the inquisitors. He had resisted conversion to the end, insisting upon the agreement signed by the Christian kings.

When the news of his death became known, appeals to resist resounded in the streets. Alone of all the notables of al-Baisin, Hamid had stayed where he was, not to make accommodation with the enemy, but to continue the mission to which he had devoted his life, to free the captured Muslims. The noble nature of his activities, the fact of his great age, and the suppressed hatreds coming to the surface combined to provoke an immediate reaction on the part of the Muslims. Barricades were put up; soldiers, civil servants and clergy were massacred. It was an insurrection.

Of course, the citizenry was in no condition to take on the army of occupation. With a few crossbows, swords, lances and clubs they managed to prevent the Castilian troops from getting into al-Baisin, and tried to organize themselves into a small army to wage the holy war. But after two days of fighting they were wiped out, and then the massacre began. The authorities proclaimed that the entire Muslim population would be executed for rebellion against the sovereigns, adding insidiously that only those who would accept conversion to Christianity would be spared. Thus the population of Granada became baptized by whole streets. In some villages in the Alpujarra mountains the peasants struck back; they managed to hold out for several weeks and even, it was said, killed the seigneur of Granada who led the expedition against them. But even there it was impossible to resist for long. The villagers were forced to seek terms; several hundred families were allowed to leave, and set themselves up in Fez; some took refuge in the mountains, swearing that no one would ever find them; all the others were baptized. The words *'Allahu akbar'* could no more be pronounced upon the soil of Andalus, where for eight centuries the voice of the muezzin had called the faithful to prayer. A man could not now say the *Fatiha* over his father's corpse. At least, that is, in public, for the Muslims who had been forcibly converted refused to repudiate their religion.

They sent heart-rending despatches to Fez. *Brothers,* ran one of their letters, *if, at the time of the fall of Granada, we failed in our duty to leave, this was simply because of our lack of resources, because we are the poorest and weakest in the land of Andalus. Today, we have been obliged to accept baptism in order to save the lives of our women and children, but we are afraid of incurring the wrath of the Most High on the Day of Judgement, and of suffering the tortures of Gehenna. Thus we beseech you, our exiled brothers, to assist us with your counsel. Enquire on our behalf of the doctors of the Law what we should do, our anguish has no end.*

Deeply moved, the Granadan exiles in Fez held a number of meetings that year, some of them in Khali's house. These were attended by both notables and common people, but particularly by *'ulama'* learned in the Law. Some came from far away to deliver the fruits of their research and their consideration.

I remember having seen the mufti of Oran arrive one day, a man of about forty, with a turban only a little less impressive than that of Astaghfirullah, but worn with a good-natured air. More deferential than usual, my uncle came out to the end of the street to welcome him, and in the course of the meeting those present simply put questions to him without daring to argue with him or to challenge his answers. Of course the problem as it presented itself required great mastery both of the Law and of the Traditions of the Prophet, as well as great daring in interpretation; it was impossible to accept that hundreds of thousands of Muslims should forsake the faith of the Prophet, yet it was monstrous to expect an entire people to go to the stake.

I still remember the first words of the man from Oran, delivered in a warm and serene voice:

'Brothers, we are here, may God be praised, in the land of Islam, and we bear our faith with pride, like a diadem. Let us be wary of condemning those who have to bear their religion like a burning ember in their hands.'

He continued:

'When you send messages to them, may your words be prudent and measured; remember your letter may light their pyre. Do not seek to blame them for their baptism; ask them simply to remain, in spite of everything, faithful to Islam, and to teach its principles to their sons. But not before puberty, not before they are old enough to keep a secret, for a child may, with an incautious word, reap their destruction.'

And what if these unhappy ones should be forced to drink wine? And what if they are invited to eat the flesh of swine, to prove they are no longer Muslims?

'Then they must do it, if they are forced to do so,' said the mufti, 'but they must protest in their hearts.'

And what if they are made to insult the Prophet, may God surround him with His prayers and His salvation?

'Then they must do it, if they are forced to do so,' repeated the mufti, 'but they must say the opposite in their hearts.'

To those who, through having not left their land, had to endure the cruellest tortures, the mufti gave the name of *Ghuraba*, Strangers, recalling the words of the Messenger of God: 'Islam began as a religion for outsiders and it will become once again a religion for outsiders just as it began. Blessed are the outsiders.'

★   ★   ★

To launch an appeal to Muslims of the world to save these unfortunates, the Granadan community of Fez decided to send emissaries to the great sovereigns of Islam, the Grand Turk, the new Sophy of Persia, the Sultan of Egypt and several others of lesser importance. Because of the functions which he used to exercise at the court of Alhambra, Khali was chosen to compose these letters, using the customary formulae; he was also charged with carrying the most important of these messages, the one addressed to the lord of Constantinople the Great. After he had been sounded out about this mission, my uncle paid visits to the Sultan of Fez and to Boabdil, and obtained letters of recommendation and credit from them both.

Each time that I recall that journey, I feel the pain of anguish, even today, although I have since then come to know the strangest lands and the most inaccessible places. I had always dreamed of Constantinople, and on hearing that Khali was to go there, I could scarcely contain myself. I turned it round and round in my head, asking whether I could possibly hope, at the age of ten, to take part in such a journey. Rather diffidently, I confided in my uncle. Great was my surprise when he replied, his arms open wide in welcome:

'Where could I find a better travelling companion?'

In spite of his ironical tone, he was clearly captivated by the idea. It only remained to convince my father.

That year again, Muhammad was often away from the city, still looking for a plot of land to rent where he could live peacefully away from noise, gossip and reproachful eyes. For two long weeks I waited for him every day, asking Warda and Mariam incessantly for news of him, although they knew nothing. Like me, they were waiting.

When he finally returned, I threw myself upon him and began to talk so fast that he had to make me start again several times. Alas, he refused immediately in a manner which brooked no further questioning. I should perhaps have waited for Khali to broach the subject of the journey in his own way, as he would have known how to extol the advantages of such a journey with eloquence. Perhaps Muhammad would have agreed so as not to annoy my uncle, with whom he had just become reconciled. But to me he could say 'No' straight out. As a pretext he pointed out the dangers of the journey, told me of people who had never returned, mentioned my studies, which I would have had to interrupt if I went away. However, I think the real reason was that he felt that I was too close to my uncle, and to my mother's family in general, and that he feared that he would lose me. Unable to argue with him, I begged him to talk it over with Khali, but he refused even to meet him.

For a whole week, I woke up each morning with my eyes bloodshot and my pillow damp. In an effort to console me my uncle swore that I would accompany him on his next journey; he would keep his word.

The day of his departure came. Khali was going to join a caravan of merchants which was leaving for Oran, where he would take ship. From first light the Granadans came in great number to wish him luck on his mission and to contribute several gold pieces for his expenses. For my part I was moping in my corner until an old man with impish eyes came and sat down next to me. It was none other than Hamza, the barber who had circumcised me. He asked for news of my father, and lamented the death of the deliverer whom he had seen for the last time in our house in al-Baisin. Then he asked after my studies, about the *sura* which I was studying at the time, and even began to recite it. It was pleasant to be in his company, and I chatted to him for an hour. He told me that he had lost the bulk of his fortune by going into exile, but that by the grace of God he was still able to look after the needs of his womenfolk. He had begun to work again, but only as a barber, because his razor was no longer sure enough for circumcisions. He had just rented a part of the local hammam in order to ply his trade.

Suddenly, an idea lit up his eyes.

'Wouldn't you like to give me a hand when you aren't at school?'

I accepted without demur.

'I'll pay you one dirham a week.'

I hastened to say that I had a friend and that I would very much like him to come with me. Hamza had nothing against it. He would receive the same pay, there were lots of things to do in the hammam.

When, some minutes later, Khali came to give me the traveller's kiss, he was surprised to see my eyes dry and smiling. I told him that I was going to work, that I would earn one dirham a week. He wished me success in my labours; I wished him success in his.

The Year of the Hammam
905 A.H.
8 August 1499 – 27 July 1500

'When I think that all these people are washing themselves with manure!'

It took me a few moments to grasp what Harun had just said. Then we both broke into loud peals of laughter. My friend was quite right, because it was indeed manure that was used to heat the water in the hammams of Fez.

That day we were paid to know it, as the owner of the bath had sent us, equipped with a pair of mules and several dirhams, to go the rounds of the stables of the quarter and buy up the accumulated manure. Then we took it outside the city, to a place to which he had directed us. A man was waiting there to receive the load; his task was to spread out the precious harvest to dry it, a process which took a month in summer and three months in winter. On the way back we brought a pile of manure with us, as hard as wood and ready to burn; it was with this that the boiler of the hammam was fed. Of course, once we had delivered the final load, Harun and I had about us the colouring and the smell of the stuff we had been carrying.

So we hurried to scramble out of our clothes and run into the warm water chamber. Our trip had been fun. Whenever we recognized a friend in the steam room we would delight in asking him whether the water did not seem different that day.

For all the people of the city, the hammam was the most pleasant of meeting places. They left their clothes in cabins near the entrance door, then met together naked, without the slightest shame. Young schoolboys would chatter about their teachers, and tell each other about their pranks, passing over their beatings in silence. Adolescents would talk about women, each accusing the other of pining for one woman or another, each boasting of his amorous exploits. Adults would be more circumspect on that subject, but would exchange advice and recipes to improve their bodily vigour, an inexhaustible topic and a gold mine for charlatans. The rest of the time they would talk dinars, discuss religion and politics, out loud or in low tones according to the opinions they held.

The men of the quarter would often meet at the hammam for lunch. Some would bring their meal with them, while others would send the steam-room boy to buy something at the neighbouring market. But they would not begin their collation directly; they would go to the tepid room, where boys would wash them and rub them with oil and unguents. They would rest a while, lying on felt carpets, their heads on a sort of wooden bolster, also covered with felt, before going into the hot room, where they would sweat. Then they would go back into the warm room to wash themselves again and to rest. It was only then that they would go into the cool room and sit around the fountain, to eat, gossip and laugh, and even sing.

Most of them would remain naked until the end of the meal, except for important persons who would not deign to show themselves thus, keeping a towel round their waist and only removing it in private reserved rooms, which were always impeccably maintained. In these rooms they received their friends, or were massaged, and the barber would also come there to offer them his services.

And then there were the women. A certain number of hammams were kept entirely for women, but most of them catered for both sexes. The same places, but at different times. In the place where I used to work, the men would come from three in the morning until two in the afternoon. For the rest of the day, the steam-room boys were replaced by negresses, who put a rope across the entrance to show the men that they could not come in, and if a man needed to say something to his wife he would call one of the women attendants to deliver the message.

Each time we had to leave, each time that we used to see the rope across the entrance and the women arriving, Harun and I would ask each other what could possibly happen in the hammam when it became the women's domain. The first few times we tried to convince ourselves that exactly the same things happened as we knew from the men's sessions, the same massages, the same rubbings, the same chatter, the same feasting, the same towels to cover the notables. However, watching the entrance in the afternoons it was clear that not only did a great number of market women arrive with their shopping bags, but all sorts of mysterious women, fortune-tellers, healers, perhaps even magicians. Was it true that they were distilling magic elixirs, putting spells on men, piercing wax figurines with magic pins? It would be an understatement to say that we were intrigued; it became an almost unbearable obsession.

And a challenge.

'I'm going tomorrow, whatever happens. D'you want to come?' said Harun one day.

I looked at his eyes. He wasn't joking.

'D'you want to come?'

It took all my courage to say no.

'Better still,' said Harun. 'I'll go on my own. But be here at midday, at this very place.'

The next day it was dark and rainy. I took up my post at the place we had agreed, from which I could see the entrance to the hammam without being seen. I had not seen Harun all day, and I wondered whether he was already there, or whether he would be able to get inside. I was waiting for him to be thrown out, I was also afraid that he would leave pursued by twenty women at his heels, and that I should be forced to flee through the streets in my turn. The one thing that I was sure of was that the Ferret had not given up his mad plan. From time to time I looked up at the sun, or rather at its outline visible through the clouds. I was becoming impatient.

There was no unusual movement at the entrance to the hammam. Some women were going in, others coming out, some enveloped in black or white, others with only their hair and the lower part of their faces covered. Little girls accompanied them, sometimes even very small boys. At one point a fat woman came towards me. When she drew level with me she stopped for a moment, inspected me from head to foot, and then set off again murmuring incomprehensibly to herself. My furtive air must have made me seem suspicious. Several minutes later, another woman, entirely covered from head to foot but much more slender, came towards the place where I was waiting. I was most uneasy. In turn, she stopped and turned towards me. I was going to take to my heels.

'You're here, in perfect safety, and you're trembling?'

It was Harun's voice. He barely left me the time to express my surprise.

'Don't make any sign, don't make any noise! Count to a hundred and then meet me at the house.'

He was waiting for me at the door.

'Tell me!' I exploded.

He took his time before replying, in the most careless tone:

'I arrived, I went in, I pretended to look for someone, I went round all the rooms and then I came out again.'

'Did you undress?'

'No.'

'Did you see anything?'

'Yes, lots.'

'Tell me, may God shatter you into pieces!'

He said nothing. His mouth did not express the slightest smile, the slightest grin. But his eyes sparkled with satisfaction and malice. I was crestfallen. I wanted to beat him black and blue.

'Do you want me to beg you, to press my forehead against your slippers?'

The Ferret was not in the slightest impressed by my sarcasm.

'Even if you beg me, even if you prostrate yourself at my feet I shall tell you nothing. I have taken risks which you refused to take. If you want to know what goes on when the women are there you must come with me next time.'

I was aghast.

'So you're thinking of going again?'

This seemed so obvious to him that he did not even deign to reply.

The next day I was in position, and I saw him go in. He had improved his get-up considerably. He was not satisfied with wrapping himself in a thick black robe, but he had a white scarf around his neck which covered his hair, a part of his forehead and his cheeks, with its ends tied together under his chin. Above this was a transparent white veil. The disguise was so perfect that I would have been taken in a second time.

When I met up with him again he seemed bothered. I asked him to tell me about his escapade, but he refused to do so, in spite of my insistence and my pleas. He remained obdurately silent, and I soon forgot the whole thing. However, it was Harun himself who would remind me of it, many years later and in a way which would remain for ever in my memory.

Towards the end of that year my uncle came back from his travels. When they learned of his return the Andalusians of Fez came in groups, one after the other, to hear what he had to say and to inform themselves of the results of his mission. He told them in detail of his sea voyage, his fear of shipwreck and pirates, the sight of Constantinople, the palace of the Grand Turk, the janissaries, his travels in the lands of the Orient, in Syria, Iraq, Persia, Armenia and Tartary.

However, he soon came to the most important part.

'Everywhere my hosts declared themselves convinced that one day soon the Castilians will be beaten, by the leave of the Most High, that Andalus will become Muslim once more, and that each one of us will be able to return to his home.'

He did not know when, or under what circumstances, he admitted, but he could testify to the invincible power of the Turks, of the terror which the sight of their vast armies would strike in the heart of every man. He was convinced of their profound concern for the fate of Granada, and their desire to deliver it from the unbelievers.

Of all those present, I was not the least enthusiastic. When we were alone together that evening, I insisted on asking my uncle:

'When do you think we shall return?'

He seemed not to understand what I wanted to say.

I told myself that he must be weary after his journey.

'To Granada, isn't that what you were talking about?'

He looked at me for a long time, as if sizing me up, before saying, in a slow and emphatic voice:

'Hasan, my son, you are now in your twelfth year and I must speak to you as if I were speaking to a man (he hesitated a moment further). Hear me well. What I have seen in the Orient is that the Grand Sophy of Persia is preparing to wage war against the Turks, who are themselves primarily preoccupied with their own conflict with Venice. As for Egypt, she has just received a consignment of corn from the Castilians as a token of friendship and alliance. That is the reality. Perhaps, in several years' time, things will have changed, but, today, none of the Muslim sovereigns whom I have met seemed to me to be concerned with the fate of the Granadans, whether of ourselves, the exiles, or the poor Strangers.'

In my eyes there was less disappointment than surprise.

'You will ask me,' Khali continued, 'why I should have told those people who were here the opposite of the truth. You see, Hasan, all those men still have, hung up on their walls, the key to their houses in Granada. Every day they look at it, and looking at it they sigh and pray. Every day their joys, their habits and a certain pride come back to their memory, and these things they will never rediscover in exile. The only reason for their existence is the thought that soon, thanks to the Great Sultan or to Providence, they will find their house once again, with the colour of its stones, the smell of its garden, the water of its fountain, all intact, unaltered, just as it has been in their dreams. They live like this, they will die like this, and their sons will do so after them. Perhaps one day it may be necessary for someone to dare to teach them to look unflinchingly at their defeat, to explain to them that in order to get on one's feet again one must first admit that one is down on the ground. Perhaps someone will have to tell them the truth one day. But I myself do not have the courage to do so.'

The Year of the Raging Lions
906 A.H.
28 July 1500 – 16 July 1501

My sister Mariam had grown up without my being aware of it. Two long separations had turned her into a stranger. We no longer shared the same roof, or the same games. When I crossed her path our words had lost their old complicity, and our glances no longer said anything to each other. It was only when she called out to me from the back of a mule that year that I came to see her again, gaze at her and remember the little girl whom I used to love and fight until she wept.

It happened in early summer in an olive grove on the road to Meknes. My father had decided that I should accompany him, together with Warda and Mariam, on a tour of the countryside behind Fez. He was still looking for suitable land to rent. His plan was that with the assistance of some Andalusian agriculturalists whom he knew he would introduce various crops which were little known and poorly cultivated on African soil, notably the white mulberry, the food of the silkworm.

In the most minute detail, he told me about a huge enterprise in which one of the richest men in Fez would take part. Listening to him I had the impression that he had somehow emerged from the despondency and world-weariness which had afflicted him after he left Granada behind, a terrible wrench which had been made worse by the loss of one of his wives after the other. Now he was scheming, challenging, his fists ready to fight, his eyes once more alight with purpose.

For the journey, he and I were on horseback and the women on mules, which meant that we had to go at their pace. At one point, Warda came alongside Muhammad. I dropped back level with Mariam. She slowed down imperceptibly. Our parents drew further away.

'Hasan!'

I had not addressed a word to her since we left Fez four hours earlier. I gave her a glance which meant at most 'Is your animal being a nuisance?' But she had taken off her light sand-coloured veil, and a sad smile covered her pale face.

'Your uncle cherishes you as if you were his own son, doesn't he?'

The question seemed pointless and out of place. I agreed brusquely, not wanting to discuss my relations with my mother's family with Warda's daughter. But that was not her purpose.

'When I have children, will you love them as he loves you?'

'Of course,' I said.

But my 'Of course' was too quick, too gruff. And embarrassed.

I was afraid of what might follow. It took a long time. I glanced towards Mariam; her silence irritated me only a little less than her questions. She no longer looked at me, but she had not put on her veil again, in spite of the dust of the road. I turned towards her and looked at her properly, for the first time for a long time. She was no less appealing than on the day when I saw her coming towards me in her mother's arms in the galley which brought us into exile. Her skin was no less pink, her lips no less shining. Only the kohl on her eyelids gave her the air of a woman. And her silhouette. As I looked at her, she sat up, and I could make out the line of her bosom. Her heart was beating, or was it mine? I lowered my eyes. In a single year, she had ripened, she had become beautiful and arousing.

'When I have children, will you love them?'

I should have been annoyed, but I smiled, because I suddenly remembered her habit, since she was a year old, of asking for the same toy three, four, ten times, in the same tone without giving up.

'Of course I shall love them.'

'Will you also talk to their mother like your uncle talks to Salma?'

'Yes, certainly.'

'Will you visit her often? Will you ask her if all is well with her? Will you listen to her sorrows?'

'Yes, Mariam, yes!'

She pulled sharply on her bridle; her mule reared up. I stopped; she looked straight at me:

'But why do you never speak to me? Why do you never come and ask me if I weep at night? I must fear all other men: my father today, my husband tomorrow, all those who are not related to me and from whom I should hide myself.'

She gave the mule its head, and it set off at a trot. I hurried to stay at her side. I still did not speak to her, but oddly enough, I was frightened for her, and a sudden affection for her radiated from my eyes. It seemed as if some danger awaited her.

★   ★   ★

Halfway between Fez and Meknes we stopped for the night in a village called 'Ar, Shame. The imam of the mosque offered to accommodate us in return for a donation for the orphans whom he looked after. He was without great learning, but with a very pleasant manner, and lost no time in telling us why this village should have such a name.

The inhabitants, he informed us, had always been known for their greed, and used to suffer from this reputation. The merchant caravans avoided it and would not stop there. One day, having learned that the King of Fez was hunting lions in the neighbour-hood, they decided to invite him and his court, and killed a number of sheep in his honour. The sovereign had dinner and went to bed. Wishing to show their generosity, they placed a huge goatskin bottle before his door and agreed to fill it up with milk for the royal breakfast. The villagers all had to milk their goats and then each of them had to go to tip his bucket into the container. Given its great size, each of them said to himself that he might just as well dilute his milk with a good quantity of water without anyone noticing. To the extent that in the morning such a thin liquid was poured out for the king and his court that it had no other taste than the taste of meanness and greed.

However, what I remember of my stay in that village had nothing to do with the incurable fault of its inhabitants but far more with the indescribably frightening experience which I had there.

The imam had received us well, and suggested that we should sleep in a wooden hut near the mosque, which had a pen next to it for our animals. Warda and Mariam slept inside, while my father and I preferred to sleep on the roof, where we could take advantage of the cool air of the summer night. So we were there on the roof when, around midnight, two huge lions, evidently attracted by the smell of the horses and the mules, came up to our door and tried to tear down the rough fence of thorns which protected our beasts. The horses began to neigh as if possessed, and threw themselves against the walls of the hut, which threatened to collapse with each charge. This continued for two hours or more, until one of the lions, no doubt enraged by the thousands of needles which pricked him every time he tried to get over the fence, turned towards the door and began to scratch it and slash at it with his claws. My father and I watched all this, powerless to intervene, knowing full well that the animals might break their way through to the women and eat them up without us being able to do anything other than watch from the roof, apart from wanting to throw ourselves at their jaws as a matter of honour. From below we could hear Mariam's screams and Warda's prayers, calling upon the Madonna in Castilian.

In a trembling voice, Muhammad made a vow: if we survived, he would break his journey to make a pilgrimage to the village of Taghya, and place an offering upon the tomb of *wali* Bu 'Izza, a saint famous for his many miracles involving lions.

I do not know whether it was the intercession of the saint or that of the mother of the Messiah which was the more effective, but in any case the lions eventually seemed to become weary and lose interest, and in the first glimmers of dawn they went away, although their roars, which were only a little less frightening, still reached us from the nearby mountain. It was only when the village came to life in the early hours of the morning that we had the courage to leave our shelter. However, before continuing our journey, we had to wait for a long caravan to come past. Determined to fulfil his vow immediately, Muhammad wanted to find a group of pilgrims at Meknes who were leaving for Taghya.

Arriving there a week later, and seeing the vast crowd of people who, like ourselves, were visiting the *wali*'s tomb, I understood the perpetual dread which lions strike in the hearts of the inhabitants of Africa. I was to experience this even more profoundly during my travels. How many times, on arriving at a village, have I seen the inhabitants gathered together, in deep distress, because a family has just been devoured by these savage beasts! How many times, when wishing to go in a particular direction, have the guides directed me another way, simply because a pride of lions had just decimated a whole caravan! It has even happened that one of these beasts alone attacked a detachment of two hundred armed horsemen, and managed to kill five or six of them before beating a retreat.

Certainly, the lion is the bravest of all animals, and I say this unreservedly, because I bore the name of this beast for the eight years of my stay in Italy. However, I must make it clear that those who live in the cold lands are far less fierce than those who live in the hotter ones. In order to silence a braggart in Fez, one says to him 'You are as brave as the lions of Agla; even the calves can nibble at their tails.' It is true that in the place of this name a child only has to run shouting behind a lion for the latter to run away. In another village in the mountains, called Red Stone, the lions wander between the houses to eat the bones which are left out for them, and everyone mixes with them without fear. I have also heard that when a woman finds herself alone with a lion in an isolated place she has only to uncover a certain part of her body in front of him for the animal to roar loudly, lower his eyes and slink away. May everyone be free to believe what he will!

★ ★ ★

On the way back from this makeshift pilgrimage, I remembered the vague feeling of apprehension that I had experienced for Mariam. A premonition of the lions' attack on our hut? For the time being, I thought so. At the age of twelve I still believed that as between beasts and men the former could do the most damage.

The Year of the Great Recitation
907 A.H.
17 July 1501 – 6 July 1502

Mariam's fiancé was four times her age and twice her height, had an ill-gotten fortune and the smile of those who have learned at an early age that life is a perpetual swindle. At Fez he was called the Zarwali, and many envied him, since this former shepherd had built the largest palace in the city, the largest, that is, after that of the ruler, a piece of elementary common sense for anyone who wanted to make sure that his head remained attached to his body.

No one knew how the Zarwali's fortune had grown so vast. For the first forty years of his life, it was said, he and his goats had roamed over the mountain of Bani Zarwal in the Rif, thirty miles from the sea. Many years later I happened to pay a visit to the area, where I observed a strange phenomenon. At the bottom of the valley there was an opening in the earth, rather like a cave, from which a huge flame issued continuously. All round it was a brownish coloured pool full of a thick liquid with a pervasive smell. Many travellers came to marvel at this wonder, and threw in branches or pieces of wood, which were burnt up on the spot. Some believe that it is the mouth of Hell.

Not far from this intimidating place, it was said, were the secret wells where the Romans had buried their treasure before leaving Africa. Had the shepherd accidentally stumbled on one of these hiding places while pasturing his flocks? That was what I had heard at Fez long before the Zarwali burst upon my life. Whatever the truth was, having discovered his treasure, instead of squandering it at once as happens to so many who become rich unexpectedly, he slowly worked out a long-term strategy. Having sold off part of the treasure bit by bit, he appeared one day, richly accoutred, at the public audience of the Sultan of Fez.

'How many gold dinars do you obtain from the Bani Zarwal each year?' he asked the monarch.

'Three thousand,' replied the sovereign.

'I will give you six thousand in advance if you will farm the taxes to me.'

And our Zarwali got what he wanted, including a body of soldiers to help him collect the taxes, extracting all the savings of the local population by threats or torture. At the end of the year he went back to the monarch:

'I was mistaken. I managed to get twelve thousand, not six thousand.'

Deeply impressed, the master of Fez farmed the whole of the Rif to the Zarwali, and assigned him a hundred bowmen, three hundred cavalrymen and four hundred foot soldiers to assist him to fleece the population.

For five years the amount of tax extracted was higher than it had ever been, but the people of the Rif gradually became impoverished. Many fled to other provinces of the kingdom; some of the coastal cities even considered handing themselves over to the Castilians. Sensing that things might begin to change for the worse, the Zarwali resigned his office, left the Rif and set himself up at Fez with the money he had extorted. Having retained the trust of the monarch he set about building a palace and began to devote himself to all manner of business. Greedy, pitiless but exceedingly clever, he was always on the lookout for new schemes.

My father had got to know him through a rich Andalusian émigré, and had told him about his plan to raise silkworms. Showing great interest, the Zarwali had plied him with questions about the caterpillars, the cocoons, the slime and the spinning, and asked one of his advisers to make a note of all the details. He declared that he was delighted to work with a man as capable as Muhammad.

'Well,' he said with a laugh, 'it's a partnership of money and brains.'

When my father replied that all Fez knew how astute and intelligent the Zarwali was, the latter replied:

'Don't you know, you who have read so many books, what the mother of one of the sultans of long ago said when her son was born?

"I do not want you to be endowed with intelligence, because you will have to put your intelligence at the service of the powerful. I want you to have good fortune, so that intelligent people may serve you." That's probably the same thing as my mother wanted for me when I was born,' laughed the Zarwali, showing all his teeth.

My father was encouraged by the meeting, although the Zarwali asked for some time to think it over. He wanted to inform the monarch about the project, obtain his consent, and consult various weavers and exporters. However, as an earnest of his genuine interest in the matter, he advanced Muhammad four hundred pieces of gold and also held out to him the dazzling prospect of a marriage alliance between the two families.

After several months, I think in Sha'ban of that year, the Zarwali summoned my father. He told him that his project was accepted and that he should begin the preparations, choosing various fields of white mulberries, planting others, recruiting skilled workers and building the first cocooneries. The king himself was full of enthusiasm for the project. He wanted to flood Europe and the Muslim lands with silks, to discourage the merchants from going as far as China to import the precious material.

My father was ecstatic with joy. His dream would come to fruition, on a scale which went far beyond his wildest hopes. He already saw himself rich, lying on immense silken cushions in a palace covered with majolica; he would be the first among the notables of Fez, the pride of the Granadans, a confidant of the sultan, a benefactor of schools and mosques . . .

'To seal our agreement,' pursued the Zarwali, 'what better than a blood alliance? Don't you have a daughter to marry?'

Muhammad immediately promised his backer Mariam's hand in marriage.

It was quite by chance that, several days later, I came to hear about this conversation, which was to change many things in my life. Gaudy Sarah had been to the harem of the Zarwali to sell her perfumes and trinkets, just as she had done in the houses and palaces of Granada. All through her visit, the women had spoken of nothing else than of their master's new marriage, making jokes about his inexhaustible vigour, and discussing the consequences of this latest acquisition for the favourites of the moment. The man already had four wives, the most that the Law would allow him to take at the same time; he must therefore repudiate one of them, but he was used to doing so, and his wives were used to it as well. The divorcee would get a house nearby, sometimes even staying within the walls, and it was whispered that some of them even became pregnant after the separation without the Zarwali showing the least surprise or taking offence.

Naturally, Sarah hastened to my mother's house the same afternoon to tell her the gossip. I had just come back from school, and was munching some dates, listening to the women's chatter with only half an ear. Suddenly I heard a name. I came closer:

'They've even had time to give Mariam a nickname: the silk-worm.'

I made Gaudy Sarah repeat her story word for word, and then asked her anxiously:

'Do you think my sister will be happy with this man?'

'Happy? Women only seek to avoid the worst.'

The reply seemed too vague and evasive.

'Tell me about this Zarwali!'

It was the command of a man. She gave a rather sardonic grin, but replied:

'He hasn't a good reputation. Crafty, unscrupulous. Immensely rich . . .'

'It's said that he plundered the Rif.'

'Princes have always plundered provinces, but that has never been a reason for anyone to refuse them the hand of his daughter or his sister.'

'And how does he treat women?'

She looked me up and down from head to toe, looking intently at the light down on my face.

'What do *you* know about women?'

'I know what I ought to know.'

She began to laugh, but my determined look interrupted her. She turned towards my mother, as if to ask her whether it was all right to continue a conversation about such matters with me. When my mother nodded, Sarah took a deep breath and laid her hand heavily on my shoulder.

'The Zarwali's women live shut up in their harem; young or old, free or slaves, white or black; there are no less than a hundred of them, each intriguing ceaselessly to spend a night with the master, or gain some privilege for their sons, a carpet for their bedroom, a jewel, perfume, an elixir. Those who expect the affection of a husband will never have it, those who look for affairs end up strangled, but those who simply want to live in peace, protected from all want, without having to make any effort, without cooking or chores, without a husband asking them for a water-cooler or a hot water bottle, such women might be happy. What category does your sister belong to?'

I was fuming with rage:

'Don't you think it's scandalous that a little girl of thirteen should be given away to an old merchant as a goodwill gesture to seal a business arrangement?'

'At my age, only naïveté still manages to scandalize me sometimes.'

I turned towards my mother aggressively:

'Do you also think that this man has the right to filch the money of the Muslims, to take a hundred women instead of four, to hold the Law of God in such contempt?'

She took refuge behind one of the verses of the Qur'an:

'Man is rebellious as soon as he sees himself well off.'

Without even saying goodbye to either of them, I got up and went out. Straight to Harun's house. I needed someone around me to show indignation, someone who would tell me that the world had not been created so that women and the joys of life should be handed over to the Zarwali and people like him. The frown which came over my friend's face at the mere mention of the name reconciled me with life again. What he had heard about Mariam's fiancé differed little from that which I had heard myself. The Ferret gave a solemn undertaking to make enquiries among the porters of the guild to find out more about him.

$$\star \quad \star \quad \star$$

To be friends at thirteen, with just the suggestion of a beard, and to declare war against injustice; from the distance of twenty years it looks like the picture of bliss. But at the time, what frustration, what suffering! It was true that I had two sound reasons for throwing myself into the fray. The first was the subtle appeal for help which Mariam had made to me on the way to Meknes, whose suppressed anguish I could now fully measure. The second was the Great Recitation, an occasion to inspire my adolescence with the pride of knowing the precepts of the Faith and the determination that they should not be ridiculed.

To understand the significance of the Great Recitation in the life of a believer, one must have lived at Fez, a city of learning which seems to have been constructed around the schools, the *madrasas*, just as some villages are built around a fountain or a saint's tomb. When, after several years of patient memorization, one reaches the point of knowing by heart each *sura* and each verse of the Qur'an, when one is pronounced ready for the Great Recitation by the schoolmaster, one immediately passes from childhood to man's estate, from anonymity to fame. It is the time when some start work, and others are admitted to the college, the fount of knowledge and authority.

The ceremony organized on this occasion gave the young Fassi the sense of having entered the world of the might. That was in any case what I felt on that day. Dressed in silk like the son of an amir, mounted on the back of a thoroughbred, followed by a slave carrying a large umbrella, I passed through the streets surrounded by the pupils in my class singing in unison. At the side of the road, several passers-by waved at me, and I waved at them in turn. From time to time a familiar face: Khali, my mother, two girl cousins, some neighbours, Hamza the barber and the boys from the hammam, and, a little to one side under a porch, Warda and Mariam.

My father was waiting for me in the reception room, where a banquet was to be held in my honour. He was carrying under his arm the new robe which I was to present to the schoolmaster as a token of gratitude. He gazed at me with disarming emotion.

I looked back at him. All at once, so many images of him clustered in my head: moving, when he told me the story of Granada; affectionate, when he caressed my neck; terrifying, when he repudiated my mother; hateful, when he sacrificed my sister; pitiable, slumped at the table in a tavern. How many truths did I want to shout down at him from the back of my horse! But I knew that my tongue would be tied once more when my feet touched the ground, when I would have to return the horse and silks to the person who lent them, when I would cease to be the short-lived hero of the Great Recitation.

The Year of the Stratagem
908 A.H.
7 July 1502 – 25 June 1503

'The Zarwali was never the poor shepherd that he claims. And he never discovered any treasure. The truth is that for many years he was a bandit, a highway robber and a murderer, and the fortune he started off with was simply the result of a quarter of a century of plunder. But there is worse to come.'

Harun had ferreted wonderfully week after week, but, in spite of my frequent entreaties he had refused to give me the slightest inkling until he had completed his investigation.

That day he had come to wait for me in front of the Qarawiyyin Mosque. I had a lecture from three until five in the morning given by a learned Syrian who was visiting Fez. Harun had given up his studies and was already wearing the short grubby habit of the porters; he was just about to begin his day's work.

'The worst thing,' pursued the Ferret, 'is that this character is insanely jealous, always convinced that his wives are trying to betray him, particularly the youngest and most beautiful ones. A denunciation, a slander, an insinuation on the part of one of her rivals is enough for the poor unfortunate to be strangled. The Zarwali's eunuchs then make the crime look like an accident, a drowning, a fatal fall, an acute tonsilitis. At least three women have died in circumstances which are suspicious to say the least.'

We paced up and down under the arcades of the mosque, which were bright with the light from countless oil lamps. Harun remained silent, awaiting my reaction. I was too overcome to make the slightest sound. Admittedly, I knew that the man whom my sister was going to marry was capable of many misdeeds, and it was for that reason that I sought to prevent the marriage. But it was now no longer a question of sparing an adolescent girl from a dull and dreary existence; it had become a matter of saving her from the grip of an assassin, a bloodthirsty monster. The Ferret was no less worried than I, but he was not the kind to waste time in lamentation.

'When is the ceremony to take place?'

'In two months at the most. The contract is signed, the preparations are already under way, my father is collecting the dowry, he has ordered the sheets for the bed and the ceremonial mattresses, and Mariam's dress is already made.'

'You must talk to your father, to him alone, for if anyone else becomes involved he will become obstinate and nothing will prevent this evil coming to pass.'

I followed his advice, except in one small detail: I asked my mother for confirmation from Sarah that Harun's information was correct. Gaudy Sarah indeed confirmed it in its entirety a week later, after having made me swear on the Qur'an that I would never mention her name in any connection with the matter. I needed this additional evidence to be able to confront my father without the least shred of doubt lurking in my mind.

In spite of this I spent the whole night turning in my head how I could best first bring up the subject, then withstand the attacks which it would provoke, and finally, if the Most High showed Himself understanding towards me, somehow carry the day. A thousand arguments and counter-arguments went backwards and forwards in my head, from the cleverest to the tritest, but none remained convincing until morning, so that I had to face my father the next day without the slightest idea, without even the beginnings of a case.

'I want to say something to you which may displease you.'

He was in the middle of eating, as was his custom every morning, his bowl of wheat gruel, sitting on a leather cushion in a corner of the yard.

'Have you done something stupid?'

'It has nothing to do with me.'

I took my courage in both hands:

'Ever since people have become aware that my sister is going to marry the Zarwali, I have been told the most disturbing things about him.'

The bowl at his lips, he inhaled loudly.

'By whom? There's no lack of jealousy in this town!'

I turned a deaf ear.

'It's said that several of his wives have been strangled!'

'If anyone says anything like that to you again, you can tell him that if those women were punished, they deserved it, and that in our family the girls have always been beyond reproach.'

'Are you sure that Mariam will be happy with –'

'Mind your own business.'

He wiped his mouth with the back of his sleeve and got up to go. I clung to him miserably:

'Don't go like that! Let me speak to you!'

'I have promised your sister to this man, and I am a man of my word. Furthermore, we have signed the contract, and the marriage will take place in a few weeks' time. Instead of staying here listening to these lies, make yourself useful! Go to the mattress-makers and see if they are getting on with the job.'

'I refuse to have any part in anything to do with this marr–'

A slap. So violent that my head went round and round for several long seconds. Behind me I heard the muffled cries of Warda and Mariam who had heard the entire conversation, hidden behind a door. My father held my jaw in his hand, gripping it tightly and shaking it feverishly.

'Never say "I refuse" to me again! Never speak to me again in this tone!'

I do not know what came over me that moment. I was as if another person was speaking through my mouth:

'I would never have spoken to you like that if I had not seen you seated in a tavern!'

Seconds later I regretted what I had said. To the end of my days I shall regret having pronounced those words. I would rather he had slapped me again, that he had beaten me all over, than see him collapsing on his cushion with a dazed air, his head in his hands. What good would it have done to try to apologize? I went out of his house, chasing myself away; I walked straight on for hours, not greeting anyone, not seeing anyone, my head empty and aching. That night I slept neither at my father's nor at my uncle's. I arrived at Harun's house in the evening, lay down on a mat, and did not get up again.

Until morning. It was Friday. Opening my eyes, I saw my friend staring at me. I had the impression he had been in the same place for hours.

'A little longer and you would have missed the midday prayer.'

He was scarcely exaggerating as the sun was high in the sky.

'When you arrived last night you looked as if you had just killed your father, as we say.'

I could manage only a twisted grimace. I told him what had happened.

'You were wrong to say that to him. But he is at fault as well, and more so than you, because he is handing over his daughter to a murderer. Are you going to let him commit a crime against your sister to make up for your own offence?'

That was precisely what I was about to do. But put like that it seemed despicable.

'I could go to Khali, he will find ways of convincing my father.'

'Open your eyes, it's not your father who has to be convinced.'

'But Mariam can't refuse to marry him! If she dared to make the slightest sound he would break her bones!'

'There's the fiancé.'

I didn't understand. I mustn't have woken up properly.

'The Zarwali?'

'Himself, and don't look at me like that. Get up and follow me.'

On the way, he explained his idea to me. We were not going to knock on the rich bandit's door, but on the door of an old man who had nothing whatever to do with my sister's marriage. But who was the only one who could still prevent it.

Astaghfirullah.

He opened the door to us himself. I had never seen him without his turban; he seemed almost naked, and twice as gaunt. He had not been out all day, because he had been suffering from a pain in his side since two Fridays past. He was seventy-nine years old, he told us, and he thought he had lived long enough, 'but God is the only judge'.

The arrival of two downcast-looking boys puzzled him.

'I hope that you have not come to bring me bad tidings.'

Harun began to speak, and I let him do so. It was his idea, and up to him to take it to its conclusion.

'Bad tidings, indeed, but not a death. A marriage against the Law of God, is that not bad tidings?'

'Who is getting married?'

'Hasan's sister, Mariam . . .'

'The Rumiyya's daughter?'

'Her mother doesn't count. Since the weigh-master is a Muslim, his daughter is also a Muslim.'

The shaikh looked at the Ferret approvingly.

'Who are you? I don't know you.'

'I am Harun, son of Abbas the porter.'

'Go on. Your words are pleasing to my ears.'

Thus encouraged, my friend explained the purpose of our mission. He did not linger over the fate of the Zarwali's wives, because he knew that this argument would not strike home with Astaghfirullah. On the other hand, he mentioned the fiancé's debauchery, his relations with his former wives, and then he dwelt at length on his past, on his massacres of travellers, 'particularly the first emigrants from Andalus', on his plunder of the Rif.

'What you have said would be enough to send a man to the fires of Hell until the end of time. But what proofs do you have? Which witnesses can you summon?'

Harun was all humility.

'My friend and I are too young, we have only just completed the Great Recitation, and our word does not carry much weight. We do not know a great deal about life, and it may be that we are indignant about matters which appear perfectly normal to other people. Now that we have said all that we know, and now that we have acted according to our consciences, it is up to you, our venerated shaikh, to see what must be done.'

When we were outside again I looked at the Ferret dubiously. He seemed quite certain about what he had done.

'I really believe what I said to him. We have done everything we could. Now we just have to wait.'

But his playful air indicated otherwise.

'I think you're gloating,' I said, 'but I don't at all understand why.'

'Perhaps Astaghfirullah doesn't know me, but I have known him for years. And I have every confidence in his atrocious character.'

The next day, the shaikh seemed to have been restored to health. His turban could be seen circulating feverishly in the suqs, fluttering under the porticos, before sweeping into a hammam. The following Friday, at the hour when the largest crowds were gathered, he spoke in his usual mosque, the one most attended by the emigrants from

Andalus. In the most candid manner he began to describe 'the exemplary life of a greatly respected man whom I shall not name', mentioning his banditry, his plunderings and his debauchery in such precise terms that eventually all the audience was whispering the Zarwali's name although he himself had never mentioned it once.

'Such are the men that the believers respect and admire in these degenerate times! Such are the men to whom you proudly open the doors of your houses! Such are the men to whom you sacrifice your daughters, as if to the deities of the time before Islam!'

Before the day was over the whole town was talking of nothing else. The words of the shaikh were reported to the Zarwali himself. Immediately, he sent for my father, insulted Granada and all the Andalusians, and, stuttering with rage, made it clear to him that there was no question of contract, marriage or silkworms, that he charged him immediately to pay back the dinars which he had advanced him, and that the weigh-master and all his family would soon have cause for bitter regret at what had come to pass. Utterly dismayed, Muhammad tried to protest his innocence, but he was thrown out unceremoniously by the Zarwali's bodyguards.

Often, when a marriage is called off at the last moment in an atmosphere of resentment, and particularly when the fiancé feels that he has been made a fool of, he circulates the rumour that his betrothed was not a virgin, or that she had loose morals, to make it impossible for her to find a husband. I would not have been surprised if the rejected bandit had done this, such was his humiliation.

But never, in my worst nightmares, could I have imagined the vengeance that the Zarwali was contemplating.

The Year of the Knotted Blade of Grass
909 A.H.
26 June 1503 – 13 June 1504

That year had begun slippery, peaceful and studious. On the first day of the year, which came in high summer, we splashed through the streets which had been drenched with water during the preceding nights because of the festival of Mihrajan. Each time I missed my footing, at each muddy pool, I thought of my father, who so detested this festival and the customs connected with it.

I had not seen him since our dispute, may God pardon me one day! But I constantly asked Warda and Mariam for news of him; their replies were rarely reassuring. Having ruined himself to give my sister a rich dowry, and finding himself simultaneously deeply in debt, frustrated in his dreams and deprived of the affection of his family, he sought oblivion in the taverns.

However, for the first weeks of the year he seemed to be recovering slowly from the breach with the Zarwali. He had eventually managed to rent an old residence at the top of a mountain six miles from Fez. It was a bit ramshackle, but had a marvellous view over the city, and had ample land attached to it on which he swore he would produce the best grapes and the best figs of the kingdom; I suspect that he also wanted to produce his own wine, even though the mountain was part of the domain of the Great Mosque. These projects were certainly less grandiose than producing silk; at least they did not put my father at the mercy of a bandit like the Zarwali.

There had been no sign of the latter for months. Had he forgotten his misfortune, would he let bygones be bygones, the man whom it

143

was said had the slightest insult graven in marble? I sometimes asked myself such questions, but these were passing worries which were swept aside by my deep absorption in my studies.

I spent my time in the lecture halls, in the Qarawiyyin Mosque, from midnight to half-past one, in accordance with the summer timetable, the rest of the day at the most famous college in Fez, the *madrasa* Bu Inania; I slept in the meantime, a little at dawn, a little in the afternoons; inactivity was unbearable, rest seemed superfluous. I was barely fifteen, with a body to shake up, a world to discover, and a passion for reading.

Each day our professors would make us study the commentaries on the Qur'an or the Tradition of the Prophet, and a discussion would commence. From the Scriptures we would often go on to medicine, geography, mathematics or poetry, sometimes even to philosophy or astrology, in spite of the ban on such subjects issued by the sovereign. We had the good fortune to have as teachers men who were learned in all fields of knowledge. To distinguish themselves from the common herd some wound their turbans around high pointed skull caps, like those which I saw worn by doctors during my stay in Rome. We students wore a simple cap.

In spite of their knowledge and their apparel, teachers were for the most part friendly men, patient in explanation, and mindful of the talents of everyone. Sometimes, they would invite us to their homes, to show us their libraries; one had five hundred volumes, another a thousand; yet another had more than three thousand, and they always encouraged us to pay careful attention to our calligraphy in order to be able to copy the most precious books, for it was thus, they said, that knowledge was spread.

When I had a moment between lectures, I would walk as far as the place where the porters stood. If I found Harun there, we would go and drink curdled milk or saunter around the Place of Marvels, where our curiosity was rarely disappointed. If the Ferret was away on an errand I would cross the flower market to go and see Mariam.

We had agreed that each time my father went to the country for the week she would put a knotted blade of grass in a crack in the outside wall. One day, towards the end of Safar, the second month of the year, I went past the house; the knotted blade was there. I pulled the bell rope. Warda shouted from within:

'My husband is away. I am alone with my daughter. I cannot open the door.'

'It's me, Hasan!'

She explained confusedly that some men had come a few minutes before; they had knocked on the door insistently, saying that she must let them in. She was afraid, and Mariam, who looked pale and weak, seemed afraid too.

'What's going on here? You both look as if you've been crying.'

Their tears began again, but Warda quickly pulled herself together:

'For the last three days it has been like hell. We dare not go out into the street. The neighbours come all the time to ask if it's true that . . .'

Her voice choked, and Mariam continued vacantly:

'They are asking if I am suffering from the illness.'

When people say 'the illness' at Fez they mean leprosy; when they talk of 'the quarter' without further designation they mean the leper quarter.

I still had not taken in what they had just told me when I heard a drumming on the door.

'The police, in the sultan's name! You are not alone now! A man has just gone inside. He can speak to us.'

I opened the door. There were at least ten people outside, an officer, four women veiled in white, the rest soldiers.

'Does Mariam, the daughter of Muhammad al-Wazzan the Granadan live here?'

The officer unfolded a piece of paper.

'This is an order from the shaikh of the lepers. We are to bring the aforesaid Mariam to the quarter.'

A single idea turned over in my head: 'If this could be an ordinary nightmare!' I heard myself saying:

'But this is slander! She has never had a single mark on her body! She is as pure as one of the verses revealed in the Qur'an!'

'We shall see about that. These four women have been appointed to examine her on the spot.'

They went into one of the rooms with her. Warda tried to follow them but someone stopped her. I stayed outside, my mind in a fog, but trying at the same time to make the officer listen to reason. He answered me calmly, appearing to see my point of view, but ended by replying to each of my outbursts that he was an official, that he had orders to carry out, and that I must speak to the shaikh of the lepers.

After ten minutes, the women came out of the room. Two of them were holding Mariam under her arms and dragging her along. Her eyes were open but her body was limp. No sound came from her throat; she seemed unable to take in what was happening to her. One of the women whispered something in the officer's ear. He made a sign to one of his men, who covered Mariam with a coarse earth-coloured cloth.

'Your sister is ill. We must take her with us.'

I tried to intervene; they thrust me roughly aside. And the sinister procession set off. At the end of the cul-de-sac a few idlers were gathered. I cried out, threatened, gesticulated. But Warda came after me, pleading:

'Come back, by Heaven, you mustn't bring out the whole neighbourhood. Your sister can never be married.'

I went back towards the house, slammed the door, and began to hammer the walls with my fists, oblivious to the pain. Warda came up to me. She was weeping, but her mind was clear.

'Wait until they have gone and then go and talk to your uncle. He has good relations with the palace. He can get her back.'

She held me by the sleeve and pulled me back.

'Calm yourself, your hands are raw.'

My arms fell heavily on Warda's shoulders; I embraced her fiercely, without unclenching my fists, as if I was still hammering at the wall. She subsided against me. Her tears ran down my neck; her hair covered my eyes; I could only inhale her breath, burning, humid and perfumed. I was not thinking of her; she was not thinking of me. Our bodies did not exist for us. But they suddenly came into existence for themselves, kindled by anger. I had never before felt conscious of myself as a man, nor been conscious of her as a woman. She was thirty-two, old enough to be a grandmother, but her face had no lines, and her hair was jet black. I no longer dared to move, for fear I might give myself away, or to speak, for fear of sending her away, nor even to open my eyes, for fear of having to recognize that I was entwined with the only woman rigorously forbidden to me, my father's wife.

Where did her mind wander during those moments? Did she feel herself drifting like me towards the intermingling of pleasure? I don't think so. Was she just numb, body and soul all swollen up? Did she simply need to clutch hold of the only human being who would share her anguish? I shall never know, for we never spoke of it; never did our words or actions ever recall that a moment had existed in which we were man and woman, bound together by the pitiless fingers of Destiny.

It was incumbent upon her to withdraw. She did so imperceptibly, with these words of tender parting:

'Go, Hasan my son, God will come to our aid. You are the best brother that Mariam could have!'

I ran, counting my steps to myself so that my mind would not dwell on anything else. As far as Khali's house.

* * *

My uncle listened to me without showing any signs of emotion, but I could see that he was moved, more than I had expected, given the complete absence of relations between himself and my sister. When I finished my story, he explained:

'The shaikh of the lepers is a power in the land. He alone is entitled to remove from Fez those who have been infected, and he alone has authority over the denizens of the quarter. Few qadis dare oppose his decisions, and the sultan himself only rarely takes it upon himself to interfere in his gruesome domain. Furthermore, he is extremely rich, for many among the believers bequeath their properties for the benefit of the quarter, either because the illness has afflicted their family, or because they take pity at the sight of these unfortunates. And the shaikh administers all the revenues. He uses part of it to provide food, lodging and treatment for the sufferers, but there are substantial sums left over which he uses in all sorts of shady ways to increase his personal wealth. It is highly likely that he has some business association with the Zarwali, and that he has agreed to help him to take vengeance upon us.'

I had distinctly heard my uncle say 'us'! My surprise did not elude him.

'You have known for a long time what I think of your father's obsession with this Rumiyya. He lost his head one day, because she very nearly left him, because he thought his honour was at stake, because he wanted, in his way, to take revenge on the Castilians. Since then, he has never recovered his good judgement. But what has just happened concerns neither Muhammad nor Warda, nor even poor Mariam; the whole Granadan community of Fez is being held up to ridicule by the Zarwali. We have to fight, even for the daughter of the Rumiyya. A community begins to fall apart the moment it agrees to abandon the weakest of its members.'

His arguments mattered little; his attitude gave me new hope.

'Do you think we shall be able to save my sister?'

'Ask the Most High to bring you hope and patience! We have to fight the most powerful and devilish individuals. You know that the Zarwali is a friend of the sultan?'

'But if Mariam has to stay in the quarter for long, she really will become a leper.'

'You must go and see her, tell her that she must not mix with the others, and bring her turtle flesh to eat, which helps to fight the illness. Above all, she should always keep her face covered with a veil impregnated with vinegar.'

I carried these counsels to Warda. She obtained the appropriate items and when my father returned to town a few days later she went with him to the edge of the quarter. A watchman called Mariam, who came to see them. She looked disoriented, overwhelmed, haggard, with bloodshot eyes in her pallid face. A stream separated her from her parents, but they could speak to her, promise her a speedy deliverance and give her their advice. They gave the things they wanted taken to her to the watchman, slipping a few dirhams into his hand.

I was waiting for them in front of the door of the house when they returned. My father made as if not to see me. I knelt on the ground and took his hand, pressing it to my lips. After several long seconds he took it away, passed it over my face, and then patted my neck. I got up and threw myself into his arms.

'Make us something to eat,' he said to Warda in a broken voice. 'We need to discuss the matter.'

She hastened to do so.

Neither he nor I said very much. At that point, the important thing was to be together, man to man for the first time, seated on the same mat, dipping our hands in the same fashion into the same dish of couscous. Mariam's engagement had torn us apart; her ordeal hastened our reconciliation. It would also reunite Muhammad with my mother's family.

That evening, Khali came to my father's house, whose threshold he had not crossed since our arrival at Fez ten years earlier. Warda treated him as an honoured guest, offered him orgeat syrup and placed an enormous basket full of grapes, apricots, pears and plums in front of him. In return, he gave her kindly smiles and words of comfort. Then she withdrew behind a door to let us discuss the matter together.

★　★　★

The rest of the year was entirely taken up with endless undertakings and interminable secret meetings. Sometimes, people outside the family would join us, contributing their advice, and sharing our disappointments. They were mostly Granadans, but there were also two of my friends. One was Harun, of course, who was soon going to make my problem his own, to the point of taking it away from me altogether. The other was called Ahmad. At the college he was called the Lame One. Calling him to mind, I cannot prevent my pen from ceasing its tortuous scratchings, and to stop for a moment thoughtful and perplexed. As far away as Tunis, Cairo, Mecca, even Naples, I have heard men speak of the Lame One, and I always wonder whether this old friend of mine will leave any traces on the pages of history, or whether he will pass across the memory of men as a bold swimmer crosses the Nile, without affecting its flow or its floods. However my duty as chronicler is to forget my resentment and to recount, as faithfully as I can, what I have known of Ahmad since the day that year when he came into the classroom for the first time, greeted by the laughter and sarcastic remarks of the other students. The young Fassis are merciless towards outsiders, especially when they seem to have come straight from the province where they were born, and particularly if they have some physical infirmity.

The Lame One had let his eyes wander round the room, as if taking note of every smile, every grin, and then came to sit down next to me, whether because it was the nearest place for him to sit or because he had seen that I was looking at him differently. He shook me vigorously by the hand, but his words were not a simple greeting:

'Like me, you are a foreigner in this accursed city.'

His tone was not questioning, his voice not low. I looked round with embarrassment. He started again:

'Don't be afraid of the Fassis, they are too crammed with knowledge to retain a drop of courage.'

149

He was almost shouting. I felt that I was becoming involved unwillingly in a dispute that had nothing to do with me. I tried to extricate myself, saying light-heartedly:

'How can you say that, if you are coming to seek knowledge in one of the *madrasas* of Fez?'

He gave me a condescending smile.

'I do not seek knowledge, because it weighs the hands down more certainly than a chain. Have you ever seen a doctor of the Law command an army, or found a kingdom?'

While he was talking, the professor came into the room, his gait dignified, his silhouette imposing. As a mark of respect, the whole class stood up.

'How do you expect a man to fight with that thing wobbling on his head?'

I was already regretting that Ahmad had come and sat next to me. I looked at him in horror.

'Lower your voice, I beg you, the master will hear.'

He gave me a fatherly slap on the back.

'Don't be so timid! When you were a child, didn't you speak out the truth that the oldest ones kept secret? Well, you were right then. You must find the time of innocence in yourself again, because that was also the time of courage.'

As if to illustrate what he had just said, he got up, limped towards the professor's raised chair and addressed him without respect, in a manner which silenced the slightest noise in the room:

'My name is Ahmad, son of Sharif Sa'di, descendant of the House of the Prophet, on whom be prayers and peace! If you see me limp, it is because I was wounded last year fighting the Portuguese when they invaded the territories of the Sous.'

I don't know if he was more closely related to the Messenger of God than I am; as far as his deformity was concerned, he had been lame since birth, as I was to learn later from one of his friends. Two lies, then, but they intimidated everyone present, including the professor.

Ahmad went back to his seat, his head high. From his first day at the college, he became the most respected and admired of all the students. He always went about surrounded by a host of devoted fellow students, who laughed at his jokes, trembled at his rages, and shared all his enmities.

And these were very tenacious. One day, one of our teachers, a

Fassi from an old family, had dared to cast doubt on the ancestry to which the Lame One laid claim. This opinion could not be disregarded lightly, since this professor was the most famous in the college, and had recently obtained the honour of giving the weekly sermon in the Great Mosque. At the time, Ahmad did not reply, and simply smiled enigmatically at the students' questioning looks. The following Friday, the whole class took itself off to hear the preacher. He had hardly uttered the first words when the Lame One was seized with an interminable fit of coughing. Gradually, other coughers took over, and after a minute or so thousands of throats were being noisily cleared in unison, a strange infection which lasted to the end of the sermon, to the extent that the faithful went back to their homes without having understood so much as a word. Henceforth the professor took care not to speak of Ahmad, nor of his noble but doubtful ancestry.

I myself never followed in the Lame One's wake, and he certainly respected me for it. We only saw each other alone, sometimes at my house and sometimes at his quarters in the *madrasa* itself, where there were rooms reserved for students whose families did not live in Fez; his people lived on the edges of the kingdom of Marrakesh.

I must say that even when we were alone together, some of his attitudes repelled me, bothered me, even sometimes frightened me. But he could also appear generous and faithful, and that was how he seemed to me that year, attentive in my periods of dejection, always finding the right tone to get me back on my feet again.

I greatly needed his company, and that of Harun, even if they both seemed unable to save Mariam. Only my uncle seemed in a position to take the necessary steps. He met lawyers, amirs of the army, the dignitaries of the kingdom; some were reassuring, others embarrassed, still others promised a solution before the next feast. We only let go of one hopeful possibility to cling on to another, equally in vain.

Until, that is, Khali succeeded, after a thousand intercessions, in approaching the sovereign's eldest son, Prince Muhammad, called the Portuguese, because he had been taken prisoner at the age of seven in the town of Arzila and led away to captivity in Portugal for many years. He was now forty, the same age as my uncle, and they stayed a long time together, discussing poetry and the misfortunes of Andalus. And when, after two hours, Khali brought up the problem of Mariam, the prince seemed very indignant and promised to bring the matter to the ears of his father.

He had no time to do so, for, by a strange coincidence, the sultan died the very next day after my uncle's visit to the palace.

To say that my relations wept for long over the old monarch would be a pure lie, not only because the Zarwali was his friend, but also because the connections just established between his son and Khali seemed to augur well for us.

The Year of the Caravan
910 A.H.
14 June 1504 – 3 June 1505

That year was the occasion of my first long journey, which was to take me across the Atlas, Sijilmassa and Numidia, towards the Saharan expanse, and then towards Timbuktu, mysterious city of the land of the Blacks.

Khali had been commanded by the new Sultan of Fez to take a message to the powerful sovereign of the Soudan, Askia Muhammad Touré, announcing his accession and promising to establish the most cordial relations between their two kingdoms. As he had promised me five years earlier, at the time of his journey to the Orient, my uncle invited me to come with him; I had discussed it with my father, who, out of consideration for my beard, which was silky but already thick, no longer thought of standing in my way.

The caravan had set off in the first cool days of autumn, two hundred animals strong, carrying men, provisions and presents. We had camel guards to protect us for the whole length of the journey, as well as cavalrymen who would return when we reached the Sahara. There were also camel drivers and experienced guides, as well as enough servants to make the embassy appear important in the eyes of our hosts. To the official procession were also attached, with my uncle's permission, several merchants with their wares, intending to take advantage both of the royal protection for the duration of the journey and of the favourable treatment which we would surely receive at Timbuktu.

The preparations had been too meticulous, too long drawn out for my liking. During the last days before departure, I could neither sleep nor read. My breathing was difficult and heavy. I needed to leave at once, to hold on tightly high up on the camel's hump, to be engulfed in the vast wastes where men, animals, water, sand and gold all have the same colour, the same worth, the same irreplaceable futility.

I discovered very soon that one could also become immersed in the caravan. When the wayfarers know that, for weeks and months, they must proceed in the same direction, confront the same perils, live, eat, pray, enjoy themselves, grieve, and sometimes die, together, they cease to be strangers to each other; no vice remains hidden, no artifice can last. Seen from afar, a caravan looks like a procession; from close to, it is a village, with its stories, jokes, nicknames, intrigues, conflicts, reconciliations, nights of singing and poetry, a village for which all lands are far away, even the land one comes from, or the land one is crossing. I badly needed such distance to forget the crushing miseries of Fez, the relentlessness of the Zarwali, the faceless cruelty of the shaikh of the lepers.

★   ★   ★

On the same day that we left, we passed through the town of Sefrou, at the foot of the Atlas mountains, fifteen miles from Fez. The inhabitants were rich, but they were shabbily dressed, their clothes all stained with oil, because a prince of the royal house had built himself a residence there and overburdened with taxes anyone who gave the slightest sign of prosperity. Passing down the main street, my uncle brought his horse up level with me to whisper in my ear:

'If anyone tells you that avarice is the daughter of necessity, tell him that he is mistaken. It is taxation which has begotten avarice!'

Not far from Sefrou, the caravan took the pass through which the road to Numidia runs. Two days later we were in the middle of a forest, near the ruins of an ancient city called 'Ain al-Asnam, the Spring of the Idols. There was a temple there where men and women used to meet in the evening at a certain time of the year. Having finished the ritual sacrifices, they would put out the lights, and each man would take his pleasure with the woman whom providence had placed by his side. They passed the night together in this fashion, and in the morning they were reminded that for a year none of the women present was allowed to go to her husband. The children who were born during that period were brought up by the priests of the temple. The temple had been destroyed, and the whole city as well, after the Muslim conquest; but the name had survived as sole witness of the age of ignorance.

Two days later we passed near a mountain village which was strewn about with ancient remains. It is called 'The Hundred Wells', because there are wells in the vicinity of such depth that they are thought to be caves. It is said that one of them had several levels, with walled rooms on the inside, some large, others small, but all fitted out. That is why treasure seekers come specially from Fez to make the descent, with the help of ropes and lanterns. Some never come to the surface again.

A week after leaving Fez we went through a place called Umm Junaiba, where a curious custom survives: there is a water course, along which the caravans walk, and it is said that anyone who passes along there must jump and dance as he walks, otherwise he will be struck with quartan ague. Our whole company set to it cheerfully, even myself, even the guards, even the great merchants, some from a spirit of fun, others out of superstition, still others to avoid the insect bites, all except my uncle who considered that his dignity as ambassador prevented him from taking part in such pranks. He was to regret it bitterly.

We were already in the high mountains over which, even in autumn, an unpredictable icy wind blows from the north. In such high places, where the climate is so harsh, I did not expect to find people so well dressed and certainly not so well educated. In particular, in one of the coldest mountain ranges, there is a tribe called Mestasa whose principal occupation was to copy books, in the most beautiful handwriting, and sell them in the Maghrib and abroad. In one village alone, an old Genoese merchant living in Fez, Master Thomasso de Marino, who had come along with the caravan, and with whom I often conversed, bought a hundred of these volumes, each with marvellous calligraphy and bound in leather. He explained to me that the *ulama* and the notables in the land of the Blacks bought many such books, and that it was a very lucrative trade.

As we had stopped for the night in this area, I accompanied the Genoese to a dinner given by his supplier. The house was well built, with marble and majolica, with fine woollen hangings on the walls, the floor covered with carpets, also made of wool, but in pleasing colours. All the guests seemed extremely prosperous, and I could not forbear to ask my host, choosing my words with extreme care, a question which was burning on my lips: how did it come to pass that the people of this cold and mountainous country were so well endowed with possessions and knowledge?

The master of the house burst out laughing:

'In short you want to know why the people of these mountains are not all boors, beggars or tramps?'

I would not have put it like that, but that was really what interested me.

'Know, my young visitor, that the greatest gift that the Most High can bestow upon a man is to cause him to be born in a high mountain across which the caravans pass. The highway brings knowledge and riches, the mountain provides protection and liberty. You, the people of the cities, have all the gold and all the books within reach, but you have princes, before whom you bow your heads . . .'

He suddenly became circumspect:

'May I talk to you like an old uncle talking to his nephew, like an old shaikh to a disciple, without deviating in any way from the teachings of life? Will you promise me not to take offence?'

My broad smile encouraged him to continue.

'If you live in a city, you agree to set aside all dignity, all self-respect in exchange for the protection of a sultan, who makes you pay dearly for it even when he is no longer capable of assuring it. When you live far from the cities, but in the plains or on the hills, you escape the sultan, his soldiers and his tax-collectors; however, you are at the mercy of marauding nomadic tribes, Arabs, sometimes even Berbers, who overrun the country, and you can never even build a wall without fearing that it will soon be pulled down. If you live in an inaccessible place far off the highway, you are of course safe from subjugation and attack, but, if you have no exchanges with other regions, you end up by living like an animal, ignorant, impoverished and frightened.'

He offered me a goblet of wine, which I refused politely. He poured one for himself, and swallowed a mouthful before continuing:

'We alone are privileged: we see passing through our villages the people of Fez, of Numidia, of the land of the Blacks, merchants, notables, students or *ulama*; they each bring us a piece of gold, or a garment, a book to read or copy, or perhaps only a story, an anecdote, a word; thus, with the passing of the caravans we accumulate riches and knowledge, in the shelter of these inaccessible mountains which we share with the eagles, the crows and the lions, our companions in dignity.'

I recounted these words to my uncle, who sighed without saying anything and then raised his eyes to heaven. I do not know whether this was to put himself in the hands of the Creator or to observe the flight of a bird of prey.

Our next stage was through the mountains of Ziz, so called because a river of that name has its source within them. The inhabitants of that region belong to a formidable Berber tribe, the Zanaga. They are sturdy men, wearing woollen tunics next to the skin, and wrapping rags around their legs which serve as shoes. Summer and winter, they go about bare-headed. I can never describe these people without remembering something extraordinary about them, which seems almost miraculous: a vast number of snakes go round among the houses, as mild and friendly as cats or little dogs. When anyone begins to eat, the snakes gather around him to eat up the crumbs of bread and other food which is left for them.

During the third week of our journey we hurtled down the Ziz mountains, through countless palm-gardens full of delicious tender fruit, towards the plain which leads to Sijilmassa. Or rather, I should say, to where this town so admired by previous generations of travellers was located. It was said that it had been founded by Alexander the Great himself, that its main street used to run the length of half a day's march, that each of its houses was surrounded by a garden and an orchard, and that it used to contain prestigious mosques and *madrasas* of renown.

Of its walls, once so high, only a few sections remain, half-ruined, and covered with grass and moss. Of its population, there remain only various hostile clans, each living with its chief in a fortified village near to the ruins of the former Sijilmassa. Their main concern is to make life difficult for the clan living in the neighbouring village. They seem merciless towards each other, going so far as to destroy the water channels, cutting the palm trees down to the ground, encouraging the nomadic tribes to lay waste the lands and houses of their enemies, so that it seems to me that they deserve their fate.

We had planned to stay three days on the territory of Sijilmassa, to rest men and beasts, to buy some provisions and repair some of our tackle; but it was written that we should stay there several months, since, the very day after our arrival, my uncle fell ill. He sometimes shivered during the day, although the heat was stifling, and sometimes sweated from all his pores during the night, when it was as cold as it had been in the high mountains. A Jewish merchant from the caravan, who was well versed in the science of medicine, diagnosed a quartan ague, which seemed a punishment for Khali's refusal to make obeisance to the custom of dancing at Umm Junaiba. God alone is master of reward and chastisement!

★   ★   ★

I was constantly at my uncle's bedside, attentive to his slightest movement, the smallest sign of pain on his face, watching over him sometimes for hours at a time, while he slept restlessly. I felt that he had suddenly aged, become weak and helpless, while two days earlier he had been able to hold an audience spellbound with his tales of the Rum, of lions or of serpents. Thanks to his gifts as a poet and orator, and also to his vast knowledge, he had impressed Muhammad the Portuguese, who had summoned him to his presence every week since his accession. There was talk that he would be appointed a counsellor, or secretary, or provincial governor.

I remember, one day when he came back from the palace, I asked Khali whether he had spoken of Mariam again. He replied in a rather embarrassed voice:

'I am gradually gaining the sovereign's confidence, and I shall soon be able to obtain your sister's release without the slightest difficulty. For the time being I must act as delicately as possible; it would be a mistake to ask him anything at all.'

Then he added with a laugh by way of apology:

'That is how you will have to behave when you go into politics!'

A little after Khali's appointment as ambassador I had returned to the attack. He had then spoken to the sovereign, who had promised him that when he returned from Timbuktu the young girl would be at home once more. My uncle had thanked him warmly and had given me the news. I had then decided to go to the quarter for the first time to tell Mariam about the monarch's promise and about my journey.

I had not seen her for a year, out of excess of affection, but also out of cowardice. She did not utter a single word of reproach. She smiled as if she had just left my side, asked me about my studies, and seemed so serene that I felt intimidated, contrite, off balance. Perhaps I would have preferred to see her in tears and to have to comfort her, even though we were separated by a stream. I told her triumphantly about the sultan's promise; she reacted just enough not to upset me. I spoke about my departure, and she gave the appearance of enthusiasm, without me knowing whether she did so out of sudden playfulness or out of mockery. The water course, which a strong man could have crossed in two strides, seemed deeper than a ravine, wider than an arm of the sea. Mariam was so far away, so inaccessible, her voice came to me as if in a nightmare. Suddenly, an old leper woman whom I had not seen approaching put a hand with no fingers on my sister's shoulder. I shouted and gathered up some stones to throw at her, telling her to go away. Mariam stood between us, protecting the leper with her body.

'Put those stones down, Hasan, you will hurt my friend!'

I complied, feeling myself about to faint. I made a gesture of farewell, and turned to leave, with death in my soul. My sister called my name again. I looked at her. She came up to the edge of the water. For the first time since my coming the tears ran down her face.

'You will get me out of here, won't you?'

Her voice was imploring, but somehow reassuring. With a gesture which I was the first to be surprised at I put my hand out in front of me as if I was swearing on the Book, and delivered this oath in a slow loud voice:

'I swear that I shall not marry before I have got you out of this accursed quarter.'

A smile lit up her whole face. I turned round and ran away as fast as my legs would carry me, because it was this image of her that I wanted to keep before me for the duration of my journey. The same day, I went to see my father and Warda to give them news of their daughter. Before knocking at the door I remained motionless for a moment. There in a crack in the wall, dry and faded, lay the knotted blade of grass which Mariam had tied together the day of her capture. I took it in my fingers and laid it stealthily on my lips. Then I put it back in its place.

★   ★   ★

I was thinking once more of this blade of grass when Khali opened his eyes. I asked if he felt better; he nodded, but went back to sleep immediately. He was to remain in this condition, hovering between life and death, unable to move, until the beginning of the hot season, when it was impossible to cross the Sahara. So we had to wait several months in the vicinity of Sijilmassa before continuing our journey.

The Year of Timbuktu
911 A.H.
4 June 1505 – 23 May 1506

My uncle seemed fully recovered when we took to the road again that year at the beginning of the cool season, towards Tabalbala, which lies in the middle of the desert of Numidia, three hundred miles from the Atlas, two hundred miles south of Sijilmassa, in a country where water is scarce and meat too, save for that of the antelope and the ostrich, and where only the shade of a palm tree occasionally alleviates the tyranny of the sun.

We had reckoned that this stage would take nine days, and from the first evening Khali began to speak to me about Granada, somewhat in the way my father had done a few years earlier. Perhaps the illness of the one and the despondency of the other had had the same effect, of making them wish to pass on their witness and their wisdom to a younger and somehow less endangered memory, may the Most High preserve my pages from fire and from oblivion! From one night to another I awaited the continuation of his story, whose only interruptions were the howlings of nearby jackals.

On the third day, however, two soldiers came to meet us. They brought a message from a lord whose lands lay to the west of our route. He had heard that the ambassador of the King of Fez was passing this way, and he insisted on meeting him. Khali made enquiries of one of the guides, who told him that the detour would delay us by at least two weeks. He made his excuses to the soldiers, saying that an envoy of the sovereign on a mission could not make visits to noblemen whose lands lay out of his way, all the more since his illness had already delayed him considerably. However, to show in what esteem he held this lord – of whom as he told me later, he had never heard spoken before – he would send his nephew to kiss his hand.

Hence I suddenly found myself entrusted with an embassy when I had not yet reached my seventeenth year. My uncle ordered two horsemen to accompany me, and provided me with several gifts which I was to offer in his name to this friendly nobleman: a pair of stirrups decorated in the Moorish fashion, a magnificent pair of spurs, a pair of silk cords braided with golden thread, one violet, the other azure, a newly-bound book containing the lives of the holy men of Africa and a panegyric poem. The journey lasted four days, and I took advantage of it to write some verses myself in honour of my host.

Having reached the town, which was I believe called Ouarzazate, I was told that the lord was hunting lions in the neighbouring mountains, and that he had given instructions that I should join him there. I kissed his hand and conveyed the greetings of my uncle. He appointed quarters where I could rest until his return. He came back before nightfall and summoned me to his palace. I presented myself, kissed his hand again, and then offered him the presents one by one, which pleased him exceedingly. Then I gave him Khali's poem, which he had read by a secretary who translated it for him word for word, since he knew little Arabic.

Then it was time for the meal, which I was awaiting impatiently, since my stomach had been empty since morning except for a few dates. We were brought roast and boiled mutton, coated with extremely fine flaky pastry, something like Italian lasagne, but firmer. Then we had couscous, *ftat*, another mixture of meat and pastry, and several other dishes which I can no longer remember. When we were all amply satisfied I stood up and declaimed my own poem. The lord had several phrases translated, but for the rest of the time he merely watched me, with a tender and protective eye. When I had finished, he retired to bed, because the hunt had fatigued him, but very early the next morning he asked me to breakfast with him, gave me through his secretary a hundred pieces of gold to take to my uncle, and two slaves to attend on him during the journey. He commanded me to tell him that these presents were simply an acknowledgement of his poem, and not an exchange for the gifts which he had presented to him. He also gave me ten pieces of gold for each of the horsemen who accompanied me.

For me, he was keeping a surprise. He began by giving me fifty pieces of gold, but, when I left, the secretary indicated that I should follow him. We went along a corridor until we reached a low door which led us into a small courtyard. In the middle was a horse, fine-looking but small, on which was sitting a beautiful brown rider, her face uncovered.

'This young slave is the lord's gift for your poem. She is fourteen, she speaks Arabic well. We call her Hiba.'

He took the bridle and put it in my hand. I took it, my eyes looking up, incredulous. My gift smiled.

Overjoyed to have met so courteous and generous a lord, I returned immediately to Tabalbala, where the caravan awaited me. I told my uncle that I had fulfilled my mission perfectly, and I reported each word and each gesture in detail. I gave him the presents which were intended for him, and the remarks that had accompanied them, and I ended by telling him about my delicious surprise. At this point in my story his face clouded over.

'Did they really tell you that this slave girl spoke Arabic?'

'Yes, and I was able to check this on the way back.'

'I don't doubt it. But if you were older and wiser you might have heard something else behind the secretary's words. To offer you this slavegirl was perhaps a way of honouring you, but it may just as well have been a way of insulting you, of showing you the abasement of those who speak your language.'

'Should I have refused?'

My uncle laughed good-naturedly.

'I can see that you are going to faint at the mere suggestion that you should have left that girl in the courtyard where you found her.'

'Then I can keep her?'

My tone was like that of a child hanging on to a toy. Khali shrugged his shoulders and signalled to the camel-drivers to make ready to depart. As I was leaving he called me back:

'Have you already touched this girl?'

'No,' I replied, my eyes lowered. 'On the way back we slept in the open air, and the guards were close by me.'

There was some malice in his grin.

'You are not to touch her now either, since before we will sleep under a roof again the month of Ramadan will have begun. As a traveller, you are not required to fast, but you must show your submission to your Creator in other ways. You must cover your slavegirl from head to toe, and forbid her to perfume herself, to use make up, to do her hair, or even to wash.'

I did not protest, for I knew immediately that religious zeal was not the only reason for this counsel. Very often in the caravans there were disputes, attacks of madness and even crimes committed because of the presence of a beautiful servant girl, and my uncle wanted at all costs to avoid any temptation or provocation.

The next part of our journey took us towards the oases of Touat and Ghurara, the points of arrival and departure of the Saharan caravans. It was there that the merchants and other travellers waited to leave together.

Many Jewish traders were settled in these oases, but they had suffered a strange persecution. The very year of the Fall of Granada, which was also the year when the Spanish Jews were expelled, a preacher from Tlemcen came to Fez, and encouraged the population to massacre the Jews of the city. When he came to hear of this, the sovereign ordered this trouble-maker to be expelled; he sought refuge in the oases of Touat and Ghurara, and succeeded in stirring up the inhabitants there against the Jews. They were almost all massacred and their goods looted.

In this region, there are many cultivated fields, but they are dry, since they can only be irrigated by water from wells. The soil is also very poor, and the inhabitants have an unusual way of improving it. When visitors come, they invite them to stay without payment, but they take the manure of their horses, and they explain to the men that they will offend them if they relieve themselves anywhere but in their houses. In consequence, travellers are obliged to hold their noses when they pass anywhere near a cultivated field.

These oases are the last places where it is possible to stock up adequately before crossing the Sahara. The waterholes become further and further apart, and it takes over two weeks to reach the next inhabited place. Furthermore, at the place which is called Taghaza, there is nothing except some mines where salt is extracted. The salt is kept until a caravan comes to buy it in order to sell it at Timbuktu, where it is in constant demand. A camel can carry up to four bars of salt. The miners of Taghaza are dependent on the supplies which they receive from Timbuktu, which is twenty days' journey away, or from other towns equally far off. It sometimes happens that a caravan, arriving late for some reason, finds that some of these men have starved to death in their huts.

But it is beyond that place that the desert becomes a real inferno. There one sees only the whitened bones of men and camels that have died of thirst, and the only living creatures visible in any number are snakes.

In the most arid part of the desert are two tombs, topped by a stone on which there is an inscription. It says that two men are buried there. One was a rich merchant, tortured by thirst, who bought from the other, a caravaneer, a cup of water for ten thousand pieces of gold. But after having taken a few steps, the seller and the purchaser collapsed together, having died of thirst. God alone dispenses life and benefits!

★ ★ ★

Even if I were more eloquent, even if my pen were more obedient, I would be incapable of describing the sensation when, after weeks of exhausting journeying, one's eyes lashed by sandstorms, one's mouth swollen with tepid salty water, one's body burning, filthy, racked with a thousand aches, one finally sees the walls of Timbuktu. Indeed, after the desert, all cities are beautiful, all oases seem like the Garden of Eden. But nowhere else did life appear so agreeable to me as in Timbuktu.

We arrived there at sunset, welcomed by a troop of soldiers despatched by the ruler of the city. As it was too late for us to be received at the palace, we were escorted to the quarters which had been reserved for us, each according to his rank. My uncle was accommodated in a house near the mosque; I was given the use of a huge room there overlooking a lively square which gradually began to empty. That evening, after a bath and a light supper, I called Hiba, with Khali's permission. It must have been ten o'clock at night. Sounds of tumult reached us from the street; a group of young people had gathered, playing music, singing and dancing on the square. I would soon get used to these strollers, who returned throughout my stay there. That night, I was so unaccustomed to the spectacle that I stood watching at the window without moving. Perhaps I was also filled with some trepidation at finding myself for the first time in a room with a woman who belonged to me.

She had made good the ravages of the road, and was as sweet, smiling and unveiled as she had been on the day she had been given to me. She came up to the window and began to watch the dancers like me, her shoulder pressing imperceptibly against my own. The night was cool, even chilly, but my face was burning.

'Do you want me to dance like them?'

Without waiting for me to reply, she began to dance with her whole body, first slowly, then faster and faster, but without losing her gracefulness; her hands, her hair, her scarves flew around the room, carried by the breeze she created, her hips swaying to the rhythm of the negro music, her bare feet tracing arabesques on the floor. I drew away from the window to let the moonlight flood into the room.

It was only towards one o'clock in the morning, perhaps even later, that the street became silent once more. My dancer lay stretched out on the ground, exhausted and breathless. I pulled the curtain across the window, trying to find courage in the darkness.

Hiba. Even if the land of Africa had only offered me this gift, it would have earned my nostalgia for ever.

In the morning, as she lay asleep, my beloved had the same smile that I had imagined all night, and the same odour of ambergris. Bending over her smooth serene forehead, I covered her with silent tender promises. Noises came once more from the window, the gossiping of the market women, the crunching of straw, the ringing of copper, the cries of animals, and smells wafting on a light fresh wind which gently ruffled the curtain. I treasured everything, blessed everything, Heaven, the desert, the journey, Timbuktu, the lord of Ouarzazate, and even that painful sensation which was shooting discreetly through my body, the fruit of my first journey, eager and clumsy, into the unknown.

She opened her eyes, then closed them immediately, as if fearing to interrupt my reverie. I murmured:

'We shall never part!'

She smiled doubtfully. I put my lips to hers, my hand slipping along her skin again to rekindle the memories of the night. But someone was already knocking on the door. I replied without opening it. It was a servant sent by my uncle to remind me that we were expected at the palace. I was to be present, in ceremonial dress, at the presentation of the letters of credence.

★ ★ ★

At the court of Timbuktu the ritual is exact and magnificent. When an ambassador obtains an interview with the master of the city, he must kneel before him, his face brushing against the ground, and then take some earth in his hand which he sprinkles over his head and shoulders. The subjects of the prince must do the same, but only on the first occasion on which they address him; in subsequent interviews the ceremonial becomes much simpler. The palace is not large, but of a very harmonious appearance; it was built nearly two centuries ago by an Andalusian architect known as Ishaq the Granadan.

Although he is the vassal of Askia Muhammad Touré, King of Gao, Mali and many other lands, the master of Timbuktu is an important individual, respected throughout the land of the Blacks. He has at his command three thousand cavalrymen and a vast number of footsoldiers, armed with bows and poisoned arrows. When he moves from one town to another, he rides on a camel, as do the people of his court, accompanied by horses led by the hand by attendants. If he encounters enemies and has to give battle, the prince and his soldiers jump on their horses, while the attendants hobble the camels. When the prince wins a victory, the entire population which has made war upon him is captured and sold, both adults and children. This is why, even in the more modest houses of the city, there are a large number of household slaves, male and female. Some masters use their female slaves to sell various products in the suqs. They can easily be recognized, for they are the only women in Timbuktu not to veil themselves. They control a good part of the retail trade, particularly foodstuffs and everything connected with that, which is a particularly lucrative activity as the inhabitants of the city eat well; cereals and stock can be found in abundance, and the consumption of milk and butter is extensive. The only rarity is salt, and rather than scattering it over food the inhabitants take pieces in their hands and lick them from time to time between mouthfuls.

Many of the citizens are rich, particularly the merchants, who are very numerous at Timbuktu. The prince treats them with respect even if they are not of the country; he has even given two of his daughters in marriage to two foreign merchants because of their wealth. All sorts of things are imported to Timbuktu, particularly European textiles which are sold far more dearly than at Fez. For commercial transactions minted money is not used, but little pieces of gold; smaller payments are made with cowries, shells from Persia or the Indies.

I passed my days wandering round the suqs, visiting the mosques, endeavouring to enter into conversation with anyone knowing a few words of Arabic, and sometimes in my room in the evenings noting down what I had observed, under the admiring gaze of Hiba. Our caravan should have stayed a week at Timbuktu, before making for Gao, the residence of Askia, on the last stage of our journey. But, most likely because of the exigencies of the journey, my uncle fell ill once more. The quartan fever seized him once more on the evening before we were due to depart. Once more I was at his bedside night and day, and I must say that more than once I lost hope that he would be cured. The lord of the city sent his own physician, a very old negro with a white beard around his face, who had read the works of the Orientals as well as those of the Andalusians. He prescribed a strict diet and prepared various concoctions of which I cannot say whether they were effective or simply harmless, since over a period of three weeks my uncle's state of health exhibited neither permanent improvement nor fatal deterioration.

At the end of the month of Shawwal, although still extremely weak, Khali decided to return to Fez without delay; the summer heat was about to begin, which would prevent us from crossing the Sahara before the following year. When I tried to dissuade him, he explained that he could not stay away for two years on a mission which was supposed to have been accomplished in six months, that he had already spent all the money which he had been allotted as well as his own, and in any case, if the Most High had decided to call him unto Him, he would prefer to die among his own family than in a foreign land.

Was his reasoning sound? I cannot allow myself to judge after so many years. I cannot deny however that the return journey was an ordeal for the whole caravan, because after the seventh day my uncle was unable to keep himself on the back of his camel. We would still have retraced our steps, but he forbade us to do so. Our only recourse was to lay him on a makeshift stretcher, which guards and servants took it in turns to carry. His soul departed from him before we reached Taghaza, and we had to bury him in the burning sand at the side of the road; may God reserve him in His ample gardens a more shady haven!

The Year of the Testament
912 A.H.
24 May 1506 – 12 May 1507

I had left Fez in my uncle's baggage train, with no other function than to follow him, listen to him and learn as I went behind him; I returned that year in charge of an unaccomplished mission, a caravan adrift and the most beautiful woman who had ever grown up in the Numidian desert.

But the heaviest thing to bear was a letter. On the way from Timbuktu I had seen Khali writing it. He took advantage of the briefest stop to take out his pen and inkwell from his belt and scribble slowly with a hand that his fever made trembling and uncertain. All our companions watched him from a distance, without disturbing him, thinking that he was putting down his impressions of the journey for the benefit of the sultan. After his death I found the letter while looking through his papers, rolled up and enclosed with a golden thread, which started with these words:

In the name of God, the Compassionate, the Merciful, Master of the Day of Judgement, He who sends to men whose lives are drawing to a close signs in their body and in their mind to enable them to learn to know His resplendent face.

It is you, Hasan, my nephew, my son, to whom I address myself, you to whom I leave as an inheritance neither my name nor my small fortune, but only my cares, my mistakes and my vain ambitions.

His first bequest was the caravan.

Its resources are running out, its way home is still long, its commander is dying, and it is towards you that the men will turn, from you that they will expect the most just orders, the wisest opinion, and that you lead them home safe and sound. You must make every sacrifice to ensure that this voyage ends in dignity.

By the time we reached the first oases, I had to replace three sick camels, purchase fresh provisions, pay for the services of two guides who left us at Sijilmassa, give several dirhams to the soldiers to make this stage of the journey agreeable and pacify them until the next one, present several gifts to the notables with whom we stayed, and all this out from a purse that contained only eighteen dinars, all that was left of a sum which my uncle had borrowed from an Andalusian merchant who had come part of the way with us on the journey out. I could also have borrowed some money myself, but because of our hasty departure from Timbuktu no merchant had had the opportunity to come with us, so that I became, with my lack of means, the least poor of travellers. I resolved to sell some of the various presents received by Khali along the way, particularly the two slaves given him by the lord of Ouarzazat, and they fetched about forty dinars. In order to be able to keep Hiba without incurring reproaches or sarcastic remarks, I let the rumour circulate that she had become pregnant by me without my knowing it, but I had to sell her horse, a piece of useless adornment which would only hinder our crossing of the desert.

My uncle presented his second bequest to me by means of a parable from former times. 'A bedouin woman was asked one day which of her children she loved the most. She replied: "The sick one until he is cured, the smallest one until he grows up, and the traveller until he returns."' I knew that Khali had long been concerned for the future of Fatima, the youngest of his daughters, who had been born in Fez the year before we came, and whose mother, the only wife whom Khali had ever had, had died while bringing her into the world. The child had been brought up by my grandmother, and then after her death by my mother, as my uncle never remarried, probably fearing that a stepmother would not treat his daughters fairly. Aged twelve at the time of her father's death, Fatima had always seemed sickly, grumpy and entirely unattractive. Khali had never asked me directly to marry her, but I knew that she was intended for me, since it is part of the natural order of things that a cousin should take one of his girl cousins for his own, sometimes the fairest, but often the one who could least easily find another husband.

I therefore resigned myself to doing so, knowing that I would thus fulfil one of my uncle's dearest wishes, that he should not leave any of his daughters unmarried when he died. For the four eldest ones he had proceeded methodically; the oldest had been assigned the largest room in the house, and her sisters had no other charge but to attend to her, like servants. She was the only one entitled to new clothes, or jewels, until the time came for her to be married. Her place in the best room had then been taken by the next youngest, who took all the honours; the others had followed, except for Fatima, who was still too young and had been reserved for me.

My final bequest concerns you by right, since it is about your mother, who has already lived under my roof for ten years, refusing, like myself, to remarry. She is no longer young, and her only happiness would be if your father were to take her back. I know that he would like to do so, but Muhammad has the failing of taking wrong decisions hastily and correct ones too slowly. I did not tell you before, but, the evening before we left, casting all pride aside, I put the question to him directly. He replied that he had thought about it constantly since the time of our reconciliation. He had even consulted an imam, who explained to him that he could not remarry a woman whom he had divorced, unless she herself had remarried in the meantime. I then suggested that Salma should contract a marriage with one of our friends, who would agree not to consummate it and would repudiate her immediately. I also told him the story of a prince of Andalus, who wanted to take back his former wife and could not bear the idea of seeing her united to another, even in a fictitious fashion. He asked a qadi in his entourage who found a solution for him which was more worthy of a poet than of a doctor of the law. The woman was to go to a beach at night, and lie down naked, letting the waves flow over her body as if giving herself to the embraces of a man. The prince could then take her back without infringing the Law. Our discussion became drowned in laughter.

Far from laughing, I stood there in horror, my hand clenching the letter. Before my fixed gaze ran the faraway memories of myself as a child, with my mother and Sarah, in the shop of the astrologer-bookseller, whose words were ringing in my ears:

Death will come, and then the waves of the sea.
Then the woman will return with her fruit.

On my return to Fez, my parents were married again, and they were all astounded and disappointed that I was not surprised. I forebore to ask them how they had managed to circumvent the interdiction.

★   ★   ★

Khali's letter continued:

I also leave my embassy in your hands, although it is not mine to bestow since it belongs to the sovereign who invested me with it. As a result of this mission, I was hoping to be able to approach him, but, by the soil that covers my father's grave! this was less from a desire to gain favours and riches than to assist my own family. Was it not through my intercession for your sister that I came to know the prince? You must also think of her when you pay court to the monarch. When you go into his presence, give him the gifts that are his due, and then report to him, in measured terms, the fruits of your observations on Timbuktu. Tell him in particular that in the land of the Blacks there are many kingdoms, that they constantly fight one another, but that they do not seek to extend themselves beyond. When you have held his attention and won his esteem, you should speak to him of Mariam, unless she is already free at the time that I am writing these lines.

But she was not free, as Harun told me, when he came to welcome me as the caravan arrived at the gates of the palace. It was there that I had to give back the mounts to the superintendent of camels, hand over the gifts to the captain of the orderlies while waiting for my interview with the monarch. Having discharged these duties I went home on foot, gossiping with Harun, telling him of my uncle's illness and death, recalling my experiences in Sijilmassa and Timbuktu, without forgetting Hiba, who was following me at a respectful distance carrying my luggage. The Ferret told me the latest news of Fez: Astaghfirullah had died, as well as Hamza the barber, may God lavish His mercy upon them! Ahmad the Lame had gone back to his region south of Marrakesh where he and his brother were leading a group of *mujahidin* who were fighting against the Portuguese.

At Khali's house the women were already dressed in black, as the sad news had arrived well in advance of the caravan. Salma was there, delighted at my return, hastening to whisper the news of her remarriage. She still lived in my uncle's house, so as not to leave my young cousin on her own, but also perhaps to avoid being under the same roof as Warda. Muhammad divided his time between the three houses, those of his two wives and his house in the country, where his crops were flourishing.

I also saw Fatima, whom mourning had made neither less grumpy nor sweeter, and who gave a tearful look in my direction. I turned instinctively to see whether Hiba was behind me. A strange sensation: I found myself repeating my father's actions, caught between two women, a radiant slavegirl and a cousin in tears.

The next day I left for the palace, where I was given an audience the same day, out of respect for my family's bereavement. I was not however received in private. The sovereign was accompanied by the captain of the orderlies, the chancellor, the keeper of the royal seal, the master of ceremonies and other courtiers, all far more sumptuously dressed than the monarch himself and who were talking quietly among themselves while I, deeply moved, poured out my carefully prepared sentences. From time to time the sultan pricked up his ears in the direction of some murmur or other, while motioning me to continue with a wave of his hand. Given the immense interest that my account aroused, I cut it as short as possible and then was silent. Several whisperings later the monarch became aware that I had finished, and declared himself impressed by my eloquence, a way of reminding me of my youth. He asked me to convey his condolences to my family, addressed several words on the subject of my uncle, 'our faithful servant', and finished by expressing the hope that he would see me on another occasion. The interview was over. However, I lingered where I was, in spite of the frowns of the master of ceremonies.

'If you would grant me a minute more, I should like to ask you a favour.'

And I began to speak of my sister, as quickly as possible, repeating the word 'injustice' two or three times, recalling the promise made to Khali. The monarch looked away; I began to think he was not listening to me. But a single word convinced me otherwise:

'The leper?'

The chancellor whispered a word in his ear, and then said to me with a little tap on my shoulder:

'I will deal with it. You will not be disappointed. Do not bother His Majesty with the matter.'

I kissed the monarch's hand and withdrew. Harun was waiting for me outside the railings.

'Do you know that you have just committed an offence against the Law of God?'

He had seen immediately that I had been made to look ridiculous, and he was trying to console me in his fashion. I walked faster without saying a word. He continued:

'I recently heard an eminent shaikh put forward the view that most if not all of the sovereigns of our time increase their revenue by taxes which are forbidden by the Law of God, and that they are all therefore thieves and ungodly men. It follows that anyone who eats at their table, or who accepts the smallest gift, or who establishes family relations with them is an accessory in their thefts and their ungodliness.'

My reply was accompanied by an outburst of anger:

'That kind of notion has been responsible for starting all the wars which have torn the lands of Islam apart. Moreover, you can rest assured: the sultan did not invite me to his table, gave me no present, and has not offered me his daughter's hand. Hence I am neither a thief nor an ungodly man, and I am in no danger of finding myself in the fire of Gehenna. But my sister is still with the lepers!'

Harun's face clouded over.

'Will you go and see her soon?'

'I am waiting for a reply from the chancellor. I would rather see her after that, as I may perhaps have some good news for her.'

In the weeks that followed I went back to some of the courses at the *madrasa* Bu Inania. I was asked to talk about my travels to my fellow students, and in particular to describe to them some of the mosques which I'had seen in the land of the Blacks, as well as the saints' tombs which I had visited. Since I had taken copious notes, I was able to speak for two whole hours, and the professor was delighted. He invited me to his house and encouraged me to write down my observations, as Ibn Batuta and other famous travellers had done before me. I promise to do so one day, if God allows me.

The professor also asked me if I was seeking work, because his brother, who was director of the *maristan* of the city, wanted to employ a young student as secretary, at a salary of three dinars a month. I accepted eagerly, as I had always been interested in the work of hospitals and hospices. It was agreed that I would start work in the autumn.

★ ★ ★

I let two months pass before returning to the palace, since I did not wish to give the chancellor the impression I was rushing him. He seemed extremely friendly, told me that he had been awaiting me for weeks, offered me some syrup, spoke tearfully of my departed uncle and then told me in an almost triumphant tone that he had managed to arrange that my sister would be examined again by four officially designated women.

'You will understand, young man, that our sultan, however powerful he is, cannot bring anyone back into the city who is suspected of being infected with this dreadful disease. If your sister is declared healthy and unmarked, a letter from the sovereign will have her removed from the quarter within a day.'

This solution seemed reasonable, and I decided to convey it to Mariam, in the most confident manner to give her new hope. Harun asked if he could accompany me. I said 'yes' immediately, not without some surprise.

Mariam claimed to be happy to see me return in good health after such a long journey, but she seemed even further away than at our last meeting, and deathly pale. I looked hard at her.

'And how do you feel?'

'Much better than most of my neighbours.'

'I had hoped that you would be free when I came back.'

'I had too much to do here.'

The bitter sarcasm which had so exasperated me two years earlier was even more pronounced.

'Do you remember my oath?'

175

'If you keep to it, if you do not marry, I shall have neither children nor nephews.'

Harun was standing behind me, looking now at the stream, now at the guard. He had only given my sister a timid and furtive greeting, and was giving the impression of not paying attention to what we were saying. Suddenly he cleared his throat noisily and looked straight into Mariam's eyes:

'If you react in this way, if you let yourself give way to discouragement, you will come out of here insane, and rescuing you will be pointless. Your brother has come to bring you good news, the result of his efforts at the palace.'

At his words she calmed herself immediately and listened to me without a trace of mockery or sarcasm.

'When shall I be examined?'

'Very soon. Be always ready.'

'I am still healthy. They will not find the smallest mark.'

'I have no doubt. All will be well!'

★ ★ ★

As we were leaving that accursed place, I looked at Harun beseechingly:

'Do you think she will ever leave?'

Instead of replying, he walked on, gazing at the ground with a pensive air for several minutes. Suddenly, he stood still, pressed his hands to his face and then spread them out, his eyes still closed.

'Hasan, I have made my decision. I want Mariam to be my wife, the mother of my children.'

The Year of the Maristan
913 A.H.
13 May 1507 – 1 May 1508

In the hospice of Fez there are six nurses, a maintenance man, twelve attendants, two cooks, five refuse collectors, a porter, a gardener, a director, an assistant and three secretaries, all decently paid, as well as a large number of sick people. But, as God is my witness, there is not a single doctor. When a sick person arrives, he is put into a room, with someone to look after him, but without receiving any treatment at all, until he either dies or is cured.

None of the sick there is from Fez itself, since the people of Fez prefer to take care of themselves at home. The only people from the city in the hospice are madmen, for whom several rooms are set aside. Their feet are always kept in chains, for fear that they might otherwise do some damage. Their ward is at the end of a corridor whose walls are strengthened with thick joists, and only the more experienced attendants dare to go near them. The one who gives them their meals is armed with a stout stick, and if he sees that one of them is excited, he gives him a good beating which either calms him down or knocks him out.

When I began working at the *maristan* I was warned very strongly about these unfortunates. I was supposed never to speak to them, or even to show that I acknowledged their presence. However, some of them made me feel very sorry for them, especially one old man, who was thin and half bald, who passed his time in prayer and chanting, and used to embrace his children tenderly when they came to see him.

One evening I had stayed late at my office to recopy the pages of a register over which I had unintentionally spilt a cup of syrup. As I was leaving I cast my eyes in this man's direction. He was weeping, leaning on his elbows at the narrow window of his room. When he saw me he hid his eyes. I took a step towards him. He began to tell me, quite calmly, that he was a God-fearing businessman who had been confined to the hospital because a jealous rival had denounced him, and that his family were unable to free him because his enemy was powerful and well received at the palace.

His story could not fail to move me. I came closer to him, murmuring some words of comfort and promising to make enquiries of the director the very next morning. When I was quite close to him he suddenly leapt at me, grabbed hold of my clothes with one hand and smeared dirt on my face with the other, shrieking with demented laughter. The attendants who rushed to my aid reproached me vigorously for my folly.

Very fortunately, the hammam near the *maristan* was still open for men at that hour. I spent an hour there scrubbing my face and my body, and then went to Harun's house. I was still extremely perturbed.

'It has taken a madman to make me understand at last!'

My words were jerky and confused.

'I understand why all our efforts end in failure, and why the chancellor has such a suave voice and such an affected smile when he receives me, and why he always makes promises he does not keep.'

My friend remained impassive. I took another breath.

'There are thousands of people in this city interceding on behalf of a relative who they claim is innocent but who is often a savage murderer, or who they claim is sane but who is often just like the madman who deceived me, or who they claim is cured of leprosy when he is almost eaten away by the disease. How is it possible to distinguish between them?'

I was waiting for the Ferret to contradict me, as he usually did. But he did not. He remained silent, deep in thought, his brow furrowed, and his reply was also a question.

'What you say is true. What should we do next?'

His reaction was strange. When Mariam was merely the sister of his friend he did not hesitate to take initiatives, regardless of my misgivings, appealing to Astaghfirullah, for instance, and deliberately causing a scandal. Now he seemed less sure of himself, although he was now the one of us most directly concerned about the fate of

178

the fair prisoner. Indeed, after having intimated to me that he intended to marry my sister, Harun had not wasted any time. He had sought out my father since his return from the countryside in order to pay him a visit, wearing his Friday clothes, and ask him formally for Mariam's hand in marriage. In other circumstances Muhammad the weigh-master would have considered that a porter with no other fortune than the good name of his guild would have been a very poor match. But Mariam was already in her nineteenth year, an age at which of all the women of Fez only a few slaves or prostitutes would not yet have celebrated their marriages. Harun was an unhoped-for saviour, and were it not for the loss of dignity it might entail, my father would have kissed the hands of this heroic fiancé. Several days later the marriage contract was drawn up by two lawyers; it stipulated that the bride's father was to hand over one hundred dinars to his future son-in-law. The very next day Warda went to bring the news to Mariam, who started to hope again and smile once more for the first time since her confinement.

But it was Harun who lost all his jollity, cheerfulness and sparkle, from one day to the next. His face always wore a worried look. That evening I finally understood the thoughts which were running through my friend's head. He insisted on having my opinion.

'But even so we can't leave Mariam with the lepers for ever! Since all our efforts have been to no avail, what do you think we should do next?'

I had no idea, and this made me reply even more angrily:

'Every time I think of her, the victim of blackguardly injustice for four years, I want to seize the Zarwali by the throat and strangle him, as well as his accomplice the shaikh of the lepers.'

I suited the action to my words. Harun seemed not the slightest impressed:

'Your stone is too big!'

I did not understand. He repeated with a tone of impatience:

'I tell you that your stone is too big, far too big. When I am in the street with the other porters I often see people shouting, insulting each other and attracting a crowd around themselves. Sometimes one of them picks up a stone. If it is the size of a plum or a pear, someone must hold his hand back, because he risks giving his adversary a bloody wound. But, on the other hand, if he takes hold of a stone the size of a water-melon you can go away in peace, because he has no intention of throwing it; he just wants to feel a weight in his bare hands. Threatening to strangle the Zarwali and the shaikh of the lepers is a stone the size of a minaret, and if I was in the street I should go off shrugging my shoulders.'

Without seeming to notice that I was blushing with embarrassment, Harun continued, spacing out his words as if passing each one of them through a filter:

'There must be a way of helping Mariam to escape without risking her recapture and without her family being worried. Of course she will not be able to live in Fez for several years at least, and since I intend to marry her, I must run away with her.'

I had know him long enough over the years to realize that a plan was bubbling away in his head and that he would not unfold it to me prematurely. However, I was unable to understand what motivated him to act in this way. In the name of our friendship I had to speak to him about it.

'How can you forsake your city, your family, your guild of your own free will, to go and live in exile, like a criminal, fleeing from one mountain to another for fear of being clapped in irons, all this for a girl to whom you've only ever once said a word in your life?'

The Ferret put the palm of his right hand on the top of my head, as he used to do when we were younger before telling me a secret.

'There is something which I could not tell you before, and even today I want you to swear that you will not be offended by it.'

I swore, fearing the worst, some sort of dishonour for my family. We were sitting on the ground in the patio of his house. The Ferret was leaning his back against the little stone fountain in which the water was not running that day.

'Do you remember the time that I went secretly into the women's hammam?'

Seven or eight years had gone by, I think, but I still remembered the merest wink, the slightest heartbeat. I assented with a smile.

'Then you will also remember that at the time, in spite of your pestering, I had obstinately refused to tell you what I had seen. I went in, draped in a veil, with a scarf tied round my head. I had wooden sandals on my feet and I was wrapped in a towel. I was eleven years old then, and there was no hair on my body to betray my sex. I walked around inside until I came across Warda and Mariam. Mariam's eyes met mine, and I knew immediately that she had recognized me. She had often seen us together, so she could not be mistaken. I was paralysed, waiting to hear a scream, to be roughly handled, and have blows rained upon me. But your sister did not cry out. She took up her towel, nimbly wrapped it round her body, while a conspiratorial smile formed on her lips. Then, on some pretext or other, she led her mother into another room. I hastened to leave, still not quite able to believe that I was safe. That day, I regretted that Mariam was not my sister; it was only three years later that I rejoiced that I was only the friend of her brother, and could dream of her as a man dreams of a woman. It was then that misfortunes began to rain down upon the head of the girl with the silent eyes.'

Until that point the Ferret's face was radiant with happiness, but it darkened at the last sentence. Before it lit up once more.

'Even if the whole world had betrayed her, the memory of the hammam would have prevented me from abandoning her. Today, she is my wife, I shall save her as she saved me, and we shall make verdant the land that makes us welcome.'

★   ★   ★

Harun came round to see me again a week later to say farewell. His entire luggage consisted of two woollen purses, the larger one containing the gold of the dowry, the other his modest savings.

'The smaller one is for the guard of the quarter, so that he will close his eyes while Mariam escapes; the other is for us, enough to live on for more than a year, with the protection of the Most High.'

They would go to the Rif, hoping to stay for some time in the mountains of the Bani Walid, the most valiant and most generous men in the kingdom. They were also very rich, since although their lands were fertile, they refused to pay a single dirham in taxes. Anyone unjustly banished from Fez knew that he could always find refuge and hospitality among them, even that some of his expenses would be defrayed, and that if his enemies sought to pursue him, the inhabitants of the mountain would attack them.

I held Harun tightly to me, but he quickly tore himself away, eager to discover what Destiny had in store for him.

The Year of the Bride
914 A.H.
2 May 1508 – 20 April 1509

In that year the first of my marriages was celebrated, desired by my uncle as he lay dying as well as by my mother, anxious to separate me from Hiba, who always had the most tender of my caresses although she had given me neither son nor daughter in three years of love. So, as custom demanded, I had to place my foot solemnly upon the foot of Fatima, my cousin, at the moment when she entered the bridal chamber, while a woman of the neighbourhood waited at the door for the linen stained with blood, which she would then brandish, laughing and triumphant, under the noses of the guests, proof of the virginity of the bride and the virility of the husband, the sign that the festivities could begin.

The ritual seemed to last for ever. Since early morning, dressmakers, hairdressers and depilators, including the irreplaceable Sarah, had been bustling around Fatima, painting her cheeks red, her hands and her feet black, with one pretty triangular design between her eyebrows and another beneath her lower lip, elongated like the leaf of an olive tree. Made up in this fashion she was seated on a platform, so that all could admire her, while those who had dressed and prepared her were given a meal. Since the end of the afternoon, friends and relations had gathered outside Khali's house. Finally the bride departed, more troubled than troubling, almost stumbling in her dress at each step, and then got into a kind of octagonal wooden coffer covered with silks and brocades which four young porters, friends of Harun, lifted on their shoulders. The procession then set off, preceded by flutes, trumpets and tambourines as well as a great number of burning torches brandished by the employees of the *maristan* and my old friends from the college. The latter walked along at my side in front of the coffer on which the bride was sitting, while behind her were the husbands of her four sisters.

We had first paraded noisily through the suqs – the shops were already shut and the streets were emptying – before halting in front of the Great Mosque, where a few friends had sprinkled us with rose water. At this stage my oldest brother-in-law, who was taking my uncle's place for the ceremony, had whispered to me that the time had come for me to leave. I had embraced him before running off towards my father's house where a room had been decorated for the night. It was there that I had to wait.

The procession caught up with me an hour later. Fatima had been entrusted to my mother, and it was she who led her by the hand to the threshold of the room, where, before leaving us, Salma reminded me with a wink what I was supposed to do first of all if I wished immediately to assert my authority as a man. So I stepped heavily on the foot of my wife, which was admittedly protected by her wooden shoe, and then the door closed. Outside there were shouts and laughter, some quite close by, as well as the clattering of saucepans, as the first marriage feast should be prepared while the marriage was being consummated.

Draped in red and gold, Fatima stood before me, deathly pale in spite of the make up, without moving, petrified, suffocating, doing her best to smile, her eyes so pitiful that I drew her towards me with a spontaneous movement, which was less of an embrace than an attempt to reassure her. She buried her head against my breast and burst into tears. I shook her to keep her quiet, fearing that she could be heard. She collapsed against me, gradually choking back her tears, but her body was trembling, and she sank slowly to the ground. Soon she was no more than a bundle of sticks awkwardly held up by my arms.

My friends had warned me that on the wedding night many girls did their utmost to appear more ignorant, surprised or alarmed than they really were, but no one had ever mentioned fainting. Moreover, I had often heard it said at the *maristan* that widows or women who had long been deserted suffered from fainting fits which some people put down to hysteria, but never girls of fifteen, and never in the arms of their husbands. I shook Fatima and tried to help her up again; her head fell back, her eyes closed, her lips half open. I began to tremble in my turn, less, I must confess, from concern for my cousin than out of the fear of the ridicule which would cling to me indelibly until the end of my days, if I were suddenly to open the door and shout: 'Help! The bride has fainted!'

I had no other recourse than to carry my cousin to the bed, lay her on her back, take off her shoes, and slacken the scarf tied under her chin. She looked as if she had merely fallen asleep, and her breathing, which had previously been spasmodic, became regular. I sat down beside her, thinking up ways to extricate myself from the situation. I could cut my finger with a pin, and smear the linen with blood, and forget about the marriage night until the next day. But did I know how to soak the white material in the way it ought to be done, without the woman at the door, who had witnessed countless deflorations, discovering the trick? I cast desperate, beseeching, woeful glances at Fatima. Her glowing red hair was spread out on the bolster. I passed my hand over her hair, seizing a clump in my hand, then let go with a sigh, before slapping her cheeks, faster and faster, harder and harder. A smile hovered on her lips, but she did not emerge from her slumber. I shook her shoulder, vigorously, until she began to toss about. She seemed not to be aware of it; the smile did not even leave her face.

Exhausted, I lay down, stretched out, my fingers brushing against the candlestick. For a brief moment I thought of snuffing it out, and going to sleep as well, come what may. But, a minute later, a scratching at the door, impatient, fortuitous, or perhaps merely imagined, recalled me to my duties. The noises outside suddenly seemed more urgent, more insistent. I did not know how long I had already spent in this nightmarish room. I put my hand to Fatima again, feeling for her heartbeats, and shut my eyes. A faint smell of ambergris brought back the negro music of Timbuktu to my ears. Hiba was before me in the moonlight; her dance ended, her arms opened, her skin sleek and smooth. And perfumed with the ambergris of the sea. My lips trembled at the *b* of her name, my arms repeated the same embraces, my body found once more the same distractions, the same landmarks, the same hiding places.

Fatima became a woman in her absence. I opened the door, the woman from next door seized the precious linen and began her ululations, the guests bustled about, the music began to rise, and the ground began to vibrate beneath the feet of the dancers. It was not long before someone came to call me to come quickly and join in the feast. I had to; I had all the time in the world to see my wife, since, according to tradition, I should not leave the house for seven days.

★　★　★

When I awoke, my bride was standing in the courtyard, leaning against the fountain, nonchalantly watching my mother, crouching on the ground two paces away from her, who was busily polishing an immense copper dish in preparation for the second feast of the wedding, which would take place that evening, to which, according to the custom, only women were invited, and at which only servant girls sang and danced. Salma was speaking in a low voice, with a worried air. When I came nearer, she stopped speaking abruptly and began to shine the dish a little more energetically. Then Fatima turned round and saw me. She was smiling blissfully, as if we had spent the most marvellous of nights of love together. Her feet were bare, she was wearing the same dress as the previous day, slightly crumpled, with the same make up, a little less obvious. I made an obviously disenchanted face before going to sit in the salon next to my father, who embraced me proudly and called in a loud voice for a basket of fruit. My mother brought it to us, and as she put it down said quietly into my ear in a reproachful tone:

'Be patient with the poor girl!'

In the evening I made a brief appearance at the women's feast, a chance to see the outline of Hiba, of whom I was to be deprived for a week more. As I left, Fatima followed me to the bedroom, no doubt at my mother's prompting. She took my hand and covered it with kisses.

'I displeased you last night.'

Without answering, I lay down on the left-hand side of the bed and closed my eyes. She leant over me and said in a hesitant, stammering voice that was barely audible:

'Don't you want to visit my little sister?'

I jumped up, incredulous. Hiba had indeed mentioned this expression to me in a mocking voice, used by certain women of this country to refer to the intimate parts of their bodies. But how could I have expected to hear it from the mouth of Fatima, who, as recently as the previous day, had fainted at the mere sight of the marriage chamber? I turned towards her. Her two hands were flat against her face.

'Who has taught you to say that to me?'

She was ashamed, frightened, weeping. I reassured her with a prolonged laugh and held her against me. She was forgiven.

The week ended with a final banquet, for which I received from my four brothers-in-law the gift of four whole sheep as well as earthenware vessels full of sweets. The next day, I left the house at last, and headed straight to the suq to perform the last act of the endless marriage ceremony; to buy some fish and give them to my mother, so that she should throw them at the feet of the bride, wishing her health and fertility.

★　★　★

Before the end of that year, Fatima was pregnant, and I immediately found it necessary to find some better-paid work than my job at the *maristan*. The daughter of a bookseller, my mother encouraged me to launch out into business, which displeased me not at all because of my taste for travelling. She accompanied her advice with a prediction which made me smile at the time:

'Many men discover the whole world while seeking only to make their fortune. But as for you, my son, you will stumble on your treasure as you seek to discover the world.'

The Year of Fortune
915 A.H.
21 April 1509 – 9 April 1510

Fatima bore me a daughter in the last days of the summer; I called her Sarwat, Fortune, for that year saw the beginning of my prosperity. If the latter was short-lived, I could not complain, as it was taken away from me just as it had been given to me, by the sovereign will of the Most High; my only contributions were my ignorance, my arrogance and my passion for adventure.

Before committing myself to a career in business I paid a visit to Master Thomasso de Marino, the old Genoese whom I had got to know on the way to Timbuktu, and who, of all the foreign merchants living in Fez, was the most respected for his wisdom and straightforwardness. I wanted to ask his advice, and perhaps work with him for a while, or go with him on some journey. Although bedridden, he received me with great friendliness, recalling with me the memory of my uncle as well as more agreeable recollections of our caravan.

The reason for my visit sunk him into deep thought. His eyes seemed to be sizing me up, moving from my green felt hat to my carefully trimmed beard, and then to my embroidered jacket, with its wide and imposing sleeves; his white eyebrows seemed like scales, weighing for and against. Then, after having apparently put aside his hesitations, he made me an unexpected offer:

'Heaven has sent you to me, my noble friend, because I have just received from Italy and Spain two large orders for black burnouses, one of a thousand items and the other of eight hundred, for delivery at the beginning of autumn. As you know, the most appreciated burnouses in Europe come from Tafza, where I would go to look for them myself if I were in better health.'

He explained the transaction to me: I would receive two thousand dinars, one thousand eight hundred to buy the stock, at one dinar per burnous at the wholesale price, the remainder for my expenses and my trouble. If I managed to get a better price from the suppliers, my share would be greater; if I had to buy more dearly, I would be obliged to pay out of my own pocket.

Without really knowing whether I had made a good bargain or a bad one, I accepted eagerly. He gave me the money in gold pieces, lent me a horse, two servants and nine mules for the journey and counselled speediness and prudence.

In order not to leave with the pack animals empty, I had collected all the money that I could lay my hands on, my own savings, those of my mother, and a part of Khali's bequest to Fatima, which amounted to a total of four hundred dinars. With this I bought four hundred of the most ordinary sabres, of exactly the same sort as the Fassis were wont to sell to the inhabitants of Tafza. However, when I proudly told my father of my bulky acquisition on my return from the suq, he almost tore his robes from consternation and despair:

'You will need at least a year to get rid of so many sabres in a little town! And when people know that you are in a hurry to return, they will buy them off you at the lowest possible price.'

His words made sense, but it was too late to withdraw, since I had gone round all the artisans to collect my consignment together, which I had paid for in cash in full. I had to resign myself to coming back the loser from my first business journey, telling myself that no one could learn a profession without bruising either his hands or his purse.

The evening of my departure my mother, panic-stricken, came to tell me the rumours she had heard in the hammam. Serious incidents were taking place at Tafza; there was talk of an expedition led by the army of Fez to re-establish order there. But instead of discouraging me, her words kindled my curiosity, so much so that I left the next day before sunrise, without even having tried to find out about it. Ten days later I arrived at my destination without incident, only to find the place seething with unrest.

I had not yet entered the town gate when the people congregated around me, some shouting at me aggressively, others questioning me insistently. I tried to keep calm; no, I had not seen the troops from

Fez coming in this direction; yes, I had heard rumours, but I had not paid any attention to them. While I was vainly endeavouring to force my way through the crowd, a tall man appeared, dressed like a prince. The crowd parted in silence to let him through. He greeted me with an elegant movement of his head and introduced himself as the elected chief of the town. He explained to me that Tafza had existed hitherto as a republic, governed by a council of notables, not under the protection of any sultan, nor any nomadic tribe, paying neither taxes nor ransoms, maintaining its prosperity by the sale of woollen burnouses, which were valued the world over. But ever since a bloody conflict had broken out between two rival clans, a succession of deadly fights and gang battles had taken place, to such an extent that in order to stop the slaughter the council had decided to ban the members of the clan which had started the fighting from the town. In order to take vengeance, those who had been expelled appealed to the sovereign of Fez, promising that they would hand over the town to him. Hence the townspeople feared an imminent attack. I thanked this man for his explanation, stated my name and the reason for my visit, repeated to him the little that I had already heard about the incidents of Tafza, adding that I did not intend to linger there, only long enough to sell my sabres, purchase my burnouses and go back again.

The notable asked me to forgive his countrymen's apprehension and ordered the crowd to let me through, explaining in Berber that I was neither a spy nor a messenger from Fez, but a simple Andalusian merchant working on behalf of the Genoese. I was then able to enter the city and make for the hostelry. However, before I could get there, I saw two richly dressed men in my way, talking loudly to each other while watching me closely. When I drew level with them, they were both talking at once; each begged me to do them the honour of staying in his house, promising also to take charge of my servants and my animals. As I did not wish to offend either of them, I refused both invitations, thanking them for their hospitality, and went to the hostelry, which was fairly uncomfortable in comparison with those of Fez, but I did not complain, since I had known no other roof than the starry vault for several nights.

I had barely settled in when the biggest fortunes in the town began to parade through my room. A rich businessman suggested I should barter my four hundred sabres for eight hundred burnouses. I was going to accept, when another merchant bounced up to my ear and quietly suggested a thousand. Having no experience, it took me some time to understand the reason for all this concern: at the approach of the hostile army the inhabitants thought only of getting rid of all their stock, to protect it from the pillage which would certainly follow the capture of the town. In addition, the arms which I was carrying could not have arrived at a more opportune moment, since the whole population was preparing to face the attackers. So I could dictate my own conditions; in exchange for my sabres I therefore required one thousand eight hundred burnouses, not one less; after some discussion, one of the merchants, a Jew, eventually accepted. So, the very day of my arrival I already had all the stock requested by Master de Marino in my possession without having spent any of the money which he had entrusted to me.

Having no more to sell, I made ready to leave the next day. But, like a lover in the middle of the night, fortune had made up her mind not to let go of me. Once more the great merchants of Tafza came to seek me out, some suggesting indigo or musk, others slaves, leather or cordovan, everything sold at a tenth of its proper price. I had to find forty mules to carry everything. The figures skipped about in my head; from my very first deal I was rich.

On my third day of business the criers announced the arrival of the army of Fez. It consisted of two thousand light cavalry, five hundred crossbowmen, and two hundred mounted pistoleers. Seeing them arrive, the terrified inhabitants decided to treat with them. And, since I was the only Fassi in the town, I was begged to act as intermediary, which, I must say, seemed most amusing. From our first meeting, the officer commanding the royal army took a liking to me. He was an educated and cultivated man, assigned, however, to carry out the most frightful task: to hand over the town and its notables to the vengeance of the opposing clan. I tried to dissuade him.

'Those who have been banished are traitors. Today, they have handed over the town to the sultan; tomorrow they will give it to his enemies. It is far better to negotiate with brave men who know the price of devotion, sacrifice and fidelity.'

I could see in his eyes that he was convinced by my reasoning, but his orders were clear: to gain possession of the town, to punish those who had borne arms against the sultan and hand over authority to the head of the exiled clan, with a garrison to assist him. However, there was one argument which he could not set aside:

'How much does the sultan hope to gain in exchange for his protection?'

'The exiled clan has promised twenty thousand dinars a year.'

I made a little calculation in my head.

'There are thirty notables on the town council, and a further twelve rich Jewish merchants. If each one of them were to pay two thousand dinars, that would make eighty-four thousand –'

The officer interrupted me:

'The annual income of the whole kingdom barely comes to three hundred thousand dinars. How do you imagine that a little town like this one could collect such a sum?'

'There are undreamed-of riches in this country, but the people hide them and do not seek to make them bear fruit; they fear being stripped of them by the rulers. Why do you think the Jews of this country are accused of being miserly? Because the least expenditure, the slightest ostentation, puts their fortune and their lives in danger. For the same reason so many of our cities are dying and the kingdom is becoming impoverished.'

As the sovereign's representative the man I was speaking to could not let me speak in this way in his presence. He asked me to come to the point:

'If you promise the notables of Tafza that their lives will be spared and the customs of the city respected, I will persuade them to hand over that amount.'

Having obtained the officer's word, I went to see the notables and informed them of the agreement. Seeing them hesitate, I told them that a letter had just arrived from Fez bearing the sultan's seal, demanding the immediate execution of all the leading figures in the town. They began to wail and to lament, but, as I have recounted in my *Description of Africa*, within two days the eighty-four thousand dinars were deposited at the officer's feet. I had never seen such a huge quantity of gold, and I learned afterwards from the mouth of the sultan himself that neither he nor his father had ever possessed such a sum in their treasuries.

★　★　★

When I left Tafza, I received valuable presents from the notables, happy to have saved their lives and their town, as well as a sum of money from the officer, who promised to tell the monarch about the role I had played in this strange business. He also gave me a detachment of twelve soldiers who accompanied my caravan back to Fez.

Before even going home, I went to see Master de Marino. I gave him the consignment he had ordered, and returned him his servants, his horse and his mules. I also gave him presents worth two hundred dinars and told him my adventure without omitting a single detail, showing him all the goods I had amassed for myself; he said it was worth fifteen thousand dinars at least.

'It has taken me thirty years to collect such a sum,' he said to me without the slightest trace of jealousy or envy.

I had the feeling that the whole world belonged to me, that I needed nothing and no one, that henceforth fortune would obey me implicitly. I was no longer walking, I was flying. As I took my leave of the Genoese, he shook my hand for a long time, leaning forwards slightly; I stood up straight, my head high, my nose raised. The old man held my hand firmly in his, longer than usual, then, without straightening himself up, looked into my eyes:

'Fortune has smiled upon you, my young friend, and I am as happy for you as if you were my own son. But be on your guard, as riches and power are the enemies of sound judgement. When you see a field of corn, do you not see that some ears are straight and others bent? It is because the straight ones are empty! So keep that humility which has led you towards me, and which has thence opened to you, by the will of the Most High, the paths to fortune.'

★   ★   ★

In that year took place the most effective attack ever launched against the Maghrib by the Castilians. Two of the main coastal cities were taken, Oran during the month of Muharram and Bougie in Ramadan. Tripoli in Barbary would fall in the following year.

None of these three cities has been recaptured since by the Muslims.

The Year of the Two Palaces
916 A.H.
10 April 1510 – 30 March 1511

I have made a rose flower upon your cheeks,
I have made a smile open out upon your lips.
Do not push me away, for our Law is clear:
Every man has the right to pick
What he himself has planted.

I had from that time a court poet, fond of my wine and of my servant girls, greedy for my gold, ready to sing the praises of my visitors and above all of myself, at each feast, each time a caravan returned, sometimes even simply at meal times, when friends, relations, attentive employees, busy merchants, passing *ulama*, and masons engaged in the construction of my palace were gathered around me.

Since my journey to Tafza my fortune had multiplied, my agents were travelling all over Africa, from Badis to Sijilmassa, from Tlemcen to Marrakesh, laden with dates, indigo, henna, oil and textiles; I took part myself only in the larger caravans. The rest of the time I ran my business from my *diwan*, and used to supervise, a cane in my hand, the construction of my new residence, on a hill not far from my uncle's house, where I had settled as master after the birth of my daughter, but which day by day seemed more confined, more modest, more unworthy of my fortune. I waited impatiently for the day when I would be able to live in my palace, my superb incomparable palace which I dreamed about and talked about incessantly, and for whose construction I had employed the best artisans, charged with the task of carrying out to perfection each of my costly desires: ceilings of carved wood, arches covered with mosaics, fountains in black marble, without thinking of the expense. When, sometimes, a figure caused me to hesitate, my poet was there to pronounce the words: 'At the age of twenty, wisdom is not to be wise.' Of course he was carving these words with my gold.

The day when the building work began was one of the most magnificent in my life. At dusk, surrounded by a horde of courtiers, I went to deposit some precious talismans and some child's hair, cut carefully from my daughter's head, at the four corners of the new building; I had suddenly become very susceptible to magic and superstitions, and I was the first to be amazed at this. This is probably the fate of rich and powerful men: aware that their wealth owes less to their merits than to luck, they begin to court the latter like a mistress and venerate it like an idol.

Throughout the night, Khali's house resounded to the sound of an Andalusian orchestra, and trembled under the muffled steps of the dancers, all slavegirls, two of whom had been bought specially for the occasion. I forbade Hiba to dance, because since Timbuktu I could never bring myself to allow her to display her intoxicating charms in front of others. I made her sit close to me, on the softest of cushions, and put my arm around her; Fatima retired early to her room, as was fitting.

I was happy to see Hiba happy and carefree for the first time for months; she felt humiliated by the birth of my daughter, and one night, going into her room, I came upon her wiping away a tear with the end of her scarf; when I ran my fingers through her hair, stealthily caressing her ear, she pushed me away with a gentle but firm hand, murmuring in a sorrowful voice which was unfamiliar to me:

'In my country, when a woman is sterile, she does not wait until her husband repudiates her or abandons her. She goes away, hides herself, and makes herself forgotten.'

I tried to adopt a playful tone, the way she normally spoke herself:

'How do you know that you won't give me a fine boy next Ramadan?'

She did not smile.

'Even before I came to puberty, the soothsayer of my tribe said that I should never become pregnant. I had not believed it, but I have been with you for five years, and you have had a child by another.'

Not knowing what else to say, I drew her close to me; she freed herself, her face twisted with pain.

'Would you agree to set me free?'

'To me you are my beloved, not my slave. But I don't want you to stop belonging to me.'

I put my hands tightly around her wrists as if they were claws to draw her palms to my lips, one after the other.

'Have you forgotten our night at Timbuktu, have you forgotten all our nights together, and our promises never to leave one another?'

A cool breeze swept in through the open window, blowing out the candle in the bronze holder. It was dark and gloomy, and I could no longer see Hiba's eyes. Her voice came to me from afar, shuddering, like some plaintive cry from the desert.

'Often, lovers hold each other by the hand and dream together of happiness to come. But as long as they live their happiness will never be greater than at that moment when their hands were clasped together and their dreams melted into one.'

Eventually she opened her arms to me that night; out of weariness, duty, remembrance, I do not know. But since then a light veil of sadness had never left her eyes.

So I was happy to see her laugh again and clap her hands in time to the music of the Andalusian orchestra. In the middle of the meal my poet stood up to declaim, from memory, verses he had composed in my honour. From the first couplet, my palace was already the Alhambra and its gardens those of Eden.

'May you enter there, on the blessed day of its completion, your heir seated upon your shoulders!'

A shiver from Hiba ran through my arm which was around her. She sighed in my ear:

'God, how I should like to give him to you, that heir!'

As if he had heard her, the poet looked towards her with compassion as well as desire, and interrupting the flow of his verse, improvised two lines, uttered in a singing voice:

Love is thirst at the edge of a well
Love is flower and not fruit.

With a spontaneous movement I picked up my purse and threw it towards him; it must have contained more than fifty dinars. But the smile which radiated from Hiba's face had no price. I spent the whole night gathering its fruit.

★ ★ ★

Six months after this banquet, I had a visit from an officer of the royal guard; the sultan wished me to see him that very day, just after the siesta. I put on suitable clothes and left for the palace, intrigued, but not without a slight pricking of unease.

The sovereign welcomed me with a torrent of courtesies, and his familiars imitated him, fawning and grimacing. He recalled my first visit on my return from Timbuktu, and my mediation at Tafza, which had brought into his treasury in that year more gold than did all the city of Fez. After having sung the praises of my uncle, my ancestors, and of Granada, he began to extol my prosperity, my eloquence and my brilliance to his companions, as well as my vast knowledge, acquired in the most prestigious schools in Fez.

'Didn't you know Ahmad the Lame at the *madrasa*?'

'Indeed, my lord.'

'I have been told that you were one of his best friends, the only one he would listen to with respect and attention.'

I immediately understood the reason for the summons and the unexpected praise. Ahmad was beginning to assume some importance, and many young students at Fez and Marrakesh had left their homes to take up arms at his side in the struggle against the slow invasion by the Portuguese which was threatening the whole Atlantic coast. The Lame One was travelling up and down the country with his supporters, sharply criticizing the Sultan of Fez, who was becoming worried by this and wished to parley with the dangerous rebel. Using me as mediator.

I decided to take advantage of the occasion to settle some old accounts which were close to my heart.

'Sharif Ahmad often came to my house, when we were at college. He proved himself a real brother to me when my sister was imprisoned in the lepers' quarter, may God efface remembrance of it from my memory and from hers!'

The sovereign cleared his throat to hide his embarrassment.

'What became of that unfortunate woman?'

'A worthy young man, a porter, took her hand in marriage, and then took refuge somewhere with her, without daring to give us any news of them, as if they were criminals.'

'Do you want a safe-conduct for them? A pardon? My secretary will prepare one.'

'Your goodness has no limits! May God grant you long life!'

I had to utter these hallowed formulae, but I was determined not to let go. I leaned towards the monarch's ear.

'My friend Sharif Ahmad was deeply concerned at the unjust fate suffered by my sister, victim of the hateful vengeance of the Zarwali.'

'I have been told of the role played by that man.'

I was greatly surprised to know that the sovereign had been told of these matters in detail; I forebore from asking him why he had done nothing at the time, since I wanted to keep him on my side. Thus I continued, still in a low voice:

'In Ahmad's eyes, the Zarwali had become the example of the depravity, which, he said, is corrupting the morals of the people of Fez. I have even heard that he had mentioned this man frequently in his harangues. May God guide him along the way of Truth,' I added cautiously, not wishing to seem to share the Lame One's opinions.

The sultan thought to himself and hesitated. Then, without saying anything, he adjusted his turban and sat up straight on his throne.

'I want you to go to see Ahmad.'

I inclined my head to show I was listening. He continued:

'You must try and calm him down, to rekindle in him more cordial feelings towards me, our dynasty, and the city of Fez, may God protect her from the unbelievers and the ambitious! I am ready to help this young Sharif, with money and arms, in his struggle against the Portuguese invaders, but I need peace on my flanks if I am to engage in my turn in the fight to defend my kingdom, which is now greatly weakened. Tangier has fallen to the Portuguese, as well as Arzila and Ceuta; Larache, Rabat, Chella and Salé are threatened, Anfa is destroyed and its inhabitants have fled. In the north the Spaniards are occupying the coastal towns one by one.'

He pulled me towards him and lowered his voice. His courtiers drew back, although pricking up their ears imperceptibly.

'In a few months I am going to send my army against Tangier and Arzila once more, in the hope that this time the Most High will send me victory. I would like to have the Sharif as an ally in this undertaking, and rather than raising the provinces against the Muslim kings, I would like him to attack the Portuguese at the same time as me, because both of us are warriors in the holy war. Can I entrust you with this mission?'

'I shall do my best, for nothing is dearer to me than the unity of the Muslims. As soon as you give me the command, I shall leave for the Sous to meet Ahmad, and I shall do everything to make him more amenable.'

The sovereign tapped me on the shoulder to show his satisfaction, and asked the captain of the orderlies and the chancellor, the keeper of the royal seal, to approach him.

'You will send a messenger this very evening to the house of the Zarwali. You will order him to leave our city for at least two years. Tell him that he should go on the pilgrimage, and then return for some time to the village of his birth.'

All the courtiers were listening avidly. In a few hours the rumour was going the rounds of the city, from mouth to mouth. No one would dare to greet the exile, no one would dare to visit him, and it was not long before grass began to grow on the road to his house. I was savouring my just vengeance, little knowing that it would bring down additional unhappiness upon my family.

When I took leave of the sultan, he asked me to return the next day, as he wished to consult me about the financial affairs of the kingdom. Henceforth I was with him every day, attending his audiences, even receiving certain petitions myself, which did not fail to arouse the jealousy of the other dignitaries. But I was quite indifferent to this, because I intended to leave for the Sous in the spring, and when I returned to busy myself with my caravans, and above all with my palace, which was growing large and more beautiful in my head, but which was making little progress on the ground, because the last months of that year had been rainy and cold, and the building site of my dreams was no more than a lake of mud.

The Year of the Lame Sharif
917 A.H.
31 March 1511 – 18 March 1512

That year, according to plan, the Sultan of Fez and the Lame Sharif each launched separate attacks against the Portuguese, the former seeking to recapture Tangier, the latter trying to relieve Agadir. Both were repulsed, with heavy losses, no trace of which can be found in the poems composed in their honour.

I had arranged to be present at the time of these days of fighting, making myself record my impressions in writing each evening. Re-reading them in Rome several years later, I was astonished to see that I had not devoted a single line to the progress of the battles. The only thing to capture my attention was the behaviour of the princes and their courtiers in face of the defeat, behaviour which did not fail to surprise me, although my attendance at court had relieved me of a number of illusions. I will cite a brief extract from my notes by way of illustration.

Written this day, the penultimate day of the month of Rabi' al-Awwal 917, corresponding to Wednesday 26 June of the Christian year 1511.

The corpses of the three hundred martyrs fallen before Tangier were brought back to the camp. To flee this sight, which caused my heart to crumble, I went to the sovereign's tent, where I found him conferring with the keeper of the royal seal. On seeing me, the monarch beckoned me to come nearer. 'Listen,' he said to me, 'to what our chancellor thinks about what has happened today!' The latter explained for my benefit: 'I was saying to our master that what has just come to pass is not such a bad thing, because we have shown the Muslims our ardour for the holy war without making the Portuguese feel bruised enough to take vengeance.' I nodded my head as if in agreement, before asking: 'And is it true that the dead are counted in hundreds?' Sensing some recalcitrance or irony, the chancellor said no more, but the sovereign himself took over: 'There were only a small number of cavalrymen among the dead. The others were only infantrymen, beggars, louts, good for nothings, of whom hundreds of thousands exist in my kingdom, far more than I could ever arm!' His tone wavered between heedlessness and joviality. I took my leave on some pretext or other and left the tent. Outside, by the light of a torch, some soldiers were gathered around a corpse which had just been brought in. Seeing me come out of the tent, an old soldier with a reddish beard came up to me: 'Tell the sultan not to weep for those who have died, for their reward is guaranteed on the Day of Judgement.' His tears flowed, his voice choked abruptly. 'My eldest son has just died, and I myself am ready to follow him to Paradise when my master commands it!' He took hold of my sleeves, his hands, clenched with despair, telling a story very different from the one on his lips. A guard came to warn the soldier not to bother the sultan's adviser. The old man slipped moaning away. I returned to my tent.

I had to leave for the Sous several days later, to meet Ahmad again. I had already met him at the beginning of the year to bring him the sultan's message of peace. This time, the master of Fez wanted to inform the Lame One that the Portuguese had suffered more losses than ourselves, and that the sovereign was safe and sound, by the grace of the Most High. When I rejoined him, the Lame One had just besieged Agadir, and his men were bubbling over with enthusiasm. Many were students, from all corners of the Maghrib, who longed for martyrdom as they would have languished for a mysterious lover.

After three days the battle was still raging, and spirits had become inflamed with the intoxication of blood, vengeance and sacrifice. Suddenly, to the amazement of everyone, Ahmad ordered that the siege should be lifted. A young man from Oran who criticized the order to retreat in a loud voice was beheaded immediately. When I showed my surprise at seeing the Lame One so easily discouraged, so quick to abandon his undertaking, he shrugged his shoulders:

'If you want to mix yourself up in politics, and negotiate with princes, you will have to learn to scorn the appearance of things.'

His nervous laugh reminded me of our long conversations in the *madrasa*. As we were alone under a field tent, I questioned him directly. He took some time to explain to me:

'The inhabitants of this region want to get rid of the Portuguese who are occupying Agadir and overrunning the plain around it, making it impossible to work in the fields. Since the master of Fez is far away, and the master of Marrakesh never leaves his palace except for his weekly hunting expedition, they have chosen to send for me. They have collected enough money to enable me to equip five hundred cavalrymen and several thousand infantrymen. It was then my duty to launch an attack against Agadir, but I had no desire to take possession of it, as I would have lost half my troops in the battle, and, even worse, I would have been obliged to station the rest of my army here for years to defend the town against the continual assaults of the Portuguese. I have better things to do today. I must mobilize and reunify the whole of the Maghrib, by subterfuge or by my sword, for the struggle against the invader.'

I clenched my fists as hard as I could, telling myself that I should make no reply; but as I was still in my twenties I could not control myself.

'So,' I said, spacing out my words as if I was only trying to understand, 'you want to fight against the Portuguese, but you are not going to throw your troops against them; you need these men who have answered your call for the holy war for your conquest of Fez, Meknes and Marrakesh!'

Without stopping at my sarcasm Ahmad took me by the shoulders:

'By God, Hasan, you don't seem to realize what is happening! The whole Maghrib is in uproar. Dynasties will disappear, provinces will be sacked, cities razed to the ground. Observe me, gaze upon me, touch my arms, my turban, because tomorrow you will no longer be able to stare at me nor brush your fingers against my face. In this province, it is I who cut off men's heads, it is my name that makes the peasants and the people of the cities tremble. Soon, this whole country will bend the knee as I pass, and one day you will tell your sons that the Lame Sharif was your friend, that he came to your house, and that he was worried about the fate of your sister. As for me, I shall remember nothing of it.'

Both of us were trembling, he with impatient rage, me with fear. I felt myself threatened, because, since I had known him before the days of his glory, I was in some sense his property, as beloved, scorned, and loathed as my old patched white coat had been for me on the day that I encountered fortune.

Thus I decided that the time had come to go away from this man, since I could no longer ever speak to him as one equal to another, since I would henceforth have to shed my self-esteem in his antechamber.

★   ★   ★

Towards the end of the year an event took place whose details I only came to know much later, but which was to have a serious effect on the lives of my family. I shall tell the story as I have been able to reconstruct it, without omitting any detail and leaving it to the care of the Most High to trace the line separating crime and just punishment.

The Zarwali had left on the pilgrimage to Mecca as he had been ordered, and was then going in the direction of the area where he was born, the Bani Zarwal mountains in the Rif, where he was to spend his two years of banishment. He did not return to the province where he had carried out so many exactions in the past without some apprehension, but he had made contact with the principal clan chiefs, distributed some purses, and had seen to it that he was accompanied on the journey by some forty armed guards and by a cousin of the ruler of Fez, an alcoholic and fairly impoverished prince whom he had invited to live with him for a while, hoping in this way to give the mountain people the impression that he was still well in at court.

In order to reach the Bani Zarwal, the caravan had to go through the territory of the Bani Walid. There, on a rocky route between two shepherd villages, the silhouette of an old woman was waiting, a dirty black mass, out of which all that emerged was a palm opened carelessly for the generosity of passers-by. When the Zarwali drew near, riding a horse with a harness, followed by a slave holding an immense umbrella over him, the beggar woman took a step towards him and began to mumble some pious entreaties in a voice that was barely audible. A guard called to her to go away, but his master made him be silent. He needed to re-establish his reputation in the land he had robbed. He took several pieces of gold from his purse and held them out in a conspicuous manner waiting for the old woman to cup her hands to receive them. In a second, the beggar woman gripped the Zarwali by the wrist and pulled him violently. He fell from his horse, with only his right foot staying in the stirrup, so that his body was upside down, his turban brushing the ground, and the point of a dagger at his neck.

'Tell your men not to move!' cried the sham beggar woman in a male voice.

The Zarwali complied.

'Order them to go off as far as the next village!'

A few minutes later only an impatient horse, two motionless men and a curved dagger remained on the mountain road. Slowly, very slowly, they began to move. The highwayman helped the Zarwali to his feet, and then led him, on foot, far off the road, between the rocks like a beast dragging his prey in his jaw, and then disappeared with him. It was only then that the aggressor revealed himself to his trembling victim.

Harun the Ferret had lived for three years in the mountain of the Bani Walid, who protected him as if he was one of their own. Was it only the desire for vengeance which prompted him to act like a bandit, or the fear of seeing his enemy established in the neighbourhood, once more hounding himself, Mariam and the two boys she had already given him? In any case, his method was that of an avenger.

Harun dragged his victim towards the house. Seeing them arrive, my sister was more terrified than the Zarwali; her husband had told her nothing of his plan, nor of the arrival of her former fiancé in the Rif. Besides, she herself had never seen the old man and could not understand what was happening.

'Leave the children here and follow me,' ordered Harun.

He went into the bedroom with his prisoner. Having rejoined them, Mariam pulled back the woollen hanging which was used to close the room.

'Look at this woman, Zarwali!'

Hearing this name, my sister let out an oath. The old man felt the blade of the dagger pressing against his jaw. He flinched imperceptibly, without opening his mouth.

'Undress, Mariam!'

She looked at the Ferret, her eyes unbelieving, horrified. He shouted again:

'It is I, Harun, your husband, who order you to undress! Obey!'

The poor girl uncovered her cheeks and her lips, and then her hair, with clumsy and halting movements. The Zarwali closed his eyes and visibly lowered his head. If he were to see the naked body of this woman, he knew what fate would await him.

'Stand up and open your eyes!'

Harun's order was accompanied by an abrupt movement of the dagger. The Zarwali straightened up, but kept his eyes hermetically sealed.

'Look!' commanded Harun, while Mariam was undoing her clothes with one hand and wiping her tears with the other.

Her dress fell to the ground.

'Look at that body! Do you see any trace of leprosy? Go and examine her more closely!'

Harun began to shake the Zarwali, pushing him towards Mariam, then pulling him back, before pushing him violently again and then letting go of him. The old man collapsed at the feet of my sister, who cried out.

'That's enough, Harun, I implore you!'

She looked with a mixture of fear and compassion at the evil wreck of a man stretched out at her feet. The Zarwali's eyes were half open, but he no longer moved. Harun went up to him suspiciously, felt his pulse, touched his eyelids, and then stood up, unperturbed.

'This man deserved to die like a dog at the feet of the most innocent of his victims.'

Before nightfall, Harun had buried the Zarwali under a fig tree, without removing his clothes, his shoes or his jewels.

The Year of the Storm
918 A.H.
19 March 1512 – 8 March 1513

That year, my wife Fatima died in childbirth. For three days I wept more intensely for her death than I had ever loved her in life. The child, a boy, did not live.

A little before the condolence ceremonies of the fortieth day I was summoned urgently to the palace. The sultan had just come back from his latest summer campaign against the Portuguese, and although he had indeed suffered only reverses, I could not understand the impassive faces which greeted me as soon as I had stepped through the main entrance.

The monarch himself showed me no sign of hostility, but his welcome lacked warmth and his voice was sententious.

'Two years ago you asked for a pardon for your brother-in-law Harun the porter. We granted it. But instead of mending his ways, instead of showing his gratitude, this man never returned to Fez, preferring to live beyond the law in the Rif, waiting for the chance to avenge himself on the old Zarwali.'

'But there is no proof, Majesty, that Harun was the assailant. The mountains are full of highway robb–'

The chancellor interrupted me, his tone louder than that of the sovereign.

'The Zarwali's corpse has just been found. He was buried near a house where your sister and her husband used to live. The soldiers recognized the victim; his jewels had not been taken. Is that the crime of an ordinary highwayman?'

I must say that since the first news of the disappearance of the

Zarwali, which had reached Fez four months earlier, although I did not know the slightest compromising detail, the possibility of Harun taking vengeance had crossed my mind. I knew that the Ferret was capable of pursuing his hatreds to the end, and I was not unaware that he had chosen to live in that part of the Rif. Thus it was not easy for me to declare his innocence. However I had to defend him because, coming from me, the least hesitation would have condemned him.

'His Majesty has too keen a sense of justice to agree to condemn a man without him being able to plead his own case. Particularly when it concerns a respected member of the porters' guild.'

The sultan seemed irritated:

'It does not concern your brother-in-law any more, but you, Hasan. It was you who asked for the Zarwali to be banished, it was at your insistence that he was ordered to go into exile in his village, and it was while going there that he was attacked and assassinated. You bear a heavy responsibility.'

While he was speaking, my eyes clouded over, as though they were already resigned to the darkness of a dungeon. I saw my fortune confiscated, my property scattered, my family humiliated, my Hiba sold on some slave market. My legs began to give way, and sweat overcame me, the cold sweat of helplessness. I forced myself to speak, with difficulty, miserably.

'What am I accused of?'

The chancellor broke in once more, made aggressive by my too evident fear:

'Of complicity, Granadan! Of having left a criminal at liberty, of having sent his victim to his death, of having held the royal pardon up to ridicule and of having abused the benevolence of Our Master.'

I tried to rally myself:

'How could I have guessed the moment that the Zarwali would return from his pilgrimage, or the route he would take? As for Harun, I have lost sight of him for more than four years, and I have not even been able to communicate to him the pardon which has been conferred upon him.'

In fact I had sent message after message to the Ferret, but in his obstinacy he had not bothered to reply. However, my defence did not leave the sovereign unmoved, and he adopted a more friendly tone:

'You are certainly not guilty of anything, Hasan, but appearances indict you. And justice lies in appearances, at least in this world, at least in the eyes of the multitude. At the same time, I cannot forget that in the past, when I have entrusted you with various missions, you have served me faithfully.'

He was silent. In his mind a debate was in progress which I forbore to interrupt, since I felt him slipping towards clemency. The chancellor leaned towards him, evidently seeking to influence him, but the monarch silenced him abruptly, before decreeing:

'You will not suffer the fate of the murderer, Hasan, but that of the victim. Like the Zarwali, you are condemned to banishment. For two whole years, you will not present yourself any more at this palace, you will not live any more at Fez, nor in any other of the provinces which belong to me. After the twentieth day of the month of Rajab, anyone who sees you within the boundaries of the kingdom will bring you here in chains.'

In spite of the harshness of these last words, I had to make an effort not to make my relief too evident. I had escaped ruin and the dungeon, and a long journey for two years did not frighten me in the least. In addition I was allowed a month to put my affairs in order.

★   ★   ★

My departure from Fez was flamboyant. I decided to go into exile with my head high, dressed in brocade, not at night but right in the middle of the day, passing through the swarming alleys, followed by an imposing caravan: two hundred camels, loaded with all sorts of merchandise, as well as twenty thousand dinars, a treasure protected by some fifty armed guards, dressed and paid for out of my own pocket, in order to discourage the bandits who roamed the roads. I stopped three times: in front of the *madrasa* Bu Inania, in the courtyard of the Mosque of the Andalusians, and then in the street of the Potters, near the ramparts, to shower the passers-by with pieces of gold, reaping praise and ovations in return.

I was taking risks by organizing such a show. Some spiteful words whispered into the ear of the chancellor, then into the ear of the monarch, and I could have been arrested, accused of having mocked the royal punishment which had struck me. However I had to run this risk, not only to flatter my self-esteem, but also for my father, my mother, my daughter, for all my family, so that they should not live in disgrace through the period of my banishment.

Of course, I also left them the wherewithal to live safe from need for years, nourished, with servants, and always dressed in new clothes.

When I was two miles from Fez, on the road to Sefrou, sure that all danger had now passed, I went up to Hiba, perched on her mount in a palanquin covered with silk.

'In the memory of the people of Fez there has never been such a proud retreat,' I called out contentedly.

She seemed worried.

'One should not defy the decrees of Destiny. One should not make light of adversity.'

I shrugged my shoulders, not at all impressed.

'Did I not swear that I would take you back to your tribe? You will be there in a month's time. Unless you wish to accompany me to Timbuktu, then to Egypt.'

Her only reply was an enigmatic and anguished '*Insha' allah*'.

Four days later we were going through the pass of the Crows, in weather appreciably colder than I had expected in the month of October. When we had to stop for the night, the guards set up the encampment in a little depression between two hills, hoping in this way to shelter from the freezing winds of the Atlas. They made the tents into a rough circle, with mine rising up in the middle, a real palace of cloth, its sides decorated with artistically calligraphed verses from the Qur'an.

It was there that I was to sleep with Hiba. I awaited this moment with anything but displeasure, but when dusk fell my fair companion obstinately refused to sleep in the tent, without any obvious reason, but with an expression of such fear that I gave up arguing. She had found the entrance to a cave half a mile from the camp. There she would sleep, and nowhere else.

To spend the night in a cave in the Atlas mountains, in the company of hyenas, lions, leopards, perhaps even those huge dragons that were said to be found in such numbers in the neighbourhood, and so poisonous that if a human body came into contact with them it would crumble like clay? It was impossible to instil such fears into Hiba. Only my marvellous tent could terrify her on that cold autumn night.

I had to give in. Overcoming my own misgivings, I let myself be led towards the cave, in spite of the entreaties of the guards and their irreverent winks. Seeing Hiba absurdly weighed down with a large pile of woollen blankets, a lantern, a goatskin full of camel's milk and a long bunch of dates made me feel that my respectability was somewhat in jeopardy.

Our shelter turned out to be cramped, more of a hollow in the rock than a real gallery, which reassured me, since I could easily touch the bottom and thus assure myself that no creature was in residence. Apart from my indomitable Hiba, who was behaving more and more strangely, piling up stones to make the entrance smaller, carefully clearing the earth away, wrapping up the goatskin and the dates in wool to protect them from frost, while I, idly mocking, continued to shower her with sarcasm and reproaches, without succeeding either in cheering her up or in irritating her, still less in diverting her from her feverish antlike bustling.

Eventually I became silent. Not from weariness, but because of the wind. From one moment to another it began to blow so strongly that it became deafening. It was accompanied by a thick swirling snowstorm which threatened to surge in spurts into our hideout. Not in the least perturbed, Hiba now surveyed her defence and survival system with an expert eye.

Wonderful Hiba! It was not this occasion that caused me to begin loving her. But she had never been anything else for me than the jewel of my harem, a brilliant, capricious jewel, who knew how to remain elusive from one embrace to the other. However, during the storm in the Atlas a different woman emerged. My only home was in her eyes, her lips, her hands.

I have always been ashamed to say 'I love you', but my heart has never been ashamed to love. And I loved Hiba, by Almighty God, dispenser of storms and calm, and I called her 'My treasure', without knowing that henceforth she was all that I possessed, and I called her 'My life', which was only right, since it was by her intervention that God enabled me to escape death.

The wind howled for two days and two nights, and the snow piled up, very soon blocking the entrance to the cave and keeping us prisoner.

On the third day, some shepherds came to unblock the opening, not to save us, but to shelter in the cave while eating their meal. They did not seem at all pleased to see us, and it did not take long for me to discover the terrible reason for this. Taken by surprise in the storm, guards and camels had perished, swallowed up in the ice. As I came nearer I could see that the goods had fallen victim to marauders, and the bodies to vultures. The encampment of my caravan was nothing but desolation and ruin. I had the presence of mind not to show myself concerned either at the death of the men I had engaged or at the loss of my fortune. I had actually grasped at the first glance that the shepherds were no strangers to looting. Perhaps they had even finished off the wounded. A word from Hiba or myself could have brought us the same fate. Suppressing my rancour, I assumed an air of extreme detachment and said:

'Such is the judgement of the Most High!'

And, since my listeners had approved this dictum, I carried on:

'Could we partake of your hospitality while waiting to resume our journey?'

I was well aware of the strange morals of these nomads. They would kill a believer without a moment's hesitation to seize a purse or a riding animal, but an appeal to their generosity was sufficient to transform them into considerate and attentive hosts. A proverb says that they always have a dagger in their hands, 'either to slit your throat, or to slit the throat of a sheep in your honour'.

★ ★ ★

'Two gold dinars and five silver dirhams! I have counted them over and over again, weighed them and shaken them. That's all that is left of my huge fortune, all I have left to cross the Sahara as far as the land of the Nile and to begin my life again!'

Hiba met my repeated lamentations with an inscrutable smile, mischievous, mocking and gentle at the same time, which only stirred up my anger.

'Two gold dinars and five silver dirhams!' I cried again. 'And not even an animal to ride, and no clothes to wear except for these which the journey has made filthy!'

'And what about me, don't I belong to you? I'm certainly worth fifty pieces of gold, perhaps more.'

The wink which accompanied this remark emptied it of the slightest trace of servility, as well as the landscape in front of us which Hiba was indicating with a lordly air, a field of indigo plants on the banks of the river Dara, at the entrance to the village where she was born.

Some urchins were already running towards us, and then it was the turn of the chief of the tribe, black-skinned, with fine features, his face surrounded with a white beard, who recognized my companion immediately in spite of ten years' absence, and hugged her to him. He spoke to me in Arabic, saying that he was honoured to offer me the hospitality of his humble dwelling.

Hiba introduced him as her paternal uncle; as for me, I was her master, which was certainly true but of no significance in the circumstances. Was I not alone, impoverished, and surrounded by her people? I was about to say that as far as I was concerned she was no longer a slave, when she silenced me with a frown. Resigning myself to saying nothing further, I found myself taking part, with as much surprise as delight, in the most extraordinary scene.

I had gone with Hiba and her uncle into her uncle's house, and we were sitting in a long low room on a woollen carpet, around which about twenty people were assembled, the elders of the tribe, their expressions showing no rejoicing at the reunion they were supposed to celebrate.

Hiba began to speak. She described me as an important notable of Fez, well acquainted with the Law and with literature, described the circumstances in which she had been given to me by the lord of Ouarzazate, and gave a graphic and moving account of the snowstorm which had brought about my ruin, finishing with these words:

'Rather than selling me to some passing merchant, this man undertook to bring me back to my village. I have sworn to him that he will not regret it.'

With an outrageous impudence, she called out to one of the elders:

'You, Abdullah, how much are you ready to pay to buy me back?'

'Your worth is beyond my means,' he answered in confusion. 'But I can contribute ten dinars.'

She cast her eyes around the company, looking for her next victim:

'And what about you, Ahmad?'

The one called Ahmad rebuked Abdullah disdainfully before declaring:

'Thirty dinars, to cleanse the honour of the tribe.'

And she continued to go around the room in this fashion, cleverly making use of jealousies and quarrels between families and clans in order to obtain a larger contribution each time. The figures were adding up in my head. My two wretched dinars became twelve, forty-two, ninety-two . . . The last person to be appealed to was Hiba's uncle, who, as chief of the tribe, had to vindicate his rank by going higher than the most generous of his subjects.

'Two hundred dinars!' he called out proudly to the assembled company.

I could not believe my eyes, but in the evening, as I was lying down in the room where the chief had invited me to spend the night, Hiba came to see me with the entire amount, more than one thousand eight hundred dinars:

'By the God which has made you so beautiful, Hiba, explain it to me! What on earth is this game? How can the people of this village have so much money? And furthermore, why should they give it to me?'

'To buy me back!'

'You know very well that they could obtain your freedom without handing over the smallest copper coin.'

'To make amends as well.'

When I continued to show the most utter incomprehension, she finally condescended to explain:

'For generations, my tribe were nomads on the west of the Sahara, until the time when my grandfather, enticed by the prospect of profit, began to cultivate indigo and sell it. Hence this village earns far more money than it needs to spend, and there is more gold buried in the ground under each little hut than in the finest residence in Fez. But, in choosing the sedentary life, my relatives lost all their warrior virtues. One day, when I was just coming to maturity . . .'

She sat down beside me, leaning her head back, before continuing:

'A large number of us, young and old, men and women, had gone to make a pilgrimage to the tomb of a *wali* about a day's journey from here. Suddenly, some riders from the guard of the lord of Ouarzazate swooped down upon us. There were four of them, while there were about fifty of us, including more than twenty men bearing arms. But none of my companions thought of using them. All of them ran away without exception, giving each of the four horsemen the opportunity to carry off the girl of his choice. During the strange ceremony in which you have just taken part, the elders of the tribe have done no more than pay their debt, atoning for the shame of themselves and their sons.'

She rested her head on my shoulder:

'You can take this money without shame or remorse. No other man deserves it as much as my beloved master.'

So saying, she had brought her lips close to mine. If my heart was thumping, my eyes glanced uneasily towards the thin curtain which separated us from the adjoining room where her uncle was.

Without the slightest embarrassment Hiba undid her dress; offering her carved ebony body to my gaze and my caresses, she whispered:

'Until now, you have taken me as a slave. Today, take me as a free woman! For one last time.'

★ ★ ★

When I left Hiba, I had only one object in view: to find some memory of her in Timbuktu, perhaps even to find some trace of her in that room which witnessed our first kiss. The building was still there. Although it belonged to the ruler of the city who kept it for important visitors, a dinar served to open its doors for me. So that on the evening of my arrival I was leaning out of the same window, inhaling the air from outside to recapture the ambergris which had once perfumed it, waiting for the rhythms of the negro orchestra, which I was certain would soon be resounding in the street. Then I would turn round to face the middle of the room, where I would see the shadow of my Hiba dancing once again. A strong gust of wind lifted the curtain which began to flutter and whirl round gracefully.

Outside, the sound of running feet and cries drifted closer. The orchestra of my memories, perhaps? But why was it making such a noise? My bewilderment was alas short-lived; the market place suddenly became alive as if it was broad daylight, invaded by a crazed and motley crowd which filled the heavens with its cries. How could I not be overwhelmed with fear? I called down from my window to an old man who was running more slowly than the others. He stopped and uttered a few breathless words in the language of the country. Seeing that I had not understood him at all, he ran off again, making a sign that I should follow him. I was still hesitating to do so when I saw the first glows of the blaze in the sky. Making sure that my gold was securely about me I jumped out of the window and ran.

I spent at least three hours wandering in this fashion, submitting to the moods of the panic-stricken crowd, picking up news of the disaster more from gestures than from words. More than half Timbuktu had burnt down, and it seemed that nothing could stop the fire, fanned by the wind, from spreading across the countless thatched huts, each dangerously close to the other. I had to get away as quickly as possible from this gigantic inferno.

I had heard the previous evening that a caravan of merchants of diverse origins had collected outside the city, ready to leave at dawn. I caught up with it. The forty of us travellers spent the whole night standing up on a hillock, fascinated by the sight of the fire and by the fearful clamour that rose from the flames, in which we could faintly discern the terrible screams of people burning to death.

I shall never recall Timbuktu without that image of hell coming back to me. When we were about to leave, a cloud of mourning veiled its face, and its body was racked with endless crackling. My most treasured memory was consumed in flames.

★ ★ ★

When our geographers of old spoke of the land of the Blacks, they only mentioned Ghana and the oases of the Libyan desert. Then came the conquerors with veiled faces, the preachers, the merchants. And I myself, who am only the last of the travellers, know the names of sixty black kingdoms, fifteen of which I crossed one after the other that year, from the Niger to the Nile. Some have never appeared in any book, but I would not be telling the truth if I would claim to have discovered them myself, since I only followed the ordinary route of the caravans which left from Jenne, Mali, Walata or Timbuktu for Cairo.

It took us no more than twelve days, following the course of the Niger, to reach the town of Gao. It had no defensive wall, but no enemy dared to go near it, so great was the renown of its sovereign, Askia Muhammad, the most powerful man in all the land of the Blacks. The merchants in the caravan were delighted to stop there. They explained that the citizens of Gao had so much gold that the most mediocre cloth from Europe or from Barbary could be sold there for fifteen or twenty times its value. On the other hand, meat, bread, rice and marrows were available in such quantities that one could purchase them extremely cheaply.

The next stages of the journey took us across several kingdoms, among which I will mention those of Wangara, Zagzag and Kano, as well as Bornu, which was far more important than the others, but where we did not linger. In fact, as we entered the capital city, we met another group of foreign merchants who hastened to tell us of their misfortunes, as I have reported in my *Description of Africa*. The king of this country had some extremely strange habits. He took such pleasure in displaying his wealth that all the harnesses of his horses were made of gold, as well as all the dishes in his palace. The leashes of his dogs were all made of fine gold, I have confirmed it with my own eyes! Having been attracted by so much luxuriousness, and, to their misfortune, having confused generosity and ostentation, these merchants had come from Fez, Sous, Genoa and Naples, with finely chased swords encrusted with jewels, tapestries, thoroughbreds and all kinds of precious goods.

'The king seemed delighted,' one of these unfortunates told me. 'He took everything immediately without even discussing the price. We were overjoyed. Since then, we have waited to be paid. We have now been at Bornu for more than a year, and every day we go to the palace to complain. We are answered with promises, and when we insist we are answered with threats.'

That was not the behaviour of the sovereign whom we visited next, the master of Gaoga. I was in his palace paying my respects to him when an Egyptian merchant from the town of Damietta came and presented the king with a fine horse, a Turkish sabre, a coat of mail, a blunderbuss, several mirrors, some coral beads and some chased knives, worth altogether some fifty dinars. The sovereign accepted this gift politely, but in return he gave the man five slaves, five camels, about a hundred huge elephants' tusks, and, as if all this were not enough, he added the equivalent of five hundred gold dinars in the money of his country.

After leaving this generous prince, we came to the kingdom of Nubia, where the great city of Dongola is situated, standing on the bank of the Nile. I was considering hiring a boat to take me to Cairo, but I was told that the river was not navigable at this point, and that I should follow the river bank as far as Aswan.

The very day of my arrival in that town, a sailor offered to take me on his *jarm*. He was already taking a large quantity of grain and livestock in this flat-bottomed vessel, but he could still manage to clear a very comfortable place for me.

Before going on board I lay down on my stomach on the bank and plunged my face deeply into the waters of the Nile. As I stood up, I was suddenly certain that after the tempest which had destroyed my fortune a new life was awaiting me in this land of Egypt, a life of passion, danger and honour.

I hastened to seize hold of it.

III
The Book of Cairo

When I arrived in Cairo, my son, it had already been for centuries the renowned capital of an empire, and the seat of a caliphate. When I left it, it was no more than a provincial capital. No doubt it will never regain its former glory.

God has ordained that I should be witness to this decline, as well as to the calamities that preceded it. I was still floating on the Nile, dreaming of adventures and joyful conquests, when misfortune presented itself. But I had not yet learned to respect it, nor to decipher its messages.

Stretched out lazily on the wide *jarm*, my head slightly raised on a wooden bolster, lulled by the chatter of the boatmen which mingled harmoniously with the lapping of the water, I was looking up at the sun, already reddening, which would disappear in three hours' time over the African bank.

'We shall be in Old Cairo at dawn tomorrow,' a negro crewman shouted to me.

I replied with a smile as wide as his own. Henceforth, no obstacle would separate me from Cairo. I had only to let myself be borne along by the inexorable flow of time and the Nile.

I was on the point of dozing off to sleep when the voice of the boatmen rose, and their conversation became more animated. As I stood up I saw a *jarm* which was going up the river and was just arriving at our level. It took me some time to see what was peculiar about this craft, which I had not seen approaching. A number of beautiful women, richly apparelled, were crammed aboard it, with their children, a vacant air about them, in the middle of hundreds of sheep whose odour was now reaching me. Some had strings of jewels on their foreheads, and high narrow fluted caps on their heads.

Sometimes a drama springs from a single strange sight. The boatmen came up to me in procession, with long faces and their palms turned towards heaven. There was a long silence. Then, out of the lips of the oldest crawled a single word:

'Plague!'

The Year of the Noble Eye
919 A.H.
9 March 1513 – 25 February 1514

The epidemic had broken out at the beginning of that year, on the morrow of a violent storm and torrential rains, manifest portents to the Cairenes of the anger of God and the imminence of chastisement. The children had been affected first, and the notables had hastened to evacuate their families, some to Tur, at the south of Sinai, where the air is healthy, and some to Upper Egypt if they had residences there. Soon countless boatloads passed us, carrying pitiful clusters of fugitives.

It would have been unwise to go further without knowing the extent of the disease. We drew alongside the eastern bank of the river in a deserted place, resolving to stay there as long as was necessary, sustaining ourselves from the goods we were carrying, changing our mooring each night to put possible looters off the scent. We went out five or six times a day in search of news, rowing close up to those travelling up the Nile to question them. The epidemic was devastating the capital. Every day, fifty, sixty, a hundred deaths were recorded in the register of births and deaths, and it was known from experience that ten times more would have gone unrecorded. Each craft quoted a new figure, always an exact one, often accompanied by explanations which permitted no discussion. Thus, on the Monday after the Christian Easter, there were three earth tremors; on the following day two hundred and seventy-four deaths were recorded. The following Friday there was a hailstorm, unheard of at that time of year; on that very day there were three hundred and sixty-five deaths. On the advice of his doctor, the Sultan of Egypt, an old Circassian Mameluke named Qansuh, decided to wear two ruby rings on his fingers to protect himself from the plague. He also decreed a ban on wine and hashish and dealing with prostitutes. In all the quarters of the city new basins were fitted to wash the dead.

Of course the victims were no longer only children and servants. Soldiers and officers began to succumb by the hundred. And the sultan hastened to proclaim that he himself would inherit their equipment. He ordered that the widows of all the soldiers who had died should be arrested until they had handed over to the arsenal a sword encrusted with silver, a coat of mail, a helmet and a quiver, as well as two horses or the equivalent of their value. Furthermore, calculating that the population of Cairo had been considerably reduced by the epidemic, and would continue to drop, Qansuh decided to confiscate a substantial quantity of corn from the new harvest, which he sent immediately to Damascus and Aleppo, where he could sell it at a price three times higher. From one day to the next the price of bread and corn increased inordinately.

When, shortly after the announcement of these measures, the sultan left his citadel and crossed the city to inspect the costly reconstruction of the college which would bear his name, which he had designed himself and whose cupola had just cracked for the third time, the people of the capital shouted at him in derision. Cries reached his ears: 'May God destroy those who starve the Muslims!' On his return the sovereign avoided the popular quarter of Bab Zuwaila, preferring to reach the citadel through streets which were not swarming with people.

This news was conveyed to us by a rich and educated young merchant, fleeing the capital with his family on his private boat, who drew up alongside us for a few hours before continuing his journey. He took an immediate liking to me, asked about my country and my recent travels, and his questions were weightier with knowledge than my replies. When I brought back the conversation to Egypt, he said to me privately in a serene voice:

'Thank goodness rulers sometimes go too far, otherwise they would never fall!'

Before adding, his eyes sparkling:

'The folly of princes is the wisdom of Destiny.'

I believed I had understood.

'Will there soon be a revolt, then?'

'We would not use such a word. It is true that in times of epidemic the people of the streets show great courage, since the power of the sultan appears very weak in comparison to that of the Most High, who mows down whole regiments of soldiers. But not even the smallest weapon can be found in people's houses, hardly even a knife to cut the cheese. When the time for an upheaval comes, it is always one Circassian Mameluke replacing another.'

Before continuing his journey, the merchant made me an unexpected proposition which I accepted with gratitude, although at the time I had no idea how generous it was.

'I am going to live for some months in Assyut, the town where I was born, and I do not want my house in Cairo to stay unoccupied for such a long time. I should be honoured if you would live there while I am away.'

While I was making a combined gesture of gesture of gratitude and refusal, he took me by the wrist:

'I am not doing you a favour, noble traveller, since, if my house remains without a master, it will be a prey for looters, especially in these difficult times. If you accept you will be obliging me, and you will solve a problem that has been bothering me.'

In these circumstances I could not but accept. He continued, in the confident tone of a man who has nurtured a decision for a long time:

'I will write out a deed certifying that you can have free use of the property until my return.'

He went to get paper, pen and ink from his boat and then came back and squatted by my side. As he was writing he asked me my name, my surnames and occupation, which seemed to satisfy him. As well as the document he gave me a bunch of keys, and told me the purpose of each of them. Then he explained very precisely how to find the house and how I should recognize it.

'It is a white building, surrounded by palm trees and sycamores. It is on a slight rise, at the extreme north of the old city, directly on the Nile. I have left a gardener there who will be at your disposal.'

This made me even more impatient to reach my destination. I asked my interlocutor when the end of the plague might be expected.

'The previous epidemics have all come to an end before the beginning of Mesori.'

I asked him to repeat the last word, because I thought I had misheard it. He smiled benevolently.

'In the Coptic year Mesori is the month when the Nile floods reach their peak.'

I murmured:

'Egypt has much merit to be Muslim when the Nile and the plague still follow the calendar of the Pharaohs.'

From the way he lowered his eyes and from his confused smile I understood that he himself was not a Muslim. He busied himself immediately:

'It's getting late. I think we must hoist up the sails.'

Addressing one of his children, who was running incessantly around a palm tree, he called out:

'Sesostris, get back into the boat, we're leaving!'

He shook my hand for the last time, adding in an embarrassed voice:

'There is a cross and an icon in the house. If they offend you, you can take them down and put them in a coffer until my return.'

I promised him that on the contrary nothing would be moved and thanked him for his extreme thoughtfulness.

While I was talking to the Copt, the boatmen were standing in the background, gesticulating animatedly. When my benefactor had gone away, they came to tell me, in solemn tones, that they had decided to leave the next day for the capital. Although they were all Muslims, they knew that the plague would not go away before Mesori. But other reasons impelled them:

'The man said that the price of food has risen suddenly. Now is the time to go to the old port, sell the cargo and return to our homes.'

I did not think of protesting. I myself was like a lover weary of sleeping night after night a few strides away from the object of his desires.

★ ★ ★

Cairo at last!

In no other city does one forget so quickly that one is a foreigner. The traveller has scarcely arrived before he is caught up in a whirlwind of rumours, trivialities, gossips. A hundred strangers accost him, whisper in his ear, call him to witness, jostle his shoulder

226

the better to provoke him to the curses or the laughter which they await. From then on he is let into the secret. He has got hold of one end of a fantastic story, he has to know the sequel even if it means staying until the next caravan, until the next feast day, until the next flood. But, already, another story has begun.

That year, when I disembarked, worn out and haggard a mile from my new home, the whole town, although scarred by the plague, was poking fun without restraint at the 'noble eye', meaning that of the monarch. The first syrup seller, guessing my ignorance and delighting in it, took it upon himself to tell me about it forthwith, pushing away his thirsty clients with a disdainful air. The account which merchants and notables gave me later on was no different from that of this man.

'It all began,' he told me, 'with a stormy interview between Sultan Qansuh and the caliph.'

The caliph was a blameless old man who lived peacefully in his harem. The sultan had treated him harshly and insisted that he should abdicate, on the pretext that his sight was failing, that he was already almost blind in his left eye and that his signature on the decrees was just a scrawl. Apparently Qansuh wanted to frighten the Commander of the Faithful in order to extort a few tens of thousands of dinars from him in exchange for keeping him in office. But the old man did not go along with this game. He took a piece of glazed paper and without trembling wrote out a deed of abdication in favour of his son.

The whole matter would have gone no further, merely another act of injustice that would have been soon forgotten, had the sultan himself one morning not felt pain in his left eye. This had happened two months before my arrival, when the plague was at its most deadly. But the sovereign was losing interest in the plague. His eyelid kept closing. Soon it would close so firmly that he had to hold it open with his finger to be able to see at all. His doctor diagnosed ptosis and recommended an incision.

My informant offered me a goblet of rose syrup and suggested that I should sit down on a wooden box, which I did. There was no longer a crowd around us.

'When the monarch refused categorically, his doctor brought before him a senior officer, the commander of a thousand, who had the same disease, and operated on him forthwith. The man returned a week later with his eye completely restored.'

It was useless. The sultan, said my narrator, preferred to have recourse to a female Turkish healer, who promised to cure him without surgery, only applying an ointment based on powdered steel. After three days of treatment the disease spread to the right eye. The old sultan no longer went out, no longer dealt with any business, did not even manage to carry his *noria* on his head, the heavy long horned headdress which had been adopted by the last Mameluke rulers of Egypt. To such an extent that his own officers, convinced that he was going to lose his sight, began to look around for a successor.

The very evening before my arrival in Cairo, rumours of a plot were spreading through the city. They had naturally reached the ears of the sultan, who decreed a curfew from dusk to dawn.

'Which is why,' finished the syrup vendor, pointing out the position of the sun on the horizon, 'if your house is far off, you really ought to run, because in seven degrees anyone caught in the streets will be flogged in public until the blood runs.'

Seven degrees was less than half an hour. I looked around me; there was no one there except soldiers, on every street corner, peering nervously at the setting sun. Not daring either to run or to ask the way for fear of being suspected, I merely walked along the river bank, quickening my pace and hoping that the house would be easily recognizable.

Two soldiers were coming towards me, with enquiring steps and looks, when I saw a path on my right. I turned into it without hesitation, with the strange impression of having done so every day of my life.

I was at home. The gardener was sitting on the ground in front of the door, his face immobile. I greeted him with a wave and made a great show of taking out my keys. Without a word, he drew aside to let me in, not appearing at all surprised to see a stranger going into his master's house. My self-assurance reassured him. However, feeling obliged to explain the reason for my presence, I took out of my pocket the deed signed by the Copt. The man did not look at it. He could not read, but trusted me, resumed his place and did not move.

★ ★ ★

The next day, when I went out, he was still there, so that I did not know whether he had spent the night there or whether he had resumed his post at dawn. I walked about in my street, which seemed extremely busy. But all the passers-by looked at me. Although I was used to this annoyance which afflicts all travellers, I felt the sensation particularly strongly, and put it down to my Maghribi clothing. But it was not that. A greengrocer stepped out of his shop to come over and give me advice:

'People are astonished to see a man of your rank walking about humbly on foot in the dust.'

Without waiting for my reply, he hailed a donkey-driver, who offered me a sumptuous beast, equipped with a fine blanket, and left me a young boy as an orderly.

So mounted, I made a tour of the old city, stopping especially at the famous mosque of Amr and at the textile market, before pushing on towards New Cairo, from which I returned with my head full of murmurings. Henceforth this excursion would take place every day, taking a longer or shorter time according to my mood and what there was for me to do, but always fruitful. I used to meet various notables, officers, palace officials and do business. Already in the first month I arranged to have a load of Indian crepe and spices for the benefit of a Jewish merchant in Tlemcen conveyed in a camel caravan chartered by some Maghribi traders. At my request, he sent back a casket of amber from Massa.

Between two deals, people confided in me. In this way I learned a week after my arrival that the sultan was now in a better mood. Persuaded that his illness was a chastisement from the Most High, he had summoned the four Grand Qadis of Egypt, representing the four rites of the Faith, to reproach them for having let him commit so many crimes without reprimanding him. He had, it was said, burst into tears before the judges, who were dumbfounded by the sight; the sultan was indeed a stately man, very tall and very stout, with an imposing rounded beard. Swearing that he bitterly regretted his treatment of the old caliph, he had promised that he would immediately make amends for the wrong he had done. And he had dictated forthwith a message for the deposed pontiff which he had had conveyed at once by the commander of the citadel. The note was worded thus: 'I bring you the greetings of the sultan, who commends himself to your prayers. He acknowledges his responsibility for his behaviour towards you and his wish not to incur your reproach. He was unable to resist an evil impulse.'

That very day the provost of the merchants came down from the citadel, preceded by torch-bearers who went around the city announcing: 'According to a decree of His Royal Majesty the Sultan, all monthly and weekly taxes and all indirect taxes without exception are abolished, including the rights upon the flour mills of Cairo.'

The sultan had decided, whatever the cost, to attract the Compassion of the Most High towards his eye. He ordered that all the unemployed of the capital, both men and women, should be assembled in the hippodrome, and gave each of them two half-fadda pieces as alms, which cost four hundred dinars altogether. He also distributed three thousand dinars to the poor, particularly those who lived in the mosque of al-Azhar and in the funerary monuments of Karafa.

After having done all this Qansuh summoned the qadis once more and asked them to have fervent prayers for the healing of his noble eye said in all the mosques. Only three of the judges could answer his call; the fourth, the Maliki qadi, had to bury that day two of his young children who had fallen victim to the plague.

The reason why the sultan set such store by these prayers was that he had eventually accepted that he should be operated on, and this took place, at his request, on a Friday just after the midday prayer. He kept to his room until the following Friday. Then he went to the stands of Ashrafiyya, had the prisoners kept in the four remand prisons, in the keep of the citadel and in the Arkana, the prison of the royal palace, brought forth, and signed a large number of releases, particularly of favourites who had fallen in disgrace. The most famous beneficiary of the noble clemency was Kamal al-Din, the master barber, whose name quickly went the rounds of Cairo, provoking several ironical comments.

A handsome youth, Kamal al-Din had long been the sultan's favourite. In the afternoons, he used to massage the soles of his feet to make him sleep. Until the day when the sultan had been afflicted by an inflammation of the scrotum which had necessitated bleeding, and this barber had spread the news across the city with graphic details, incurring the ire of his master.

Now, he was pardoned, and not only pardoned but the sultan even excused himself for having ill-treated him, and asked him, since this was his particular vice, that he should go about and tell the whole city that the august eye had been cured. In fact the eyelids were still covered with a bandage, but the sovereign felt sufficiently strong to have his audience once more. The more so since a series of events of exceptional gravity had come to pass. He had just received, one after the other, an envoy from the Sharif of Mecca and a Hindu ambassador who had arrived in the capital a few days earlier to discuss the same problem: the Portuguese had just occupied the island of Kamaran, they were in control of the entrance to the Red Sea and had landed troops on the coast of Yemen. The sharif was afraid that they would attack the convoys of Egyptian pilgrims who usually passed through the ports of Yanbu' and Jidda, which were now directly threatened. As for the Hindu emissary, he had come in great pomp, accompanied by two huge elephants caparisoned in red velvet; he was particularly concerned about the sudden interruption of trade between the Indies and the Mameluke Empire brought about by the Portuguese invasion.

The sultan pronounced himself most concerned, observing that the stars must have been particularly unfavourable for the Muslims that year, since the plague, the threat to the Holy Places and his own illness had all occurred at the same time. He ordered the inspector of granaries, the Amir Kuchkhadam, to accompany the Hindu ambassador in procession back as far as Jidda, and then to stay there in order to organize an intelligence service to report on the intentions of the Portuguese. He also promised to arm a fleet and command it himself if God granted him health.

★ ★ ★

It was not before the month of Sha'ban that Qansuh was seen wearing his heavy *noria* again. It was then understood that he was definitively cured, and the city received the order to rejoice. A procession was organized, at the head of which walked the four royal doctors, dressed in red velvet pelisses trimmed with sable, the gift of a grateful sovereign. The great officers of state all had yellow silk scarves, and cloths of the same colour were hanging from the windows of the streets where the procession passed as a sign of rejoicing. The grand qadis had decorated their doors with brocaded muslin dotted with specks of amber, and the kettledrums resounded in the citadel. As the curfew had been lifted, music and singing could be heard at sunset in every corner of the city. Then, when the night became really dark, fireworks sprang forth on the water's edge, accompanied by frenzied cheering.

On that occasion, in the general rejoicing, I suddenly had an overwhelming urge to dress in the Egyptian fashion. So I left my Fassi clothes, which I put away carefully against the day when I would leave, and then put on a narrow gown with green stripes, stitched at the chest and then flared to the ground. On my feet I wore old-fashioned sandals. On my head I wrapped a broad turban in Indian crepe. And it was thus accoutred that I called for a donkey, on which I enthroned myself in the middle of my street, surrounded by a thousand neighbours, to follow the celebrations.

I felt that this city was mine and it gave me a great sense of well-being. Within a few months I had become a real Cairene notable. I had my donkey-man, my greengrocer, my perfumer, my goldsmith, my paper-maker, prosperous business dealings, relations with the palace and a house on the Nile.

I believed that I had reached the oasis of the clear springs.

The Year of the Circassian
920 A.H.
26 February 1514 – 14 February 1515

I would have slumbered for ever in the delights and the torments of
Cairo if a woman had not chosen, in that year, to make me share her
secret, the most dangerous that there was, since it could have
deprived me of life and of the beyond at the same time.

The day that I met her began in the most horrible manner. My
donkey-boy had strayed from our usual route a little before entering
the new city. Thinking that he wanted to avoid some obstacle, I let
him do so. But he led me into the middle of a crowd, and then,
putting the reins into my hand, muttered an excuse and ran off,
without my even being able to question him. He had never behaved
like this before, and I resolved to speak to his master.

It was not long before I understood the reason for all the
excitement. A detachment of soldiers was proceeding through Saliba
Street, preceded by drummers and a torch-bearer. In the middle, a
man was dragging himself along, his torso bare, his hands
outstretched, attached to a rope pulled along by a horseman. A
proclamation was read ordaining that the man, a servant accused of
stealing turbans in the night, was condemned to be cleft in two. This
form of execution was, I knew, generally reserved for murderers,
but there had been a spate of thefts over the preceding days and the
merchants were demanding an exemplary punishment.

The unfortunate man did not cry out, but just moaned dully,
nodding his head, when, all of a sudden, two soldiers threw
themselves upon him, causing him to lose his balance. Before he was
even stretched out on the ground, one of them seized him by the

233

armpits while the other simultaneously grabbed hold of his feet. The executioner approached, carrying a heavy sword in both hands, and with a single blow cut the man in two across the waist. I turned my eyes away, feeling such a violent contraction in my stomach that my paralysed body almost fell to the ground in a heap. A helping hand rose towards me to support me, with an old man's voice:

'One should not gaze upon death from the back of one's mount.'

Rather than jump to the ground, which I did not feel capable of doing, I clung on to my donkey, turned back and went away, causing protest from those whom my manoeuvre prevented from seeing the next part of the spectacle: the upper part of the victim's body was just being put on a pile of quicklime, raised upright facing the crowd where it remained delirious for several minutes before expiring.

In an effort to forget, I decided to attend to my affairs, to go and inform myself about the departures and arrivals of the caravans, to listen to various gossip. But as I proceeded my head became heavier and heavier. It was as if I had been overcome by a fit of dizziness; I drifted this way and that, from one street to another, from one suq to another, half conscious, inhaling saffron and fried cheese, hearing as if from afar the din of the hawkers who were accosting me. Without his attendant, who was still watching the gruesome spectacle, my donkey began to roam about according to his moods and his habits. This lasted until a merchant, noticing that I was not well, took the reins and handed me a cup of sugared water, perfumed with jasmin which immediately relieved my stomach. I was in Khan al-Khalili, and my benefactor was one of the richest Persian traders there, a certain Akbar, may God extend His benefits to him! He made me sit down, swearing that he would not let me go until I had fully recovered.

I had been there for at least an hour, my mind emerging slowly from the fog, when the Circassian made her entrance. I do not know what struck me about her first. Was it her face, so beautiful yet so uncovered, with only a black silk scarf holding back her blonde hair? Was it her waist, so slim in this city where only copiously nourished women were appreciated? Or perhaps the ambiguous manner, deferential but not over-zealous, with which Akbar said: 'Highness!'

Her retinue did not distinguish her from the simplest bourgeoise woman: a single servant, a peasant woman with stiff gestures, and an air of being constantly amused, who was carrying a flat object wrapped clumsily in an old worn-out sheet.

My gaze was evidently too persistent, because the Circassian turned her face away with a conspicuous movement. Seeing this, Akbar confided in me in a deliberately ceremonious voice:

'Her Royal Highness Princess Nur, widow of the Amir 'Ala al-Din, nephew of the Grand Turk.'

I forced myself to look elsewhere, but my curiosity was only stronger. Everyone in Cairo was aware of the drama of this 'Ala al-Din. He had taken part in the fratricidal war which had set the heirs of Sultan Bayazid against one another. It even seemed at one point that he had triumphed, when he had seized the city of Bursa and had threatened to take Constantinople. But his uncle Salim had eventually gained the upper hand. A relentless man, the new Ottoman sultan had had his brothers strangled and their families decimated. However, 'Ala al-Din managed to flee and take refuge in Cairo, where he was received with honour. A palace and servants were put at his disposal, and it was said that he was now preparing to encourage a rising against his uncle with the support of the Mameluke empire, the Sophy of Persia, and the powerful Turkish tribes in the very heart of Anatolia.

Would the coalition have got the better of the redoubtable Salim? It will never be known: four months after his arrival 'Ala al-Din was carried away by the plague. He was still not twenty-five years old, and had just married a beautiful Circassian with whom he had fallen in love, the daughter of an officer assigned to his guard. The Sultan of Egypt, apparently saddened by the prince's death, presided himself over the prayer for the dead man. The funeral ceremonies were imposing, the more noteworthy because they took place according to the Ottoman custom, which was hardly known in Cairo: 'Ala al-Din's horses walked in front, their tails cut and their saddles turned round; on the bier above the body were his turban and his bows, which had been broken.

Nevertheless, the master of Cairo took back the palace of 'Ala al-Din two months later, a decision for which he was rebuked by the population. The widow of the Ottoman was granted a modest house and such a derisory pension that she was obliged to auction the few objects of value that her husband had left her.

All these matters had been reported to me at the time, but they had not assumed any particular significance for me. While I was going over them in my mind, Nur's voice came to me, heart-rending but dignified:

'The prince draws up plans in his palace, without knowing that at the same moment, in a cottage, an artisan's fingers are already weaving his shroud.'

She had spoken these words in Arabic, but with that Circassian accent which no Cairene could fail to recognize, since it was that of the sultan and the Mameluke officers. Before I could reply, the merchant came back, with his offer of a price:

'Seventy-five dinars.'

She turned pale:

'This piece has no equal in the world!'

It was a wall tapestry worked in needlework of rare precision, surrounded by a frame in carved wood. It showed a pack of wolves running towards the summit of a snowy mountain.

Akbar called me to witness:

'What Her Highness says is the absolute truth, but my shop is full of valuable objects which I am forced to sell cheaply. Buyers are rare.'

Out of politeness I inclined my head slightly. Feeling that he had gained my trust, he went further:

'This year is the worst since I began working thirty years ago. People do not dare to show the merest hint of their dinars, for fear that they will be accused of hiding their riches and that someone will come and extort it from them. Last week, a singer was arrested merely on the strength of a denunciation. The sultan himself submitted her to questioning while the guards crushed her feet. They got a hundred and fifty pieces of gold out of her.'

He continued:

'Please note that I understand perfectly well why our sovereign, may God protect him, is forced to act in this manner. He no longer receives the revenues from the ports. Jidda has not had a boat for a year because of the Portuguese corsairs. The situation is not much better at Damietta. As for Alexandria, it has been deserted by the Italian merchants who can no longer find any business to transact there. And to think that this city had, in the past, six hundred thousand inhabitants, twelve thousand grocers open until night and forty thousand Jews paying the canonical *jizya*! Today, it's a fact that Alexandria gives the treasury less than it costs it. We see the results of this every day: the army has not had meat for seven months; the regiments are in ferment, and the sultan looks for gold wherever he thinks he can find it.'

The entrance of a client interrupted him. Seeing that the new arrival was not carrying anything in his hands, Akbar must have thought that he was a customer and asked us to excuse him for a moment. The princess prepared to leave, but I held her back:

'How much did you hope to get for it?'

'Three hundred dinars, no less.'

I asked her to let me see the tapestry. I had already made up my mind, but I could not take it without looking at it, for fear that the purchase might appear to be an act of charity. But I also did not want to examine it too closely, for fear of being thought to be bargaining. I gave it a hasty glance before saying, in a neutral tone:

'Three hundred, that seems a fair price to me. I'll buy it.'

She was not mistaken:

'A woman does not accept a present from a man to whom she cannot show her gratitude.'

The words were firm, but the tone was less so. I replied, with false indignation:

'It is not a gift. I am buying this because I want it!'

'And why should you want it?'

'It's a souvenir.'

'But it's the first time you've seen it!'

'Sometimes one glance is enough for an object to be irreplaceable.'

She blushed. Our looks met. Our lips parted. We were already friends. The servant woman, more cheerful than ever, walked between us, trying to overhear our whisperings. We had arranged to meet: Friday, at midday, Azbakiyya Square, in front of the donkey showman.

★ ★ ★

Since my arrival in Egypt, I had never missed the solemn Friday prayer. But, that day, I did so without much remorse; after all, it was the Creator who had made this woman so beautiful, and it was He who had put her in my path.

Azbakiyya Square was filling up slowly as the mosques emptied, because it was the custom of all the Cairenes to gather there after the ceremony to play dice, listen to the patter of the story-tellers, and sometimes lose themselves in the neighbouring alleys where certain taverns were offering a short cut to Eden.

I did not yet catch sight of my Circassian, but the donkey showman was there, already surrounded by a swelling cluster of idlers. I joined them, glancing frequently at the faces which surrounded me and at the sun in the hope that it had moved a few degrees.

The clown was dancing with his beast, without anyone knowing which was following the steps of the other. Then he began to talk to his donkey. He told him that the sultan had decided to undertake a great construction work, and that he was going to requisition all the donkeys in Cairo to transport lime and stones. At that very moment the animal fell to the ground, turned round on to his back, his legs in the air, puffed out its stomach and shut its eyes. The man began to lament in front of the audience, saying that his donkey was dead, and he took a collection to buy himself another one. Having collected several dozen coins, he said:

'Don't believe that my donkey has given up the ghost. He is a glutton who, aware of my poverty, acts a part so that I can earn some money and buy him something to eat.'

Taking a big stick he gave the beast a good beating.

'Come on, get up now!'

But the donkey did not move. The clown continued:

'People of Cairo, the sultan has just issued an edict: the whole population is to go out tomorrow to be present at his triumphal entry into the city. The donkeys have been requisitioned to carry the women of high society.'

Thereupon the donkey leaped to its feet, began to preen himself, showing great happiness. His master burst out laughing as did the crowd.

'So,' he said, 'you like pretty women! But there are several here! Which one would you like to carry?'

The beast went round the audience, seemed to hesitate and then made for a rather tall lady spectator who was standing a few paces away from me. She was wearing veils so thick that her face was invisible. But I recognized her bearing immediately. She herself, frightened by the laughter and the looks, came up to me and clutched my arm. I hastened to say to the donkey in a jocular voice: 'No, you won't be carrying my wife!', before going off with her in a dignified fashion.

'I didn't expect to see you veiled. Had it not been for the donkey, I wouldn't have recognized you.'

'It is precisely in order not to be recognized that I am veiled. We are together in the street, in the middle of an inquisitive gossiping crowd, and no one is aware that I am not your wife.'

And she nodded teasingly:

'I take off the veil if I want to please all men; I wear it if I only want to please a single one.'

'Henceforth, I should hate it if your face were to be uncovered.'

'Will you never want to look at it?'

It is true that we could not be alone in a house, neither hers nor mine, and that we had to be satisfied with walking in the city side by side. The day of our first meeting Nur insisted that we visit the forbidden garden.

'It has been given this name,' she explained to me, 'because it is surrounded by high walls and the sultan has prohibited access to it in order to protect a wonder of nature; the only tree in the world to produce real balsam.'

A piece of silver in the hand of the guard enabled us to go inside. Leaning over the balsam tree, Nur drew aside her veil and stayed still for a long time, fascinated, as if in a dream. She repeated, as if to herself:

'In the whole world there is only this one root. It is so slender, so fragile, but so precious!'

As far as I could see, the tree seemed quite ordinary. Its leaves were like those of a vine, perhaps a little smaller. It was planted right in the middle of a spring.

'It is said that if it was watered with different water it would dry up immediately.'

She seemed moved by this visit, although I did not understand why. But the next day we were together again, and she seemed happy and considerate. Henceforth our walks were daily, or almost so, because in the middle of the week, Mondays and Tuesdays, she was never free. When, at the end of a month, I pointed this out to her, her reaction was sharp:

'You might never have seen me, or only once a month. Now I am with you two, three, five days a week, you complain about my absences.'

'I don't count the days that I see you. It is the others than seem interminable to me.'

It was a Sunday, and we were close to the mosque of Ibn Tulun, in front of the women's hammam where Nur was preparing to enter. She seemed to hesitate:

'Would you be ready to come with me, without asking the slightest question?'

'As far as China, if I must!'

'Then meet me tomorrow morning, with two camels and full waterskins, in front of the Great Mosque of Giza.'

★ ★ ★

Intent on keeping my promise, I did not ask her about our destination, so much so that at the end of two hours on the road we had only exchanged a few words. However I did not think that it would be against the spirit of our agreement to say:

'The pyramids can't be far from here.'

'Exactly.'

Encouraged by this information I continued:

'Is that where we're going?'

'Exactly.'

'Do you come here each week to see those round buildings?'

She was overcome by a frank and devastating laugh at which I could only feel offended. To show my disapproval, I got down to the ground and hobbled my camel. She hastened to come back towards me.

'I'm sorry that I laughed. It was because you said that they were round.'

'I didn't invent it. Ibn Batuta, the great traveller, says exactly that they have a "circular shape".'

'That was because he never saw them. Or perhaps from very far off, or at night, may God forgive him! But do not blame him. When a traveller tells of his exploits, he becomes a prisoner of the admiring chuckles of those who listen to him. He no longer dares to say "I don't know", or "I haven't seen" for fear of losing face. There are lies of which the ears are more guilty than the mouth.'

We had recommenced our progress. She went on:

'And what else did he say about the pyramids, this Ibn Batuta?'

'That they were built by a sage who was well acquainted with the movements of the stars, and who had foreseen the Flood; that was why he built the pyramids, on which he depicted all the arts and sciences, to preserve them from destruction and oblivion.'

Fearing further sarcasms, I hastened to add:

'In any case Ibn Batuta stated that these were only suppositions, and that no one really knows what these strange structures were built for.'

'For me, the pyramids have been built only to be beautiful and imposing, to be the first of the wonders of the world. They must certainly have had some function, but that was only a pretext provided by the prince of the time.'

We were just reaching the summit of a hill, and the pyramids stood out clearly on the horizon. She held back her camel and stretched out her hand to the east, in a gesture which was so touched with emotion that it became solemn.

'Long after our houses, our palaces and ourselves have disappeared, these pyramids will still be there. Does that not mean, in the eyes of the Eternal One, that they are the most useful?'

I put my hand on hers.

'For the time being, we are alive. And together. And alone with each other.'

Casting a look around her, she suddenly adopted a mischievous tone:

'It's true that we are alone!'

She pushed her mount up against mine, and, lifting her veil, kissed me on the lips. God, I could have stayed thus until the Day of Judgement!

It was not I who left her lips; nor was it she who separated herself from me. It was the fault of our camels who went away from each other too soon, threatening to overbalance us.

'It's getting late. What if we were to have a rest?'

'On the pyramids?'

'No, a little further on. A few miles from here there is a little village where the nurse who brought me up lives. She waits for me every Monday evening.'

A little to the side of the village there was a fellah cottage, covered in mud, at the end of a little raised path which Nur took, begging me not to follow her. She disappeared into the house. I waited for her, leaning against a palm tree. It was almost dark when she returned, accompanied by a stout easygoing old peasant woman.

'Khadra, this is my new husband.'

I jumped. My staring eyes encountered a frown on Nur's face, while the nurse was beseeching Heaven:

'Widowed at eighteen! I hope that my princess will have better luck this time.'

'I hope so too!' I cried spontaneously.

Nur smiled and Khadra mumbled an invocation, before leading us towards an earthen building near her own, and even more cramped.

'It isn't a palace here, but you will be dry and no one will disturb you. If you need me, call me through the window.'

There was only one rectangular room, lit by a flickering candle. A faint smell of incense floated around us. Through the unshuttered window came a long lowing of buffaloes. My Circassian put the door on the latch and leaned against it.

Her tousled hair fell first, then her dress. Around her bare neck lay a ruby necklace, the central stone hanging proudly between her breasts. Around her bare waist, a slender belt in plaited golden thread. My eyes had never looked upon a woman so richly undressed. She came up and whispered in my ear:

'Other women would have sold off their intimate jewellery first. But I keep them. Houses and furniture can be sold, but not the body, not its ornaments.'

I held her to me:

'Since this morning I have resigned myself to one surprise after another. The pyramids, your kiss, this village, the announcement of our marriage, and now this room, this night, your jewels, your body, your lips . . .'

I kissed her passionately. Which dispensed her from confessing that as far as surprises went I had only heard the '*Bismillah*' and the rest of the prayer was to follow.

But that did not come to pass before the end of the night, which was deliciously endless. We were lying down beside one another, so close that my lips trembled at her whisperings. Her legs formed a pyramid; her knees were the summit, each pressed close to the other. I touched them, they separated, as if they had just been quarrelling.

My Circassian! My hands sometimes still sculpt the shape of her body. And my lips have forgotten nothing.

★   ★   ★

When I awoke, Nur was standing up, leaning against the door as she had been at the beginning of the night. But her arms were heavy and her eyes had a false smile.

'Here is my son Bayazid whom I conceal as though he were a child of shame!'

She came forward and placed him, like an offering, on my hands which were open in resignation.

The Year of the Rebels
921 A.H.
15 February 1515 – 4 February 1516

This son was not of my blood, but he had appeared to bless or to
punish the deeds of my flesh. He was thus mine, and I would have
needed the courage of Abraham to have sacrificed him in the name of
the Faith. Is it not in the blade of a knife brandished by the Friend of
God above a pyre that the revealed religions meet? I did not dare to
commit this sacred crime, which I praise each year in the feast of
al-Adha. However, that year, duty called me to do so straight away,
because a Muslim empire was in the process of being born before my
eyes, and this child was threatening it.

'One day, Bayazid, son of 'Ala al-Din, will make the throne of the
Ottomans tremble. Only he, the last survivor of the princes of his
line, will be able to raise the tribes of Anatolia. Only he will be able
to reunite the Circassian Mamelukes and the Safavids of Persia
around him and cut down the Grand Turk. Only he. Unless the
agents of Sultan Salim strangle him.'

Nur was leaning above her son's cradle, without knowing what
torture her words were inflicting upon me. This empire whose
destruction she was thus predicting was the one which my prayers
had been invoking even before I knew how to pray, since it was the
instrument which I had always expected would bring about the
deliverance of Granada.

Now this empire was there, in the process of moulding itself
before my eyes. It had already conquered Constantinople, Serbia
and Anatolia, it was preparing to invade Syria, Iraq, Arabia Deserta,
Arabia Felix, Arabia Petraea as well as Egypt. Tomorrow it would be

master of Barbary, Andalusia, perhaps Sicily. All the Muslims would be reunited again, as in the time of the Umayyads, within a single caliphate, flourishing and formidable, which would impose its law on the nations of the unbelievers. Was I going to put myself at the service of this empire, dream of my dreams, hope of my hopes? Was I going to contribute to its emergence? Not at all. I was condemned to fight it or to flee. Facing Salim the Conqueror, who had just sacrificed, without the hand of God restraining him, his father, his brothers with their descendants, and who would soon sacrifice three of his own sons, facing this sword of the divine wrath, there was a child whom I was determined to protect, to nourish at my breast, until he became man, amir, destroyer of empire, and would kill according to the law of his race. Of all this I had chosen nothing; life had chosen for me, as well as my temperament.

Henceforth I had to leave Egypt, where Bayazid and his mother were in danger. Nur had kept her pregnancy secret, except from Khadra, who had helped her deliver the baby and had kept him since the first day. What if the nurse, already old, should die, and the child should be taken to Cairo, where his identity would be quickly discovered? He would then be at the mercy of Salim's agents, of whom there were many in Egypt; he might even be handed over by Sultan Qansuh himself who, while distrusting the Ottomans to the utmost, was too afraid of them to refuse them the head of a child.

My solution was easily found: to marry Nur and leave for Fez with the child, where I could produce him as my own, in order to return to Egypt when he was older and when his age would no longer betray his origin.

As Nur was a widow, the marriage was a simple one. Some friends and neighbours gathered in my house for a meal, among them an Andalusian lawyer. At the moment that the contract was being drawn up, he noticed the icon and the cross on the wall. He asked me to take them down.

'I cannot,' I said. 'I promised the owner of the house not to touch them until his return.'

The lawyer seemed embarrassed, and the guests as well. Until Nur intervened:

'If it is not possible to take these objects down, nothing prevents them being covered.'

Without waiting for a reply she drew a damask screen up to the wall. Satisfied, the notary officiated.

We did not stay more than two nights in the house, which I left with regret. Chance had offered it to me, and left it with me for nearly two years; the Copt had never reappeared or given me any news of himself. I had only heard that an epidemic of plague had struck Assyut and its neighbourhood, decimating a large part of the population, and I imagined that my benefactor had probably fallen victim to it. May it please God that I may be wrong, but I see no other explanation for his absence, nor especially for his silence. Nevertheless, before leaving I handed the keys into the keeping of my goldsmith, Da'ud the Aleppine. As the brother of Ya'qub, master of the Mint, a good friend of the sultan, he was better placed than anyone else to prevent some Mameluke from taking over the empty house.

Our voyage began in the month of Safar, on the eve of the Christian Easter. The first stop was Khadra's cottage, near Giza, where we spent a night, before returning with Bayazid, then aged sixteen months, towards Bulaq, the great river port of Cairo. Thanks to a judicious bakshish, we were able to embark immediately on a *jarm* which was transporting a cargo of refined sugar from the sultan's personal factory to Alexandria. There were numerous craft at Bulaq, and some were very comfortable, but I was anxious to arrive at the port of Alexandria under the sovereign's flag, having been warned by friends of the difficulties encountered at the customs. Some travellers were searched down to their underclothes, on arrival and departure, by over-zealous officials who used to tax dinars as well as goods.

Avoiding this annoyance, I was better able to appreciate the grandeur of this ancient city, founded by Alexander the Great, a sovereign of whom the Qur'an speaks in laudatory terms, and whose tomb is a place of pilgrimage for the pious. It is true that the town is no more than the shadow of what it once was. The inhabitants still recall the time when hundreds of ships lay permanently to anchor in the harbour, from Flanders, England, Biscay, Portugal, Puglia, Sicily, and especially from Venice, Genoa, Ragusa and Turkish Greece. That year, only memories still crowded into the harbour.

In the middle of the town, facing the port, is a hill which did not exist, it is said, at the time of the Ancients, and has been formed only from the accumulation of ruins. Rummaging through it, vases and other objects of value can often be found. On the top a small tower has been built, where there lives a watchman all day and all night, whose job is to keep a watch for passing ships. Each time he signals one to the customs men he receives a bonus. In return, if he sleeps or leaves his post and a ship arrives without him having signalled it, he pays a fine equal to twice his bonus.

Outside the city, some imposing ruins can be seen, in the middle of which rises a very high and massive column which the ancient books say was built by a sage named Ptolemy. He had placed a great steel mirror at the top of it, which, it was said, used to burn all enemy boats which tried to approach the coast.

There were surely many other things to visit, but we were all eager to depart, promising ourselves to come back one day to Alexandria when our minds would be at peace. Then we embarked in an Egyptian vessel making for Tlemcen, where we rested a whole week before taking to the road.

★　★　★

I had put on my Maghribi clothes once more, and going through the walls of Fez I had covered my face with a *taylassan*. I did not want my arrival to be known until I had met my family, that is to say my father, my mother, Warda, Sarwat, my six-year-old daughter, as well as Harun and Mariam, whom I had no hope of seeing but of whom I expected to hear news.

However, I could not prevent myself from beginning by stopping in front of the site of my palace. It was exactly as it was when I had left it, except that the grass had grown, covering the unfinished walls. I turned my gaze away quickly as well as the drier gaze of my mule, which I directed towards Khali's house, several paces away. I knocked. From inside a woman answered whose voice I did not recognize. I called my mother by her first name.

'She doesn't live here any more,' said the voice.

Mine was too choked with emotion to ask further questions. I left for my father's house.

Salma was standing in front of the door and duly clasped me to her bosom, as well as Nur and Bayazid, whom she covered with kisses, not without marvelling that I should have given my son such an uncommon name and such clear skin. She said nothing. Only her eyes spoke, and it was in them that I saw that my father had died. She confirmed it with a tear. But it was not there that she wanted to begin:

'We do not have much time. You must listen to what I have to say to you before you go away again.'

'But I have no intention of going away!'

'Listen to me and you will understand.'

And thus she spoke for more than an hour, perhaps two, without hesitating or interrupting herself, as if she had already turned over in her mind a thousand times what she would say to me on the day when I returned.

'I do not want to curse Harun, but his actions have cursed us all. No one at Fez has blamed him for the death of the Zarwali. Alas! he did not stop there.'

Shortly after my banishment, she explained, the sovereign had despatched two hundred soldiers to seize the Ferret, but the mountain people had taken up cudgels on his behalf. Sixteen soldiers were killed in an ambush. When the news became known, a proclamation was stuck up and read in the streets of Fez, announcing that there was a price on Harun's head. Our houses were put under police guard; the police were there day and night, closely questioning each visitor, so much so that even very close friends hesitated to associate with the outlaw's relatives. Ever since, a new proclamation had been read out each week, accusing Harun and his band of having attacked a convoy, robbed a caravan, or massacred travellers.

'That's not true!' I exclaimed. 'I know Harun. He might have killed in vengeance or self-defence, but not to steal!'

'The truth is only important for God; what concerns us is what the people believe. Your father was thinking of emigrating again, to Tunis or some other city, when his heart stopped suddenly, in Ramadan last year.'

Salma breathed for a long time before continuing:

'He had invited several people to come and break the fast in his company, but no one dared to enter the house. Life had become a heavy burden for him to bear. The next day, during the siesta, I was awoken by the sound of something falling. He was stretched out on the ground, in the courtyard where he had been pacing up and down since morning. His head had struck the edge of the pool. He had stopped breathing.'

A terrible heat filled my breast. I hid my face. My mother continued without looking at me:

'In the face of adversity, women bend and men break. Your father was prisoner of his self-esteem. I had been taught to submit.'

'And Warda?'

'She left us after the death of Muhammad. Without her husband, without her daughter, she no longer had anyone in this country. I believe that she has returned to her village in Castile, to end her life among her own people.'

Then she added in a low voice:

'We should never have left Granada!'

'Perhaps we are going to go back there.'

She did not deign to reply. Her hand brushed at the wind before her eyes, as if chasing a persistent fly.

'Ask me instead about your daughter.'

Her face lit up. And mine too.

'I was waiting for you to speak of her. I did not dare to ask you. I left her when she was so young!'

'She is chubby and cheeky. At the moment she is with Sarah, who takes her sometimes to play with her grandchildren.'

They both arrived an hour later. Contrary to my expectations, it was Gaudy Sarah who flung herself around my neck, while my daughter stood at a respectful distance. We had to be introduced. My mother was too moved, so Sarah took care of it:

'Sarwat, this is your father.'

The little girl took a step towards me and then stopped.

'You were in Timb—'

'No, not in Timbuktu, but in Egypt, and I've brought you back a little brother.'

I took her on my knees, covering her with kisses, breathing in deeply the smell of her smooth black hair, dreamily caressing her neck. I had the impression of repeating in the most minute detail a scene which I had seen a hundred times: my father seated on his cushion, with my sister.

'Is there any news of Mariam?'

It was Sarah who replied:

'It's said that she's been seen with a sword in her hand, at her husband's side. But there are so many stories about them . . .'

'And do you think that Harun is a bandit?'

'There are rebels in every community. One curses them in public and prays for them when one is alone. Even among the Jews. There are Jews in this country who do not pay the tribute, who ride horses and bear arms. We call them the Karayim. You probably know that.'

I agreed:

'There are hundreds of them, organized like an army, who live in the mountains of Damansara and Hintata near Marrakesh.'

But I wanted to go back to my first concern.

'Do you really think that there are people in Fez who pray secretly for Harun and Mariam?'

This time it was Salma who exploded:

'If Harun was only a simple bandit, he would not be pursued so relentlessly in proclamation after proclamation. When he attacked the Zarwali, he almost became a hero. But they wanted to make him out to be a thief. In the eyes of the common people, gold soils more easily than blood.'

Then, speaking more slowly, as if another person was speaking from within her:

'It is useless to try to clear your brother-in-law. If you try to defend him you will be treated as his accomplice once again.'

My mother was afraid that my desire to defend Harun and Mariam would impel me to commit new follies. She was probably right, but I had to try. The very way in which my banishment had been decided led me to think that the Sultan of Fez would listen to me now.

The sultan was then on campaign against the Portuguese, beside Bulawan. For months I went up and down the country following the royal àrmy, sometimes bearing arms and taking part in some skirmishes. I was ready to do anything to wring out a pardon. Between two battles I spoke to the monarch, his brothers and a number of his advisers. But why go into details when the results were so disappointing? An intimate of the sultan finally agreed with me that many crimes had been attributed unjustly to Harun, adding, in a tone of disarming sincerity:

'Even if we could pardon your brother-in-law for what he has done, how could we pardon him for the things we accuse him of having done?'

One day I suddenly decided to abandon my efforts. I had indeed not managed to get what I wanted, but through chance conversations I had gleaned a piece of information that I wanted to confirm. I returned to Fez, took Salma, Nur, Sarwat and Bayazid, and set off, without disclosing my purposes to them, having decided no longer to look back. At Fez I possessed nothing more than a half-completed building, a ruin inhabited by regrets and empty of memories.

★   ★   ★

Our journey lasted for weeks without me revealing our destination, which was not a place but a man: 'Aruj the corsair, called Barbarossa. I had actually heard that Harun was with him. So I made straight for Tlemcen, then followed the coast road towards the east, avoiding the cities held by the Castilians, such as Oran or Mars al-Kabir, stopping in places where I could meet Granadans, at Algiers for example, and particularly at Cherchell, where the population consisted almost entirely of refugees from Andalus.

Barbarossa had taken as his base the little port town of Jijil, which he had wrested from the Genoese the previous year. However, before reaching there, I heard that he was besieging the Castilian garrison at Bougie. As this town lay on my way, I decided to go there, leaving my family several miles away in the charge of the imam of a small village mosque, promising myself to come back and collect them after having inspected the battlefield.

It was at Bougie that I met Barbarossa, as I have written in my *Description of Africa*. He did indeed have a very red beard, of its own natural colour but also reddened with henna, because the man was past fifty but looked older and seemed only to be kept standing upright by the lust for conquest. He limped badly, and his left arm was made of silver. He had lost his arm at Bougie itself, in the course of a previous siege which had ended in disaster. This time the battle seemed better joined. He had already occupied the old citadel of the town and was undertaking the investment of another fortress near the beach where the Castilians were continuing to resist.

The day of my arrival there was some respite in the battle. Guards were standing in front of the commander's tent, one of whom came originally from Malaga. It was he who ran to call Harun, with a deference which made me realize that the Ferret was a lieutenant of Barbarossa. In fact he arrived accompanied by two Turks, whom he dismissed with a confident gesture before throwing himself upon me. We stayed joined together for a long moment, exchanging vigorous slaps which conveyed all our friendship, our surprise and the sadness of estrangement. Harun first made me enter the tent and presented me to 'Aruj as a poet and diplomat of renown, for which I only understood the reason later. The corsair spoke like a king, in short and measured sentences whose apparent meaning was trite but whose hidden meaning was difficult to define. Thus he recalled the victories of Salim the Ottoman and the increasing arrogance of the Castilians, remarking sadly that it was in the East that the sun of Islam was rising while it was setting in the West.

When we had taken our leave, Harun brought me to his own tent, less imposing and less embellished, but which could nevertheless accommodate about ten people and was very well supplied with fruit and drinks. It was not necessary for me to ask any questions for the Ferret to begin to answer them.

'I have killed only murderers, I have robbed only thieves. I have not ceased to fear God for a moment. I have ceased only to fear the rich and the powerful. Here I am fighting the unbelievers to whom our princes are paying court, I defend the towns which they abandon. My companions in arms are the exiles, outlaws and lawbreakers from all lands. But does not ambergris issue forth from the entrails of the sperm whale?'

He had poured out these words one after the other, as if he was reciting the *Fatiha*. Then, in a very different voice:

'Your sister has been wonderful. A lioness of the Atlas. She is in my house in Jijil, sixty miles from here, with our three sons, the youngest of whom is called Hasan.'

I did not try to conceal my emotion.

'I have never doubted you for a moment.'

Since we were children, I had always given in very quickly in all arguments with the Ferret. But this time I had to explain to him how his actions had affected our family. His face darkened.

'At Fez I was a torture to them. Here, I shall be their protector.'

A week later, we were all at Jijil. The remnants of my family were reunited, ten fugitives under a corsair's roof. However, I remember it as a moment of rare happiness, which I would willingly have prolonged.

The Year of the Grand Turk
922 A.H.
5 February 1516 – 23 January 1517

I, who ran across the world to save Bayazid from the vindictiveness of the Ottomans, found myself, that year, with wife and child in the very heart of Constantinople and in the most extraordinary position possible: bending over the outstretched hand of Salim the Grim, who was favouring me with a protective nod of his head and the suspicion of a smile. It is said that the prey is often attracted by the fangs which are preparing to destroy it. Perhaps that was the explanation of my insane rashness. But, at the time, I did not see it thus. I was content to follow the course of events to the best of my judgement, endeavouring to start my life anew on the little piece of ground from which I did not yet feel banished. But I should explain how this happened.

Barbarossa prospered before my very eyes, and Harun in his shadow. The attack against Bougie eventually failed, but in the first days of the year the corsair had succeeded in taking power at Algiers, having killed the former master of the city by his own hand, while this unfortunate was being massaged in his hammam.

Of course Algiers was not as big a city as Oran or Bougie, and would not have covered a single quarter of Tlemcen, but it had nevertheless the appearance of a city, with its four thousand hearths, its ordered suqs, ranged by trades, its avenues flanked with fine houses, its bath houses, its hostelries and above all its splendid walls, constructed from huge stones, which extended towards the beach in a vast esplanade. Barbarossa had made it his capital, he had assumed a royal title, and he meant to have himself recognized by all the princes of Islam.

For my part, after the reunion at Jijil, I had taken to the road once more. Tired of wandering and frustrated by my experience in Cairo, which had been interrupted too abruptly, I hoped to cast my anchor at Tunis, for several years at least. I began to dress immediately in the fashion of the country, wearing a turban covered with a veil, feeding on *bazin* and sometimes even on *bassis*, even going so far as to inhale an infamous concoction called al-hashish, a mixture of drugs and sugar, which produced drunkenness, gaiety and appetite. It was also a noted aphrodisiac, greatly appreciated by Abu 'Abdullah, the ruler of Tunis.

Thanks to Harun, who had close connections in the city, including the *mizwar*, the commander in chief of the army, I had easily been able to find a house in the suburb of Bab al-Bahr, and I began to make contact with several textile manufacturers with the idea of establishing a small trading business.

But I did not have time. Less than a month after my arrival, Harun came one evening and knocked on my door, accompanied by three other lieutenants of Barbarossa, one of whom was a Turk whom I had greeted at Bougie in the tent of the corsair. The Ferret was as serious as a judge.

'We have a message for you from His Victorious Lordship al-Qa'im bi-'Amr Allah.'

This was the title which Barbarossa had earned for strangling the Amir of Algiers. He asked me to go to Constantinople to take a message to the sultan, announcing the creation of the kingdom of Algiers, showing him obedience and allegiance and beseeching him for his assistance against the Castilians who were still occupying a marine fort at the entrance to the port of Algiers.

'I am most honoured to receive so much confidence. But there are already four of you. What need do you have of me?'

'Sultan Salim will not accept an ambassador who is not a poet and does not address him in verses of praise and thanksgiving.'

'I can write a poem which you can read yourself.'

'No. We are all warriors, while you have already carried out the missions of an ambassador. You have a better appearance, and that is important; our master must appear like a king, not like a corsair.'

I was silent, seeking some pretext to evade such a dangerous task, but Harun badgered me relentlessly. His voice seem to come straight from my own conscience.

'You do not have the right to hesitate. A great Muslim empire is in the process of coming to life in the East, and we in the West should stretch out our hand to it. Until now, we have been subjected to the law of the unbelievers. They have taken Granada and Malaga, then Tangier, Melilla, Oran, Tripoli and Bougie, tomorrow they will seize Tlemcen, Algiers, Tunis. To confront them we need the Grand Turk. We are asking you to assist us in this task and you cannot refuse. No business that you may have here can be more important. And your family is secure. Moreover, your expenses will be paid in full and you will be generously recompensed.'

He did not forget to add, with a pirate's smile on the corner of his lips:

'Of course, neither I nor my companions would dare to tell Barbarossa that you have refused.'

I had as much room for manoeuvre as a fledgling being pursued by a falcon. Being unable to reveal the real reason for my hesitation without betraying Nur's secret, I could not put up an argument.

'When must we embark?'

'This very night. The fleet is awaiting us at La Goulette. We have made a detour to fetch you.'

As if expressing the last wish of a condemned man I asked to speak to Nur.

Her reaction was wonderful, not that of the wife of a bourgeois which she had become by our marriage, but that of a soldier's daughter which she had always been. And of the mother of the sultan which she hoped to become. She was standing in our bedroom, her face and hair uncovered, her head high, her expression direct.

'You must go there?'

It was halfway between a question and a statement.

'Yes,' I said simply.

'Do you think it may be a trap?'

'Not at all. I would put my head on the block for it!'

'That's exactly what must be avoided. But if you have such great faith in Harun, let us all go there.'

I was not sure that I had understood. She explained to me in a determined voice:

'Bayazid's eyes must be able to gaze upon his city and his palace. Perhaps he will have no other opportunity while he is young. The sea voyage has its dangers, certainly, but my son should get used to them. It is up to God to preserve him or let him perish.'

She was so sure of herself that I did not dare to discuss her reasons, preferring to prevaricate:

'Harun will never accept that I should bring my wife and child.'

'If you comply with his request he cannot refuse you yours. Talk to him, you know how to find the words.'

At dawn we had already passed Gammarth. With the assistance of my sea-sickness I had the impression of drifting in the middle of a nightmare.

★ ★ ★

A strange city, Constantinople. So weighed down with history, but at the same time so new, both in its stones and in its people. In less than seventy years of Turkish occupation its face had completely changed. Of course Santa Sophia is still there, the cathedral turned mosque, where the sultan goes in procession each Friday. But most of the buildings have been put up by the new conquerors, and others spring up each day, palaces, mosques and *madrasas*, or even simple wooden huts into which thousands of Turks are coming to cram themselves, newly arrived from the steppes where they used live as nomads.

In spite of this exodus, the conquerors remain in their capital a minority among others, not in any way more affluent, except for the ruling family. In the most splendid villas, in the best-stocked shops in the bazaar are seen mostly Armenians, Greeks, Italians and Jews, some of the latter having come from Andalus after the fall of Granada. There are not less than forty thousand of them and they are united in their praise for the equity of the Grand Turk. In the suqs, the turbans of the Turks and the skull caps of the Christians and Jews mingle without hatred or resentment. With only a few exceptions, the streets of the city are narrow and muddy, so that people of rank can only move about if they are carried on men's backs. Thousands of people follow this dreadful employment, for the most part new arrivals who have not yet found any better occupation.

The day that we disembarked we were all too tired to go out of the harbour area. The voyage had taken place at a bad time of year, since we had to reach Constantinople before the sultan left the city on his spring campaign. So we spent the first night in a hostelry run by a Greek from Candia, a distant cousin of Barbarossa. The next morning we presented ourselves at the seraglio, the sultan's residence. Nur remained outside the portcullis, talking in low tones into Bayazid's ear, quite indifferent to his age, his occasional groans and his untimely laughter. I suspect her of having studiously narrated to him on that day the entire bloody and glorious history of his dynasty until his birth two years earlier.

As for me, I was a few steps away on the other side of the Sublime Porte, dressed in a long silk gown studded with gold, my eyes reading and re-reading the poem which I was to recite before the sultan, which I had had to compose at sea, between two fits of dizziness. Around me were thousands of soldiers and civil servants, but also citizens of all ranks, all silent out of respect for the person of the sultan. I waited for over two hours, sure that I would be asked to come back later.

This was to underestimate the importance of Barbarossa and the interest which the Ottoman was taking in him. A page soon came to fetch me, with Harun and his companions, to make us go through the Middle Gate towards the courtyard of the *diwan*, a broad park with flowers in bloom, where I could see ostriches running. In front of me, a few steps away, I saw a row of sipahis, motionless on their harnessed horses. When, all of a sudden, my eyes misted over, my ears began to buzz, and my throat tightened so sharply that I felt myself unable to utter the slightest word. Was it fear? Was it the fatigue of the journey? Or simply the closeness of the sultan? Passing by the row, I could see only sparkling lights. I tried to maintain a normal pace, imitating the page who was going before me, but I felt I was about to trip over, to collapse; I feared above all that I might find myself struck dumb at the feet of Salim the Grim.

He was there, seated in front of me, a pyramid of silk on cushions of brocade, a vision expected but nevertheless sudden, with a cold look which dispersed the fog from my eyes without calming my fear. I was no more than an automaton, but an automaton which was functioning with precise movements which seemed to be dictated by the impassive sultan. Then my poem burst forth from my memory, without eloquence but without faltering, accompanied during the last verses by a few hesitant movements which cost me effort and sweat. The sultan nodded his head, sometimes exchanging a brief word with his courtiers. He had no beard but a bushy moustache which he fingered endlessly; his complexion seemed ashen, his eyes too large for his face and slanting slightly. On his turban, which he wore small and tightly wound, was a ruby encrusted in a golden flower. At his right ear hung a pearl in the shape of a pear.

My poem finished, I leaned over the noble hand, which I kissed. Salim was wearing a silver ring on his finger, rather roughly made, the gift, I was told, of his astrologer. As I stood up again a page dressed me in a long gown of camel's hair and then asked me to follow him. The interview was over. The discussion could now take place, in another room, with the counsellors. I hardly took part. My role was to represent, not to negotiate, especially as the conversations, which began in Arabic, continued in Turkish, a language which I knew imperfectly before my stay in Rome.

However, I was able to obtain a piece of information of very great importance, thanks to a mistake on the part of one of the counsellors. 'Nothing is worse for a man than he should make a slip of the tongue' the Caliph 'Ali used to say, may God honour his face! But the tongue of this dignitary was slipping incessantly. So that when the citadel of Algiers, occupied by the unbelievers, was being discussed, this man kept talking about the 'citadel of Cairo', even going so far as to talk about the Circassians instead of the Castilians, until another counsellor, although very much younger, gave him such a furious look that the other turned pale, feeling his head shaking on his shoulders. It was indeed this look and this turning pale more than the slips of the tongue which made me realize that something of extreme gravity had been revealed. In fact, Sultan Salim wanted it believed that his war preparations that year were directed towards the Sophy of Persia; he had even invited the master of Cairo to join together with him in the struggle against the heretics. But in fact it was against the Mameluke Empire that the Ottoman had decided to march.

As soon as the meeting ended, I hastened to discuss its purport with Nur, which was far worse than a slip of the tongue on my part. As I should have foreseen, my Circassian became inflamed with passion, not in her outward aspect but in her heart. She definitely wanted to warn the brothers of her race of the danger which was threatening them.

'Sultan Qansuh is a sick, vacillating old man, who will go on listening complacently to Salim's promises of friendship right up to the moment when the Ottoman sabre cuts his throat and those of all the Circassians as well. He was probably a valiant soldier in his youth, but at the moment the only thing that concerns him is his eyelids and to extort gold from his subjects. He must be warned of the intentions of Constantinople; only we can do it, since we are the only ones aware of them.'

'Do you know what you are suggesting to me? To do the job of a spy, to come out of Salim's antechamber to go and tell Qansuh what has been said there. Do you know that the words that have passed between us, you and me, here in this room, would be sufficient to have our heads cut off?'

'Don't try to frighten me! I am alone with you and I am speaking in a low voice.'

'I left Egypt for your sake and now you are asking me to go back there!'

'We had to leave to save Bayazid; today we must return to save my brothers, as well as the future of my son. All the Circassians will be massacred, Sultan Salim is going to catch them unawares, take possession of their lands, and build an empire so powerful and so extensive that my son will never be able to covet it. If anything can be attempted, I must do it, at whatever danger to my life. We can go to Galata and take the first boat for Alexandria. After all, the two empires are not yet at war, they are even supposed to be allies.'

'And if I say no to you?'

'Say to me "No, you are not to try to save the people of your race from massacre", "No, you are not to fight so that your son will one day be the master of Constantinople", and I shall obey. But I will have lost the taste for living and loving.'

I said nothing. She went further:

'What substance are you made of that you accept the loss of one town after another, one homeland after another, one woman after another, without ever fighting, without ever regretting, without ever looking back?'

'Between the Andalus which I left and the Paradise which is promised to me life is only a crossing. I go nowhere, I desire nothing, I cling to nothing, I have faith in my passion for living, in my instinct to search for happiness, as well as in Providence. Isn't it that which united us? Without hesitating, I left a town, a house, a way of life, to follow your path, to indulge your relentless obsession.'

'And why have you stopped following me now?'

'I am weary of obsessions. Of course I shall not abandon you here, surrounded by enemies. I shall bring you back to your own people so that you may be able to warn them, but there our ways will part.'

I was not sure that I had struck a good bargain, nor that I would have the courage to stick to it. At least I believed that for myself I had set the limits of the venture I had let myself be dragged into. As for Nur, she seemed the picture of radiance. My reservations were of small concern, as long as they did not stand across her way. From my very detailed words she heard only the 'Yes' which I had not even uttered. And already, without waiting, while I was weaving the lie in my head which I would serve up to Harun in order to give him the slip, she began to speak of boats, quays and luggage.

★　★　★

When, on my return to the land of the Nile, the customs official at the port of Alexandria asked me, between two searches, whether it was true that the Ottomans were preparing to invade Syria and Egypt, I replied with an oath against all the women in the world, blonde Circassians in particular, which my questioner approved with gusto, as if that was the obvious explanation of the misfortunes to come.

Throughout the journey to Cairo, Nur had to put up with reproach and sarcasm. But after our third day in the capital I had to admit that she had not been entirely wrong to undertake her dangerous initiative. The rumours which were going around were so contradictory that the most utter confusion reigned in men's minds, not just among the common people but also at the Citadel. The sultan had decided to leave for Syria, to engage with the Ottoman troops, and then, having had reassuring news, he had cancelled his expedition. Those regiments who had received the order to set off were now told to return to their barracks. The caliph and the four grand qadis were asked, twice, to prepare to accompany the sovereign to Aleppo; twice, their processions had taken the road to the Citadel in expectation of a grand departure; twice they had been told that they should go back to their homes.

To add to the turmoil, an Ottoman plenipotentiary had arrived with great pomp to renew promises of peace and friendship, proposing, once again, an alliance against the heretics and the unbelievers. This waiting and uncertainty blunted the combative edge of the army, which is probably what the Grand Turk intended. So it was important that testimony from Constantinople should open the eyes of those in authority. It was even more important that it should be conveyed in a manner which would inspire confidence without revealing the source of the information.

Nur had the idea of writing a letter and leaving it secretly at the house of the secretary of state, Tumanbay, the second most influential person after the sultan and the most popular of the rulers of Egypt. She believed that a message from a Circassian woman would be forwarded immediately to the great Mameluke.

That very night, someone knocked at my door. Tumanbay had come alone, an extraordinary thing in this town where the merest commander of ten men would never think of moving without a numerous and noisy escort. He was a man of about forty, tall, elegant, with a clear complexion, a long moustache in the Circassian style, and a short and carefully trimmed beard. At my first words of welcome his face darkened. My accent had worried him, as the Maghribi community in Cairo was well known for its sympathy towards the Ottomans. I hastened to call Nur to my side. She appeared with her face uncovered. Tumanbay recognized her. A sister of his race and the widow of an opponent of Salim, she could not but inspire the fullest confidence.

So the secretary of state sat down without ceremony to listen to my story. I repeated to him what I had heard, without adding a flourish or omitting a detail. When I had finished, he began by reassuring me:

'It is not a matter of having a testimony that I can produce. The important thing is the inner conviction of those in authority. My mind is made up, and after what I have just heard I will struggle even more vigorously so that the sultan will share my opinion.'

He seemed to be thinking intently. A wry expression hovered over his lips. Then he said, as if continuing a private conversation:

'But with a sultan, nothing is ever simple. If I press him too much, he will say to himself that I am trying to get him away from Cairo, and he will no longer want to leave.'

His confidence made me bolder:

'Why shouldn't you leave with the army yourself? Aren't you thirty years younger than he is?'

'If I won a victory, he would fear my return at the head of the army.'

Letting his eyes wander round him, the secretary of state noticed the icon and the Coptic cross on the wall. He smiled and scratched his head in a conspicuous fashion. He had good reasons to be puzzled: a Maghribi, dressed in the Egyptian style, married to a Circassian woman, the widow of an Ottoman amir, and who decorated his house like a Christian! I was about to explain to him how the house had come to me, but he interrupted:

'The sight of these objects does not offend me. It is true that I am a Muslim by the grace of God, but I was born a Christian and baptized, like the sultan, like all the Mamelukes.'

With these words he jumped to his feet and took his leave, repeating his thanks.

Seated in a dark corner of the room, Nur had not taken part in the conversation. But she seemed satisfied with it.

'For this meeting alone I do not regret having come so far.'

Events seemed to prove her right quickly enough. We learned that the sultan had finally decided to leave. His battalion was seen leaving the hippodrome, crossing Rumaila Square before going up the Hill of the Oxen and Saliba Street, where I had gone that day in expectation of a spectacle. As the sultan moved forward, greeted with cheers, a few paces away from me, I noticed that the openwork golden bird, the emblem of the Mamelukes, on the top of his parasol, had been replaced by a golden crescent; it was murmured around me that the change had been ordered as the result of a letter from the Ottoman casting doubt on Qansuh's religious ardour.

At the head of the interminable procession of the sultan were fifteen lines of camels, harnessed with bobbles in gold brocade, fifteen others harnessed with bobbles in many-coloured velvet. The cavalry came next, with two hundred chargers at its head, covered with steel caparisons encrusted with gold. Further away one could see palanquins on mules decked out with yellow silk coverings, to carry the royal family.

The previous evening, Tumanbay had been appointed lieutenant-general of Egypt, with full powers; but it was rumoured that the sultan had taken all the gold in the treasury with him, several million dinars, as well as precious objects from the royal warehouses.

I had asked Nur to come with me to be present at the event which she had worked for. She begged me to go alone, saying that she felt unwell. I thought that she did not wish to show herself too much in public; I soon discovered that she was pregnant. I did not dare to rejoice too much, because although, at the approach of my thirtieth year, I ardently desired a son of my blood, I realized that Nur's condition would henceforth prevent me from leaving her, and even from fleeing from Cairo with her, which prudence was commanding me to do.

Three months passed, during which we received regular news of the sovereign's progress: Gaza, Tiberias, then Damascus, where an incident was reported. The master of the mint, a Jew named Sadaqa, had thrown some newly-minted silver pieces at the sultan's feet at the time of his triumphal entry into the city, as was the custom. Qansuh's guards had rushed forward to pick up the coins, in such a way that the sultan, severely jostled, had almost fallen off his horse.

It was known that after Damascus the sultan went to Hama and then Aleppo. Then there was silence. For three weeks. A silence which at the beginning was not interrupted by the slightest rumour. It was only on Saturday, the sixteenth of Sha'ban, 14 September 1517, that a messenger arrived at the Citadel, out of breath and covered with dust; a battle had taken place at Marj Dabiq, not far from Aleppo. The sultan had taken part in it, wearing his little hat, dressed in his white cloak, with his axe on his shoulder, with the caliph, the qadis and the forty bearers of the Qur'an around him. In the beginning, the army of Egypt had had the upper hand, taking seven flags from the enemy and some large artillery pieces mounted on carriages. But the sultan had been betrayed, particularly by Khairbak, the governor of Aleppo, who was in league with the Ottomans. While he was commanding the left flank, he had turned back, which immediately spread discouragement throughout the whole army. Realizing what was happening, Qansuh suffered a stroke. Falling from his horse, he died at once. In the confusion, his body had not even been recovered.

The inhabitants of Cairo were appalled, the more so as other rumours soon followed one another about the advance of the Ottomans, who followed the route of the Egyptian army in reverse. Thus Aleppo had fallen into their hands, then Hama. At Khan al-Khalili, several shops belonging to Turks from Asia Minor or to Maghribis were looted, but order was energetically restored by Tumanbay who announced the abolition of all taxes and reduced the prices of all essential goods in order to alleviate the effect of this news.

Although the secretary of state had the situation in hand, he waited a month before having himself proclaimed sultan. That very day, Damascus had just fallen in its turn into Salim's hands; Gaza would soon follow it. Lacking sufficient soldiers, Tumanbay ordered the setting up of popular militias for the defence of the capital. He emptied the prisons and announced that the crimes of all those who enlisted would be pardoned, including homicides. In the last days of the year, when the Ottoman army was approaching Cairo, the Mameluke sultan drew up his troops in Raydaniyya camp, to the east of the city. He also brought several elephants and some newly-cast cannons, and had a long deep trench dug, in the hope of sustaining a long siege.

However, this was not the Ottoman's intention. After having given his army two days to rest after the long crossing of Sinai, Salim ordered a general assault, with such a profusion of cannons and such an overwhelming numerical advantage that the Egyptian army scattered in a few hours.

It was thus that on the very last day of the year the Grand Turk made his solemn entry into Cairo, preceded by criers who promised the inhabitants that their lives would be spared, calling on them to resume their normal lives the next day. It was a Friday, and the caliph, who had been captured in Syria and brought back in the suite of the conqueror, had a sermon pronounced in all the mosques in the capital in the name of 'the sultan son of the sultan, sovereign of the two continents and the two seas, destroyer of the two armies, master of the two Iraqs, servant of the holy sanctuaries, the victorious King Salim Shah.'

Nur's eyes were bloodshot. She was so distressed by the triumph of the Grand Turk that I feared for the life of the child she was carrying. As she was a few days from her time, I had to make her swear to stay still on her bed. As for me, I found consolation in promising myself to leave this country as soon as she recovered. In my street, all the notables had hidden their precious possessions and their flags in their family vaults out of fear of looting.

Nevertheless, that day my orderly and his donkey presented themselves outside my door as usual to take me into the city. The boy told me with some hilarity that on the way he had stumbled over the severed head of a Mameluke officer. As I did not laugh at all, he permitted himself to voice the opinion that I was taking things too seriously. Which earned him a blow from the back of my hand.

'So,' I growled in a fatherly way, 'your city has just been occupied, your country has been invaded, its rulers have either been massacred or have fled, others replace them, coming from the ends of the earth, and you reproach me for taking things too seriously?'

His only reply was a shrug of his shoulders and this phrase of centuries-old resignation:

'Whoever takes my mother becomes my step-father.'

Then he started laughing again.

One man, however, was not at all resigned. It was Tumanbay. He was girding himself to write the most heroic pages in the history of Cairo.

The Year of Tumanbay
923 A.H.
24 January 1517 – 12 January 1518

Master of Cairo, the Grand Turk strutted about as if he was intent on brushing over each holy place, each quarter, each door, each frightened look with his indelible shadow. In front of him, the heralds never wearied of proclaiming that no one should fear for their life or property, while at the same time massacres and looting were taking place, often a few paces from the sultan's retinue.

The Circassians were the first victims. Mamelukes or descendants of Mamelukes, they were hunted down relentlessly. When a high dignitary of the old regime was captured, he was perched upon a donkey, facing backwards, his hair in a blue turban and decked out with little bells which were hung around his neck. Thus accoutred, he was paraded around the streets before being decapitated. His head was then displayed upon a pole, and his body thrown to the dogs. In each camp of the Ottoman army hundreds of these poles were planted in the earth, each alongside the other, macabre forests through which Salim liked to wander.

Of course the Circassians, deceived for a moment by the Ottoman promises, did not take long to get rid of their customary headdresses, skull caps or light turbans, and put on large turbans in order to merge with the rest of the population. In consequence the Ottoman soldiers began to arrest all passers-by indiscriminately, accusing them of being Circassians in disguise and forcing them to pay a ransom to be allowed to go. When the streets were empty the soldiers forced open the doors of houses, and under the pretext of flushing out escaping Mamelukes, gave themselves over to pillage and rape.

The fourth day of that year, Sultan Salim was in the suburb of Bulaq, where his army had set up the largest of its camps. He had attended the executions of several officers and had then ordered that the hundreds of decapitated corpses which were cluttering up the camp should immediately be thrown into the Nile. Then he had gone to the hammam to purify himself before going to the evening prayer at a mosque near the landing stage. By nightfall he had returned to the camp and called several of his aides around him.

The meeting had just begun when an extraordinary tumult broke out; hundreds of camels, laden with burning tow, rushed towards the Ottoman positions setting fire to the tents. It was already dark, and in the ensuing chaos thousands of armed men invaded the camp. Tumanbay was at their head. There were certainly regular troops among his soldiers, but it was mostly the common people, sailors, water carriers, former criminals who had joined the popular militia. Some were armed with daggers, others had only slings, or even clubs. However, with the assistance of nightfall and surprise, they sowed death among the ranks of the Ottomans. In the most intense moment of the battle, Salim himself was surrounded on all sides, and only the determination of his bodyguard enabled him to force his way out. The camp was in the hands of Tumanbay, who, without losing a moment, ordered his partisans to throw themselves into the pursuit of the occupation troops in all the quarters of Cairo, and to take no prisoner.

Street by street the capital was reconquered. The Circassians set about chasing the Ottoman soldiers, with the active assistance of the population. The victims, now turned executioners, were merciless. I saw with my own eyes, not far from my house, the execution of seven Turks who had fled into a mosque. Chased by twenty Cairenes, they had taken refuge at the top of the minaret, and had begun to fire shots on the crowd. But they were caught, their throats cut and their bloody bodies thrown from the top of the building.

The battle had begun on Tuesday evening. On Thursday Tumanbay went to set himself up in the Shaikhu Mosque in Saliba Street, which he turned into his headquarters. He seemed so much in control of the city that the next day the Friday sermon was once more pronounced in his name from the tops of the pulpits.

But his position was no less precarious. Once they had got over the surprise of the initial attack, the Ottomans had rallied. They had retaken Bulaq, infiltrated into old Cairo as far as the area around my street, and, in their turn gradually recaptured the lost ground step by step. Tumanbay mostly controlled the popular quarters of the centre, to which he had prevented access by hastily-dug trenches or barricades.

Of all the days which Allah has created, it was on that Friday and no other that Nur chose to feel the pains of confinement. I had to creep out and edge my way across my garden to call the neighbourhood midwife, who only agreed to come at the end of an hour's entreaty, and then for gold: two dinars if it was a girl, four dinars if it was a boy.

When she saw the fragile pink cleft between the baby's swollen thighs, she called out to me in a vexed tone:

'Two dinars!'

To which I replied:

'If everything ends well, you'll get four all the same!'

Overjoyed at such generosity, she promised to return several days later to perform the excision, which she would do for nothing. I asked her not to do so, explaining that this practice did not exist in my country, at which she seemed surprised and upset.

To me my daughter seemed as beautiful as her mother, and as pale-skinned. I called her Hayat, Life, for whom my dearest wish, as for all my family, was simply to be able to escape alive from the murderous orgy of Cairo, where two empires confronted one another, the one intoxicated by its triumph, the other determined not to die.

In the streets the battle was still raging. The Ottomans, who had regained control of most of the suburbs, tried to push towards the centre, but they only advanced slowly and sustained heavy losses. However, the outcome of the battle was no longer in doubt. Soldiers and militiamen gradually deserted Tumanbay's camp, while at the head of a handful of faithful followers, some black fusiliers and the Circassians of his personal bodyguard, the Mameluke sultan struggled on through another day. On the Saturday night he decided to leave the city, although without having lost any of his determination. He said that he would soon return with more troops to flush out the invaders.

How can I describe what the Ottomans did when they were able to enter the quarters of Cairo once more? This time it was no longer a question of eliminating the Circassian troops who had opposed them as it had been after their first victory. They now had to punish the entire population of Cairo. The soldiers of the Grand Turk poured into the streets with orders to kill anything that breathed. No one could leave the accursed city, since all the roads were cut; no one could find themselves a refuge, since the cemeteries and the mosques were themselves turned into battlefields. People were forced to crouch in their own homes, hoping that the hurricane would pass. On that day, between dawn and the last quarter of the night, it is said that more than eight thousand were slain. The streets were all covered with corpses, men, women, children, horses and donkeys, mingled together in an endless bloody procession.

The next day, Salim had two flags hauled up outside his camp, one white, the other red, signifying to his men that vengeance had henceforth been taken and that the carnage should stop. It was high time, because if the reprisals had continued for several days with the same intensity, the Grand Turk's only conquest in this country would have been an enormous charnel-house.

Throughout these bloody days, Nur had not stopped praying for victory for Tumanbay. My own sentiments were scarcely different. Having welcomed the Mameluke sultan under my roof one evening, I admired his bravery even more. Above all, there was Bayazid. Sooner or later, a suspicion, a denunciation, an indiscretion, would hand him over to the Ottomans, with all his family. For the security of the outlawed child, and for our own, Tumanbay had to be victorious. When I realized, in the course of the Sunday, that he had definitely lost the fight, I flared up against him, from suppressed disappointment, fear and rage, declaring that he should never have thrown himself into such a hazardous enterprise, dragging the population in his wake and bringing down the wrath of Salim upon them.

Although she was still very weak, Nur sat up with a start, as if she had been awoken by a bad dream. Only her eyes could be seen in her pallid face, staring at nothing.

'Remember the pyramids! How many men have died to build them, men who could have passed many more years working, eating and mating! Then they would have died of the plague, leaving no trace behind them. By the will of Pharaoh they have built a monument whose silhouette will perpetuate the memory of their labour for ever, their suffering, their noblest aspirations. Tumanbay has done no different. Are not four days of courage, four days of dignity, of defiance, worth more than four centuries of submission, of resignation and meanness? Tumanbay has offered to Cairo and to its people the finest gift that exists: a sacred flame that will illuminate and kindle the spirit in the long night that is beginning.'

Nur's words left me only half-convinced, but I did not try to contradict her. I simply put my arms around her gently to put her back to bed. She was speaking the language of her people; I had no other ambition than to survive, with my family, no other ambition than to go away, in order one day to relate on a piece of glazed paper the fall of Cairo, of her empire, of her last hero.

★   ★   ★

I could not leave the city for several weeks, until Nur was in a position to travel. In the meantime, life in Cairo became increasingly difficult. Provisions became rare. Cheese, butter and fruit could not be found, and the price of cereals rose. It was said that Tumanbay had decided to starve out the Ottoman garrison by preventing the provisioning of the city from the provinces which he still controlled; in addition, he had made agreements with the nomad Arab tribes, who had never submitted to any authority in Egypt, that they should come and lay waste the surroundings of the capital. It was said at the same time that Tumanbay had brought the materials of war, arrows, bows and powder from Alexandria, that he had assembled fresh troops and was preparing to launch a new offensive. In fact clashes multiplied, particularly around Giza, making impassable the road to the pyramids which we needed to take to fetch Bayazid.

Should we, in spite of everything, try to flee, at the risk of being intercepted by an Ottoman patrol, by Mameluke deserters or some band of looters? I hesitated to do so until I learned that Sultan Salim had decided to deport several thousand inhabitants to Constantinople. At first it was the caliph, the Mameluke dignitaries and their families, but the list continued to lengthen: masons, carpenters, monumental masons, pavers, blacksmiths, and all kinds of skilled workers. I soon learned that the Ottoman civil servants were drawing up lists of the names of all Maghribis and Jews in the city with a view to deporting them.

My decision was taken. Promising myself to leave within three days, I was making a last trip to the city to settle various matters when a rumour reached me: Tumanbay had been captured, betrayed by the chief of a bedouin tribe.

Around midday cries rang out, mingling with the calls to prayer. A word was uttered near me, Bab Zuwaila. It was towards that gate that thousands of citizens were hurrying, men and women, old and young. I did likewise. There was a crowd there, continually increasing in size, and the more impressive because it was almost silent. Suddenly it parted to allow an Ottoman column to pass through, of a hundred or so cavalrymen and twice as many infantrymen. With backs to the crowd, they formed three concentric circles, with a man on horseback in the middle. It was not easy to recognize Tumanbay from this silhouette. His head bare and his beard shaggy, he was dressed only in scraps of red cloth ill concealed by a white cloak. On his feet he had only a bulky wrapping of blue material.

At the command of an Ottoman officer, the deposed emperor dismounted. Someone untied his hands, but twelve soldiers surrounded him immediately, sabres at the ready. However, he was clearly not considering flight. He waved with his free hands to the crowd, which cheered him bravely. All eyes, including his own, then turned towards the famous gate where a hangman was in the process of fixing a rope.

Tumanbay appeared surprised, but the smile did not leave his lips. Only his gaze lost its sharpness. His only cry to the crowd was:

'Recite the *Fatiha* three times for me!'

Thousands of murmurs could be heard, a rumbling which became more vibrant each moment.

'Praise be to God, Lord of the Universe, the Compassionate, the Merciful, Master of the Day of Judgement . . .'

The last *Amin* was a long drawn out cry, furious, rebellious. Then nothing more, silence. The Ottomans themselves seemed taken aback, and it was Tumanbay who shook them:

'Hangman, do your job!'

The rope was tied round the condemned man's neck. Someone pulled at the other end. The sultan rose a foot, then fell back to the ground. The rope had broken. The rope was tied once more, pulled again by the hangman and his assistants, and broke once more. The tension became unbearable. Only Tumanbay maintained his amused manner, as if he felt himself elsewhere already, in a world where courage receives quite a different reward. The hangman tied the rope for the third time. It did not break. A clamour broke out, sobbing, moaning and prayers. The last Emperor of Egypt had expired, the bravest man ever to have governed the valley of the Nile, hung at the Zuwaila gate like a vulgar horse thief.

★ ★ ★

All night, the vision of the condemned man remained fixed before my eyes. But in the morning, emboldened by bitterness and insomnia and insensitive to danger, I took the road to the pyramids.

Without being aware of it, I had chosen the best moment to escape; the Ottomans, put at ease by the execution of their enemy, had relaxed their vigilance, while the associates of Tumanbay, stunned by their defeat, had taken flight. Of course, we had to stop five or six times to answer various suspicious questions. But we were neither molested nor robbed, and night found us lying peacefully once more at Khadra's house, in the cottage of our first loves.

There, several months of simple and unexpected happiness passed by. Too small and too poor to attract covetous eyes, the nurse's village existed cut off from wars and disturbances. But this quiet existence could only serve for me as a shady oasis between two long stages. Noises from afar were calling me, and it was written that I should not remain deaf to their temptations.

The Year of the Abduction
924 A.H.
13 January 1518 – 2 January 1519

I emerged with no certainties from my long rural retreat, studded with contemplations and silent walks. All cities were perishable; all empires devouring, Providence unfathomable. The only things which comforted me were the Nile flood, the movement of the stars, and the seasonal births of the buffaloes.

When the hour to leave arrived, it was towards Mecca that I turned my face. A pilgrimage was a necessity for my life. As Nur was apprehensive about the journey with two children, one aged one year and the other four, I asked Khadra to come with us, which gave her great joy, swearing that she awaited no other reward than the privilege of expiring in the Holy Places. A sailing ship took us from the African shore of the river, half a day from Giza, towards the south. It belonged to a rich manufacturer of sesame oil, who was taking his merchandise to Upper Egypt, stopping a day or two in every town of any importance. Thus we visited Bani Suwaif, al-Minya, then Manfalut, where an old man joined us. That same night, taking advantage of the silence and the fact that the children were asleep, I was beginning to write, by the light of a candle, when this new passenger called out to me:

'Hey, you! Go and wake one of the sailors! I can see a big piece of wood in the water which will be very useful for cooking tomorrow!'

I did not like his janissary tone, nor his hoarse voice, nor his suggestion in the middle of the night. However, out of consideration for his age I replied to him without any disrespect:

'It's midnight, it would be better not wake anyone. But I can probably help you myself.'

I put my pen down reluctantly, and went a few steps towards him. But he called out touchily:

'I don't need anyone. I'll manage fine on my own!'

He was leaning overboard, holding a rope in his hand with which he was trying to catch the floating plank, when suddenly a long tail shot up from the water, coiled around him and threw him into the Nile. I began to shout, rousing passengers and crewmen savagely from their sleep. The sail was struck in order to stop the craft, which was moored for a whole hour on the bank, while the brave sailors threw themselves into the water. But to no avail. Everyone agreed that the unfortunate man had been eaten by a crocodile.

Throughout the rest of the voyage I heard the most extraordinary tales about these enormous lizards which terrorize Upper Egypt. It seems that at the time of the pharaohs, then of the Romans, and even at the beginning of the Muslim conquest, the crocodiles did relatively little damage. But in the third century of the *hijra* a most strange event occurred. In a cave near Manfalut a life-size statue cast in lead representing one of these animals was found, covered with pharaonic inscriptions. Thinking that it was some sort of ungodly idol, the governor of Egypt at the time, a certain Ibn Tulun, ordered that it should be destroyed. From one day to the next the crocodiles unleashed their fury, attacking men with hatred and sowing terror and death. It was then understood that the statue had been put up under certain astrological conjunctions in order to tame these animals. Most fortunately, the curse was confined to Upper Egypt; below Cairo, the crocodiles never eat human flesh, probably because the statue which inhibits them has never been found again.

After Manfalut we passed by Assyut, but did not stop there, because of a further epidemic of plague that had been reported there. Our next port of call was al-Munshiya, where I visited the Berber ruler who governed it. Next was al-Khiam, a little town whose population was entirely Christian, with the exception of the chief of police. Two days later we were at Qina, a large market town surrounded by a wall of mud brick from which the heads of three hundred crocodiles were hanging triumphantly. It was there that we took the land route to go to the port of al-Qusayr, on the Red Sea, equipped with full goatskins for the journey, because there is not a single watering place between the Nile and the Red Sea. We did not take more than a week to reach Yanbu', the port of Arabia Deserta,

where we berthed at the appearance of the crescent moon of Rabi'
al-Thani, when the annual pilgrimage season was almost reaching its
end. Six days later, we were in Jidda.

In this harbour, which prosperity has passed by, there are few
things worth visiting. Most of the houses are wooden huts, apart
from two old mosques and a few hostelries. A modest dome should
also be mentioned, where it is claimed that Our Lady Eve, mother of
mankind, had spent some nights. That year, the town was
administered for the time being by an Ottoman admiral, who had got
rid of the former governor, who had remained faithful to the
Mamelukes, by throwing him out of a ship in an area infested with
sharks. The population, who were mostly poor, were expecting the
new government to deal ruthlessly with the unbelievers who were
interfering with trade in the Red Sea.

We stayed only two days at Jidda, time to make contact with a
caravan leaving for Mecca. Halfway between the two cities I took off
my clothes to put on the *ihram* of the penitents, two long seamless
strips of white material, one worn round the waist, the other round
the shoulders. My lips repeated tirelessly the cry of the pilgrims:
'*Labbaika, Allahuma! Labbaika, Allahuma!*, Here am I, Lord!' My
eyes searched for Mecca on the horizon, but it was not until the end
of another day's journey that I saw the holy city, and then only when
I arrived before its walls. The town where the Prophet was born,
peace and blessing be upon him! is situated at the bottom of a valley
surrounded by mountains which protect it from prying eyes.

I entered the city through Bab al-'Umrah, the busiest of its three
gates. The streets seemed very narrow, and the houses clinging to
one another, but better constructed and richer than those of Jidda.
The suqs were full of fresh fruit, in spite of the aridity of the
environment.

With every step I took I felt myself transported into a world of
dreams; this city, built on this sterile soil, seemed never to have had
any destiny other than contemplation; at the centre, the Noble
Mosque, the House of Abraham; and at the heart of the mosque, the
Ka'ba, an imposing building which I longed to walk round until I
became exhausted, each of whose corners bears a name: the Corner
of Iraq, the Corner of Syria, the Corner of Yemen, the Black Corner,
the most venerated, facing eastwards. It is there that the Black Stone
is embedded. I had been told that in touching it I was touching the
right hand of the Creator. Usually, so many people were pressing

themselves against it that it was impossible to contemplate it for any length of time. But as the great waves of pilgrims had passed I could approach the Stone at leisure, covering it with tears and kisses.

When it was time for me to let Nur, who was following me at a distance, take my place, I went off to drink the blessed water of Zamzam under a vault near the Ka'ba. Then, noticing that the door of the Ka'ba had just been opened for some distinguished visitor, I hastened to go inside, long enough for a prayer. It was paved in white marble streaked with red and blue, with black silk hangings covering the whole length of the walls.

The next day I went back to the same places, and repeated the same rituals with fervour, and then sat down for hours, leaning against the wall of the mosque, oblivious to what was going on around me. I was not trying to think about anything in particular. My spirit was simply open to the spirit of God as a flower to the morning dew, and I felt such well-being that all words, all gestures, all looks became futile. I rose to go with regret at the close of each day and returned with joy each morning.

Often, in the course of my meditation, verses of the Qur'an came back into my memory, particularly those of the *sura* of the Cow, which evoke the Ka'ba at length: 'We have established the Holy House to be a retreat and a place of security for mankind, and we have said: "Take the station of Abraham for a place of prayer." ' My lips were murmuring the words of the Most High, as at the time of the Great Recitation, without stammering or distortion. 'Say: We believe in God and in that which has been sent down to us from Heaven, to Abraham and Ismail, to Isaac, to Jacob, to the twelve tribes, to the Books which have been given to Moses and to Jesus, to the Books delivered to the prophets from their Lord; we make no distinction between them, and we are Muslims, resigned to the will of God.'

★ ★ ★

We left Mecca after a month, which passed by more quickly than a night of love. My eyes were still full of silence, and Nur kept the noise of the children from me. We were travelling towards the north, to visit the tomb of the Messenger of God at Medina, before reaching Tabuk, Aqaba and then Gaza, where a merchant from the Sous offered to take us on board his ship, a caravel moored in a creek to the west of the town. I had met this man during the last part of the journey, and we often rode side by side. He was called 'Abbad. He was my age and my height, shared my liking for business and travel, but where I had anxiety he had only frankness. It is true that he had read few books, so he maintained intact a certain ignorance which I had lost too early.

We were already at sea when Nur asked me for the first time: 'Where are we going?'

The answer should have been obvious, as much for her as for me. Did I not have a house in Tunis, where my mother and my eldest daughter were waiting for me? Nevertheless, I remained silent, wearing an enigmatic smile. My Circassian insisted:

'What have you said to your friend?'

'His boat will go right across the Mediterranean before going on down the Atlantic coast after Tangier. We will get off where we please.'

Instead of showing her anxiety, Nur put on a singsong voice:

'Neither in Egypt, nor in Syria, nor in Candia . . .'

I continued, amused by the game:

'Nor in the Kingdom of Fez, nor in Sus . . .'

'Nor at Bursa, nor at Constantinople . . .'

'Nor at Algiers . . .'

'Nor in Circassia . . .'

'Nor in Andalus . . .'

Both of us let out long peals of affected laughter, watching closely out of the corner of our eyes to see which one would be the first to give in to the shameful nostalgia of the exiled. I had to wait ten days before seeing the tears, black with dust and lead ore, which betrayed Nur's deepest fears.

We had put in at Alexandria in order to provision ourselves, and just as we were getting ready to depart an officer of the Ottoman garrison came on board for a last inspection, something which was nothing out of the ordinary in itself. The man probably only nurtured the suspicions which his position required, but he had a way of examining faces which gave each one the sense that he had done wrong, of being on the run, and of having been recognized.

All of a sudden Nur's son struggled free of Khadra, who was holding him, and ran straight towards the soldier.

'Bayazid!' called the nurse.

Hearing this name, the Ottoman leaned towards the child, brought him up to his own height at arm's length and began to turn him round, insistently examining his hair, his hands and his neck.

'What's your name?' he asked.

'Bazid.'

'Son of whom?'

Wretched woman, I told you so, I shouted within myself. On two occasions I had come across Nur in the process of instructing her son that he was Bayazid, son of 'Ala al-Din the Ottoman, and I had reproved her severely, explaining that at his age he could betray himself. Without saying that I was wrong she had replied that the child must know his identity and prepare to shoulder his destiny; she feared she might one day disappear without having revealed his secret to him. But at that moment she was trembling and sweating, and I as well.

'Son of 'Ala al-Din,' replied Bayazid.

At the same time he pointed an uncertain finger towards the place where I was sitting. As he did so I got up and went towards the officer with a wide smile and outstretched hand:

'I am 'Ala al-Din Hasan ibn al-Wazzan, merchant of Fez and native of Granada, may God restore it to us by the sword of the Ottomans!'

Completely intimidated, Bayazid threw himself upon me and buried his face in my shoulder. The officer let go of him, saying to me:

'Fine child! He has the same name as my oldest! I haven't seen him for seven months.'

His moustache rustled. His face was no longer terrifying. He turned round and stepped on to the gangway, signalling to 'Abbad that he could leave.

After we were half a mile from the quay, Nur went back into our cabin to cry all the tears which she had repressed until then.

★   ★   ★

It was at Jerba, a month later, that Nur experienced her second fright. But this time I did not see her weep.

We had stopped for the night, and I was glad to leave the pitching planks for a while and walk with 'Abbad on dry land. And I was also

282

curious to see something of this island whose gentle way of life people had often extolled to me. It had long belonged to the King of Tunis, but at the end of the last century the inhabitants decided to proclaim their independence and to destroy the bridge which linked them to the mainland. They were able to provide for their own needs by exporting oil, wool and raisins, but soon a civil war broke out between the various clans, and mass murders bathed the country in blood. Little by little all authority was lost.

This in no way discouraged 'Abbad from putting in there as often as possible.

'Chaos and joy in life are a good match for one another!' he remarked.

He knew a very pleasant sailors' tavern.

'They serve the biggest fish on the coast, and the best wine.'

I had no intention of stuffing myself, even less of getting drunk on my way back from a pilgrimage. But after the long weeks at sea a little celebration was called for.

We were hardly inside the door and were still looking around for a table corner to sit at, when the end of a sentence made me jump. I listened. A sailor was relating that he had seen the severed head of 'Aruj Barbarossa displayed in a public place in Oran. He had been killed by the Castilians who paraded their macabre trophy from port to port.

When we found ourselves a place, I began to tell 'Abbad my recollections of the corsair, my visit to his camp, and the embassy which I had performed in his name at Constantinople. Suddenly my companion made a sign that I should lower my voice.

'Behind you,' he whispered, 'there are two Sicilian sailors, one young, the other old, who are listening to you with rather too much interest.'

I turned round furtively. The appearance of our neighbours was scarcely reassuring. We changed the subject, and were relieved to see them leave.

An hour later, we left in our turn, gay and satisfied, happy to walk along the beach on the wet sand, under a radiant moon.

We had just passed some fishermen's huts when some suspicious shadows lengthened in front of us. In an instant we found ourselves surrounded by about ten men, armed with swords and daggers, among whom I easily recognized our neighbours at table. One of them spat out some orders in bad Arabic, but I understood that we should neither speak nor move if we did not want to be stabbed. A moment later we were flung to the ground.

The last image that I can remember is that of the fist which crashed down on 'Abbad's neck before my eyes. Then I sank into a long tormented night, stifling, shipwrecked.

Could I have guessed that the most extraordinary of my travels would begin thus?

IV
The Book of Rome

I no longer saw land, nor sea, nor sun, nor the end of the journey. My tongue was salty, my head felt sick, misty and painful. The hold in which I had been thrown smelled of dead rats, mouldy planks and the bodies of the captives who had haunted it before me.

So I was a slave, my son, and my blood felt the shame. I whose ancestors had trodden the soil of Europe as conquerors, would be sold to some prince, some rich merchant from Palermo, Naples or Ragusa, or, even worse, to some Castilian who would make me drink all the humiliation of Granada every minute.

Near me, weighed down by the same chains, the same ball, 'Abbad the Soussi lay upon the dust, like the most wretched of servants. I looked at him, a mirror of my own decline. Yesterday he was still proudly strutting about on the bridge of his caravel, distributing kicks and laughter, and the entire sea was not broad enough for him, nor the swell sufficiently raging.

I sighed noisily. My companion in misfortune, whom I thought was asleep, replied without even opening his eyes:

'*Al-hamdu l'illah! al-hamdu l'illah!* Let us thank God for all his blessings!'

This was hardly the moment for me to blaspheme. So I confined myself to saying:

'Let us give thanks to Him at all times. But what would you like to thank Him for at this very moment?'

'For having spared me from rowing like these unfortunate galley slaves whose moaning breath I can hear. I also give thanks to Him for having left me alive, and in good company. Are these not three excellent reasons for saying *al-hamdu l'illah!*'

He sat up:

'I never ask from God that He should preserve me from calamities; only that He should keep me from despair. Have faith; when the Most High leaves go of you with one hand, He catches hold of you with the other.'

'Abbad spoke the truth, my son, more so than he thought. Had I not left the right hand of God at Mecca? At Rome I was going to live in the hollow of His left hand!

The Year of San Angelo
925 A.H.
3 January 1519 – 22 December 1519

My abductor was a man of renown and of pious fears. Pietro Bovadiglia, a venerable Sicilian pirate, already in his sixties, several times a murderer, and fearing to offer up his soul in a state of plunder, had felt the need to make reparation for his crimes through an offering to God. Or rather through a gift to His representative on that side of the Mediterranean, Leo X, sovereign and pontiff of Rome, commander of Christianity.

The gift for the Pope was myself, presented with ceremony on Sunday 14 February for the feast of St Valentine. I had been forewarned of this the previous evening, and I had stayed with my back leaning against the wall of my cell until dawn, unable to sleep, listening to the ordinary noises of the city, the laughter of a watchman, some object falling into the Tiber, the cries of a newborn baby, disproportionate in the dark silence. Since arriving in Rome I often used to suffer from insomnia, and I eventually came to guess what it was that made the hours so oppressive; far worse than the absence of freedom, or the absence of a woman was the absence of the muezzin. I had never previously lived thus, week after week, in a city where the call to prayer did not rise up, punctuating time, filling space, reassuring men and walls.

I must have been shut up in the castle for a good month. After the dreadful sea journey and countless stops, I had been landed, without 'Abbad, on a quayside in Naples, the most populous of the cities of Italy, and then driven alone to Rome by road. I was only to see my companion three years later, in curious circumstances.

I was still in chains, but, to my great surprise, Bovadiglia thought it well to apologize:

'We are in Spanish territory. If the soldiers were to see a Moor without chains, they would attack him.'

The respectful tone let me hope that from now on I would be less harshly treated, an impression which was confirmed after my arrival at Castel San Angelo, an imposing cylindrical fortress to which I had been brought up by a spiral ramp. I was put into a little room, furnished with a bed, a chair and a wooden trunk, as if it was a modest hostelry rather than a prison, apart from the heavy door, duly padlocked from the outside.

Ten days later, I received a visitor. Seeing the attentiveness with which the guards welcomed him, I understood that he was a close associate of the Pope. He was a Florentine, Master Francesco Guicciardini, governor of Modena and a diplomat in His Holiness' service. I gave my own personal particulars, my names, titles and distinguished achievements, not leaving out any of my missions, however compromising, from Timbuktu to Constantinople. He seemed delighted. We spoke to each other in Castilian, a language which I understood well enough but in which I could only express myself with difficulty. So he made himself speak slowly, and when I apologized politely for the inconvenience which my ignorance involved, he replied with great courtesy:

'I do not myself know Arabic, which is nevertheless spoken all round the Mediterranean. I should also present my excuses.'

Encouraged by his attitude, I uttered several words of vulgar Italian, that is to say Tuscan, as well as I could, at which we both laughed together. After that, I promised him in a tone of friendly defiance:

'Before the end of the year, I shall speak your language. Not as well as you, but sufficiently to make myself understood.'

He acknowledged this by a motion of his head, while I continued:

'However, there are some habits which I shall need time to acquire. Particularly the Europeans' way of addressing the person they are speaking to as "you", as if there were several people, or "she" as if to a woman who is not there. In Arabic we use the familiar you to everyone, prince or servant.'

The diplomat paused, not so much to think, it seemed to me, but rather to invest the words which were going to come with due solemnity. He was sitting on the only chair in the room, dressed in a red bonnet which outlined the shape of his head, giving him the air of a conspirator. I was sitting on the trunk, a pace away from him. He leaned over, pointing a predatory nose in my direction.

'Master Hassan, your coming here is important, supremely important. I cannot say more to you about it, because the secret belongs to the Holy Father, and he alone will be able to reveal it to you when he judges it opportune. But do not think that your adventure is due to pure chance, or to the innocent caprice of a corsair.'

He pondered:

'I am not saying that the good Bovadiglia has crossed the seas in search of you. Not at all. But he knew what sort of Moor should be presented to the Holy Father: a traveller, an educated man. More than this, he has alighted upon a diplomat. We were not hoping for so much.'

Should I have felt flattered to be such a good catch? In any case, I showed neither pleasure nor annoyance. Above all, I was greatly intrigued, and intent on knowing more about it. But Guicciardini was already getting up.

He had scarcely left when an officer of the guard came into my cell to ask me whether I needed anything. Boldly, I asked for clean clothes, a little table, a lamp, and something to write with, which I obtained in the course of the day. That very evening, the character of the meals changed: instead of beans and lentils I had meat and lasagne, with red wine from Trebbiato, which I drank in moderation.

★   ★   ★

The Florentine did not take long to convey to me the news for which I was hoping: the Pope was going to receive me, from the hands of Pietro Bovadiglia. The pirate and the diplomat arrived together in front of the door of my cell on St Valentine's day. The Pope was waiting for us in the castle itself, in the library. Bursting with fervour, Bovadiglia threw himself at his feet; Guicciardini helped him to get up, confining himself to a deferential but brief kiss of the hand. I came towards him in my turn. Leo X was motionless on his armchair, his face clean-shaven, all round and pleasant, his chin pierced with a dimple, his lips thick, particularly his lower lip, his eyes at once reassuring and inquiring, his fingers smooth with the smoothness of one who has never worked with his hands. Behind him, standing up, was a priest who turned out to be an interpreter.

The Pope put the palms of both hands on my bowed back, whether as a sign of affection or of taking possession I do not know, before saying a few words of thanks for the pirate's benefit. I was still kneeling, kept thus deliberately by my new master who only permitted me to get up when the Florentine had led my kidnapper outside. For them, the audience was at an end; for me, it was just beginning. In an Arabic strongly tinged with Castilian turns of phrase, the interpreter conveyed to me:

'A man of art and learning is always welcome among Us, not as a servant but as a protégé. It is true that your arrival in this place has taken place against your will and through means which We cannot approve. But the world is so made that vice is often the arm of virtue, that the best acts are often undertaken for the worst reasons and the worst acts for the best reasons. Thus Our predecessor, Pope Julius, had recourse to a war of conquest in order to endow our Holy Church with a territory where it can feel itself safe. . . .'

He broke off, realizing that he was going to make reference to a debate of whose basic premises I was entirely ignorant. I took advantage of this to venture a timid opinion:

'In my view, there is nothing scandalous in that. The caliphs, the successors of the Prophet, have always commanded armies and governed states.'

He listened to the translation with unexpected interest. And hastened to question me:

'Has it always been thus?'

'Until the moment when the sultans supplanted them. The caliphs have since then been confined to their palaces.'

'Was that a good thing?'

The Pope seemed to attach great importance to my opinion. I thought very hard before expressing myself.

'I do not think that it was. As long as the caliphs were rulers, Islam was radiant with culture. Religion reigned peaceably over the affairs of this world. Since then, it is force which rules, and the faith is often nothing but a sword in the hands of the sultan.'

My interlocutor was so satisfied that he called his interpreter to witness:

'I have always thought that my glorious predecessor was correct.

Without his own army, the pope would only be the chaplain of the most powerful king. One is sometimes forced to make use of the same arms as one's enemies, to go through the same compromises.'

He pointed his index finger towards me.

'What you say gives Us comfort. Bovadiglia has been very lucky. Are you ready to serve Us?'

I mumbled some words of acquiescence. He acknowledged this, not without a somewhat ironic grimace:

'Let us accept with resignation the decrees of Providence!'

Before continuing, speaking faster, with the interpreter barely keeping up with him:

'Our adviser, Master Guicciardini, has spoken briefly about the importance of that which we expect from you. We shall speak about it to you again when the time comes. Know only that you arrive in this blessed city at the most difficult moment in all its history. Rome is threatened with destruction. Tomorrow, when you walk through this city, you will feel that it is growing and becoming more attractive, just as, on the branch of a majestic old tree which has dried up a few buds burst forth, a few green leaves, a few flowers resplendent with light. Everywhere, the best painters, the best sculptors, writers, musicians, artisans, produce the finest works under Our protection. Spring has just begun, but winter already approaches. Death already lies in wait. It lies in wait for us from all quarters. From which side will it reach us? With which sword will it strike us? God alone knows, unless He wishes to take such a bitter cup from Our lips.'

'God is great!' I said spontaneously.

'God protect us from all the sultans!' the Pope went further, his expression suddenly joyful.

That day, the interview went no further. Leo X promised to call me again. On returning to my cell, I found that new directives concerning me had been issued: my door would no longer be locked before nightfall, and I could wander as I pleased within the walls of the castle.

When I saw the Pope again a week later he had prepared a serious programme especially for me. Henceforth my time was to be divided between study and teaching. One bishop would teach me Latin, another the catechism, a third the Gospel and the Hebrew tongue; an Armenian priest would give me Turkish lessons every morning. For my part, I had to teach Arabic to seven pupils. For this I would receive a salary of one ducat each month. Without my having expressed the slightest protest, my benefactor admitted with a laugh that it was a refined form of forced labour, adding however that this programme was proof of his own enthusiastic interest in me. I thanked him and promised to do my best to show myself in no way unworthy.

Henceforth, he would summon me each month, alone or with my teachers to test the state of my knowledge, particularly of the catechism. In his mind the date of my baptism was already fixed, as well as the name which I should bear.

* * *

My year's captivity was thus without pain for the body and highly profitable for the mind. From one day to another I felt my knowledge increase, not only in the subjects which I studied but equally from the contact with my teachers, and with my pupils, two Aragonese priests, two Frenchmen, two Venetians, and a German from Saxony. It was the latter who first mentioned in front of me the increasingly bitter quarrel which had set Leo X against the monk Luther, an event which was already threatening to cover the whole of Europe with fire and blood and which was going to bring upon Rome the most heinous of calamities.

The Year of the Heretics
926 A.H.
23 December 1519 – 12 December 1520

'What is the Pope for? What are the cardinals for? What God is worshipped in this city of Rome, entirely given over to its luxuries and pleasures?'

Such were the words of my German pupil Hans, in religion Brother Augustine, who pursued me right into the antechamber of Leo X to win me over to the doctrines of the monk Luther, while I entreated him to keep silent if he did not wish to end his days at the stake.

Blond, bony, brilliant and obstinate, Hans would take a pamphlet or a brochure out of his bag after each lesson, which he would begin to translate and comment upon, pestering me incessantly to know what I thought about it. My reply was invariably the same:

'Whatever my feelings might be, I cannot betray my protector.'

Hans seemed upset, but not at all discouraged, and would return to the charge after the next lesson.

He realized that I listened to his words without annoyance. To certain of them at least, which sometimes brought back to my memory a *hadith* of the Prophet Muhammad, prayers and blessings upon him! Does Luther not commend the removal of all statues from places of worship, considering that they are objects of idolatry? 'The angels do not enter into a house where there is a dog or a figurative representation,' the Messenger of God has said in a well-attested *hadith*. Does Luther not say that Christianity is none other than the community of the believers, and ought not to be reduced to a Church hierarchy? Does he not affirm that the Holy

Scripture is the sole foundation of the Faith? Does he not hold up the celibacy of the priesthood to ridicule? Does he not teach that no man can escape from that which his Creator has ordained for him? The Prophet has not said otherwise to the Muslims.

In spite of these similarities, it was impossible for me to follow my own rational inclinations on this subject. A ferocious struggle was taking place between Leo X and Luther, and I could not give my support to someone unknown to me at the expense of the man who had taken me under his wing and had treated me thereafter as if he was my progenitor.

Of course I was not the only one to whom the Pope said 'My son', but he said it differently to me. He had given me his two first names, John and Leo, as well as the name of his distinguished family, the Medicis, all with pomp and solemnity, on 6 January 1520, a Friday, in the new basilica of St Peter, still unfinished. On that day it was crammed with cardinals, bishops, ambassadors and numerous protégés of Leo X, poets, painters, sculptors, glittering with brocade, pearls and precious stones. Even Raphael of Urbino was there, the divine Raphael as the admirers of his art used to call him, not seeming in any way weakened by the disease which was to carry him off three months later.

The Pope was triumphant beneath his tiara:

'On this day of Epiphany, when we celebrate the baptism of Christ at the hands of John the Baptist, and when we also celebrate, according to Tradition, the arrival of the three Magi from Arabia to adore Our Lord, what greater happiness could there be for us than to welcome, into the bosom of Our Holy Church, a new Magian King, come from the furthest corners of Barbary to make his offering in the House of Peter!'

Kneeling facing the altar, clad in a long white woollen cloak, I was bemused by the odour of incense and crushed by so many undeserved honours. None of the people assembled in this place was unaware that this 'Magian King' had been captured on a summer night by a pirate on a beach in Jerba, and brought to Rome as a slave. Everything which was said about me and everything which was happening to me was so insane, so immoderate, so grotesque! Wasn't I the victim of some bad dream, some mirage? Wasn't I really in a mosque in Fez, Cairo or Timbuktu, as on every Friday, my mind affected by a long sleepless night? Suddenly, in the heart of my doubts, the voice of the Pope rose again, addressing me:

'And you, Our well-beloved son John-Leo, whom Providence has singled out among all men . . .'

John-Leo! Johannes Leo! Never had anyone in my family been called thus! Long after the end of the ceremony I was still turning the letters and syllables over and over in my head and on my tongue, now in Latin, now in Italian. Leo. Leone. It is a curious habit which men have, thus to give themselves the names of the wild beasts which terrify them, rarely those of the animals which are devoted to them. People want to be called wolf, but not dog. Will it happen to me one day that I shall forget Hasan and look at myself in a mirror and say: 'Leo, you have shadows under your eyes?' To tame my new name I soon arabized it; Johannes Leo became Yuhanna al-Asad. That is the signature which can be seen under the works which I have written at Rome and at Bologna. But regular visitors to the papal court, somewhat surprised by the belated birth of a brown and fuzzy Medici, immediately gave me the additional surname of Africanus, the African, to distinguish me from my saintly adoptive father. Perhaps also to prevent him making me a cardinal as he had done for most of his male cousins, some at the age of fourteen.

On the evening of the baptism, the Pope called me to him. He began by telling me that I was henceforth a free man, but that I could continue to live in the castle while I found lodgings outside, adding that he was anxious that I should continue to pursue my studies and my teaching with the same assiduity. Then he took a tiny book from a table which he placed like a host on my open palm. As I opened it I saw that it was written in Arabic.

'Read it out loud, my son!'

I did so, leafing through the pages with great care:

'Book of the prayers of the hours . . . completed on 12 September 1514 . . . in the town of Fano under the auspices of His Holiness Pope Leo –'

My protector interrupted me in a trembling and unsteady voice:

'This is the first book in the Arabic language which has ever come off a printing press. When you return to your own people, take it carefully with you.'

In his eyes, I saw that he knew that I would go away again one day. He seemed so moved that I could not prevent my own tears from flowing. I bent to kiss his hand. He pressed me to himself and embraced me like a real father. By God, I have loved him since that moment, in spite of the ceremony which he had just inflicted upon me. That a man of such power, so venerated by Christians in Europe and elsewhere, should be so moved at the sight of a tiny book in Arabic, produced in the workshops of some Jewish printer, seemed to me worthy of the caliphs before the age of decadence, such as al-Ma'mun, the son of Harun al-Rashid, may the Most High bestow His mercy upon the one and the other.

When, on the morrow of this interview, I left the walls of my prison for the first time, free, my arms swinging, when I walked across the bridge of San Angelo towards the Ponte quarter, I had no feelings of resentment or bitterness about my captivity any more. A few weeks of heavy chains, a few months of soft servitude, and lo and behold I had become a traveller again, a migrant creature, as in all the lands where I had sojourned and obtained, for a while, pleasures and honours. What a lot of streets, of monuments, men and women I longed to discover, I who in a year knew of Rome only the cylindrical silhouette of Castel San Angelo and the endless corridor which connected it with the Vatican!

★ ★ ★

I was probably wrong to let myself be accompanied on my first visit by the irrepressible Hans. I immediately made my way straight ahead, towards the Via dei Banchi Vecchi before turning left into the famous Via del Pellegrino, to admire the shop windows of the goldsmiths and the displays of the silk merchants. I would have stayed there for hours, but my German was becoming impatient. Eventually he pulled me by the sleeve, like a hungry child. I forced myself, even apologizing for my frivolity. Were there not so many churches, palaces and monuments to admire in our neighbourhood? Or perhaps he wanted to take me to the Piazza Navona, quite close by, where, it was said, there was a ceaseless spectacle, of tumblers at least, at all times?

Hans was not thinking about any of this. He led me through narrow alleyways, where it was impossible to pass without stepping over heaps of rubbish. Then, in the darkest and most foul-smelling place, he stopped dead. We were surrounded by filthy, skeletal idlers. From a window, a woman called us to join her in exchange for a few *quattrini*. I felt terrible, but Hans did not move. As I glared at him he thought it as well to explain:

'I want you to keep this vision of wretchedness constantly in front of you when you see how the princes of the Church live, all those cardinals who own three palaces each, where they compete in sumptuousness and debauchery, where they organize feast after feast, with twelve kinds of fish, eight salads, five sorts of sweets. And the Pope himself? Have you seen him having the elephant which the King of Portugal gave him paraded up and down with great pride? Have you seen him throw gold pieces at his jesters? Have you seen him hunting on his estate at Magliana, in long leather boots, riding behind a bear or a wild boar, surrounded by his sixty-eight dogs? Have you seen his falcons and goshawks, brought for gold from Candia and Armenia?'

I understood his sentiment but his behaviour annoyed me:

'Show me rather the monuments of ancient Rome, those of which Cicero and Livy have spoken!'

My young friend seemed triumphant. Without saying a word, he started to walk once more, with such a firm step that I barely managed to keep up with him. When he decided to come to a halt, half an hour later, we had left the last inhabited streets far behind us. We were in the middle of a vast empty space.

'Here was the Roman Forum, the heart of the old city, surrounded by bustling quarters; today it is called the Campo Vaccino! And, in front of us, do you see Monte Palatino, and over there, to the east, behind the Coliseum, Monte Esquilino? They have been empty for years! Rome is no more than a large market town camping out on the site of a majestic city. Do you know what its population is today? Eight thousand souls, nine thousand at most.'

That was far fewer than Fez, Tunis, or Tlemcen.

Going back towards the castle, I noticed that the sun was still high in the sky, so I thought it as well to suggest to my guide to take a walk in the direction of St Peter's, going through the fine quarter of Borgo. We had hardly arrived in front of the basilica when Hans launched once more into a crazy diatribe:

'Do you know how the Pope wants to finish building this church? By taking the Germans' money.'

Several passers-by were already congregating around us.

'I have visited enough monuments for today,' I begged him. 'We shall come back another time.'

And, without waiting for him for a single moment, I ran to take refuge in the calm of my former prison, vowing never to go walking around Rome with a Lutheran guide.

On my next visit I chanced to have Guicciardini as companion, who had just returned from a long visit to Modena. I imparted to him my deep disappointment, particularly after my visit to the Campo Vaccino. He did not seem particularly affected by it.

'Eternal city, Rome, but with lapses,' he declared with wise resignation.

Before continuing:

'Holy city, but full of impieties; idle city, but one which gives the world a masterpiece every day.'

It was a joy for the spirit to walk alongside Guicciardini, to take in his impressions, his comments, his confidences. However, there were certain inconveniences: thus, to get from the Castel San Angelo to the new palace of Cardinal Farnese, less than a mile away, took us nearly two hours, so great was the fame of my companion. Some people greeted him as they passed by, while others dismounted in order to engage him in long private conversations. Having extricated himself, the Florentine would return to my side with a word of apology: 'That is a fellow countryman who has recently set up in Rome', or 'That is an extremely influential bursar', 'That is the postmaster of the King of France', and even, on two occasions, 'That is the bastard of Cardinal So and So.'

I had shown no surprise. Hans had already explained to me that in the capital of the Popes, though teeming with men of religion, nuns and pilgrims from all countries, the mistresses of the princes of the Church had palaces and servants, that their offspring were destined for the highest posts, that priests of lower rank had their concubines or courtesans, whom they flaunted without shame in the streets.

'Lust is less of a scandal than sumptuous living,' said Guicciardini, as if he had followed the development of my thoughts step by step.

He continued:

'The lifestyle of the prelates of Rome costs vasts sums, while nothing is produced in this city of clerics! Everything is bought in Florence, Venice, Milan and elsewhere. In order to finance the excesses of this city, the Popes have started to sell ecclesiastical titles: ten thousand, twenty thousand, thirty thousand ducats for a cardinal. Everything is for sale here, even the post of steward! As that was still not enough, they started to sell indulgences to the wretched Germans! If you pay, your sins are forgiven! In short, the Holy Father is seeking to sell off Paradise. It was in this way that the quarrel with Luther began.'

'So this monk was right.'

'In one sense, yes. Except that I cannot help thinking that the money collected in such a questionable fashion goes towards the completion of the Basilica of St Peter, and that part of it is devoted not to banquets but to the noblest creations of the human spirit. Hundreds of writers and artists are producing masterpieces in Rome before which the Ancients would turn pale with envy. A world is in the process of being reborn, with a new vision, a new ambition, a new beauty. It is being reborn here, now, in corrupt, venal and impious Rome, with money wrested from the Germans. Is that not a very useful sort of waste?'

I no longer knew what to think. Good and Bad, truth and untruth, beauty and rottenness were so muddled up in my mind! But perhaps that was it, the Rome of Leo X, the Rome of Leo the African. I repeated Guicciardini's formulations out loud, in order to engrave them upon my memory:

'Idle city . . . holy city . . . eternal city . . .'

He interrupted me in a voice grown suddenly despondent:

'Accursed city as well.'

While I gazed at him, awaiting some explanation, he took a crumpled piece of paper from his pocket.

'I have just copied out some lines written by Luther to our Pope.'

He read in a low voice:

'You, Leo, the most ill-fated of all, you are seated upon the most dangerous of thrones. Rome was formerly a gate of Heaven; it is now the gaping abyss of Hell.'

The Year of the Conversa
927 A.H.
13 December 1520 – 30 November 1521

What a Saturday of happiness in my life was 6 April of that year! However, the Pope was angry. He thundered so loudly that I stayed motionless for a long moment in the antechamber, protected from his shouts by the heavy carved double doors. But the Swiss who accompanied me had his orders. He opened the door of the study without knocking, almost pushed me into the room and closed the door firmly behind me.

When he saw me, the Pope stopped shouting. But his eyebrows remained knitted together and his lower lip was still trembling. He indicated that I should come nearer with a signal from his smooth fingers, which were drumming feverishly on the table. I leaned over his hand, and then over the hand of the person who was standing on his right.

'Leo, do you know our cousin Cardinal Julius?'

'How could I have lived in Rome without knowing him?'

This was not the best reply in the circumstances. Julius de Medici was certainly the most flamboyant of all the princes of the Church, and the Pope's trusted associate. But the latter had been reproaching him for some time for his escapades, his love of ostentation, his rowdy love affairs, which had made him the favourite target of the Lutherans. On the other hand, Guicciardini had spoken well of him: 'Julius has all the qualities of the perfect gentleman, a patron of the arts, tolerant, good company. Why the devil should anyone want to make a man of religion out of him?'

In a red cape and skull cap, a fringe of black hair across the breadth of his forehead, the Pope's cousin seemed engrossed in a painful meditation.

'The cardinal must speak to you, my son. Sit yourselves together on those chairs over there. I myself have some mail to read.'

I do not believe that I am mistaken in stating that the Pope did not miss a single word of our conversation that day, since he did not turn a single page of the text which he had in his hands.

Julius seemed embarrassed, seeking some sign of complicity in my eyes. He cleared his throat discreetly.

'A young person has just entered my service. Virtuous and beautiful. And intelligent. The Holy Father desires that I should present her to you, and that you should take her to wife. Her name is Maddalena.'

Having delivered himself of these words with a visible effort, he turned to other matters, asked me about my past, my travels, my life in Rome. I discovered he had the same appetite for knowledge as his cousin, the same rapture at hearing the names of Timbuktu, Fez and Cairo, the same respect for the things of the mind. He made me swear that one day I should commit an account of my travels to paper, promising to be my most eager reader.

The great pleasure which this conversation gave me did not however greatly reduce my profound suspicion towards the proposal which had been made to me. To state matters frankly, I had no desire at all to find myself the belated husband of some adolescent girl whose advanced state of pregnancy would set all the tongues of Rome wagging. However, it was difficult for me to say 'No' in a single word to the Pope and his cousin. Hence I formulated my reply in sufficiently roundabout terms to enable my feelings to show through:

'I put myself in the hands of His Holiness and His Eminence, who know better than I what is good for my body and my soul.'

The sound of the Pope's laughter made me jump. Putting down his mail, he turned round to face us squarely.

'Leo will see the girl this very day, after the requiem mass.'

★   ★   ★

In fact that day was the commemoration, in the Sistine Chapel, of the first anniversary of the death of Raphael of Urbino, whom Leo X used to cherish more than all his other protégés. He often called him to mind with an unfeigned emotion, which made me regret having known him so little.

Because of my long period of seclusion, I had only met Raphael twice; the first time briefly in a corridor of the Vatican, the second time at my baptism. After the ceremony he had come up, like so many others, to offer his congratulations to the Pope, who had put him beside me. A question was burning on his lips:

'Is it true that there are neither painters nor sculptors in your country?'

'Some people do paint or sculpt, but all figurative representation is condemned. It is considered as a challenge to the Creator.'

'It does our art too much honour to think that it can emulate the Creation.'

He made an astonished and somewhat condescending frown. I felt I had to reply:

'Isn't it true that after having made the statue of Moses Michelangelo ordered it to walk or speak?'

Raphael smiled maliciously.

'So they say.'

'That is what the people of my country seek to avoid. That a man should have the ambition to substitute himself for the Creator.'

'And the prince who decides on life and death, does he not substitute himself for the Creator in a far more blasphemous fashion than the painter? And the master who possesses slaves, who buys and sells them?'

The painter's voice rose. I tried to calm him:

'One day I should like to visit your studio.'

'If I were to decide to paint your portrait, would that be blasphemy?'

'Not at all. It would be as if the most eloquent of our poets were to write a eulogy about me.'

I had not found a better comparison. He was content with it.

'Very well. Come to my house when you wish.'

I had resolved to do so, but death had overtaken me. Of Raphael I remembered only a few words, a frown, a promise. It was my duty to think of him on that day of commemoration. But very quickly, already before the end of the ceremony, it was towards Maddalena that my thoughts turned.

I tried to imagine her, her hair, her voice, her figure; I asked myself in which language I should speak to her, with which words I should begin. I also tried to guess what Leo X and his cousin could have said to each other before summoning me. The Pope had probably discovered that the cardinal had just added a young and beautiful girl to his numerous retinue, and fearing some new scene, had ordered him to get rid of her, swiftly and in a dignified manner. In that way no one could claim that Cardinal Julius had shameful designs upon the girl; his sole concern was to find a wife for his cousin Leo the African!

A priest whom I knew, whom I saw leaving the chapel, gave me some additional information which served to confirm my suppositions: Maddalena had lived in a convent for a long time. In the course of a visit, the cardinal had noticed her, and when he was to leave at the end of the day he had quite simply taken her away in his baggage train. His behaviour had caused a scandal, and a complaint had reached the ears of Leo X, who had reacted immediately both as head of the Church and head of the Medici.

I believed that I was now in possession of the core of the facts, but I only held a little of the peel.

★ ★ ★

'Is it true that you are from Granada, like me, and that you are also a convert, like me?'

I had overestimated my strength and my serenity. When she walked slowly into the little carpeted room where the cardinal had bade me sit I immediately lost all desire to question her, for fear that a word from her lips would compel me to distance myself. For me, henceforth the truth about Maddalena was Maddalena. I had one single desire, to contemplate her gestures and her colouring for ever. She was ahead of all the women of Rome in her languor. Languidness in her gait, in her speech, in her gaze as well, at once conquering and resigned to suffering. Her hair had that deep blackness which only Andalus can distil, by some alchemy of the refreshing shadow and the burnt earth. Before she became my wife, she was already my sister, her breathing was familiar to me.

Even before she sat down, she began to tell her story, the whole of her story. The questions which I had decided not to ask she had decided to answer. Her grandfather belonged to an impoverished and forgotten branch of a great Jewish family, the Abrabanels. A humble blacksmith in the suburb of Najd, in the south of the city of my birth, he had been completely unaware of the danger which was threatening his family, until the very moment when the edict of expulsion had been promulgated. Emigrating to Tetouan with his six children, he had lived on the edge of destitution, with no other joy in life but to see his sons gain some knowledge and his daughters become more beautiful. One of them was to be the mother of the *conversa*.

'My parents had decided to go and set themselves up in Ferrara,' she explained to me, 'where some cousins had prospered. But the plague broke out on the vessel on which we had embarked, decimating crew and passengers. Landing at Pisa, I found myself alone. My mother, my father and my young brother had perished. I was eight years old. An old nun took me in. She took me with her to a convent of which she was abbess, and hastened to have me baptized, giving me the name of Maddalena; my parents had called me Judith. In spite of the sadness of having lost those most dear to me I was careful not to curse fate, since I ate my fill, learned to read and was never whipped without due cause. Until the day that my benefactress died. Her replacement was the natural daughter of a grandee of Spain, shut up there to expiate the sins of her family, who considered that this fine convent was nothing but purgatory for herself and the others. However, she reigned supreme, distributing favours and punishments. For me she reserved the worst of her heart. For seven years I had been an increasingly fervent Christian. To her, however, I was just a convert, a *conversa* of impure blood, whose very presence would bring down the worst curses upon the convent. And, under the hail of humiliations which rained down unjustly upon me, I felt myself returning to the faith into which I was born. The pork which I ate began to give me nausea, and my nights were tormented by it. I began to think up plans for escape. But my only attempt failed miserably. I never ran very fast, particularly in a nun's habit. The gardener caught me and brought me back to the convent twisting my arm as if I were a chicken thief. And then I was thrown into a dungeon and whipped until the blood came.'

Some traces of this remained, but they did not detract at all from her beauty or the sweet perfection of her body.

'When I was let out, at the end of two weeks, I had decided to change my attitude. I made a show of profound remorse, and showed myself devoted, obedient and oblivious to humiliation. I was waiting for my time to come. It came with the visit of Cardinal Julius. The mother superior was obliged to receive him with ceremony, although she would have sent him to the stake if she had had it in her power. She sometimes made us pray for the repentance of the princes of the Church, and was unsparing of her criticisms of the "dissolute life of the Medici", not in public, but in front of certain nuns in her entourage who were not slow to mention it. It was probably the vices of which he was accused that made me have faith in this cardinal.'

I agreed:

'Virtue becomes unhealthy if it is not softened by some misdemeanours, and faith quickly becomes cruel if it is not subdued by certain doubts.'

Maddalena touched my shoulder lightly as a sign of trust before continuing her story:

'When the prelate arrived, we all lined up to kiss his hand. I waited my turn impatiently. My plan was ready. The fingers of the cardinal, adorned with two rings, were held out in a princely fashion. I took them, shook them a little harder than necessary, and held them two seconds too long. That was enough to attract his attention. I held up my head, so that he could look at my face. "I need to confess myself to you," I said to him in a loud voice, so that the request would be official, heard by all the cardinal's suite as well as by the mother superior. She adopted a sugary tone: "Move away my child, you are bothering His Eminence and your sisters are waiting." There was a moment of hesitation. Would I find myself in the dungeon of revenge for ever? Was I going to be able to hold on to the hands of a saviour? I was holding my breath and my eyes were imploring. Then the sentence came: "Wait for me here! I am going to confess you." My tears flowed, betraying my happiness. But, when I knelt in the confessional, my voice was strong once more to pronounce without a mistake the words which I had repeated a hundred times. The cardinal listened silently to my long cry of despair, just nodding his head to encourage me to continue. "My daughter," he said to me when I had finished, "I do not believe that convent life is made for you." I was free.'

Thinking about it, her tears ran anew. I put my hand upon hers, pressed it affectionately and withdrew it when she resumed the thread of her story.

'The cardinal brought me to Rome with him. That was a month ago. The abbess did not want to let me leave, but my protector would not pay any heed to her objections. To take her revenge, she got up a whole cabal against him, interceded with the Spanish cardinals, who, in their turn, went to the Pope. The most dreadful accusations were made, against His Eminence and myself . . .'

She stopped speaking, because I leaped up with one bound. I did not want to hear any word of these calumnies, even from the exquisite mouth of Maddalena. Was it truth or untruth that I was fleeing in this way? I do not know. The only thing that mattered now was the love that had just been born in my heart and in that of the *conversa*. When she rose to say farewell to me there was an uneasiness in her eyes. My hurried departure had somewhat alarmed her. She had to overcome her timidity to say to me:

'Shall we see each other again sometimes?'

'Until the end of my life.'

My lips brushed against hers. Her eyes were alarmed once more, but with happiness and the giddiness of hope.

The Year of Adrian
928 A.H.
1 December 1521 – 19 November 1522

Pope Leo died of an ulcer on the very first day of that year, and I
believed for a while that it was already time for me to leave Rome,
which became suddenly inhospitable without this attentive god-
father, this generous protector, may the Heavens pour countless
riches upon him, in the image of that which he always did himself!

I was not alone in thinking of leaving. Cardinal Julius exiled
himself to Florence; Guicciardini took refuge in Modena, and all
around me hundreds of writers, painters, sculptors and merchants,
the most famous among them, prepared to desert the city as if it had
been struck by the plague. In fact there was a brief epidemic, but the
real plague was of another kind. Its name was declaimed out loud
from the Borgo to Piazza Navona with the invariable epithet: Adrian
the Barbarian.

The cardinals had elected him as if to repent. Too many
accusations had been levelled against the papacy during the last
pontificate, the Germans were supporting Luther's theses by whole
provinces, and Leo X was held responsible. Thus it was desired to
change the face of the Church; the Florentine, the Medici who had
become Pope at the age of thirty-eight and who had brought his taste
for luxury and beauty to Rome, was succeeded by an austere
Dutchman of sixty-three, 'a saintly and virtuous man, boring, bald
and miserly'. The description was Maddalena's, who never had at
any time the slightest sympathy for the new head of Christianity.

'He reminds me too much of the abbess who persecuted me. He
has the same narrow vision, the same desire to make a perpetual fast

out of life, his own and the lives of others.'

At the beginning my own opinion had been less clear-cut. Although I had always been loyal towards my benefactor, certain aspects of Roman life wounded my inner faith. That a Pope should have declared, as Adrian had done, 'I have a taste for poverty!' was not displeasing to me, and the story which so amused the courtiers after the first week of his reign did not make me roar with laughter. Entering the Sistine Chapel, the new pontiff actually cried out at the sight of Michelangelo's ceiling: 'This is not a church, but a steamroom crammed with naked bodies!' adding that he had decided to cover these blasphemous figures with whitewash. By God, I could have let out the same cry. Mixing frequently with the Romans had removed certain of my prejudices against painting, the nude, and sculpture. But not in places of worship. Such were my feelings at the accession of Adrian VI. It is true that I was not yet aware that this former tutor of Charles V had been inquisitor of Aragon and Navarre before his arrival in Rome. In a few weeks he made a complete Medici out of me, if not by the nobility of my origins at least by the nobility of my aspirations.

This Pope began by abolishing all the pensions initiated by Leo X, including my own. He also cancelled all orders for pictures, sculptures, books, and building construction. In every sermon he fulminated against art, that of the Ancients as well as that of contemporaries, against feasting, pleasure and expenditure. From one day to the next, Rome became nothing but a dead city, where nothing was created, built, or sold. In justification of his decision, the new Pope pointed to the debts accumulated by his predecessor, judging that the money had been wasted. 'With the sums squandered on the reconstruction of St Peter,' members of Adrian's circle used to say, 'a crusade could have been armed against the Turks; a whole regiment of cavalry could have been equipped with the money given to Raphael.'

Since my arrival in Rome I had often heard talk of the crusades, even from the mouth of Leo X. But this was evidently some sort of ritual which had no real meaning, rather like the way in which certain Muslim princes talk about jihad to embarrass an adversary or to calm down some false bigot. It was quite otherwise with Adrian, may God curse him and all religious fanatics! He firmly believed that by mobilizing Christianity against Islam he would put an end to the Lutheran schism and would reconcile the Emperor Charles with the

King of France.

The suppression of my pension and a call for universal bloodletting: there was certainly enough there to rid me of any desire to acclaim this Pope. And to prompt me to leave Rome as quickly as possible for Florence, whither Cardinal Julius had encouraged me to follow him.

I would probably have joined him had Maddalena not been pregnant. I had rented a three-storeyed house in the Pontine quarter. On the top floor there was a kitchen, on the second floor a living room with my desk, and on the ground floor a large bedroom which gave out on to a kitchen garden. It was in that room that my first son was born one July evening, whom I called Guiseppe, that is to say Yusuf, like the father of the Messiah, like the son of Jacob, like Sultan Salah al-Din. My wonderment was boundless. I stayed for hours caressing the child and his mother, watching them in their daily activities, particularly suckling, which never ceased to move me. So I had no desire to drag them on to the painful roads of exile. Neither towards Florence nor even towards Tunis, as was suggested to me that year, in curious circumstances.

★   ★   ★

One day I was in Cardinal Julius' house, shortly before his departure for Tuscany, when a young painter introduced himself to him. He was called Manolo, I think, and came from Naples, where he had acquired a certain reputation. He hoped to sell his paintings before going back to his city. It was not unusual for an artist to come from afar to see the Medici, as everyone who knocked at his door could be sure that they would not leave empty-handed. This Neapolitan unrolled several canvases, of uneven quality, it seemed to me. I looked at them absent-mindedly, when all of a sudden I jumped. A portrait was just passing in front of me, quickly put away by Manolo with a gesture of irritation.

'May I see that picture again?' I asked.

'Certainly, but it is not for sale. I brought it by mistake. It was ordered by a merchant and I must deliver it to him.'

Those curved lines, that matt complexion, that beard, that smile of eternal satisfaction . . . There could be no mistake! I still had to ask:

'What is the name of this man?'

'Master Abbado. He is one of the richest shipowners in Naples.'

'Abbad the Soussi! I murmured a good-humoured curse.

'Will you see him soon?'

'He is often on his travels between May and September, but he spends the winter in his villa beside Santa Lucia.'

Taking a sheet of paper, I hastily scribbled a message for my companion. And, two months later, 'Abbad arrived at my house in a carriage, accompanied by three servants. Had he been my own brother I would not have been happier to embrace him!

'I left you in chains at the bottom of a ship's hold; I meet up with you again and you are prosperous and resplendent.'

'*Al-hamdu l'illah! al-hamdu l'illah!* God has been generous towards me!'

'Not more so than you deserve! I can testify that even at the worst moments you never said a word against Providence.'

I was sincere. Nevertheless I could not keep my curiosity completely intact.

'How did you manage to extricate yourself so quickly?'

'Thanks to my mother, may God bless the earth that covers her! She always used to repeat this sentence to me which I eventually knew by heart: a man is never without resources as long as he has a tongue in his head. It is true that I was sold as a slave, my hands in chains and a ball and chain at my feet, but my tongue was not chained up. A merchant bought me, whom I served loyally, giving him all sorts of advice, enabling him to profit from my experience of the Mediterranean. In that way he made so much money that he set me free at the end of the first year and made me a partner in his business.'

When I seemed astonished that things had been so easy, he shrugged his shoulders.

'When a man has become rich in one country, he can easily become so once more elsewhere. Today our business is one of the most flourishing in Naples. *Al-hamdu l'illah!* We have an agent in every port and about ten branches which I visit regularly.'

'Would you happen to make a detour to Tunis?'

'I am going there in the summer. I shall go and visit your family. Should I tell them that you are happy here?'

I had to acknowledge that without having made a fortune I had not had to undergo the rigours of captivity. And that Rome had

made me taste of two real kinds of happiness: that of an ancient city
that was being reborn, drunk with beauty, and that of a son who was
sleeping on the knees of the woman I loved.

My friend seemed satisfied. But he added:

'If, one day, this town ceases to bring you pleasure, you must
know that my house is open for you, you and your family, and that
my vessels will carry you as far as you wish.'

I denied that I wanted to leave Rome, promising 'Abbad to
welcome him on his return from Tunis and to give him a sumptuous
feast.

★   ★   ★

I did not want to complain in front of my friend, but things had
begun to take a turn for the worse for me; Adrian had decided to
mount a campaign against the wearing of beards. 'They are suitable
only for soldiers,' he had decreed, ordering all clerics to shave. I was
not directly affected, but because of my assiduous visits to the
Vatican palace, my persistence in keeping this decoration seemed
like an insolent reminder of my Moorish origins, like a challenge to
the Pope, probably even a sign of impiety. Among the Italians whom
I met, beards were not common, and were more a sign of eccentricity
reserved for artists, an eccentricity that was elegant for some and a
sign of exuberance for others. Some were attached to them, while
others were ready to get rid of them rather than to be forbidden the
court. For me the matter could not but take on a different
significance. In my country the beard is standard. Not to have one is
tolerated, especially for a foreigner. To shave it off after one has had
a beard for many long years is a sign of abasement and humiliation. I
had no intention of undergoing such an affront.

Would anyone believe me if I were to say that I was ready to die
for my beard that year? And not only for my beard, because all the
battles were confused in my mind, as in the Pope's: the beard of the
clergy, the naked breasts on the ceiling of the Sistine Chapel, the
statue of Moses, with thunderous gaze and quivering lips.

Without having sought it, I became a pivot and symbol of
obstinate resistance to Adrian. Seeing me pass by, proudly fingering
the bushy hair on my neck, the most clean-shaven of Romans would
murmur their admiration. All the pamphlets written against the

Pope would first come into my hands before being slid under the doors of the notables of the city. Some texts were no more than a web of insults: 'Barbarian, miser, pig' and worse. Others spoke of the pride of the Romans. 'Never more shall a non-Italian come to sit upon the throne of Peter!' I stopped all my teaching, all my studies, devoting my time to the struggle. It is true that I was handsomely rewarded. Cardinal Julius sent me substantial sums of money as well as encouraging letters. He promised to show me the full extent of his gratitude when the situation changed for the better.

I awaited that moment with impatience, for my situation at Rome was becoming precarious. A friend of mine who was a priest, author of an inflammatory pamphlet, had been shut up in Castel San Angelo two hours after having visited me. Another had been attacked by some Spanish monks. I felt myself constantly spied upon. I no longer left my house, except to make a few swift purchases in the quarter. Every night I had the impression that I would sleep at Maddalena's side for the last time. And I held her even more closely.

The Year of Sulaiman
929 A.H.
20 November 1522 – 9 November 1523

That year, the Grand Turk found favour in my eyes once more. Of course, he never knew anything about it, but what does that matter? The dispute had raged inside me, and it was within me that it had to be resolved.

I had been obliged to flee the most powerful empire of Islam to protect a child from the vindictiveness of a bloodthirsty monarch, and I had found in Christian Rome the caliph under whose shadow I would so much have liked to live in Baghdad or Cordova. My mind delighted in this paradox, but my conscience was not appeased. Had the time passed when I could be genuinely proud of my own without needing to brag about them?

Then there was Adrian. Then there was Sulaiman. And above everything else this visit from 'Abbad. On his return from Tunis he had come to see me, faithful to his promise, and even before his lips had opened his eyes were already pitying me. As he hesitated to shock me with what he had learned, I felt I should put him at ease.

'One cannot reproach the messenger for something which is an act of Providence.'

Adding, with an affected smile:

'If a man has left his family for many years, he cannot expect to hear any good news. Even if you were to tell me that Nur had just had a child, that would be misfortune.'

Probably thinking that his task would become even harder if he let me go on joking further, my friend made up his mind to speak:

'Your wife did not wait for you. She only stayed a few months in

317

your house in Tunis.'

My hands were sweaty.

'She went away. And left you this.'

He handed me a letter which I unsealed. The handwriting had been executed with care, probably that of a public letter-writer. But the words were Nur's:

If it was only my own happiness that was at stake, I would have waited for you for many long years, if need be until I had seen my hair turn silver in the loneliness of the nights. But I live only for my son, for his destiny, which will come to fruition one day, if it pleases God. Then we shall summon you to our side so that you may share the honours as you shared the dangers. In the meantime I shall go to Persia where, although he has no friends, Bayazid will at least have on his side the enemies of those who are hunting him down.

I leave Hayat for you. I have borne your daughter as you have carried my secret, and it is time that each one of us takes back that which is his own. Some will say that I am an unworthy mother, but you know that it is for her own good that I leave her behind, to protect her from the dangers which attend my own steps and those of her brother. I leave her as a gift for you, when you return; as she becomes older, she will look like me, and at every moment she will remind you of a blonde princess whom you loved and who loved you. And will always love you from the depth of her new exile.

Whether I encounter death or glory, do not let my image tarnish in your heart!

When he saw the first tear fall, 'Abbad leaned his elbows on the window, pretending to be absorbed by some scene taking place in the garden. Ignoring the empty chairs which surrounded me I let myself fall to the ground, my eyes clouded over. As if Nur was in front of me, I murmured furiously to her:

'What good is it to dream of a palace when one can find happiness in a hut at the foot of the pyramids!'

After several minutes 'Abbad came and sat down at my side.

'Your mother and your daughters are well. Harun sends them money and provisions each month.'

Two sighs later, I handed him the letter. He made a gesture of pushing it away, but I insisted. Without thinking too deeply, I was anxious that he should read it. Perhaps I wanted him to refrain from condemning Nur. Perhaps, out of self-esteem, I wanted him not to pity me as if I was an ordinary husband deserted by a wife who was tired of waiting. Perhaps I also wanted to share with a friend a secret which from now on I would bear alone.

Thus I heard myself telling, in detail, the story of my Circassian, beginning with the chance meeting at a merchant's in Khan al-Khalili.

'Now I understand your terror when the Turkish officer took Bayazid in his arms in Alexandria harbour.'

I laughed. 'Abbad continued, happy to have been able to distract me:

'I could never explain to myself why a Granadan could be so afraid of the Ottomans, the only ones who promise to give him back his city one day.'

'Maddalena can't understand it either. She wants all the Andalusians, Jews and Muslims, to rejoice with her every time she hears the news of an Ottoman victory. And she's astonished that I remain so cold.'

'Are you going to light her lantern now?'

'Abbad had spoken in a low voice. I replied in the same tone:

'I will tell her everything in small doses. I could not tell her about Nur's existence before.'

I turned towards my friend. My voice became feeble and thoughtful again:

'Have you noticed how much we have changed since we came to this country? At Fez I would never have spoken of my wives in this way, even to my closest friend. If I had done so, he would have blushed to the peak of his turban.'

Laughingly, 'Abbad agreed with me.

'I myself made a thousand and one excuses before asking my neighbour after the health of his wife, and before answering me, he made sure nobody listened, fearing for his honour.'

After a long burst of laughter and some moments of silence, my companion began a sentence and then interrupted himself, hesitant and embarrassed.

'What were you going to say?'

'It's probably not yet the right moment.'

'I've told you too many secrets for you to hide from me half of what you're thinking!'

He resigned himself.

'I was going to say that henceforth you are free to love the Ottomans because Bayazid is no longer your son and because your wife is no longer a Circassian, because in Rome your protector has been replaced by an inquisitor, because in Constantinople Salim the Grim has been dead for two years and Sulaiman has replaced him.'

In a sense, what 'Abbad said was true. I was henceforth free in my feelings, in my enthusiasm, free to join with Maddalena in her spontaneous outburst. What happiness, what serenity there would be to be able to draw, amid the succession of events in the world, a dividing line between joy and grief! However, I knew that this happiness was denied me, by my very own nature.

'But I know you,' 'Abbad continued without looking at me. 'You cannot enjoy anything to its full.'

He thought for a moment.

'I think that, quite simply, you do not love princes, and sultans even less. When one of them wins a victory, you immediately find yourself in the camp of his enemies, and when some fool venerates them, that in itself is sufficient reason for you to abhor them!'

This time, what 'Abbad said was probably true. Seeing that I was not attempting to defend myself, he harried me:

'Why should you be hostile to Sulaiman?'

He spoke to me with such a moving naïveté that I could not prevent myself from smiling. At that very moment Maddalena came into the room. She heard the sentence my friend had uttered, which he hastened to translate into Italian for her, knowing that she would immediately bring him reinforcements. Which she did with vigour:

'Why on earth are you hostile to Sulaiman?'

She walked slowly towards us, still slumped against the wall like schoolboys reciting the long Sura of Women to each other. 'Abbad sat up, a confused word on the tip of his tongue. I stayed where I was, thoughtful and perplexed. As if to accompany my thoughts, Maddalena launched into a passionate eulogy of the Grand Turk:

'Since he came to power Sulaiman has put an end to the bloody practices of his father. He has strangled neither brothers, sons nor cousins. The notables who were deported from Egypt have been brought back to their homes. The prisons have emptied. Constantinople sings the praises of the young sovereign, comparing his actions to a refreshing dew, and Cairo no longer lives in fear and mourning.'

'An Ottoman sultan who does not kill!'

My tone was full of doubt. 'Abbad corrected me:

'Every prince must kill. The main thing is that he should not take pleasure in it, as was the case with the old sultan. Sulaiman is certainly from the Ottoman race, and in conquest he yields nothing to his father. For two months he has been besieging the knights of the island of Rhodes, with the largest fleet that Islam has ever seen. Among the officers who accompany him is your brother-in-law Harun, and with him his eldest son, who will, one day, marry Sarwat, your daughter, his cousin. Whether you like it or not, your family are involved in that battle. Even if you have no desire to join them, should you not at least wish for their victory?'

I turned back towards Maddalena, who was delighted at my friend's words. I asked her solemnly:

'If I were to decide that the time had come for us to take the road to Tunis with our child, what would you think about it?'

'You have only to say the word and I should leave with pleasure, to get away from this inquisitor-Pope who is only waiting for the opportunity to seize hold of you!'

'Abbad was the most excited of the three of us:

'Nothing detains you here. Leave with me at once!'

I calmed him down:

'It's only December. If we must go by sea, we cannot do so for three months.'

'Come to my house in Naples, and from there you will embark for Tunis in the first days of spring.'

'That seems possible,' I said thoughtfully.

But I hastened to add:

'I shall think about it!'

'Abbad did not hear the last part of the sentence. To celebrate my timid acceptance and to prevent me changing my mind he called from the window to two of his servants. He ordered one to go and buy two bottles of the best Greek wine, while the other had to prepare a pipe of tobacco.

'Have you already tasted this sweet poison from the New World?'

'Once, two years ago, at the house of a Florentine cardinal.'

'Is it on sale in Rome?'

'Only in certain taverns. But the *tabacchini* which run them have the worst reputations in the city.'

'Soon the whole world will be full of *tabacchini*, and their reputation will be no worse than the reputation of grocers or perfume sellers. I myself import whole cargoes from Seville which I sell in Bursa or Constantinople.'

I took a puff. Maddalena inhaled the perfume but refused to try it.

'I would be too afraid to choke myself with smoke!'

The Soussi advised her to heat the water to drink an infusion of the tobacco, with a bit of sugar.

★   ★   ★

When 'Abbad left us that day, Maddalena immediately threw her arms around my neck.

'I shall be happy to leave. Let's not linger here!'

'Be prepared! When my friend returns, we shall take the road together.'

'Abbad had been to Ancona on business, promising to be back within ten days. He kept his promise, only to be welcomed by a weeping Maddalena.

I had been arrested the previous day, 21 December, a Sunday, while I was very unwisely carrying a pamphlet which a French monk had slid into my pocket at the entrance of the church of San Giovanni dei Fiorentini.

Whether by coincidence or as a deliberate humiliation, when I was taken to the Castel San Angelo I was shut up in the same cell which I had occupied for almost two years. But, at that time I risked nothing more than captivity, while this time I could be judged and condemned to purge my crime in a far-off prison, or even in a galley.

I would probably not have been so concerned if I had not planned to leave. However, for the first part of the time my captivity was less rigorous than I had feared. In February I was even able to receive a present from 'Abbad which seemed sumptuous in the circumstances: a woollen cloak and a date cake, accompanied by a letter in which he told me in barely veiled words of the conquest of Rhodes by Sulaiman: *The sea has brought our people to the summit of the rock, the earth has shaken with our cries of triumph.*

Seen from my cell, this seemed to me to be a personal revenge against Adrian and his dreams of crusade. And when, in the course of the following months, my detention became more and more harsh, when I had nothing more to read, nothing to write with, neither pen nor ink nor even the merest lamp to dispel the darkness which pervaded from the afternoon, when I had no contact any more with the outside, when my warder pretended to understand no language beyond some vague German dialect, I began to regard 'Abbad's letter as a precious relic, and to repeat the words about the capture of Rhodes like an incantation.

One night I had a dream. I saw Sulaiman with a child's face under his turban, the face of Bayazid. He tore down a mountainside to come and rescue me, but, before he could reach me I woke up, still in my cell, unable to go back to sleep to catch hold of the end of the dream.

Darkness, cold, insomnia, despair, silence . . . In order not to succumb to madness I resumed the habit of praying, five times a day, to the God of my childhood.

I awaited from Constantinople the hand that was going to set me free. But my deliverer was much nearer at hand, may the Most High lend him His aid in the torment which is his fate today!

The Year of Clemency
930 A.H.
10 November 1523 – 28 October 1524

A rushing of feet, a tumult of voices, then the hundred dry cold noises of a key turning in the door which shook slowly on its rusty hinges. Standing near my bed I rubbed my eyes, intently watching the silhouettes which were about to be outlined against the light from outside.

A man came in. When I recognized Guicciardini I took a step towards him, preparing to throw myself round his neck, but I stopped short – I even stepped back, as if driven away by an invisible force. Perhaps it was his marble countenance, or else his silence a few seconds too long or the rigidity of his bearing. In the half light, I thought I saw a sort of smile on his lips, but when he spoke he did so in a voice which was distant, and, it seemed to me, exaggeratedly contrite.

'His Holiness wishes to see you.'

Ought I to lament or rejoice? Why did Adrian want to see me? Why had he sent Guicciardini in person? The Florentine's inscrutable face forbade me to question him. I looked towards the sky. It must have been six or seven in the morning. But of what day? And of what month? I asked a guard while we were passing through the corridor in the direction of the Vatican. It was Guicciardini who replied, as curtly as possible:

'It is Friday 20 November 1523.'

He had just reached a little door. He knocked and went in, making a sign that I should follow him. The entire furniture consisted of three empty red armchairs. He sat down, without inviting me to do likewise.

I could not explain his attitude. He who had been such a close friend, a confidant, he who, as I knew, so much enjoyed my company, with whom I had exchanged spirited words and friendly blows.

He got up abruptly.

'Holy Father, here is the prisoner!'

The Pope had come in noiselessly through the little door behind me. I turned round to look at him.

'Heavens above! Heavens above! Heavens above!'

I could not pronounce any other words. I fell to my knees and instead of kissing the hand of the sovereign pontiff I held it against me, pressed it to my forehead, to my face which was bathed in tears, to my trembling lips.

He freed himself gently.

'I must go and say mass. I will come back here in a hour.'

Leaving me on the ground, he went out. Guicciardini burst out laughing. I got up and went over to him with a threatening look.

'Should I embrace you or rain down blows upon you?'

His laughter redoubled. I collapsed into an armchair without being invited to do so.

'Tell me, Francesco, was I dreaming? Was that really Cardinal Julius who has just been in this room, dressed all in white? Was it really his hand that I have just kissed?'

'Cardinal Julius de Medici is no more. Yesterday he was elected to the throne of Peter, and he has chosen to call himself Clement, the seventh of that name.'

'Heavens above! Heavens above!'

My tears fell without restraint. However, I was able to stammer, through my sobs:

'And Adrian?'

'I would not have thought that his disappearance would have affected you to such an extent!'

I dealt him a blow on the shoulder with my fist which he did not even seek to dodge, so much did he know that he deserved it.

'It has already been two months since Pope Adrian has left us. It is said that he was poisoned. When the news of his death became known, anonymous individuals hung garlands over his doctor's door to thank him for having saved Rome.'

He murmured some conventional formula of disapproval before continuing:

'A battle then took place in the conclave between Cardinal Farnese and Cardinal Julius. The first one seemed to have the most votes, but after the trials which they had just experienced the princes of the Church wanted to encounter the generosity of a Medici again at the head of this city. After numerous ballots our friend was elected. Immediately there were celebrations in the streets. One of the first thoughts of the sovereign pontiff was for you, I can bear witness. He wanted to set you free at once, but I asked him permission to put on this charade. Will you forgive me?'

'With difficulty!'

I held him against me for a warm embrace.

'Maddalena and Giuseppe have wanted for nothing. I would have told you to go and see them, but we must wait for the Pope.'

By the time that the Florentine had informed me of everything which had taken place since my internment, Clement VII had returned. He asked not to be disturbed and came and sat down in the most simple way in the armchair which we had left for him.

'I thought that the best pranks in Rome were those of the late lamented Cardinal Bibbiena. But Master Guicciardini's inventions deserve to be remembered.'

He sat up slightly in his chair and his face became suddenly serious. He gazed at me intently.

'Last night we talked for a long time, Francesco and I. He cannot give me much advice in matters of religion, but Providence has burdened me with the additional task of running a state and of preserving the throne of Peter from the encroachments of temporal powers. In that area Francesco's counsels are precious to me, as are yours, Leo.'

With a look, he handed over to the diplomat.

'You have often asked, Leo, the real reason why you were carried off to Rome, why we decided one day to have an educated Moor kidnapped by Pietro Bovadiglia on the Barbary coasts. There was a scheme of things behind it which the late Pope Leo never had the opportunity to reveal to you. The moment has come today.'

Guicciardini was silent and Clement continued, as though they were both reciting the same text:

'Let us look at the world in which we live. In the East, there is a formidable empire, inspired by a faith which is not our own, built upon order and blind obedience, able to cast cannons and arm fleets. Its troops are advancing towards the centre of Europe. Buda and Pest are threatened, and Vienna will also be threatened before long. In the West there is another empire, Christian but no less formidable, since it already extends from the New World to Naples and dreams of universal domination. Above all, it dreams of submitting Rome to its will. The Inquisition flourishes on its Spanish lands, while the heresy of Luther flourishes on its German territories.'

The diplomat became more specific, encouraged by the approving nods of the Pope:

'On the one hand there is Sulaiman, Sultan and Caliph of Islam, young, ambitious, with limitless power, but anxious to make the crimes of his father forgotten and to appear as a man of good will. On the other hand there is Charles, King of Spain, even younger and no less ambitious, who has managed, by spending a small fortune, to get himself elected to the throne of the Holy Roman Empire. Facing these two men, the most powerful in the world, is the Papal State, with a gigantic cross and a dwarf sword.'

He made a short pause.

'Certainly, the Holy See is not alone in fearing this conjunction. There is King François, who is struggling to prevent his kingdom being dismembered. There is also Henry of England, entirely devoted to His Holiness, but too far off to be the slightest help.'

I still did not see how my humble self could be of use in this galaxy of crowned heads. But I did not want to interrupt the Florentine.

'This delicate situation, to which the Holy Father Leo alluded in your presence, was the subject of frequent discussion with Cardinal Julius and myself. Today, as before, we feel that we must be active in several directions to reduce the dangers. We must, before everything else, reconcile ourselves with François, which will not be a simple matter. For thirty years the kings of France have sought to conquer Italy. They were held justly responsible for the evils which afflicted the peninsula, and their troops were accused of leaving epidemics and devastation in their wake. We must also persuade Venice, Milan and Florence to forget their quarrels and make a common front against the empire.'

He adopted a quieter tone and leaned forward, as he always did when imparting a confidence:

'We have also thought that we should enter into negotiations with the Ottomans. But how? We have no idea, nor do we know what we might be able to obtain from them. A slowing down of the advance of the janissaries across the Christian lands of Central Europe? Probably not. The re-establishment of peace in the Mediterranean? An end to the depredations of the pirates?'

He replied to each of his own questions with a doubtful frown. Clement took over again:

'What is certain is that it is time to build a bridge between Rome and Constantinople. But I am not a sultan. If I dared to go too quickly, a thousand criticisms from Spain and Germany would rain down upon me, from my own colleagues.'

He smiled at his slip of the tongue.

'I mean from the cardinals. We have to proceed very carefully, to wait for opportunities, to see what the French, the Venetians and the other Christian powers are doing. You two will make a team. Leo now knows Turkish, as well as Arabic. Above all he knows the Ottomans well, and their ways of thought and action. He has even been on an embassy in Constantinople; Francesco is completely familiar with Our policies and can negotiate in Our name.'

He added, as if talking to himself:

'I would only have preferred one of the emissaries to have been a priest . . .'

And then, louder, in a slightly mocking tone:

'Master Guicciardini has already refused to have himself ordained. As for you, Leo, I am amazed that Our dear cousin and glorious predecessor never suggested that you should devote your life to religion.'

I was puzzled; why was the man who had introduced me to Maddalena asking me such a question? I glanced at Guicciardini; he seemed worried. I gathered that the Pope wanted to examine my religious convictions before sending me on a mission to the Muslims. Seeing that I hesitated to reply, he tried again:

'Would not religion have been the best of all ways of life for a man of learning and education like yourself?'

I was evasive:

'To speak of religion in the Holy Father's presence is like speaking of one's fiancée in her father's presence.'

Clement smiled. Without letting go of me.

'And what would you say about the fiancée if the father was not there?'

I decided to prevaricate no longer:

'If the head of the Church was not listening to me, I would say that religion teaches men humility, but that it has none itself. I would say that all religions have produced both saints and murderers, with an equally good conscience. That in the life of this city, there are the Clement years and the Adrian years, between which religion does not allow you to choose.'

'Does Islam allow a better choice?'

I almost said 'we' but caught myself in time:

'Muslims learn that "the best of men is the most useful to mankind" but in spite of such words, they sometimes honour false zealots more than real benefactors.'

'And where is the truth, in all that?'

'That is a question which I no longer ask myself. I have already made my choice between truth and life.'

'There must be one true faith!'

'That which unites the believers is not so much a common faith as the ritual actions they perform in common.'

'Is that so?'

The Pope's tone was unfathomable. Was he thinking of putting into question the mission with which he had just entrusted me? Guicciardini feared that he might, and hastened to intervene, with the broadest of smiles:

'Leo is saying that truth belongs only to God, and that men can only disfigure it, or debase it, or subjugate it.'

As if in approval, I murmured sufficiently loudly to be heard:

'May those who are in possession of the truth release it!'

Clement laughed awkwardly. Then he continued:

'Let us sum up. Brother Leo will not take religious orders. He will only be a diplomat, like Brother Francesco.'

Reassured, the latter clasped his hands together, made a pious frown and said teasingly:

'If Brother Leo has a horror of truth, he need have no fear; he will not encounter it often in our brotherhood.'

'*Amen*,' I said in the same tone.

*   *   *

A great number of friends had gathered at my house to celebrate my release, news of which had spread since dawn. Neighbours, pupils and friends all agreed that I had hardly changed after a year in prison. All, that is, except Giuseppe, who resolutely refused to recognize me and went into a sulk for a good three days before saying 'father' to me for the first time in his life.

'Abbad soon came from Naples, to greet my return, but also to exhort me to leave Rome without delay. For me, there was no longer any question of doing so.

'Are you sure you won't be shut up again in Castel San Angelo the next time you want to leave?'

'God will choose whether to leave me here or make me go.'

'Abbad's voice became suddenly severe.

'God has already chosen. Does He not say that one must not stay of one's free will in the land of the unbelievers?'

The look I gave him was heavy with reproach. He hastened to apologize.

'I know that I have no right to tell you what to do, I who live in Naples, I who offer gifts twice a year to the Church of San Gennaio, and have Biscayans and Castilians for partners. But I fear for you, by the Book! I feel that you are mixed up in disputes which have nothing to do with us. You go to war with a Pope, and you are only saved by his death.'

'This city is now my city, and having experienced imprisonment here has only made me feel more attached to its fate and to that of those who rule it. They consider me as a friend, and I cannot treat them as if they were simply Rumis.'

'But your own family is elsewhere, and you ignore them as if thirty years of your life and theirs had never existed.'

He paused before striking me with the news:

'Your mother died this summer.'

Obviously in the know, Maddalena came to warm my hand with a consoling kiss. 'Abbad continued:

'I was in Tunis during her last illness. She asked for you to come.'

'Did you tell her I was in prison?'

'Yes! I thought it better that she should save for you her last anguish rather than her last reproach.'

★ ★ ★

In an effort to be forgiven for having been the bearer of evil tidings once again, 'Abbad had brought a casket for me from Tunis, containing my voluminous notes from my travels, with which I was able to set about writing the work which had been so often requested since my arrival in Rome: a description of Africa and the remarkable things that may be found there.

But I had not yet written the first line when another project came to monopolize my writing time, a senseless but fascinating project which was suggested to me by my former pupil Hans, a month after I left prison. Having decided to go back to Saxony, he came to bid me farewell, reiterating his gratitude for the instruction which I had given him, and introducing me at the same time to one of his friends, a printer, a Saxon like himself, but who had been living in Rome for fifteen years.

Unlike Hans, this man was not a Lutheran. He was a disciple of a Dutch thinker whom Guicciardini had already mentioned to me: Erasmus. It was the latter who had suggested the mad scheme which he had adopted as his own.

This was to prepare an enormous lexicon in which each word should appear in a multitude of languages, including Latin, Arabic, Hebrew, Greek, Saxon, German, Italian, French, Castilian, Turkish and many others. For my part I undertook to provide the Arabic and Hebrew sections on the basis of a long list of Latin words.

The printer spoke with moving fervour:

'This project will probably never see the light of day, at least not in my lifetime or in the form for which I strive. Nevertheless I am ready to devote my life and my money to it. To strive so that all men may one day be able to understand each other, is that not the noblest of ideals?'

To this grandiose dream, this marvellous folly, the Saxon printer had given the name *Anti-Babel*.

The Year of the King of France
931 A.H.
29 October 1524 – 17 October 1525

Cold messenger of death and defeat, the snow fell upon my way that year for a third time. As in Granada during a certain winter of my childhood, as in the Atlas in the autumn of my fortune, it came back in a storm, this devastating blast, ill-fated whisper of destiny.

I was returning from Pavia, in the company of Guicciardini, having carried out a most extraordinary mission, a most secret one as well, since of all the princes of Christianity the Pope alone knew its import, and only the King of France had been properly forewarned.

Ostensibly, the Florentine had been appointed by Clement VII to perform a mission of mediation. The last months had been bloody. The emperor's troops had tried to take Marseilles, showering hundreds of cannon-balls over the city. Without success. King François had retaliated by seizing Milan and then by besieging Pavia. The two armies threatened to confront one another in Lombardy, and it was the Pope's duty to avert a murderous battle. It was his duty, Guicciardini explained to me, but it was not in his interests, since it was only the rivalry which existed between the two Christian powers that gave the Holy See some freedom of manoeuvre. 'To make sure that peace is not made, we must be the mediators.'

More important was the other mission, in which I was involved. The Pope had learned that an ambassador of the Grand Turk was on his way towards the camp of the King of France. Was this not the occasion so long awaited to make contact with the Ottomans? Hence Guicciardini and I had to be beneath the walls of Pavia at the same time as this emissary, and give him a verbal message from Clement VII.

In spite of the cold, we reached the French lines in less than a week. We were welcomed first by a high-ranking old gentleman, Maréchal de Chabannes, seigneur of La Palice, who knew Guicciardini very well. He seemed surprised at our visit, since another of the Pope's envoys, the bursar Matteo Giberti, had arrived a week earlier. Not in the least disconcerted, Guicciardini replied in a tone which was half ingratiating, half joking, that it was normal 'to send John the Baptist ahead of Christ'.

This bragging apparently had some effect, since the Florentine was received that very day by the king. I was not myself admitted to the interview, but I was able to kiss the monarch's hand. To do this I barely needed to bow my head, since he was at least a hand's breadth taller than me. His eyes slid over me like the shadow of a reed before dispersing in a thousand unattainable shimmers while mine were fixed in fascination on a particular point in his face, where his immense nose came to protect a moustache that was too fine, plunging valiantly over his lips. It was probably because of his complexion that François' smile appeared ironical even when he wanted to appear benevolent.

Guicciardini came out well pleased from the round tent where the meeting had taken place. The king had confirmed that the Ottoman would arrive the next day, and seemed delighted at the idea of contact between Rome and Constantinople.

'What better could he hope for than a blessing from the Holy Father when he seals an alliance with the unbelievers?' the Florentine remarked.

Before adding, apparently delighted to have caught me unawares:

'I mentioned your presence here and your knowledge of Turkish. His Majesty asked me if you could act as interpreter.'

However, when the Ottoman envoy came in and began to speak, I was struck dumb, incapable of opening my lips, incapable even of clearing my throat. The king gave me a murderous look, and Guicciardini was red with anger and confusion. Very fortunately the visitor had his own translator, who, moreover, knew François' language.

Of all those present, one man alone understood my agitation and shared it, although his office forbade him to reveal anything, at least until he had accomplished the formal ritual attached to his functions of representative. Only after having read out the letter from the sultan, and after exchanging a few smiling words with the king, did the ambassador come over to me, embrace me warmly, and say out loud:

'I knew that I should meet allies and friends in this camp, but I did not expect that I should find a brother here whom I had lost for many long years.'

When the interpreter of the Ottoman delegation had translated these words, the company had eyes only for me, and Guicciardini breathed again. I myself had only one dazed and incredulous word on my lips:

'Harun!'

I had indeed been told the previous evening that the Grand Turk's ambassador was called Harun Pasha. But I had not made the slightest connection between him and my best friend, my closest relative, my almost brother.

We had to wait until the evening to be alone in the sumptuous tent which his escort had put up for him. His Excellency the Ferret wore a high and heavy turban of white silk, embellished with a huge ruby and a peacock's feather. But he hastened to take it off, with a gesture of relief, revealing a balding greying head beneath.

Straight away he began to satisfy my evident curiosity:

'After our voyage together to Constantinople I often entered the Sublime Porte, as the emissary of 'Aruj Barbarossa, may God have mercy upon him! and then of his brother Khair al-Din. I learned Turkish and the language of the courtiers, I made friends at the *diwan* and I negotiated the incorporation of Algiers into the Ottoman sultanate. I shall be proud of that until the Day of Judgement.'

His hand made a sweeping gesture through the air.

'At present from the borders of Persia to the coast of the Maghrib, from Belgrade to the Yemen, there is one single Muslim Empire, whose master honours me with his confidence and his good will.'

He continued, with a tone of reproach he did not try to hide:

'And what have you been doing all these years? Is it true that you are now a high dignitary at the papal court?'

I deliberately repeated his own formula:

'His Holiness honours me with his confidence and his good will.'

I thought it as well to add, emphasizing every word:

'And he has sent me here to meet you. He hopes to establish a link between Rome and Constantinople.'

If I was expecting some excitement, some show of joy, some surprise at this most official pronouncement I was deeply frustrated. Harun suddenly seemed preoccupied by a speck of dirt on the rivers of his billowing sleeve. Having rubbed and blown upon it to wipe it away entirely, he deigned to reply, in tones of pious frivolity:

'Between Rome and Constantinople, do you say? And to what end?'

'For peace. Wouldn't it be wonderful if Christians and Muslims all around the Mediterranean could live and trade together without war or piracy, if I could go from Alexandria to Tunis with my family without being kidnapped by some Sicilian?'

Once more that stubborn mark on his sleeve. He rubbed it even harder and dusted it off energetically before directing towards me a look without kindness.

'Listen to me, Hasan! If you want to recall our friendship, our years at school, our family, the impending marriage of my son and your daughter, let's talk about such things in peace around a full table and, by God, I should enjoy that moment more than any other. But if you are the envoy of the Pope and I am the envoy of the sultan, then we must discuss things differently.'

I tried to defend myself:

'Why should you reproach me? I only spoke about peace. Is it not right that the religions of the Book should cease to massacre one another?'

He interrupted me:

'You must know that between Constantinople and Rome, between Constantinople and Paris, it is faith which divides, and interest, noble or base, which brings together. Don't talk to me about peace or the Book, because they are not in question, and it is not about them our masters think.'

Since we were children I had never been able to keep up an argument against the Ferret. My reply had the ring of capitulation:

'All the same I see a common interest between your master and my own; neither the one nor the other wants Charles V's empire to spread throughout Europe, or Barbary!'

Harun smiled.

'Now that we are talking the same language I can tell you what I have come to do here. I am bringing the king gifts, promises, even a hundred or so brave horsemen who will fight at his side. Our struggle is the same; do you know that the French troops have just captured Ugo de Moncada, the man whom I myself defeated before Algiers after the death of 'Aruj? Do you know that our fleet has been ordered to intervene if the imperial troops try to take Marseilles again? My master has decided to seal an alliance with King François, and to this end he will continue to multiply his gestures of friendship.'

'Will you be able to promise the king that the Ottoman offensive in Europe will not continue?'

Harun seemed exasperated by my naïveté.

'If we attacked the Magyars, whose sovereign is none other than the brother-in-law of the Emperor Charles, the King of France would not think of reproaching us for it. It would be the same if we were to besiege Vienna, which is governed by the emperor's own brother.'

'Won't the King of France be criticized by his peers if he lets Christian territories be conquered in this way?'

'Probably, but my master is ready to give him in exchange the right to protect the destiny of the churches of Jerusalem and the Christians of the Levant.'

We were silent for a moment, each immersed in our own thoughts. Harun leaned back on a carved chest and smiled.

'When I told the King of France that I had brought a hundred soldiers for him, he seemed embarrassed. I thought for a moment that he would refuse to let them fight at his side, but eventually he thanked me most warmly. And he made it known in the camp that these horsemen were Christian vassals of the sultan.'

He continued abruptly:

'When will you return to your family?'

'One day, certainly,' I said hesitantly, 'when Rome has lost its attractions for me.'

' 'Abbad the Soussi told me when I saw him in Tunis that the Pope had imprisoned you for a year in a citadel.'

'I had criticized him sharply.'

Harun was overcome by a fit of merriment.

'You Hasan, son of Muhammad the Granadan, allowed yourself to criticize the Pope right in the middle of Rome! 'Abbad even told me that you criticized this Pope for being a foreigner.'

'It was not exactly that. But my preference was certainly for an Italian, if possible a Medici from Florence.'

My friend was dumbfounded that I should answer him in all

seriousness.

'A Medici, you say? Well, as soon as I return to Constantinople I shall suggest that the title of caliph should be taken away from the Ottomans and restored to a descendant of 'Abbas.'

He cautiously stroked his neck and collar, repeating as if it were a refrain:

'You prefer a Medici, you say?'

While I was conversing with Harun, Guicciardini was concocting the most elaborate plans, convinced that my relationship with the emissary of the Grand Turk presented a unique opportunity for papal diplomacy. I had to moderate his enthusiasm, to make him aware, in particular, of the complete indifference which my brother-in-law had displayed. But the Florentine dismissed my objections with a wave of his hand:

'In his capacity as ambassador, Harun Pasha will undoubtedly report our overtures to the Grand Turk. A step has been taken, and we shall receive an Ottoman emissary at Rome before long. Perhaps you and I will also take the road to Constantinople.'

But before going further, it was time to give the Pope an account of our mission.

★　★　★

We were hastening towards Rome when the snowstorm which I mentioned took us by surprise a few miles south of Bologna. With the first blasts, the drama of the Atlas broke in upon my memory. I felt myself brought back to those terrifying moments when I had felt myself surrounded by death as if by a pack of hungry wolves, only linked with life by the hand of my Hiba, which I held savagely. I repeated over and over again to myself the name of my beautiful Numidian slave, as if no other woman had ever taken her place in my heart.

The wind redoubled its force, and the soldiers of our escort had to dismount to try to shelter. I did the same, and so did Guicciardini, but I quickly lost sight of him. I thought I heard shouts, calls, yells. From time to time I saw some fleeting figure which I tried to follow, but which vanished each time into fog. Soon my horse ran away. Running blindly, I collided with a tree, which I clung to, crouching and shivering. When, after the storm had died down, someone finally found me, I was stretched out unconscious, deep in the snow, my right leg fractured by some maddened horse. Apparently I had not remained covered up for long, which saved my leg from amputation, but I could not walk and my chest was on fire.

So we returned towards Bologna, where Guicciardini put me in a little hostelry near the Spanish College. He himself left the next day, predicting that I would be on my feet within ten days and would be able to join him at the papal court. But that was only to make me feel better, because when he arrived in Rome he immediately advised Maddalena to come and join me as soon as possible with Giuseppe, and to bring my papers and my notes so that I could overcome my boredom by writing. In fact I could not get used to being unable to move, and at first I was in a perpetual temper, all day long cursing the snow, destiny and the unfortunate hotel-keeper, who nevertheless served me patiently.

I was not to leave my bedroom until the end of that year. First I was nearly carried off by pneumonia and I had hardly recovered when my leg began to bother me again; it was so numb and swollen that I feared amputation once more. Out of rage and despair I worked and worked, day and night, and in this way I was able to finish the Arabic and Hebrew translations which I had promised the Saxon printer. I also managed to write the first volumes of my *Description of Africa* that year. After a few months I eventually began to get used to the advantages attached to my condition of sedentary scribe and penitent traveller, and to experience the everyday joys of my little family. But not without keeping an anxious eye on what was happening around me.

I was still between two fevers at the beginning of March when Maddalena told me the news that was already shaking Italy: the imperial troops had crushed the army of the King of France before Pavia. At first it was rumoured that François had been killed; I soon learned that he had only been captured. But the situation was only a little less disastrous; whatever the fate of the monarch, it was clear that the French would not be able to stand in the way of the emperor's ambitions for some time.

I thought of Clement VII. He had shown too much favour to François not to suffer his part of the defeat. How would he extricate himself from his false step? Was he going to make peace with Charles V to avert his wrath? Or would he make use of his authority to gather the princes of Christendom together against an emperor who had become too powerful, too dangerous for them all? I would have given a great deal to be able to talk to the Pope. And even more so to Guicciardini, particularly after a letter from him reached me at the beginning of summer, containing this enigmatic sentence, fearful in its irony: *'Only a miracle can save Rome now, and the Pope desires that I should accomplish it!'*

The Year of the Black Bands
932 A.H.
18 October 1525 – 7 October 1526

He was standing in front of me, a statue of flesh and iron, with a powerful laugh and enormous outbursts of rage.

'I am the armed might of the Church.'

Men though called him the 'great devil', and loved him for it, indomitable, intrepid, hot-headed, taking women and fortresses by storm. They were afraid of him, and prayed to God to protect him and to keep him far away.

'My incorrigible cousin Giovanni,' Clement VII would say, with tenderness and resignation.

Condottiere and Medici, he was the epitome of all Italy. The troops he commanded were like him, venal and generous, tyrannical and lovers of justice, indifferent to death. That year, they had entered the Pope's service. They were called the Black Bands, and their leader was soon no longer known as Giovanni di Medici but Giovanni of the Black Bands.

I met him at Bologna. For my first outing I had decided to go to the palace of Master Jacopo Salviati, a venerable gentleman of the city, who had showered me with kindness all through my illness, constantly sending me money, books, clothes and presents. Guicciardini had asked him to take me under his protection, and he acquitted himself of that office with fatherly diligence, never letting a week pass without sending one of his pages to inquire after my health. This Salviati was the most prominent person in Bologna, and he lived in a luxurious manner worthy of the Medicis. It is true that his wife was none other than Pope Leo's sister, and that his daughter

Maria had married Giovanni of the Black Bands. Unfortunately for her, it must be said, since she saw him very rarely, between two campaigns, two idylls, two affairs.

That day however he had come, less for his wife's sake than for their son, aged six. I was walking towards the Palazzo Salviati, leaning on Maddalena's shoulder, when the procession came within earshot. The condottiere was accompanied by a good forty of his faithful followers on horseback. Some passers-by murmured his name, some cheered him, others hurried past. I preferred to draw back to let him pass, as my gait was still slow and uncertain. He cried from far off:

'Cosimo.'

A child appeared in the embrasure of a window on the first floor. Giovanni set off at a trot, and then, when he was underneath the boy, drew his sword, pointed it at the boy and shouted:

'Jump!'

Maddalena almost fainted. She covered her eyes. I myself stood rooted to the spot. However, Master Jacopo, who had come out to welcome his son-in-law, said nothing. He certainly seemed extremely annoyed, but as if at some everyday misfortune rather than at a drama. Little Cosimo seemed no more surprised nor impressed. Putting his foot on the frieze, he jumped into the air. At the last moment, his father, throwing his sword away, caught him under his arms, held him at arms' length and raised him above his head.

'How is my prince?'

The child and the father laughed, as well as the soldiers in the escort. Jacopo Salviati forced himself to smile. Seeing me arrive, he took advantage of this to relieve the tension by introducing me formally to his son-in-law.

'Master John-Leo, geographer, poet, diplomat at the papal court.'

The condottiere leaped to the ground. One of his men brought him back his sword, which he put back in its sheath while presenting himself to me with excessive joviality.

'I am the armed might of the Church.'

He had short hair, a thick brown moustache cut at the sides and a look which transfixed me more surely than a lance. At the time, the man seemed to me most unpleasant. But I soon changed my mind, seduced, like so many others, by his astonishing capacity to leave his gladiatorial soul behind to become a Florentine, a Medici of astonishing sensitivity and insight as soon as he entered a salon.

'You were at Pavia, someone told me.'

'I stayed there only a few days, in the company of Master Francesco Guicciardini.'

'I was far away myself. I was inspecting my troops on the road to Milan. When I returned the Ottoman envoy had left. And you too, I think.'

He had a knowing smile. To avoid betraying the secret of my mission I decided to keep silent and to turn my eyes away from his. He continued:

'I have heard that a message left Paris recently for Constantinople asking the Turks to attack Hungary to force Charles V to divert his attention from Italy.'

'Isn't the King of France a prisoner in Spain?'

'That doesn't stop him from negotiating with the Pope and the sultan or from sending instructions to his mother, who is regent of the kingdom.'

'Wasn't it said that he is on the point of death?'

'He is no longer. Death has changed its mind.'

As I persisted in not expressing any opinion of my own, confining myself to asking questions, Giovanni asked me directly:

'Don't you think that it seems like a very curious coalition: the Pope allied to François, who is allied to the Grand Turk?'

Was he trying to sound out my feelings for the Grand Turk? Or to find out what could have taken place with Harun Pasha?

'I think that the Grand Turk, however powerful he may be, is not in a position to decide the outcome of a war in Italy. A hundred men taking part on the battlefield are more important than a hundred thousand men at the other side of the continent.'

'Who is the strongest in Italy, in your opinion?'

'There was a battle at Pavia, and we should drawn our conclusions from it.'

My reply evidently pleased him. His tone became friendly, even admiring.

'I am happy to hear these words, because, in Rome the Pope is hesitant and your friend Guicciardini is pushing him to attack Charles and ally himself with François, at the very moment when the King of France is the emperor's prisoner. In my position I cannot express my reservations without giving the impression of fearing a confrontation with the empire, but you will soon realize that this mad Giovanni is not entirely devoid of wisdom and this great sage

Guicciardini is on the point of committing a folly and of making the Pope commit one as well.'

Thinking that he had spoken too seriously, he began to tell a succession of anecdotes about his latest wild boar hunt. Before returning abruptly to the charge:

'You should say what you think to the Pope. Why don't you come back to Rome with me?'

I had in fact intended to put an end to my seemingly endless enforced stay in Bologna. I hastened to accept his offer, telling myself that a journey at Giovanni's side would be extremely pleasant, and without danger, since no brigand would dare to approach such a procession. And so, the very next day, I found myself on the road again with Maddalena and Giuseppe, surrounded by the fearsome warriors of the Black Bands, who became, on this occasion, the most attentive of companions.

★ ★ ★

After three days' march, we arrived at Giovanni's residence, a magnificent castle called Il Trebbio, where we spent a night. Early the next morning we reached Florence.

'You must be the only Medici who does not know this city!' exclaimed the condottiere.

'On the way to Pavia with Guicciardini we almost stopped here, but we had no time.'

'He must be a real barbarian, that "time" which prevents you seeing Florence!'

And he added immediately:

'Time presses on this occasion too, but I would not forgive myself if I did not show you around.'

I had never before visited a city with an army as a guide. All along the Via Larga to the Palazzo Medici, where we burst into the colonnaded courtyard, it was a regular morning parade. A servant came to invite us in, but Giovanni refused curtly.

'Is Master Alessandro there?'

'I think he is asleep.'

'And Master Ippolito?'

'He is asleep too. Should I wake them up?'

Giovanni shrugged his shoulders disdainfully and turned back.

Leaving the courtyard he went several paces to the right to show me a building under construction:

'The church of San Lorenzo. This is where Michelangelo Buonarotti works now, but I don't dare to take you there because he could easily show us the door. He has little love for the Medici and besides he has an unpleasant character. Indeed, that was why he came back to Florence. Most of our great artists live in Rome. But Leo X, who gathered so many talented people around him, preferred to send Michelangelo away and give him a commission here.'

He resumed the tour in the direction of the Duomo. On both sides of the road the houses seemed to be well laid out and tastefully embellished, but there were very few as luxurious as those in Rome.

'The Eternal City is full of works of art,' my guide acknowledged, 'but Florence is itself a work of art, and it is to the Florentines that we owe the best in all disciplines.'

I thought I was listening to a Fassi talking!

When we reached the Piazza della Signoria, and when a notable of a certain age, dressed in a long robe, came up to Giovanni to exchange a few words with him, a group of people began to chant *'Palle! Palle!'*, the rallying cry of the Medici, to which my companion replied with a salute, saying to me:

'Don't think that all the members of my family would be acclaimed in this fashion. I am the only one who still enjoys some favour with the Florentines. If, for instance, my cousin Julius, I should say Pope Clement, were to decide to come here today, he would be booed and jostled. Moreover, he knows it very well.'

'But isn't it your native city?'

'Ah, my friend, Florence is a strange mistress for the Medici! When we are far off, she calls us with loud cries; when we come back, she curses us.'

'What does she want today?'

He had a worried air. He stopped his horse in the middle of the street, at the very entrance to the Ponte Vecchio, on which the crowd had parted to let him pass through, and from which some cheers were coming.

'Florence wants to be governed by a prince, on condition that it should be governed as a republic. Every time that our ancestors forgot this, they had cause to regret it bitterly. Today the Medici are represented in the city of their birth by that presumptuous young Alessandro. He is barely fifteen, and he thinks that because he is a

Medici and the son of the Pope, Florence belongs to him, women and goods.'

'Son of the Pope?'

My surprise was genuine. Giovanni burst out laughing.

'Don't tell me that you have lived seven years in Rome without knowing that Alessandro was Clement's bastard?'

I confessed my ignorance. He was delighted to enlighten me:

'At a time when he was still neither Pope nor cardinal, my cousin knew a Moorish slavegirl in Naples, who bore him this son.'

We were going back up towards the Palazzo Pitti. Soon, we crossed the Porta Romana, where Giovanni was cheered once more. But, sunk in his thoughts, he did not reply to the crowd. I hastened to do so in his place, which amused my son Giuseppe so much that all along the road he constantly begged me to make the same gestures, bursting out with laughter each time.

★ ★ ★

The very day of our arrival in Rome, Giovanni of the Black Bands insisted that we should go to the Pope together. We found him in conclave with Guicciardini, who did not seem at all pleased at our arrival. He had probably just convinced the Holy Father to take some painful decision and feared that Giovanni might make him change his mind. To conceal his anxiety, and to sound out our intentions, he adopted, as was his wont, a jocular tone:

'So there can be no more meetings between Florentines unless a Moor is among us!'

The Pope gave an embarrassed smile. Giovanni did not even smile. For my part I replied in the same tone, with a gesture of marked irritation:

'There can be no meeting between Medici unless the people join with us!'

This time Giovanni's laugh cracked like a whip, and his hand came down on my back in a formidable friendly hug. Laughing in his turn, Guicciardini quickly passed on to the events of the moment:

'We have just received a message of the utmost importance. King François will leave Spain before Ash Wednesday.'

A discussion ensued in which Giovanni and I put forward, with due diffidence, arguments in favour of coming to terms with Charles V. But in vain. The Pope was entirely under the influence of Guicciardini, who had persuaded him to stand up to 'Caesar' and to be the soul of the anti-imperial coalition.

★ ★ ★

On 22 May 1526 a 'Holy League' came into existence in the French town of Cognac. As well as François and the Pope, it included the Duke of Milan and the Venetians. It was war, one of the most terrible that Rome would ever know. Because, though he had temporized after Pavia, this time the emperor was determined to push matters to their conclusion against François, whom he had released in exchange for a written agreement which was quickly declared null and void as soon as the latter had crossed the Pyrenees, and against the Pope, ally of 'the perjurer'. The imperial armies began to regroup in Italy, beside Milan, Trent and Naples. Against them, Clement could count only on the bravura of the Black Bands and their commanders. Judging that the principal danger would come from the north, the latter left for Mantua, determined to prevent the enemy from crossing the Po.

Alas! Charles V also had his allies, even within the papal state, a clan which was called 'la imperialista', headed by the powerful Cardinal Pompeo Colonna. In September, taking advantage of the fact that the Black Bands were far away, the cardinal burst into the quarters of Borgo and Trastevere at the head of a band of pillagers who set fire to several houses and proclaimed in public that they were going to 'deliver Rome from the tyranny of the Pope'. Clement VII hurriedly took refuge in Castel San Angelo, where he barricaded himself in while Colonna's men were sacking the palace of St Peter. I thought of taking Maddalena and Giuseppe to the castle, but I gave up the idea, considering that it would be most unwise to cross the Ponte San Angelo in the circumstances. I went to earth in my own house, letting matters take their own course in those difficult times.

In fact the Pope was obliged to accept all Colonna's demands. He signed an agreement promising to withdraw from the Holy League against the emperor, and refrain from taking any sanctions against the guilty cardinal. Of course, as soon as the attackers had gone he made it known to all that there was no question of him respecting a

347

treaty imposed under conditions of duress, terror and sacrilege.

The day after this violent incident, while Clement was still fulminating against the emperor and his allies, news arrived in Rome of the victory of Sultan Sulaiman at Mohàcs, and of the death of the King of Hungary, the emperor's brother-in-law. The Pope summoned me to ask me whether, in my opinion, the Turks were going to launch an assault on Vienna, whether they would soon push on into Germany, or move towards Venice. I had to say that I did not have the slightest idea. The Holy Father seemed extremely concerned. Guicciardini judged that the responsibility for this defeat lay entirely with the emperor, who was waging war in Italy and attacking the King of France instead of defending the lands of Christendom against the Turks, instead of fighting the heresy which was devastating Germany. He added:

'Why should one expect the Germans to go to the aid of Hungary if Luther tells them morning and night: "The Turks are the chastisement which God has sent us. To oppose them is to oppose the wish of the Creator!" '

Clement VII nodded in approval. Guicciardini waited until we were outside to let me share in his extreme satisfaction:

'The victory of the Ottoman will change the course of history. Perhaps this is the miracle which we were waiting for.'

⋆　⋆　⋆

That year I put the final touches to my *Description of Africa*. Then, without taking a single day's rest, I decided to set to work on the chronicle of my own life and the events in which I had been involved. Maddalena thought that the sight of me working with such frenzy was a bad omen.

'It's as if our time was running out,' she would say.

I would have liked to reassure her, but my mind was beset by the same obsessive apprehensions: Rome was fading away, my Italian existence was coming to an end, and I did not know when I would have the time to write again.

The Year of the Lansquenets
933 A.H.
8 October 1526 – 26 September 1527

Thus came my fortieth year, that of my last hope, of my final desertion.

Giovanni of the Black Bands was sending the most reassuring news from the front, confirming the Pope, the Curia and the whole of Rome in the false impression that the war was very far away and would remain there. *The Imperial forces are north of the Po and will never cross it,* the condottiere promised. And from Trastevere to the Trevi quarter people delighted to boast of the gallantry of the Medici and his men. Romans longstanding or of passage vied with each other in their contempt for 'those barbarian Germans', who, as everyone knows, have always looked at the Eternal City with envy, greed and a relentless lack of understanding.

I could not join in this mad euphoria, so deeply were tales of the last days of Granada engraved upon my memory, when my father, my mother, Sarah and the whole crowd of those soon to be exiled were persuaded that deliverance was certain, when they affected unanimous contempt for a triumphant Castile, when they cast deep suspicion upon anyone who dared to question the imminent arrival of assistance. Having learned from the misfortune of my own family, I had come to be distrustful of appearances. When everyone persists in the same opinion, I turn away from it; the truth is surely elsewhere.

Guicciardini reacted in the same way. Appointed lieutenant-general of the papal troops, he was in the north of Italy, together with Giovanni, whom he observed with a mixture of admiration and fury: *He is a man of great courage, but he risks his life in the merest skirmish. But if anything should happen to him, it would be impossible to contain the flood of the imperial troops.* Written in a letter to the Pope, these complaints only came to light in Rome when they already had become meaningless; struck down by a falconer's ball, the chief of the Black Bands had his leg shattered. An amputation was necessary. It was dark, and Giovanni insisted on holding the torch himself while the doctor cut off the limb with a saw. Pointless suffering, because the wounded man expired shortly after the operation.

Of all the men I have known, Tumanbay the Circassian and Giovanni of the Black Bands were certainly the most courageous. The first had been killed by the Sultan of the East, the second by the Emperor of the West. The first had been unable to save Cairo; the second could not spare Rome from the suffering which awaited her.

In the city, there was immediate panic once the news of his death became known. The enemy had only advanced a few miles, but it was as if they were already at the gates of the city, as if the disappearance of Giovanni had torn down the fortresses, dried up the rivers and flattened the mountains.

In fact, nothing seemed able to halt the advancing tide. Before his death, the chief of the Black Bands was desperately attempting to prevent two powerful imperial armies joining forces in northern Italy; the one, composed principally of Castilians, was in the vicinity of Milan, while the other, by far the more dangerous, consisted of German lansquenets, almost all of whom were Lutherans from Bavaria, Saxony and Franconia. They had crossed the Alps and invaded the Trentino with the conviction that they had been entrusted with some divine mission, to chastise the Pope, who was guilty of having corrupted Christianity. Ten thousand uncontrollable heretics, marching against the Pope under the banner of a Catholic emperor; such was the calamity which engulfed Italy that year.

The death of Giovanni, followed by the hurried retreat of the Black Bands, had enabled all the imperial troops to join forces and to cross the Po, determined to go as far as the palace of St Peter. There must have been about thirty thousand soldiers, badly dressed, badly fed and badly paid, who reckoned on living off the country and exploiting it. They came first to Bologna, which put up a considerable ransom in order to be spared; then it was the turn of Florence, where the plague had just broken out, and which also paid a heavy tribute to prevent itself being pillaged. Guicciardini, who had played a part in these negotiations, strongly advised the Pope to make a similar agreement.

Once more, there was a sense of euphoria; peace was within reach, people said. On 25 March 1527 the Viceroy of Naples, Charles de Lannoy, the special envoy of the emperor, arrived at Rome to conclude an agreement. I was in the middle of the crowd in St Peter's Square, to be present at this moment of deliverance. The weather was fine, a marvellous spring day, when the notable arrived, surrounded by his bodyguard. But at the very moment when he entered the gate of the Vatican, there was a flash of lightning, followed by a torrential outburst of rain which poured down on us with a noise which seemed to herald the end of the world. When the first shock had passed I ran to take shelter in a doorway, which was soon surrounded by a sea of mud.

At my side, a woman was soon wailing loudly, lamenting this evil portent. Hearing her, I remembered the flood at Granada, which I had experienced through the eyes of my mother, may God surround her with His mercy! Was this, once again, a sign from Heaven, a harbinger of disaster? However, that day there was no overflowing of the Tiber, nor ruinous floods, nor great slaughter. In fact the peace agreement was signed at the end of the afternoon. To ensure that the city should be spared, it stipulated that the Pope should hand over a substantial sum of money.

The money was indeed handed over, sixty thousand ducats, someone told me, and as a sign of his good faith, Clement VII decided to dismiss the mercenaries whom he had recruited. But this was not enough to stop the imperial army from moving forward. Officers who dared to mention retreat were threatened with death at the hands of their own troops; at the height of the quarrel, the chief of the lansquenets was brought down by a fit of apoplexy, and the command passed to the Constable of Bourbon, cousin and sworn enemy of the King of France. He was a man without much authority, who was following the imperial army rather than commanding it. No one else could control this mob any longer, not even the emperor, who was, besides, in Spain. Uncontrollable, unyielding, destroying everything before it, it was advancing towards Rome, where hopes for peace had given way to a panic becoming increasingly insane every day. The cardinals in particular could think only of hiding themselves or of running away with their riches.

The Pope persisted in believing that his agreement with the viceroy would eventually be respected, even if this were to be at the very last moment. It was only at the end of April, when the imperial troops reached the Tiber, a few miles upstream from the city, that the Holy Father resolved to organize its defence. As the papal coffers were empty, he elevated six rich merchants to the rank of cardinal, who handed over two hundred thousand ducats for the privilege. With this money, an army of eight thousand could be raised, two thousand Swiss guards, two thousand soldiers from the Black Bands, and four thousand volunteers from among the inhabitants of Rome.

At the age of forty, I did not feel capable of bearing arms. However, I volunteered to run the arms and munitions store at the Castel San Angelo. In order to fulfil satisfactorily a task which required my vigilant presence day and night, I decided to take up residence in the fortress, arranging to move Maddalena and Giuseppe in there as well. It was in fact the best-defended part of the whole city, and it soon became flooded with refugees. I had occupied my former room, which made me seem most affluent, since the newcomers were obliged to cram themselves by whole families into the corridors.

In the first days of May a strange atmosphere came over this makeshift encampment, fertile ground for the most bizarre excitements. I shall always remember the moment when a fife player in the papal orchestra arrived quite out of breath, shouting at the top of his voice:

'I've killed the Bourbon! I've killed the Bourbon!'

It was a certain Benvenuto Cellini from Florence. One of his brothers had fought in the ranks of the Black Bands, but he himself, a medal-maker by trade, had never belonged to any army. He had gone off to fight, he said, with two of his friends near the Porta Trittone.

'There was a thick fog,' he declared, 'but I could make out the silhouette of the constable on horseback. I fired my arquebus. A few minutes later the mist cleared, and I saw the Bourbon lying on the ground, evidently dead.'

Hearing this, I simply shrugged my shoulders. Others snapped at him harshly; the battle was raging on the city walls, especially near the Borgo, and the shooting had never been so heavy; a tumult of war, suffering and fear rose from the city; this was not the time for vain boasting.

However, I must say that to my greatest surprise before the end of the day the news was confirmed. The Bourbon had indeed been killed in the vicinity of the Porta Trittone. When a cardinal announced it to us, a broad smile lighting up his haggard face, there were several shouts of victory. At my side there was a man who did not express the slightest joy. He was a veteran of the Black Bands, and he was boiling with rage.

'Is this the way wars are fought these days? With these accursed arquebuses, the most valiant of cavalrymen can be picked off from afar by a fife player! This is the end of chivalry! The end of wars of honour!'

However, the Florentine fife player became a hero in the eyes of the multitude. He was given drinks, he was begged to tell the story of his exploit again, he was carried about in triumph. The celebration was uncalled for, because the death of the Bourbon did not delay the assault of the imperial armies for a second. Quite the contrary: it could be said that the disappearance of the commander of the army had served only to arouse his troops even further. Taking advantage of the fog, which meant that the artillery installed at Castel San Angelo could not function, the lansquenets scaled the walls in several places and poured into the streets. Some survivors were still able to get to the castle, their eyes full of the tales of the first horrors. Other accounts were to follow.

By the God who caused me to traverse the wide world, by the God who has made me live through the torments of Cairo and those of Granada, I have never encountered such bestiality, such hatred, such bloody destruction, such pleasure in massacre, destruction and sacrilege!

Would anyone believe me if I were to say that nuns were raped on the altars of the churches before being strangled by laughing lansquenets? Would anyone believe me if I were to say that the monasteries were sacked, that the monks were relieved of their habits and forced under the threat of the whip to trample on the crucifix and proclaim that they worshipped the cursed Satan, that the old manuscripts from the libraries fed huge bonfires, around which drunken soldiers danced, that no sanctuary, no palace, no house, escaped being looted, that eight thousand citizens perished, mostly from among the poor, while the rich were held hostage until their ransom was paid?

Contemplating the thick columns of smoke rising up over the city in ever growing number from the wall of the castle, I could not erase the vision of Pope Leo from my memory, who had predicted this disaster at our first meeting: Rome has just been reborn, but death already stalks her! Death was there, in front of me, spreading through the body of the Eternal City.

★　★　★

Sometimes, a few militiamen, a few survivors from the Black Bands, tried to block access to a crossroads, but they were quickly submerged under the flood of attackers. In the Borgo quarter, and especially in the immediate neighbourhood of the Vatican palace, the Swiss guards resisted with commendable valour, sacrificing themselves in tens, in hundreds, for each street, each building, and delaying the advance of the imperial armies for several hours. But eventually they yielded through sheer force of numbers, and the lansquenets invaded St Peter's Square, shouting:

'Luther Pope! Luther Pope!'

Clement VII was still in his oratory, unaware of the danger. A bishop came to pull him unceremoniously by the sleeve:

'Holiness! Holiness! They are here! They will kill you!'

The Pope was on his knees. He got up and ran towards the corridor leading to the Castel San Angelo, with the bishop holding up the bottom of his gown to prevent him tripping over. On his way, he passed in front of an open window, and an imperial soldier fired a salvo in his direction, without hitting him.

'Your white robe is too conspicuous, Holiness!' said his companion, hastening to cover him with his own cloak, which was mauve, and less visible.

The Holy Father arrived at the castle safe and sound, but worn out, covered with dust, haggard, his face drawn. He ordered the portcullises to be lowered to prevent access to the fortress, and then shut himself up in his apartments to pray, perhaps also to weep.

In the city, given over to the lansquenets, the sack continued for several long days more. But Castel San Angelo was little affected. The imperial troops surrounded it on all sides, but never risked an attack. Its defensive wall was solid; it had numerous different artillery pieces, sakers, falconets and culverines; its defenders were determined to die to the last man rather than succumb to the fate of the wretched citizenry.

During the first days, reinforcements were still expected. It was known that the Italian members of the Holy League commanded by Francesco della Rovere, Duke of Urbino, were not far from Rome. A French bishop came to whisper in my ear that the Grand Turk had crossed the Alps with sixty thousand men and that he was going to attack the imperial troops from the rear. The news was not confirmed, and the army of the league did not dare to intervene, although it could have retaken Rome without any difficulty and decimated the lansquenets, who were totally absorbed in their pillaging, orgies and drunkenness. Demoralized by the indecision and cowardice of his allies, the Pope resigned himself to negotiations. As early as 21 May he received an envoy from the imperial camp.

Another emissary followed him two days later, for a brief visit. While he was coming up the ramp of the castle, I heard his name mentioned, embellished with various offensive epithets. It is true that he was one of the heads of the Colonna family, a cousin of Cardinal Pompeo. A Florentine priest began to hurl abuse at him, but all those present bade him be silent. Many knew, in fact, like me, that this man, a person of great uprightness, could not rejoice at the disaster which had afflicted his city, that he most certainly regretted the perfidy for which his family was responsible, and that he would do everything to rectify this wrong, by trying to save what could still be saved of the soul of Rome and of the dignity of the papacy.

Hence the arrival of this Colonna did not surprise me. On the other hand, I did not have the slightest idea that the emissary was going to speak about me in the course of his meeting with the Pope. I had never met him before, and when a militiaman came to summon me immediately to the papal apartments, I had not the slightest idea of what might be demanded of me.

The two men were sitting in the library, in two armchairs close to one another. Pope Clement had not shaved for two weeks, a sign of mourning and of protest at the fate which had been inflicted upon him. He asked me to sit down and introduced me to his visitor as 'a very dear son, a precious and devoted friend'. Colonna had a message for me, which he delivered with some condescension:

'The chaplain of the Saxon lansquenets has asked me to assure you of his friendship and his grateful remembrance.'

Only one Saxon could know Leo the African. His name was on my lips like a cry of victory, perhaps somewhat indelicate in the circumstances:

'Hans!'

'One of your former pupils, I believe. He wants to thank you for all that you have taught him with so much patience, and to show you his gratitude by helping you leave the city with your wife and child.'

Before I could react, the Pope intervened:

'Of course, I will not oppose the decision which you will take in any way, whatever it may be. But I should warn you that your departure will not be without grave risks for you and yours.'

Colonna explained to me:

'Among the troops surrounding the castle are a great number of madmen who want to pursue their humiliation of the Apostolic See to the bitter end. Particularly the Germans whom Luther has made fanatical, may God pursue him with his anger until the end of time! Others, in contrast, would like to put an end to the siege and find a solution which would put a stop to the humiliation of Christendom. If His Holiness were to attempt to leave today, I know whole regiments which would not hesitate to seize his person and submit him to the vilest of tortures.'

Clement blenched, while his visitor continued:

'Neither I nor even the Emperor Charles could prevent that. We must still negotiate much longer, have recourse to persuasion and guile, using all possible means. Today we have the unhoped-for chance to enable one of the besieged to leave, at the express request of a Lutheran preacher. He is waiting for you, with a detachment of Saxons, all heretics like himself, and he says he is ready to escort you himself far away from here. If all goes well, if the whole army hears tomorrow that the chaplain of the Saxon lansquenets has freed one of those besieged in San Angelo, it will be easier for us to suggest, in a few days or a few weeks, the liberation of other people, perhaps even His Holiness himself, in conditions of dignity and security.'

Clement VII intervened again:

'I repeat, you must not be unaware of the risks. His Eminence tells me that certain fanatical soldiers could cut you into pieces, you, your family and your escort, without even sparing this chaplain. The decision which you are asked to take is not easy. In addition, you do not have the time to think it over. The cardinal is already getting ready to leave and you must go with him.'

By temperament I preferred to run a risk that was immediate but of short duration than stay for ever in this besieged prison, which could be overrun at any moment and put to fire and the sword. My sole hesitation was for Maddalena and Giuseppe. It was not easy for me to lead them, of my own free will, through hordes of murderers and looters. That said, if I were to leave them in San Angelo with or without me there, I could in no way ensure their security.

Colonna pressed me:

'What have you chosen?'

'I put myself in God's hands. I shall tell my wife to pack the few things we have here.'

'You will take nothing with you. The smallest bundle, the tiniest bag might arouse the lansquenets like the smell of blood excites wild beasts. You will leave just as you are, lightly dressed with arms swinging.'

I did not bother to argue. It was written that I should pass from one country to another as one passes from life to death, without gold, without ornament, with no other fortune than my resignation to the will of the Most High.

When I explained to her what was happening in a few brief words, Maddalena got up. Slowly, as she always did, but without the slightest hesitation, as if she had always known that I would one day come to call her into exile. She took Giuseppe's hand and walked behind me to go to the Pope, who blessed us, praised our courage and commended us to the protection of God. I kissed his hand and handed him all my writings, with the exception of this chronicle, still unfinished, which I had rolled up and slid under my belt.

Hans awaited us with open arms at the entrance to the Regola quarter, where we had often wandered in the past, and which was now no more than a heap of burnt-out ruins. He wore a short gown and discoloured sandals, and had a helmet on his head, which he promptly removed to give me an embrace. The war had made him prematurely grey, and his face was more angular than ever. Around him stood a dozen lansquenets, in baggy clothes and ragged plumes, to whom he introduced me as his brothers.

We had barely taken a few steps when a Castilian officer came to station his men across our way. Signalling that I should not move, Hans spoke to the soldier in a tone that was firm but which would brook no provocation. Then he took a letter out of his pocket, the sight of which cleared the way immediately. How many times were we stopped in this way before reaching our destination? Probably twenty times, perhaps even thirty. But at no point was Hans caught unprepared. He had organized the expedition admirably, obtaining a whole wad of safe-conducts signed by the Viceroy of Naples, Cardinal Colonna and various military leaders. In addition, he was surrounded by his 'brothers', solidly-built Saxons, who were quick to point their arms at the numerous drunken soldiers who were roaming the streets on the lookout for spoils.

When he felt reassured of the efficacy of his arrangements, Hans began to talk to me about the war. Strangely, the thoughts he put forward in no way corresponded to the image I had kept of him. He bemoaned the turn which events had taken, recalling the years he had spent in Rome with emotion, and condemned the sack of the city. At first he spoke in veiled terms. But on the third day, when we were nearing Naples, he rode along at my side, so close that our feet touched.

'For the second time we have unleashed forces which we have been unable to contain. First the revolt of the peasants of Saxony, inspired by Luther's teaching, which had to be condemned and repressed. And now the destruction of Rome.'

He had spoken the first words in Arabic, and then continued in Hebrew, the language he knew better. One thing was certain: he did not want the soldiers accompanying him to be aware of his doubts and his remorse. To me he seemed so ill at ease in his role as Lutheran preacher that when we reached Naples I felt obliged to suggest to him that he should come with me to Tunis. He smiled bitterly.

'This war is my war. I have longed for it, I dragged my brothers, my cousins, the young men of my diocese into it. I can no longer run away from it, even if it should lead me to eternal damnation. You have only been mixed up in it by a quirk of fate.'

At Naples, an urchin led us to 'Abbad's house, and it was only when the latter came to open his gate that Hans left us. I wanted to express my desire to see him again one day, somewhere in the wide world, but I did not want to cheapen the deep gratitude I felt for this man by meaningless formulae. So I simply embraced him warmly and then watched him go, not without a feeling of paternal affection.

Then it was 'Abbad the Soussi's turn to give me a warm embrace. For months he had hoped for our arrival each day. He had cancelled all his journeys that year, swearing that he would not leave without us. Now nothing held him back. After a bath, a feast and a nap, we were all at the harbour, perfumed and dressed in new clothes. The finest of 'Abbad's galleys awaited us, ready to make for Tunis.

A last word written on the last page, and we are already at the coast of Africa.

White minarets of Gammarth, noble remains of Carthage, it is in their shade that oblivion awaits me, and it is towards them that my life is drifting after so many shipwrecks. The sack of Rome after the chastisement of Cairo, the fire of Timbuktu after the fall of Granada. Is it misfortune which calls out to me, or do I call out to misfortune?

Once more, my son, I am borne along by that sea, the witness of all my wanderings, and which is now taking you towards your first exile. In Rome, you were 'the son of the Rumi'. Wherever you are, some will want to ask questions about your skin or your prayers. Beware of gratifying their instincts, my son, beware of bending before the multitude! Muslim, Jew or Christian, they must take you as you are, or lose you. When men's minds seem narrow to you, tell yourself that the land of God is broad; broad His hands and broad His heart. Never hesitate to go far away, beyond all seas, all frontiers, all countries, all beliefs.

For my part, I have reached the end of my wanderings. Forty years of adventures have made my gait heavy and my breathing burdensome. I have no longer any desire other than to live long peaceful days in the bosom of my family. And to be, of all those that I love, the first to depart. Towards the final Place where no man is a stranger before the face of the Creator.